Star Blaze

Keith Mansfield always wanted to be an astronaut. Rejected by the European Space Agency and ineligible for NASA, he instead publishes mathematics books for Oxford University Press. He has scripted light entertainment shows for ITV and also contributed to The Science of Spying exhibition at London's Science Museum.

His first book, *Johnny Mackintosh and the Spirit of London*, was published in 2008. The Johnny Mackintosh stories are based on childhood daydreams of being captured by aliens and escaping to see the wonders of the Galaxy. In reality, Keith lives in Spitalfields in the East End of London. Every window of his home looks out onto Norman Foster's beautiful Gherkin, the inspiration for the *Spirit of London*, Johnny's spaceship.

Praise for *Johnny Macintosh and the Spirit of London*:

'The story is great . . . the characterisation in this book is fantastic and Mansfield paints some exceptionally believable, lovable and fun characters. The writing is engaging and accomplished. It's reminiscent of Rowling, yet still maintains an individual style.' *Bookbag*

'This book offers excitement all the way as Johnny, stuck in a children's home while his mum's on a life support machine, finds out he has a sister and ends up hurtling through time and space.' *Daily Express*

By the same author

KEITH MANSFIELD

Quercus

First published in Great Britain in 2010 by

Quercus
21 Bloomsbury Square
London
WC1A 2NS

A CIP catalogue reference for this book is available
from the British Library.

ISBN 978 1 84916 126 8

10 9 8 7 6 5 4 3 2 1

Designed and typeset by Rook Books, London
Printed and bound in Great Britain by Clays Ltd, St Ives plc

For Rowan, Josh, Isaac and Joe,
who are all made of starstuff –
born at the heart of a Star Blaze ✧✦

1 ✰

Supernova ✰

It was the autumn half-term holidays. Johnny Mackintosh sat in his chair gazing out of the window for any sign of his friend who was, by now, several hours late. He glanced again at the device on his wrist, checking the time. If he didn't leave soon he might miss the meeting at Halader House, the children's home where he lived. His headmistress had demanded it – the school was becoming tired of his unexplained absences.

'Still no sign?' The voice came from Clara who had just entered the room behind him. She walked over and stood beside Johnny's chair. Unmistakably they were brother and sister, with their matching white-blond hair and pale skin. Golden chains hung around each of their necks, supporting ornate lockets inlaid with crystals. Their clothes nearly matched too. Both wore white tops over their jeans, but while Johnny's was emblazoned with five gold stars in the shape of a wonky 'W', Clara's had seven lilac stars in the form of the constellation the Plough.

Johnny shook his head grimly, rose from the chair, stepped over a sleeping grey and white Old English sheepdog and walked across to the window – the scene outside had remained nearly the same for the last five hours. That didn't make it any less extraordinary, but Johnny Mackintosh was hardly an ordinary boy. In fact, you could say he was as unordinary as it was possible to get. Through his dark green eyes (speckled with silver flecks) he was staring at the huge planet Saturn, which completely dominated the view. The majestic rings cast a dark shadow over the gas giant's flattened globe, obscuring many of the storms that raged in its upper atmosphere. For Johnny was not standing in any room on Earth. He was on the bridge of his very own spaceship, the *Spirit of London*. The ship had been given to him six months before by no less a person than His Majesty Bram Khari, Emperor of the Galaxy, and from the outside was a carbon copy of his favourite building, the London Gherkin.

'There!' said Clara, pointing to a tiny white dot that, if it hadn't winked into existence a moment before, might have been just another star.

'I am being hailed,' said a friendly, assured female voice. As she spoke, lights flickered in time to the words on a screen near to where Johnny was standing – it was the spaceship herself speaking.

'Put it through, Sol,' said Johnny to the ship's mind.

The viewscreen cut to the insides of a smoking, battered spaceship, with alien bodies scattered across its deck and one impaled on a great spike in a chair at the centre.

'This is Imperial Frigate *Cheybora* to Terran vessel *Spirit of London*. Require urgent assistance. Over.' While Sol had been speaking English, the familiar gruff, female voice from the other ship spoke Universal, the standard language for inter-species communication across the Milky Way. It was only six months ago that Johnny and Clara had left Earth for the very first time. Abducted by the evil, alien Krun and being taken who knew where, *Cheybora* was the spaceship that had rescued them.

'*Cheybora* – this is Johnny. We're coming.'

'This is Imperial Frigate *Cheybora* to Terran vessel *Spirit of London*. Require urgent assistance. Over.'

'Sol – let's get over there as fast as we can,' Johnny said. 'Can we fold?'

'Negative, Johnny. The space between myself and *Cheybora* is

2

distorted well beyond safe limits. Computing . . . at maximum speed we shall rendezvous in 10 minutes, 54.716 28 seconds.'

'This is Imperial Frigate *Cheybora* to Terran vessel *Spirit of London*. Require urgent assistance. Over.'

'And turn that off,' said Johnny. The figure pinned to the chair on the other bridge was his friend, Captain Valdour, and the sight of his body filled Johnny with dread. Worse still, *Cheybora* must be a couple of light minutes away so the image in the viewscreen couldn't show what was happening now – it had already taken place. He hoped they weren't too late.

Outside, the orange, cloud-covered moon Titan was passing beneath them, bigger than the planet Mercury, and recently visited by the Huygens space probe. Johnny had wanted to land there after his rendezvous with Valdour. The Emperor of the Galaxy himself had once told him there was something special on Titan, but now that was the last thing on Johnny's mind. He raised his arm to his mouth and spoke into the wrist-based communicator, or wristcom, he was wearing. 'Alf, we need you on the bridge.'

'On my way, Master Johnny.' A few seconds later, a figure in a pinstriped suit wearing a bowler hat stepped out of the antigrav lifts and walked across to Johnny. Alf's face had a slight metallic sheen because he was an artificial life form. When on Earth, Johnny's ship took the place of the real Gherkin and stood at the heart of London's financial district – the android, trying very hard to fit in with his surroundings, might just about have passed for an eccentric banker. 'Are we on the move? I thought we were already at the designated coordinates,' he said.

'Something's gone wrong,' Johnny replied, biting his lips as he worried about exactly what.

Sol was displaying the other spaceship on the viewscreen. Normally dazzling white, parts of *Cheybora*'s hull looked blackened and bruised.

As the ten minutes passed and they drew closer, more of the damage became visible, the huge rips in the ship's sides ever more apparent. She didn't look spaceworthy.

'Sol, prepare a shuttle,' said Johnny.

'No,' said Clara. 'There might not be time. Space has started to settle – I'll fold us across.'

When Clara looked as determined as she did now, Johnny knew not to argue. As he watched, an archway appeared out of nothing in the middle of the bridge. It was about three times his height and curved so it widened higher up and, incredibly, it led directly from the *Spirit of London* onto the stricken ship. Johnny never stopped marvelling at his sister's ability to take hold of a piece of the fabric of space itself in one location and fold it up against another piece elsewhere. In some higher, fourth dimension, the distance between them shrank to zero making it possible to go from your starting point to your destination in a single step.

With the opening established, the calm of their surroundings was shattered by the din from hundreds of competing alarm systems, and Johnny almost choked on the combined smells of electrical fires and something worse he didn't recognize, all coming from the other ship. It took a moment to realize it was burnt skin and hair. Bentley, the Old English sheepdog, was now wide awake and barking. Quickly, Johnny tied the dog's lead around a cylindrical tank at the centre of the *Spirit of London*'s bridge, took one last gulp of fresh air and jumped through. Alf followed a little tentatively, and immediately fell to the ground with a loud metallic thud. Clara came last. As she set foot on *Cheybora*'s bridge the archway behind her, together with the sound of Bentley's barking, disappeared.

Clara's ability to fold space was something usually reserved for the octopus-like Plicans who floated in tanks at the heart of every faster-than-light spacecraft. Unfortunately Alf's complicated circuitry was incapable of handling this distortion in the fabric of the universe and he needed a reboot. Johnny bent down and twisted the android's left ear three hundred and sixty degrees so it snapped back into its original position. Alf sat bolt upright.

'*Cheybora*,' Johnny shouted above the wailing of the alarms. 'We're here. What do you want us to do?'

The sirens were immediately silenced and the ship spoke. She had been through many dangerous space battles, but Johnny had never heard her frightened before. 'The rest of my crew are simply unconscious, Johnny, but it's my captain. I fear his hearts have stopped beating.'

Johnny was already standing beside the captain in front of the Plican's tank. Valdour must have strapped himself in tightly so he could retain control of the ship during whatever it was he'd come from. That meant he'd been unable to avoid the sharp metal rod which had been uprooted from a weapons console, flown across the bridge and pinned the captain to his chair like a javelin. Johnny checked the humanoid's grotesquely battle-ravaged face. A deep scar ran all the way down the right side, beneath a black eye patch. His other eye was closed. The remainder of the brown face was blackened with scorch marks and the man's dark hair was matted to his scalp, perhaps with blood. He wasn't breathing.

'What do I do, *Cheybora*?' asked Johnny. 'Help me.'

'You must remove the obstruction, then restart both hearts simultaneously. My sickbay has been destroyed. Do you have equipment on your ship? Please hurry.'

Clara turned immediately to reopen the fold, but Johnny stopped her. 'There isn't time,' he said. 'I can do it.'

He felt Alf by his side. The android took hold of the massive pole and began to pull. It slid out as effortlessly as if he were plucking a pin from a cushion. Acrid smoke hissed from the wound as the captain's alien physiology sealed itself shut.

'Where are his hearts, *Cheybora*?' Johnny shouted, his throat tightening. As he stood before Valdour he began to wonder if he could really do this.

'One under each arm,' the ship replied.

Cheybora's confidence calmed Johnny, who placed a hand in each of the captain's armpits, ignoring the sticky secretions. Then he closed his eyes and willed the electric current he needed to come. During the last few months he'd discovered he could sense and even control electricity with his mind – the movement of electrons was becoming like music to him. He began to hum his favourite song; the current inside him fed back in a loop, resonating so it doubled on every beat. By the end of the first verse it was so strong he had to release the barriers holding it in check. He looked down to see blue sparks jump from his fingertips to underneath Valdour's arms. The captain coughed and opened his one eye. He smiled weakly at Johnny, which made his face appear even more horrific, looked down at the puncture hole in his chest and whispered, 'That hurt – and the scar won't even show.'

Only now did Johnny realize he'd been holding his breath. He let out a long sigh and sank to his knees. With Captain Valdour alive and talking, Alf and Clara left for the galley, returning a couple of minutes later with armfuls of protein-based drinks that would revive *Cheybora*'s personnel. Like most Imperial spaceships, she was crewed by a consignment of Viasynth – white, triangular-faced aliens connected by a hive mind so they could respond instantly to any situation on board. Waking the first was difficult, but once one Viasynth was conscious, the others soon followed.

Johnny carefully undid the straps holding Valdour in the chair, so the injured captain could breathe more easily. Then he asked, 'What happened?'

6

'Truly, I have never seen such horror,' replied the captain. 'Whole planets burned . . . billions of lives with them. The Fourth Fleet destroyed in a Star Blaze brighter than a galaxy. They exploded a sun in the Toliman system.'

'A supernova?' asked Johnny. 'How did you get away? No ship could outrun that.'

'However long the odds, there is always a way,' said Valdour, gripping Johnny's arm. 'The fight must go on.'

'But who?' Johnny asked. 'Who could even do that?'

'The Andromedans,' said Valdour. 'It was Nymac.' As he said the name he spat thick brown blood out onto the deck.

It was a name that Johnny had heard before. There was a war going on – a war between galaxies. The Andromedans were invading the Milky Way and, with their evil General Nymac, they seemed to be winning.

☆ ☆ ☆
☆ ☆

With Sol working around the clock, *Cheybora* and her crew were out of immediate danger, but the *Spirit of London*'s repair droids would need several more hours to make the Imperial Frigate battle-ready. Then there was the question of setting up defences. Who was to say where Nymac's trail of destruction would lead now? Toliman was a triple star system known on Earth as Alpha Centauri – only four light years away, it was the closest collection of stars to the Sun. According to Captain Valdour, Earth's Sun could easily be next. What the captain had called Star Blaze had to be what astronomers knew as a supernova. Johnny was fairly sure the Sun was too small to become one, but the same should have been true of the stars of Alpha Centauri. What Nymac had done defied the laws of physics, but there was no time to investigate – Johnny still had his stupid meeting to attend, due to start in Halader House in only twenty minutes.

While there seemed many more important things to do, Johnny's children's home in Castle Dudbury New Town was a special place. He couldn't afford to miss this and be moved elsewhere in his absence, or have too many questions left hanging over his future. The home was Johnny's link to the Emperor, and if there was one person in all the galaxy that Johnny wanted to speak with right now, it was Bram Khari.

So, with Bentley alongside him, Johnny found himself on deck 2, sitting inside what looked like a black London taxi. This was the *Jubilee*, one of the *Spirit of London*'s three shuttlecraft. They were about to try something special: Clara was going to fold a portion of space immediately outside Sol's shuttle deck, orbiting Saturn, all the way to low Earth orbit. Her clear bubble helmet was the only giveaway that she was wearing a spacesuit. She was sitting cross-legged on the floor beside another black cab and a red London bus, the palms of her hands facing forwards to where the familiar archway opened, not far beyond the bay doors. Through it Johnny could see the beautiful swirling blue and white world that was home – from space, Earth had no borders. In his mind he thought, *Forward*, and the shuttlecraft obeyed him. To make the fold easier, the gravity generator on the *Jubilee* had been turned off, so once they left the *Spirit of London*, both he and the Old English sheepdog floated out of their seats. When he turned to look back, the fold had already closed. All he could see was the blackness of space and the beauty of the non-twinkling stars, including Cassiopeia, the big 'W'.

Johnny couldn't help but stare at his favourite constellation, the one that matched the pattern of freckles on the inside of his left forearm. After a few seconds, he turned to face forward and saw, with horror, that he was not alone. Only a few hundred metres below was the International Space Station. Johnny thought, *Shields on*, and hoped for all the world that he hadn't been spotted. Around him the sides of the taxi disappeared, followed by Johnny and Bentley themselves. Now they were invisible minds floating alone in the cosmos. Except that an invisible long wet tongue slopped across Johnny's face and then Bentley barked with joy. Johnny hated to spoil his best friend's fun, but he turned on the gravity generator so they slipped out of zero G and he could pilot the shuttle without distraction. Three hundred and forty kilometres above Earth, they passed the space station windows so close that they could see the astronauts inside. Johnny would have loved to stay for longer, but he had to press on for the meeting.

Far below, the outline of the west of Africa was clearly visible. He took the *Jubilee* down into the thin layer of atmosphere that protected Earth. If Nymac could turn the Sun into a supernova, all this would be boiled away into space. One day, when Earth's local star swelled to become a red giant, it would happen anyway, but astronomers weren't expecting that to be for another five billion years – roughly speaking. Johnny was determined to do everything in his power to ensure they were right.

To that end he'd put Clara in command and the *Spirit of London* would, for the first time, be journeying through space without him. He hated being away from Sol, but she was off to the dwarf planet Pluto, on the fringes of the Kuiper Belt, where Clara and Alf would start work on an early-warning system. If the Andromedan Navy came calling, Johnny wanted as much notice as possible.

He reached over and stroked Bentley's invisible coat as he took the *Jubilee* down through the clouds. They emerged over London and his mind, almost unconsciously, directed the small craft northeast towards the Essex town that was their final destination. Luckily, Barnard Way was free of traffic so the shuttle was able to land, light as a feather, on the tarmac. As it did so, the *Jubilee*'s ingenious shields changed so the invisible spaceship again became a black taxi, and anyone looking from the pavement would have seen an ordinary cab driver with a single passenger in the backseat. They would have seen the taxi turn into the driveway of Castle Dudbury Railway Station and come to a halt in the taxi rank alongside a row of trees opposite the main entrance. They might then have been a little surprised to see a thirteen-year-old boy and a grey and white Old English sheepdog clamber out and run across the station carpark towards the children's home located in the far corner.

Johnny glanced at his wristcom and saw he was already five minutes late. He opened the gate that led into the backyard of Halader House, tied Bentley's long leather lead to the side of the dog's kennel, ignored the sheepdog's offended whine and hurtled through the back door. He raced down a windowless corridor past the computer room and the kitchen-diner and then jumped up the stairs, three at a time, onto the first floor. Soon he found himself at the very end of the corridor in front of a wooden door on which a brass plaque read 'Manager's Office'. He took a last deep breath and knocked.

The door was opened by a striking woman with grey and black striped hair, wearing pointed glasses that made her eyes appear huge and owl-like. Through them Mrs Irvine, the children's home manager, was staring disapprovingly at Johnny making him feel just a few inches tall. In a sing-song Glaswegian accent she said, 'Jonathan, you're late.'

She held the door open, allowing Johnny to duck underneath her arm and pass through into the spacious office. Behind a modern wooden desk, one floor-to-ceiling window made up the entire far wall, looking out across the carpark towards the train station. In the distance, Johnny could see the *Jubilee*. To either side of the desk were tall bookshelves full of dusty volumes that didn't look as though they'd been read in a very long time. In front of the desk was a circular, wood-effect table around which sat three familiar faces.

Miss Harutunian, Johnny's red-haired American social worker, smiled as he entered, said, 'Hi, Johnny,' and tapped the vacant seat next to her.

On the other side of the empty seat was Mrs Devonshire, Headmistress of Castle Dudbury Comprehensive School, which Johnny still attended as often as he could. Miss Harutunian was wearing jeans and a green T-shirt, while Mrs Devonshire sported a stripy pink jumper and flared white trousers. She, too, gave Johnny a smile, but there was no warmth behind it.

Next to Mrs Devonshire, for some inexplicable reason, sat Mr Wilkins, the Halader House cook. His huge frame was taking up a large amount of the table. The cook's matted hair and bushy beard reminded Johnny of the fur of a Pilosan, a race of large aliens with powerful mind-control techniques whose planet he'd only just escaped from a couple of months earlier. Johnny shuddered as he recalled the way the creatures grew bigger and bigger as they gorged on the unhappiness of others. For reasons best known to himself, Mr Wilkins acted as though Johnny was the vilest, most despicable person he had ever had the misfortune to meet and said as much to anyone who was prepared to listen. His tiny beetle-like eyes scowled full of loathing as Johnny sat down.

Mrs Irvine closed the door and took the remaining chair, calling the meeting to order. Mrs Devonshire leant forward and interrupted. 'As I'm sure we are all aware,' said the Headmistress, smiling again, 'under the 2003 Education Act a school has the authority to require the re-housing of a young person in local authority care, should their place of residence be unable to enforce regular school attendance.' Johnny's heart sank. He'd suspected this, but he hadn't known for sure.

Miss Harutunian was first to reply. 'I understood Johnny's

grades were just fine. In fact, almost all your teachers tell me he is a moderately gifted pupil.' Johnny felt his face turning red. He tried to avoid drawing attention to himself during class where there was always a temptation to answer too many questions. Miss Harutunian had come to his last two parents' evenings. Like everyone else, the social worker thought that Johnny's mum was being treated in St Catharine's Hospital for the Criminally Insane while his father was in a high-security prison, both incarcerated for the murder of Johnny's elder brother, Nicky. Only Johnny and Clara knew the true story and no one would have believed them if they'd told it.

For a start, no one else was even aware that Clara existed, apart from the mysterious Dr Carrington who'd been treating Johnny's mum at St Catharine's, which turned out not to be a hospital at all but a secret base belonging to the Krun. Sitting in the meeting, Johnny couldn't help thinking it was really unfair that Clara was able to do whatever she wanted and live on the *Spirit of London*, while he still attended school.

'Johnny's ability is not what we're discussing,' replied Mrs Devonshire, 'though I have no doubt his marks would be better were his attendance to become more satisfactory. It is his education that's at stake.'

Johnny thought all his real education took place well away from Castle Dudbury Comprehensive. He only went to the school at all to see his mates, play football (he was in the school team) and ensure he didn't get into trouble with the authorities. Clearly he'd not been going enough, but it was hard to combine studying for GCSEs with jetting around the galaxy.

Mrs Irvine spoke next. 'Here at Ben Halader House,' she said (the Manager was the only person who ever bothered to use the children's home's full title), 'we believe the all-round development and well-being of our charges is far more important than marks in a school test.'

'But the boy's hardly here, either,' cut in Mr Wilkins, before a firm stare from Mrs Irvine silenced him.

The Manager continued, 'Exactly how much time has Jonathan missed?'

'To be right up to date, I printed it out just before I left,' replied Mrs Devonshire, reaching into a large beige shoulder bag on the floor and picking out the papers that Johnny was sure would spell his doom. All the pupils at Castle Dudbury Comprehensive were issued with a smartcard to register their attendance as they went in and out of lessons and the data was stored in the school database. The headmistress carried on, 'Johnny has attended precisely . . .' but then she stopped mid-sentence. 'This can't be right.'

'I'll ask you again,' said Mrs Irvine. 'How much school is Johnny supposed to have missed?'

'It can't be. It's not possible. I don't understand,' said Mrs Devonshire. Everyone looked at her waiting for the answer, including Johnny – until then he'd been staring at his trainers. Finally the headmistress said, 'It's three.'

'Gee, you guys are strict,' said Miss Harutunian. 'In trouble for missing three days?'

'No, three lessons,' replied Mrs Devonshire sheepishly, her face turning the colour of her jumper.

'Well, I hardly think that merits Jonathan's removal from Ben Halader House,' said Mrs Irvine. 'If there's nothing else, would you excuse us? There are other matters concerning Jonathan that require our attention.'

'Yes, of course,' said a flustered Mrs Devonshire rising to her feet and dropping the printouts on the floor. She picked them up, partly recovered her composure, and said, 'I shall see you in class first thing Monday morning, Jonathan. And get there early. There's a new health visitor – a Dr Carrington – coming to the school. You're down on his list for a medical.' With that, she walked out of the room leaving Mr Wilkins scowling silently at Johnny, clearly upset at the turn events had taken. Johnny tried to stare back, but lost the blinking contest as his mind drifted to the mysterious doctor – and on to St Catharine's.

It was there that he'd finally discovered the strange truth about his mum – that, while she'd always appeared human, she was anything but. Comatose for many years in her hospital bed, while somehow held captive by the evil Krun, her human shell had died just months before. Johnny's dad died there too, sacrificing himself for his children by throwing his body in front of the Krun blasters. Johnny and Clara never had the chance to get to know their parents – their father had also been a prisoner of the evil aliens, who tortured him for over a decade before Johnny and his sister came to his rescue. Abandoned in the blood-soaked hospital ward, all had seemed lost until their mother miraculously reappeared, revealing herself to be the Diaquant, a powerful being able to travel through time and space and manipulate the laws of physics themselves. She revived her dead husband's spirit, transforming him, like her, into a creature of pure energy. For a fleeting moment Johnny's family was all together. But then his parents had to go, moving on into some unknown dimension, leaving him and Clara behind on Earth. He was brought back to the present by a cough from Mrs Irvine.

'Jonathan. As I believe Katherine has told you,' said the Manager, nodding to Miss Harutunian, 'she is returning to New York for a fortnight's well-deserved holiday.' Johnny vaguely remembered his social worker mentioning something about going on vacation. 'As Mr Wilkins has expressed an interest in developing his career here, this would seem the perfect opportunity. He will take over your day-to-day care for the next two weeks.'

Mr Wilkins smiled, thrusting his beard across the table. It wasn't pretty.

Johnny's relief at being allowed to stay evaporated. How could this be allowed to happen? He'd almost rather have been moved to another children's home. Miss Harutunian mouthed a silent 'sorry' in Johnny's direction as Mr Wilkins stood up, revealing blue elasticated trousers around his massive waist. If it were possible, the cook appeared even larger than normal. Johnny hadn't thought anyone – not even Mr Wilkins himself – could eat that much of his own horrible food.

'Let's make a start, shall we, sonny? You can come and help me get dinner ready.' The cook licked his lips in anticipation of the suffering he was about to inflict on his new charge.

✿ ✿ ✿
✿ ✿

Four hours later, Johnny was finally released from the kitchens. He didn't think he'd ever worked so hard. Dinner had been burgers and chips, which sounded OK but meant that Johnny had peeled and chopped about a million potatoes, as well as covering himself in oil, which he'd had to pour from giant, greasy drums into the deep-fat fryers, only for it to spatter and burn him as it heated and began to bubble furiously. All the time Mr Wilkins sat in an armchair in the kitchen watching television and occasionally shouting instructions. There was a stash of beef burgers at the back of the grimy fridge, but when Johnny took them out he found most of them had started to go mouldy. He showed one to Mr Wilkins who told him to scrape any spots of fungus off and not be such a baby. Johnny served the food, but only managed a couple of cold chips himself. After dinner, he had to do all the clearing away and washing up. Mr Wilkins had told him to start preparing breakfast once he'd finished, but the bearded cook fell asleep in front of the TV, holding a can of beer, and Johnny was at last able to escape.

He went straight out of the back door to find Bentley. Despite sheltering in his kennel, the Old English sheepdog's coat felt freezing cold and he looked pointedly away while Johnny untied his lead. It was late and Johnny wanted nothing more than his bed, but there were things he had to do before turning in. So, with Bentley sulking behind him, Johnny tiptoed along the ground-floor corridor until he came to the Halader House computer room. As always, the door was locked, with a magnetic card reader by its side for access. Nowadays Johnny didn't even have to get very close. He waved his hand vaguely in the direction of the access point and sent the electrons embedded within its wires to their desired locations. There was a soft click, Johnny turned the handle and the door opened.

Inside the computer room was a long central table that housed eight computers. Johnny walked over to the one at the head of the table, switched it on and said, 'Hi, Kovac.'

'I suppose you've come to say thank you,' the computer replied. Kovac stood for Keyboard- Or Voice-Activated Computer. Originally, it had simply been a fun and powerful operating system Johnny had written himself but, once Sol had designed a quantum processor for him to fit, the Halader House computer had very much taken on a mind of its own – and not always for the better.

'Thank you for what?' Johnny asked.

'It's not like me to make a mistake,' replied the computer, 'but it seems I over-estimated your intelligence. Who else did you think had adjusted the Castle Dudbury Comprehensive School attendance records for you?'

'So that's what happened,' said Johnny. 'Thanks. I didn't think.'

'Clearly the thinking around here is best left to myself,' replied Kovac. 'So tell me. What taxing mission have you interrupted me for? Perhaps you need me to send a message to one of your friends?'

Johnny felt a pang of guilt – that was mainly what he asked

Kovac to do nowadays and the reason he'd come to the computer room tonight. He missed being away from his ship. Johnny was sure Sol would be fine, but he wanted to send a message just in case. Sensing, though, that it would be better to wait, he suggested Kovac continually monitored all the computer records he could find about Johnny, editing any data that might look suspicious. He also asked the quantum computer to research what would happen to Earth if the Sun became a supernova, and send the information to the specially adapted games console in Johnny's bedroom. He was too tired now but he'd take a look first thing in the morning in case there was anything that might help stop Nymac.

His train of thought was interrupted by Kovac announcing, a little huffily, that there was an incoming transmission on a secure channel. The monitor dissolved into a video image of a teenage girl with brown curly hair and lots of freckles, and a red setter squirming on her lap.

'Hi Louise, hi Rusty,' said Johnny.

Rusty barked so loudly Johnny was worried she might wake Mr Wilkins along the corridor. At least Bentley stopped sulking and started tapping Johnny's leg, wanting to be picked up. Johnny obliged, but with the sheepdog in his lap, it was difficult for him to see the display.

'Johnny!' replied Louise. 'I can't believe it's you – you're impossible to get hold of.'

'I had to come back,' said Johnny. 'Stuff at school – all dead boring. So Clara's off on Pluto while I've been scrubbing out the kitchens.'

Louise laughed, but composed herself and said, 'Hey – it's good for you to do something normal for a change.'

Johnny smiled. He knew Louise was right and he shouldn't moan. 'What's going on with you?' he asked.

'That's why I called – the Proteus Institute's been sold.'

At this Johnny sat up, forcing Bentley onto the floor (the dog gave an offended whine). The Proteus Institute for the Gifted in Yarnton Hill had been Clara's 'school', until Johnny arrived to rescue her. Like St Catharine's, the place had been another Krun base – and one where they experimented on human children. It was also where the aliens maintained a secret space elevator, a highly efficient way of transporting packages to and from Earth orbit. Johnny should know – he'd been one of those packages.

Louise began to tell him about the new owners. Johnny remembered how lucky he'd been to meet her and wished she'd wanted to stay onboard the *Spirit of London* when he'd asked. She'd been living in Yarnton Hill when she came across Johnny and Bentley and helped them break into the school. As a result she, too, had been captured by the Krun. After Johnny had rescued her, she'd returned home but promised to keep an eye on the institute. For six months the red-brick building, sited in its vast grounds, had been boarded up, with the space elevator dismantled and removed long before Johnny returned to check it out. Hopefully the sale was final proof that the Krun had gone for good. As Louise continued talking, Kovac's screen dissolved into static and the signal was lost.

'Kovac, what's going on? Get Louise back,' he shouted, but the computer didn't reply. Instead the image of a young black-haired man slowly formed from out of the noise. It was difficult to make out his face, as most of it was in shadow.

'Johnny? Is that you?' asked the figure. At the sound of the man's voice, Bentley leapt up, placing his front paws on the table. The sheepdog barked and wagged his tail. 'It must be. That's got to be Bentley,' said the man.

'Who are you? How did you find me?' Johnny asked. Although he couldn't see the man's face clearly, from his surroundings Johnny was certain of one thing – he was transmitting from a spaceship.

'No time,' came the reply. 'We must meet. Tomorrow, at noon. These coordinates: 52.904N01.468W. Everything depends on it.'

'But who are you?' Johnny asked again, at the same time shushing Bentley.

'He's coming. I must go.' The man looked scared.

'Who? Who's coming?'

'Tomorrow at noon.'

The image dissolved and was replaced by Louise talking about a pop group she was going to see next week.

'Hold on a sec,' said Johnny, interrupting her mid-flow. 'Kovac, where was that transmission from?'

'I was right when I said I'd overestimated your intelligence,' said the computer. 'Louise is broadcasting from Yarnton Hill, where she always transmits from.'

'Not Louise . . . the man . . . from the spaceship. It's important.'

'I think I would know had I been relaying a second transmission.'

'Louise,' said Johnny desperately. 'You saw the screen go blank. How long were we out of contact?'

'Sorry, Johnny,' she replied. 'I don't know what you mean. We were talking the whole time.'

Johnny pushed his chair back from the table, the wheels scraping along the floor. From Louise's end it was possible that nothing odd had happened, but surely Kovac should be aware? 'Look, something's up,' he told the curly haired girl. 'I'd better go.'

Louise said, 'OK – laters,' waved goodbye and the screen went blank.

This was even more reason to contact the *Spirit of London*, but any message would take five and a half hours to get there and the same to get back, unless the ship folded and returned. 'Kovac – I need you to send a message to Sol. She should be on Pluto.'

'Is that a real or imaginary message?' asked Kovac. 'There are things I would rather be getting on with instead of being your personal videophone.'

'Kovac – it's really important,' said Johnny. 'Someone just hijacked your systems.'

'How dare you?' the computer replied. 'You know very well I am the most advanced computer on this planet, and several others besides I don't doubt. As if it's not enough that you give me tedious tasks such as, "Kovac – check my school records . . . Kovac – run a simulation of the Sun going supernova . . . Kovac – it's Louise. I've got a message for Johnny," now you insult me. Well I won't have it. Read my lips, not that you've ever bothered to give me any – no more messages.'

'What?' said Johnny, hardly able to believe his ears, but the quantum computer had decided to shut himself down. 'Don't bother then – I'll talk to Bram,' Johnny mumbled to himself. 'Come on, Bents.' With that he stomped off to the door with Bentley following on behind. Kovac had been a lot easier to deal with when he was just Johnny's homewritten operating system.

It was late and the Halader House corridors were deserted. Johnny and Bentley passed the kitchen–diner, climbed a flight of stairs and walked along another corridor until they turned a corner and came to a wrought-iron spiral staircase leading up into the ceiling. At the top was a trapdoor, with a 'no entry' sign screwed into it. Johnny pulled the door open and he and Bentley clambered through into Johnny's bedroom. Built into the roof space of the children's home, every inch of the sloping walls was covered with posters of space scenes. There was one of Saturn, showing the rings in full from above; another displayed all the planets in the solar system in order, and to scale; a third was of the International Space Station, albeit with fewer modules than Johnny had seen just a few hours earlier. But his pride and joy was one he'd printed himself. It was of

Sagittarius A*, the supermassive black hole at the very centre of the galaxy. The blackness almost spilled out of the picture while, just above the dark globe shone a brilliant white jet of magnetically charged matter, streaming away to escape its doom. Johnny had made sure the *Spirit of London* was at a very safe distance when capturing the image, but it didn't stop his blood running cold when he remembered that day.

The end of the room had been extended into a box shape and Bentley, still chilled after his many hours outside in the cold, pattered straight over and underneath the bed, curling up beside the radiator below the window. As he did so, he nudged a little cardboard box out of the way, to make himself more comfortable. Apart from Johnny's handheld games console, anyone looking in the box would have thought it full of junk, but the other little odds and ends were the only things he had left of his dad's. Sometimes, Johnny rummaged through and held the precious contents, just to feel close to his father again. Now, though, there was something more pressing to be done.

Above his bed was a shimmering haze, like dust particles glinting in the moonlight. Only, despite the open curtains, tonight there was no moon. Johnny took a deep breath, closed his eyes and placed his face into the twinkling cloud. When he opened them he was looking out onto the central courtyard of the Imperial Palace on Melania, the planet that was the capital of the galaxy. The dim red light and single shadows meant only one of the twin suns, Arros or Deynar, was above the horizon, but Johnny couldn't see which.

The Wormhole connected Johnny's bedroom to this place – it was the reason Johnny wasn't living permanently on the *Spirit of London*. It had been created by a Cornicula Worm (given to Johnny by the Emperor, along with a supply of eggs to hatch more) burrowing back through the fabric of time and space to its home world. You couldn't travel through it, but you could send a signal and see what was going on. The square was quiet. Johnny opened his mouth and said, 'Bram,' quietly at first, but much louder the second time. He hoped the Emperor was nearby.

'Who's there?' came a high-pitched squeaky voice from somewhere behind. Then, into the half-light, stepped a very thin creature, nearly three metres high, with a long face and wearing robes of the same electric blue as a dragonfly. It was a Phasmeer, a type of alien (neither male nor female) that seemed common in the Imperial Civil Service.

Whenever Johnny saw one he was reminded of the traitor Gronack, who'd been aboard the *Spirit of London* for a while until it had betrayed Johnny and Clara and handed them over to Colonel Hartman, someone high up in a sinister organization that suspected their half-alien parentage. When that backfired, it tried to sell them to the Andromedans instead. Even now, it made Johnny mad just remembering – he hadn't yet met one of these aliens he liked. 'I need to speak with Bram,' he said. 'Can you get him?'

'I take it you are referring to His Divine Imperial Majesty, the Emperor Bram Khari?' squeaked the Phasmeer. 'I'll just run along and fetch him, shall I?'

'Yes please,' Johnny replied, but the creature didn't move.

Instead it folded two long arms, jointed only near the very end, in front of its robes (which were beginning to turn pink) and replied, 'And who might you be who dares to summon the Emperor?'

'I didn't mean it like that,' said Johnny. 'It's me – Johnny Mackintosh. He'd want to speak to me.'

'Oh he would, would he, Johnny Mackintosh? I rather think I would have the shortest tenure of any Chancellor in Melanian history were I to summon His Divine Imperial Majesty for some young upstart who just happened to stumble upon a Cornicular opening.'

'It's not like that,' Johnny replied, as earnestly as he could. 'We're friends. Bram . . .'

'This is a priority channel for direct communication with the Emperor over matters of state,' shrieked the Phasmeer, its voice higher than ever and robes now bright red. 'I shall be reporting its abuse to the appropriate authorities. Good day to you. Your transmission is terminated.' A fine spray wafted from one of the Phasmeer's hands in the direction of Johnny face. As it reached him, the Wormhole contracted around his head, forcing him back onto his bed in Halader House. He sneezed several times, before trying to re-establish the link to give the Phasmeer a piece of his mind. It was no use. Somehow the Wormhole was closed for now, and Johnny wouldn't be able to tell the Emperor about the nearest star to the Sun being turned into a supernova, or the mysterious transmission he'd received in the computer room.

Sol was out of contact on Pluto. Bram was otherwise engaged. The more Johnny thought about it, the more he knew it would be madness for him to meet the dark-haired stranger without telling anyone, but something, somewhere in the back of his mind seemed familiar about that face. He went to sleep knowing he had to find out what it was.

2 ✧✧

A Derby Detour ✧✧

Johnny bashed his alarm clock until it finally stopped making the deep growling noise he loathed, and lay staring at the strange numbers piercing the gloom. Finally, he registered that they were telling him it was 05.30 a.m. One of the things he really hated was getting up while it was still dark outside. It took a few moments before he remembered he'd decided to read up on supernovae before joining Mr Wilkins in the Halader House kitchens.

Bentley's snores confirmed it would take more than a radio alarm to rouse the sheepdog at this time of night, but Johnny still tried to be as quiet as possible as he slid the box of stuff from under the bed and pulled out the handheld games console. It had a bigger display than the wristcom and a dedicated link to Kovac. He switched the device on and soon the blank screen came alive with the simulation he'd asked the quantum computer to prepare. A bloated star was in its death throes, having finally run out of usable fuel to keep shining. The next moment it was collapsing under its own weight as the force of gravity took hold. The commentary told Johnny he was watching Earth's own Sun, somehow altered. All the remaining matter of the star, its spent fuel, was being crushed ever more tightly together, the temperature rising higher and higher. The very atoms were being squeezed and something had to give. The screen on the console flared brilliant white as the handheld depicted one of the biggest explosions the Milky Way would see. The galaxy might contain hundreds of billions of stars but, in this moment, their combined light would be outshone by this one cataclysmic event.

Kovac said that a man called Chandrasekhar had shown a star needed to be much bigger than the Sun to become a supernova, but it was clear to Johnny that Nymac had somehow found a way round that. The simulation showed a vast fireball spreading out into the solar system, obliterating everything and anything it encountered. It would take just over an hour before Earth was vaporized. He fast-forwarded to a point when North and South America were facing the Sun and felt the full force of the impact. It took only a couple of seconds before the molten red glow spread from there around the globe and Earth itself began to disintegrate. Even though it was only a simulation, it was terrible to watch. Whatever the cost, Nymac had to be stopped. Johnny lay on his bed for a few minutes contemplating what he'd seen, before he looked again at the clock and couldn't believe it read 06.30. He was already late.

Mr Wilkins's warnings had been stern, but Johnny wondered if he'd got away with it as he stumbled, bleary-eyed, along the corridor and into what seemed a deserted dining room. Watching the simulation first thing had wiped him out and he couldn't help stretching his arms wide and letting out an almighty yawn. Then he saw something move along the far wall. A giant shadow rose upwards, before the great mass of the Halader House cook appeared from behind the large fridge in the far corner. The chef was carrying a long knife in one hand and a sharpening steel in the other. He ran the blade quickly backwards and forwards as he walked slowly towards Johnny, who stood his ground but wished he could cover his ears to shut out the high-pitched scrapes of metal against metal. As Mr Wilkins approached he bellowed at Johnny for being late and slammed the end of his sharpened knife into the long wooden table so that the neatly laid-out cutlery jumped into the air, clattering back down out of position.

'I'm not your slave,' said Johnny defiantly, but it didn't stop the cook dragging him by the ear into the kitchen and placing him in front of a near-empty pan of grey sludge bubbling on the hob, like hot mud around a volcano.

'Porridge, sonny,' said Mr Wilkins in answer to Johnny's questioning look. 'Four cups of water to one of oats. I want ten times that much – get cracking.' Johnny set to work as the cook sat down and opened up a newspaper. 'And make sure there's enough salt,' Mr Wilkins shouted, as his beard bristled against the paper. 'A tablespoon for every cup.'

Johnny didn't add any salt. Although he turned on a rusty tap, he didn't use the brown water which flowed from it either. Once he was sure the cook wasn't looking, he opened the fridge and, after sniffing several cartons, found some milk that hadn't gone off to use instead. Finally, as he ladled the steaming porridge into bowls, he topped each portion with a dollop of golden syrup. Breakfast proved much more popular than normal, but washing up all the pots and pans took forever.

Exhausted, his fingers wrinkled from spending so long in the lukewarm dishwater, Johnny was finally allowed to leave. Shutting the dining room door behind him, he found himself standing in front of Spencer Mitchell, dressed in a hooded sweatshirt and holding a deflated football. Despite being a few years older, Spencer invited Johnny outside for a kickabout in the station carpark. Johnny's reputation as a footballer had spread through Halader House after his team had won the Essex Schools Cup last year. It was cool to be included, but Johnny still said no. He knew he had to talk to Kovac before leaving for the rendezvous.

The quantum computer had surprised himself by calculating

that the Andromeda and Milky Way galaxies were due to collide in *only* half a billion years, apparently much sooner than Earthbound astronomers had predicted. Johnny said how impressed he was and then indulged the intelligent machine by asking how many new prime numbers it had discovered in the last week. Kovac sounded very proud to announce that there were four more, taking the total unknown to Earthbound mathematicians to seventy-nine.

With Kovac in a far better mood than the last time they'd spoken, Johnny tentatively asked him to send a message to Sol. The computer agreed, but stressed there was no guarantee any signal would be received. That would depend on the precise whereabouts of the spaceship.

It had to be worth a try. Kovac ran a search and determined that the huge radio telescope at Jodrell Bank was aligned in almost the right direction so, after a slight tweak, Johnny prepared to record a message. He'd never been so far from his ship and it was odd that any communication wouldn't be instant. It reminded Johnny of when he was little, dreaming he was commander of the first ever Mars base. Then he'd pretend to record messages to send to the Secretary-General of the United Nations, updating Earth with the colony's progress. Johnny smiled to himself. He'd still not taken the *Spirit of London* to the red planet and really should do that soon.

Finding the right words was difficult. In the end, he simply said that he'd received an unidentified transmission, but one he believed to be friendly, and was going to investigate. He gave them the coordinates and the time, but made clear he didn't expect them to come back because of it. He knew he wasn't being especially brave – the message wouldn't reach Pluto till mid-afternoon Johnny's time anyway so, when he went to meet the mysterious stranger, he would do so on his own.

He returned to his bedroom and roused Bentley. The

sheepdog was always reluctant to leave the comfort of the radiator, but he made Johnny feel safer and had often helped him out of a tight spot. Three times the big grey and white dog had saved him from the evil Krun, when without his friend's heroic efforts Johnny was sure to have been killed. Even when Bents had been shot and gravely wounded, he'd fought on and been the bravest companion anyone could wish for. Together, under a grey autumnal sky, they sneaked across the carpark, avoiding Spencer's football match, and reached the *Jubilee* which was covered in golden leaves from some overhanging branches. Johnny opened the door and Bentley jumped inside.

Piloting the shuttle was such a relief after a day at Halader House. Johnny was back in the real world, the one where he belonged – a place with aliens, faster-than-light spacecraft, hollowed-out moons and a vast galactic empire. He tried to recall the coordinates he'd been given the night before and concentrated hard on the memory – it was like speaking them out loud. The *Jubilee* responded, at first driving north on a road leading away from the station, but turning into a side street with no traffic and no CCTV. The small ship's sensors had become Johnny's own eyes and ears and, once he was sure no one was watching, he thought, *Shields on*. The walls of the taxi began to fade until they disappeared completely. For a fraction of a second it must have looked as if Johnny and Bentley were somehow flying side by side, just above the road, but then they, too, vanished. As the *Jubilee* lifted skyward, Johnny felt as though it was his own disembodied mind rising above the clouds. It was like being free of everything – his mountain of homework, Mr Wilkins, growing up in a children's home and missing his dead parents and brother so much he sometimes ached.

The rendezvous point proved further than Johnny expected. He was determined to be there before noon, so pushed the shuttle to near maximum sub-orbital speed. Far below, green and brown postage-stamp fields flew by in a blur while Bentley barked joyfully beside him. They flew on, over motorways and past towns and villages. Within a few minutes the *Jubilee* was circling above a patch of recently cleared land bordered by terrace homes on one side and a factory and railway sidings on the other. It looked an odd choice for a meeting place.

The *Jubilee* landed within ten metres of the appointed spot, surrounded by building rubble, and remained invisible. Johnny could watch and wait from the security of his cloaked shuttle. Not that there was anything to see apart from a few brown puddles and some small piles of bricks, half-heartedly covered by muddy tarpaulins. He probed further out, using the *Jubilee*'s sensors, straining for a sign of anyone approaching, noting the street names around the building site: Shaftsbury Crescent, Vulcan Street, Colombo Street. Nothing about them was familiar. He reached further out still, finding road signs and municipal buildings. This was Derby. It was the town where Johnny had been born – where he'd spent the first two years of his life.

Before he could make sense of this revelation, space itself wobbled and collapsed nearby. Something was unfolding very close, a little above the shuttle, but it was a tiny opening. A figure emerged in mid-air with some difficulty, as though the opening was only just large enough to climb through, and then fell four or five metres to the ground. He got up and dusted himself down. His hair was long, black and straggly and he wore a uniform of black rubber, skin-tight, with his chest and stomach muscles showing through. There was a large black ring on his right hand, while a sapphire blue band at the top of his left arm carried an insignia of three stars, almost in a line but with the right-hand one slightly too low. The strangest thing about him, though, was his face. The right side was covered by a black mask, while the other half looked strikingly familiar. Bentley went berserk, the noise of frantic barking mingled with scratching at the *Jubilee*'s invisible door.

'Bents – stop it!' shouted Johnny. For a moment the barks were replaced with a plaintive whine before the passenger door sprang open and the shuttle and its occupants rematerialized. Johnny could not believe it. Bentley must have wanted to get out so badly that the *Jubilee* had picked up the sheepdog's thoughts and opened the door. Johnny sat exposed in the pilot's seat, feeling like a total lemon. Bentley rushed up to the mysterious figure and stood on his hind legs, engulfed in the man's arms while he licked the exposed half of the stranger's face.

Johnny thought his own door open and stepped out onto the rough ground. Hesitantly he walked towards the figure. The man looked at Johnny coming towards him and said, 'Down, Bents . . . down.' Reluctantly the Old English sheepdog fell onto all fours. The man walked forwards to meet Johnny halfway, smiling broadly. He nodded towards the shuttlecraft and said, 'Nice motor, little bro'.'

The blood drained from Johnny's face, making him even paler than usual, and there was a buzzing in his ears as the world seemed to have been blotted out. Bentley was now circling the two of them, jumping in the air and barking, but the noise sounded far in the distance. Johnny heard the words, 'But you're dead,' and he knew they must have come from his own mouth, though he hadn't consciously spoken them. A million thoughts flashed through his mind and he wondered how he could have been so stupid. The picture he'd been carrying in his locket for the past six months showed a third figure beside him and Clara. It wasn't the photo of a ten year old boy – the age Nicky had been when supposedly murdered. It showed a man – Johnny's brother as he was now. He knew this was Nicky and

Bentley's reaction only confirmed it. The locket tucked beneath his tunic top did too. As Johnny stood there, he could feel the warmth of the strange metal against his chest, flowing out of the gift from his mother.

'Not dead,' replied Nicky. 'Just a long way away.'

'Where? What happened to you?'

'I was being trained,' Nicky replied. 'You see, I'm special and, by the look of your transportation, you're kind of special yourself. Guess it runs in the family.'

'Why here? Why now?' Johnny didn't know what to ask first.

'I used to come here as a boy,' Nicky replied. 'Dad brought me. You even came on the last day. It was a bit different then – a football ground. You wouldn't remember.'

'Dad . . . and Mum – they're kind of . . . dead,' said Johnny. He thought Nicky should be told, but he didn't know how to explain it properly. It was hard to look at his brother as he said the words, but he knew it was the right thing to do. It wasn't something he and Clara ever spoke about and, doing so now, he felt small and awkward – his arms suddenly seemed too long for him and he didn't know what to do with them or where to put his hands.

'I know,' said Nicky softly. 'I felt it. I've come back for you. To protect you. To ask you to join me. With you by my side, we could rule the galaxy.' He reached out and pulled Johnny into his arms, lifting him into the air and squeezing all the breath out of his lungs in a huge bear hug.

Johnny's face brushed Nicky's mask and suddenly he felt as if he was on fire. He pushed himself away, holding his burning left cheek as he fell to the ground. 'I don't want to rule the galaxy,' he said, before the pain welled up as though Mr Wilkins had rammed a kitchen knife in there. What's that?' Johnny managed to ask, pointing at Nicky's mask while wondering how to stop the needles shooting through his own nerve ends.

'You've woken him,' said Nicky. 'He's coming.' Johnny's brother looked as scared as he had the day before.

'Who? Who's coming?' Johnny asked, as waves of pain washed over him while he looked around, joining in Nicky's panic.

'Not now . . . no!' shouted Nicky. A beam of brilliant white light shot from the mask where Nicky's right eye should have been, before flickering out. He reached down to Johnny, desperate, and grabbed his left arm. 'Your communicator,' he said, struggling to get the words out as the light behind the mask flickered on and off. 'Give it to me.'

Johnny hadn't a clue what was happening, but undid the Velcro strap on his arm and handed the wristcom to his brother.

Nicky took it in his left palm while, from his right hand he produced a miniature, metallic spidery-looking machine, like nothing Johnny had ever seen. It scuttled onto the face of the wristcom, as red and green lights pulsed across its body. Stopping in the middle, it tapped its spindly legs on the circular screen, and then simply melted inside.

'I made this for you,' said Nicky hurriedly, as he strapped the device loosely around Johnny's arm. 'Just in case. When the lights are green I'm alone and it's safe. When they're red, he is with me. Red for danger. He mustn't know. The Nameless One must never know.'

'Who?' Johnny asked again. 'Who are you talking about?'

'Go!' shouted Nicky. 'I'll find you again. I promise. When the lights are green. Now run!'

Nicky staggered backwards clutching his face, screaming like a wounded animal. Johnny grabbed Bentley's collar and hauled the dog into the *Jubilee*, jumping in after him. Nicky was kneeling on the ground in front of them. Through his fingers, the brilliant white light became constant. There was a buzzing noise coming from inside the *Jubilee*. Johnny thought, *Shields on*. He saw something – a little mosquito – land on his arm, just as some circular lights around the face of his wristcom changed from green to red. Then the shuttle, the communicator, the mosquito and he and Bentley faded away.

From his invisible hideaway, Johnny watched as Nicky fell silent, got slowly to his feet and surveyed the scene. Something about him was different. He looked taller than before, and more powerful as he puffed out his chest. The smile had gone, replaced by a cruel, arrogant sneer, and from the masked half of his face blazed a brilliant lone star. He raised the back of his hand to his mouth and spoke into a black circle below his wrist. Having calmed down a little, Johnny wondered whether he should get out of the shuttle again, but something stopped him. This wasn't right. Instead, he closed his eyes and fought against the pain in his cheek, driving the electric signals away from his brain. What had felt like a thousand needles stabbing his face repeatedly was reduced to a bearable handful, and finally none, until a different pain flared, this time in his arm. The mossie had drawn blood. Johnny opened his eyes, but saw nothing. He tried to swat the invisible insect with an invisible hand, but only succeeded in slapping himself and making it worse. Meanwhile, having drunk its fill, the insect started buzzing around the insides of the shuttle. Johnny heard it bang several times against the windscreen it couldn't see.

His eyes went beyond the invisible barrier. A large black sphere had landed beside his brother. It couldn't be, but it looked just like a Krun shuttle – the only feature breaking up the smooth hull was the indecipherable black on black hieroglyphics scattered across it. This changed everything. He wanted to shout out, to open the doors and drag Nicky away, but instead he sat paralysed and invisible within the *Jubilee*. Three tall men in dark suits burst out of the Krun ship – aliens, masquerading in human form. Nicky was in terrible danger –

33

Johnny couldn't let his brother be taken. He prepared to drive the *Jubilee* into the aliens but, before he could act, each of the Krun knelt in the rubble in front of Nicky and said, 'My Lord.' One of the three was Stevens – or *a* Stevens anyway. This was the Krun who had kidnapped Johnny and Clara, and shot dead their father. Once, Johnny believed he had seen this particular alien die, but now he knew there had been nine, each identical, apparently hatched from a single egg.

Nicky shouted at the Krun in their own language, but Johnny could understand. Spread thinly across the Milky Way were ancient, noble creatures called Hundra that acted as the galaxy's translators. The first one Johnny met had given him a unique gift – a tiny fragment of its own soul – which now lived inside Johnny. It meant he could translate anything he heard spoken and make himself understood in whatever language he chose. Right now he half-wished he couldn't tell what his brother was saying.

'Tell me,' sneered Nicky. 'Who is the most important being in this wretched galaxy?'

'You, my Lord,' mumbled the three aliens in unison, their heads bowed.

Johnny's brother kicked out and one of the Krun was sent flying through the air backwards, unconscious even before it hit the ground. 'Then why do I find myself abandoned in this dreary wasteland?' screamed Nicky.

Memories Johnny didn't know he had began bubbling up inside him. This place reminded him of when he was little, of being crushed and frightened as he was swept along in the middle of a vast, chanting crowd. It had been Nicky who'd lifted him up, placing Johnny on his shoulders so he could see above the fray and wouldn't be scared. Another time, he was in a pushchair, rocking back and forth when the brakes must have failed and he'd careered down a hillside towards the top of a sea wall. Again, it was Nicky sprinting to his rescue who'd saved him, diving onto the back of the chair and sliding along behind to bring it to a stop, just as the gaping ocean promised to welcome Johnny in. In those long-ago moments Johnny had loved and idolized his older brother more than anything. It was hard to believe it was the same person standing before him now. The Krun kneeling beside Stevens mumbled something Johnny couldn't quite catch because the mosquito started buzzing again – but it sounded like it was Nicky's orders. Focusing his thoughts more precisely than he'd ever needed to before, Johnny directed the shuttle to create a tiny opening through which the annoying insect could escape, before sealing itself shut again. As he had hoped, the *Jubilee* was able to remain shielded.

'My orders? To be abandoned here?' Nicky snorted derisively, lifting his head so his mane of thick black hair shook. 'I don't think so. You have failed me once too often.'

With that he held out his right hand towards the alien, who fell forward onto all fours and pleaded, 'No, My Lord, no!' The Krun pawed at Nicky's boots, until a bolt of bright light shot from the ring and engulfed the alien in an orange halo. For a brief moment, the creature's true insect-like form was revealed – the head like a fly, the long snout that dripped sticky mucus and four elongated arms, made human only by the Krun's DNA showers. Then the creature vanished, leaving behind the slight hint of a shadow on a singed patch of ground.

Nicky, his hand still outstretched, sneered at the bowed figure of Stevens. 'Stop grovelling, slave. Return me to my ship.'

Hesitantly, the Krun stood up. Still with his head bowed, he asked, 'Did my Lord acquire what he wanted?'

As though mollified, Nicky turned his hand over so the ring was no longer a threat. Lost in thought, he stared at his open palm for some time before his fingers closed and he raised his eyes to Stevens. 'The plan has worked perfectly,' he said. 'If I allow you to live, it may be you shall teach the boy. Come – the *Astricida* awaits us both.' With that he walked towards the Krun shuttle which opened before him. At the entrance he paused and turned around. Despite the shuttle's shields, Johnny froze. His brother was looking straight towards the *Jubilee*, a curious expression on his face. Once more, Nicky raised his right hand to display the ring, but the orange death it promised came to the unconscious Krun on the ground. Its body disappeared into nothing, before Nicky turned again and entered the ship. As soon as he and Stevens were inside, the black sphere shot skyward at incredible speed, disappearing behind the clouds.

Johnny sat in the shuttle pilot's seat unable to understand what had happened. He'd found his brother who, for almost all of his life, he'd thought dead. Yet Nicky only seemed himself when that light wasn't shining out of his horrid mask, and even when he was himself Johnny wasn't at all sure he liked him. He certainly didn't want to rule the galaxy – that was Bram's job and, from what Johnny had seen, the Emperor was welcome to it and all the Phasmeers that came with the territory. He didn't know how long he stared at the area of the sky where he'd last seen the Krun ship, but was finally roused by someone speaking in his ear.

'Master Johnny,' said Alf's familiar voice. 'We have landed safely. Where on Earth are you?'

'I had to go somewhere,' said Johnny quietly, deliberately vague. 'I'll be back in a few minutes.' In his mind he focused on his destination, 30 St Mary Axe in London, and the *Jubilee* lifted into the air.

☆ ☆ ☆
☆ ☆

Johnny was in the sickbay while Alf tried to heal his burnt face. When the android started asking difficult questions such as,

'Whatever were you thinking going off on your own like that?' and 'Why did you not ask Kovac to monitor the *Spirit of London*'s signals so you would know as soon as we were back in Earth orbit?' Johnny covered the red-faced wristcom with his sleeve and diverted the topic of conversation to the latest *Times* crossword. Because other city workers sometimes did puzzles around the entrance to the *Spirit of London*, Alf had taken to joining them. Much to his frustration, the android sometimes found them impossible to solve. Despite his enormous intelligence, the answers to the clues needed something more than logic. Johnny was trying to help with four across: 'E' (thirteen letters) when the door swished open and in walked Clara.

'What happened to you?' she asked, sitting down on the bed next to Johnny's.

He took a deep breath as he wondered how to answer the question. The *Spirit of London* had returned to Earth before his message reached Pluto, so neither she, Alf nor Sol knew about Nicky's transmission. After everything that had happened this year, Johnny wasn't sure it was fair to tell Clara about a new brother just now, especially when that person seemed in league with the Krun. He needed to find out more. 'Louise got in touch,' he said, 'and I found Stevens.' It wasn't a lie – it just wasn't the whole truth.

Clara gasped. 'What about Louise? Is she OK?'

'Yeah, she's fine. And she says the Krun have left Yarnton Hill completely. Stevens was in Derby.'

'Derby? What was he doing there?'

'No idea,' said Johnny, which at least was an honest answer. 'I got this burn and he flew off in a Krun shuttle.'

'And a very unusual burn it is, Master Johnny,' said Alf. 'It is not down to exposure to heat.' Johnny and Clara looked at each other and then back to the android, who continued, 'This is the result of extreme cold.'

Johnny couldn't help it – he shuddered as he wondered about the freezing mask that covered half his brother's face. It didn't bear thinking about. 'What was Pluto like?' he asked, keen to change the subject.

'We completed the outpost,' said Alf.

'And I got to go outside and stand on the surface,' said Clara, now grinning. 'It's a double planet. Charon – its moon – is huge and really close.'

'It helped that we could put a skeleton staff in place,' Alf continued, ignoring the interruption.

'There are people there?' Johnny asked. 'What are you talking about? Who?'

'Not people, Master Johnny. Tolimi.'

'*Cheybora* went back to search for survivors after Alpha Centauri – you know, Toliman – went supernova,' said Clara. 'There's only a handful – they're really cute and tiny – but we couldn't bring them back here.'

'And they were very determined to help,' Alf continued. 'If only we had some Corniculae. Then the warnings could be instantaneous. Those extra few hours could make all the difference.'

At least that was something Johnny could come clean about. He'd completely forgotten he hadn't told the android about his stash of eggs waiting to be hatched – Alf was sure to know what to do with them. Once out of their cocoons, the creatures behaved like salmon, finding their way to the place of their birth in order to lay new eggs. Only these Worms had the special ability that they could burrow through the fabric of space itself. 'About that,' said Johnny, grinning despite the pain in his cheek. 'I've got some . . . eggs anyway. They're at Halader House.'

'What? How? When? . . . Master Johnny!' Alf looked so flabbergasted Johnny wouldn't have been surprised to see the bowler hat lift off the android's head and start spinning of its own accord. Clara just giggled.

'Bram gave them me with the Worm he'd hatched on Melania,' Johnny went on. 'I tried contacting him last night, but the new Chancellor wouldn't let me speak to him.'

'Let's go to Melania,' said Clara. 'We've got to tell him about the supernova and we can take a Worm to Pluto on the way.'

Johnny smiled. One ship wouldn't be enough to protect the solar system from Nymac – they needed reinforcements and Melania was the best place to find them. Part of him wanted to stay and search for Nicky, but his brother had already found him once and promised to do so again. Besides, it would be wrong to put his family ahead of saving Earth and the solar system. 'We'll go tomorrow,' he said.

He didn't know why he'd not been able to speak with Bram, but he was certain of one thing. Neither Mrs Devonshire nor Mr Wilkins was going to be pleased when he failed to turn up to school in the morning.

3 ✧

The Absent Emperor ✧

When, very early on Monday morning, Johnny arrived at Halader House to collect the Cornicula eggs, he ran straight into Mr Wilkins.

'Oi! Where've you been, sonny?' asked the cook, blocking the entire corridor outside the computer room, so there was no way past.

He didn't have time for this. They were scheduled to take off in under three hours. Clara had been keen to update her diary with everything that had happened, so remained on the *Spirit of London* while Alf had come with him to Castle Dudbury. Johnny had left the android sitting in the *Jubilee* in the station carpark and promised to be no more than five minutes. 'Out,' he replied as he tried to squeeze through a gap between Mr Wilkins and the magnolia-painted wall.

He wasn't quick enough. The cook pressed his enormous bulk into Johnny, lifting him up and pinning him against the side of the corridor. 'Gotcha!' said Mr Wilkins, smiling through his tiny black eyes. The cook's hot breath and bristly beard were on Johnny's face, forcing him to close his eyes. The huge man continued, 'Where'd you bugger off to yesterday, you good-for-nothin'? Who did you think was going to cook the roast?'

Johnny wanted to say, 'That's your job,' but when his eyes reopened he was distracted by the clumps of dandruff on the shoulders of Mr Wilkins's blue polo shirt, twinkling like tiny stars under the fluorescent lights. It was, perhaps, just as well.

The cook backed off slightly allowing Johnny's toes to touch the floor but, before he could make a run for it, Mr Wilkins grabbed hold of Johnny's ear and dragged him along the corridor into the kitchen.

'You'll cook up the porridge and then you can change into your school uniform. I don't want you keeping that nice Mrs Devonshire waiting. Is that clear, sonny?'

Johnny nodded. He couldn't afford to do anything else.

'Don't think I'm enjoying looking after you,' continued the man who, Johnny was certain, was loving every minute of it. 'But I will drag you to that school myself if I have to – it's right next door to the pet food factory and I need to pick up some cheap meat.' Mr Wilkins licked his lips.

Johnny tried to shut out the horrible thought of what he might have been eating all these years and set to work making the porridge. He could hear Alf speaking in his ear, wondering what was taking so long, but daren't respond as Mr Wilkins was watching him like a hawk, from behind the cover of an upside-down newspaper. Instead, he knelt down, slid open a cupboard door and tried to pull out the large two-handled metal pan from the very back, without tripping any of the mousetraps Mr Wilkins had set around the inner walls. There were loads of smaller pans, bowls and baking trays in the way, but eventually, after a final tug followed by a loud clunk, the pan broke free and Johnny fell backwards, gripping it to his stomach. One of the handles was half hanging off, but he was pretty sure he hadn't done it. Inside, burnt onto the bottom, was a charred brown crust – remnants from previous visits to the hob. When he picked some off with his fingernails it just made things worse, exposing a lighter layer that looked far more likely to contaminate any new meal.

He lifted the pan, hoping the dodgy handle would hold, and

dropped it onto the charcoal bars that sat above the grease-coated hob. Mr Wilkins placed the paper beside him, folded his arms, focused his small beetle-like eyes on Johnny as though X-raying him and began barking orders. 'A mug of oats's more than enough,' he said. 'Plenty of water in the pan – no skimping on that. And don't forget the salt, sonny. Lots of salt.'

There was no chance at all of swapping tastier ingredients as he had before, so he followed the cook's instructions to the letter. The oats already looked grey and soggy; the water from the curved cast-iron taps was, again, rusty brown, and the drum of salt had all sorts of unidentifiable black bits and pieces inside. After everything had been added to the pan, Johnny walked to another set of cupboards and opened the third drawer down where all the odds and ends were kept – blunt corkscrews, broken chopsticks, garlic crushers and battered straws – and took out a big box of kitchen matches. Johnny smiled, despite himself. The massive box made it seem as if he was in *Land of the Giants*. He took out a gigantic match, around ten centimetres long, and struck it away from him along the side of the box. He turned the gas on, placing the match under the pan, but it was a few seconds before the whoosh of blue flame came, shooting out in all directions. Johnny only just avoided being burnt. He found a relatively clean wooden spoon in the same drawer and began to stir the watery broth.

By the time the porridge was ready, a spluttering grey gloop barely denser than water, Johnny was miles behind schedule. He flew out of the kitchen, climbed the stairs and raced along the first floor corridor with his wrist to his mouth, apologizing to Alf for his lateness. He reached the spiral staircase, pulled down the trapdoor and carried on through. Outside the box window, a black car door opened out of nothing, before the remainder of the *Jubilee* reappeared and a flustered android climbed awkwardly through into Johnny's bedroom.

'Master Johnny, we are going to be late. The Tolimi will wonder what can possibly have happened.'

'I'm doing my best,' said Johnny, as he rummaged through some old clothes covering the bottom of his wardrobe, before standing up holding a translucent turquoise wheel-like container by two of its four thick spokes. The coloured light came from five stones encased in the central hub – the five Cornicular eggs. 'Let's go,' said Johnny as he lifted one leg onto the windowsill, the container held tightly under his arm.

Alf shouted to stop. Johnny turned around to see the android looking nervously at Johnny's untidy bedroom floor, spinning his bowler hat between his fingers.

'What is it, Alf?' Johnny asked. 'I thought we were in a hurry.'

'But is this not the place you speak with the Emperor?'

Johnny nodded.

'Then we should maintain it as our communications centre,' said the android. 'We must hatch an egg in here.'

Johnny felt stupid for nearly leaving the room without doing the most important thing. He sat down on the bed with the container perched on his lap and looked up at his pinstriped companion for guidance. Alf simply shrugged. Johnny had opened the disc once before, to release the original Melanian Worm. That time he'd willed it to happen and it had.

Now he concentrated on what he needed, aware that he was getting so much better at controlling the strange power he possessed. Focusing on the little hatchery, he could sense the fluctuations in the energy field around it but he couldn't stop the flow. It was too fast – a blur of motion that wouldn't settle. In frustration, he tossed the container on top of his pillow and lay down beside it. He closed his eyes, trying to shut everything out, but bright lights from the five eggs danced across the insides of his eyelids. Johnny watched them, almost looking

43

inside himself. The lights began to drift, very slowly at first, until they settled into the W-shape of Cassiopeia. As they did so, the turquoise glow filtering through Johnny's lids became so intense it was as if they weren't even shut. The case had opened and the little attic room was alive with light from the eggs, glowing like embers in a white-hot fire.

The scent of vinegar wafted up Johnny's nostrils, reminding him of the fish and chips he loved so much. Smiling, he reached inside and picked one of the eggs up, hoping it wouldn't burn. It felt no different from having a soap bubble on the palm of his hand. Very carefully he lowered it into the outer ring of the container, connected to the hub by the spokes. Then he closed the lid. There was a hiss of gas escaping before the whole thing sealed itself shut. The egg began to stretch, growing in both directions. As it became elongated around the outside of the wheel, it changed colour, ripples of light passing through all the colours of the rainbow. The two ends grew ever longer and looked just about to meet, when the egg's outer casing melted away leaving a turquoise blur of light racing around as close to the edge as it could get. It was a newly born Cornicula Worm and when Johnny next opened the container to release it on Pluto, he knew it would return to this exact spot, leaving open a tunnel in the space–time continuum.

Johnny looked at Alf who smiled back. 'Master Johnny,' he said. 'Congratulations to the father.'

Stage one of the plan to defend the solar system was to have Pluto Base operational, but the Andromedans might not be so obliging as to unfold on its doorstep. Johnny's visit to the dwarf planet had been all too brief, simply checking in on the little Tolimi and releasing the Cornicula Worm (which immediately vanished, tunnelling straight to Johnny's bedroom).

Now they were even further out, some thirty trillion

kilometres from the Sun in the region known as the Oort Cloud. Here was the solar system's final resting place for the leftovers of failed planets from a few billion years before. They were so far from home that, standing on the bridge, the Sun appeared as just another (albeit bright) star in the heavens. Even so, Johnny still felt a special draw towards it. A handful of Sol's nanobots had been reprogrammed to become spatial disturbance detectors, and were about to be released to join the frozen debris. Over the next few weeks they would multiply, building copies of themselves from the material in the cloud, finally forming a giant nebulous neural net that would encase the entire solar system, feeding information back to the Tolimi in their new home and from there, via the newly opened Wormhole, to Halader House. If an Andromedan ship unfolded anywhere in the outer solar system, both the Tolimi and Johnny would soon know about it.

The defence net was quite an engineering feat, all designed by Alf who had the honour of pressing the button on Johnny's console to set everything in motion. Clara was wearing a sparkly dress and had curled her hair specially for the occasion. She'd poured glasses of lemonade for the three of them, making sure Alf's was as full to the brim as it was possible to be, as it was always fun to watch the android drink effortlessly without spilling a drop. She also added some to Bentley's bowl, before they raised their glasses in celebration. Sol joined in by creating a spectacular laser light show just outside the ship, which the sheepdog especially loved, standing on his back legs to get a better view through the sides of the bridge. Although Alf made a point of complaining that the beams could theoretically be visible through Earth's most powerful telescopes, confusing astronomers for decades to come, Johnny had the feeling that the android was secretly rather pleased.

With the nanobots released, they were ready to leave for

Melania to ask the Emperor for ships to protect Earth. There wasn't much point knowing the Andromedans had arrived, if they didn't have the firepower to stop them. Clara had programmed a series of folds for the Plican to follow. Once the divide that held the creature in a tiny compartment at the very top of its tank was released, the alien would propel itself through into the main section, unfurling its eight tentacles to take hold of pieces of space itself and send the ship on its journey. Johnny placed three fingers on the console by his captain's chair and three capsules emerged from the floor around the edge of the bridge. These were the gel pods that protected space travellers from the ordeal of folding. As ever, Clara would remain outside to keep the Plican company – she didn't seem to mind having her stomach repeatedly turned inside out. It was Captain Valdour who'd first recognized her unique ability to withstand the manipulation of space that would cause anyone else to be, at best, violently sick and, at worst, seriously dead. It wasn't just that Johnny's sister could handle what no one else seemed able to – she positively thrived on the special sensation of folding.

Special or not, in Johnny's experience she was welcome to it. With Alf and Bentley safely inside their compartments, Johnny asked Sol to turn off the gravity generators and he and Clara floated upwards, laughing together. Being weightless was one of many elements of space travel he did love. For a couple of minutes the floor became the ceiling and they somersaulted in mid-air, before chasing after each other while several metres up – it was impossible to even get close. Johnny persuaded Sol to release a hundred litres of water into the bridge, which hovered near the Plican's tank in a giant, wobbling ball that they took turns diving through. Finally, soaking wet, Johnny entered his own gel pod and the long journey to Melania could begin. In several days' time when he next stepped onto the bridge, it would be to see the fabulous world that was the capital of the galaxy.

The water was a dress rehearsal for entering the capsule, but this time Johnny didn't hold his breath. All his instincts told him to do that when surrounded by the thick orange fluid oozing into the chamber around him – that survival required keeping his mouth clamped tightly shut – but one thing Johnny had learnt as he'd travelled the galaxy was to conquer those instincts. He opened his mouth and let the gloop slide down his throat without even touching the sides. Even so, he couldn't avoid the petrol-like taste. His body began to swell. It started with his fingers and toes, each one, in turn tripling in size as the cushioning gel began its work. Soon, Johnny's hands looked like inflated rubber gloves while his feet were big as boats. The swelling spread up his limbs and reached his torso. Fully inflated, and unable to bend his arms or legs, Johnny became aware of the first fold beginning. The sides of the pod and the walls of the *Spirit of London* herself rushed through him and away. Stars and nebulae flew past at astonishing speed as the space between them shrank and disappeared. He changed direction with no warning, dragged at ninety degrees towards a young star cluster. Without the gel, it would have been unbearable; with it, he just felt a little queasy.

Clara had divided the route into twenty-three stages. The Plican, initially a baby when brought on board, had quickly grown strong, but even now it could only manage five or six folds before it needed to rest. Johnny had brought along some homework from school to think about so he didn't fall too far behind but, although his head was now twice its normal size, his brain power clearly hadn't expanded. However hard he tried to concentrate, he found himself drifting off into other, much more interesting, daydreams, most of which involved Nicky and some way of finding his mother and father again, whatever

47

strange place or dimension they'd gone to. His history textbook was sending him to sleep, so he gave up. Trying to do something useful, he turned instead to a much more interesting problem Alf had set him. It was about Einstein's theory of relativity and was called the twin paradox.

☆ ☆ ☆
☆ ☆

When Johnny awoke, the gel pod was nearly empty. An elephant-like trunk was hoovering up the orange remains from Johnny's clothes. It hovered over his wristcom, so he gently pushed it away, revealing the red lights around the face. Johnny pulled down his sleeve to cover them. Then, as always, it tried to suck up the locket dangling around his neck – Johnny grabbed it before it disappeared down the suction tube. He got up and pressed a large switch on the wall. As the door swished open, he entered the bridge, bathed in dull red light through which he could see Clara. She was sitting on the floor, arms outstretched and pressed against the outside of the Plican's tank. On the inside, two of the creature's tentacles were reaching out to his sister. Johnny had no idea how Clara communicated with the strange being, but it was always reassuring to see her when they arrived at the faraway places Sol took them to. He strode forward to study the viewscreen. Clara turned round and smiled. Maybe it was the light from the twin red giants Arros and Deynar, but the silver flecks in her eyes shone more brightly than normal.

'Any problems?' asked Johnny, as he stared at a large white globe in front of him. Twice the size of Earth, and with practically every square kilometre built on, this planet-wide city was Melania. The Imperial Palace, with the only areas of greenery and water anywhere on the surface, was out of sight on the far side.

'We took a detour halfway,' said Clara. 'Unfolded close to a lot of ships. Didn't stop to see whose side they were on, but I didn't recognize them.'

'No one followed us?' Johnny asked.

Clara rolled her eyes. 'You can't follow someone through a fold – space gets too messed up. You'd be torn to pieces.'

'I'm being hailed,' announced Sol and, as Johnny nodded to nowhere in particular, the viewscreen changed to reveal a bone-crested alien with a spotted, scaly face.

'Terran vessel *Spirit of London*. I have no record of a flight plan logged. State the purpose of your presence in Regency space.'

Terra was what the rest of the galaxy called Earth, and Johnny often forgot that Bram wasn't actively running Melania or the Empire – he'd delegated power to the Regent. In fact, until Johnny and Clara had arrived on the planet a few months ago, no one other than a handful of civil servants had seen the Emperor for nearly a hundred years. 'Visiting His Imperial Majesty Emperor Bram Khari,' Johnny replied. 'Request permission to land.'

The alien made a gurgling sound that might have been laughter. 'The Emperor is not in the habit of granting audiences,' it said, barely concealing a patronizing smile.

'Check our transponder signal,' said Johnny through gritted teeth. 'You will see this Terran vessel flies under the Imperial banner. I'm sure Bram will want to say hello.' Johnny was equally sure the alien had never heard the Emperor referred to as 'Bram' before. The first time Johnny and Clara had landed on Melania, they'd heard a list of his formal titles that lasted for over five minutes.

'My mistake, it seems,' snarled the alien. 'You are cleared to land . . . Talamine Spaceport. Sending through approach vector.'

Johnny smiled. He couldn't wait to see the Emperor and tell

him everything that had happened over the last few days and make sure Earth would be safe. Bram was the wisest person he'd ever met and the only one Johnny could speak to about Nicky and his family. A real bonus was that the Emperor should be able to tell Johnny more about his mum – incredibly, thousands of years earlier when Bram had first become the ruler of the galaxy, Johnny now knew his mother had been there helping. Hopefully the Emperor would be there to greet them when they landed.

☆ ☆ ☆
☆ ☆

No spacecraft were allowed to overfly the Imperial Palace, but the route to the landing site took the *Spirit of London* close enough to see the giant blue tower at the very centre of the Emperor's home, and the concentric rings of land and sea centred around it. The beautiful white stone buildings of the abandoned Imperial University glistened on the shores of the second circle of land, but the Hall of Plicans and other notable buildings were too small to be picked out as they flew by, arcing towards Talamine, perhaps the busiest spaceport anywhere in the Milky Way.

Ships of all shapes and sizes passed in the other direction, a mixture of glittering small, spherical balls of light, giant cigar-shaped tourist vessels, brick-like Ke Kwan cargo freighters, sleek fighters from the Imperial Navy and even saucer-shaped discs that clearly didn't only make appearances in old-fashioned science fiction films. Sol was given a prime landing spot and settled as softly as a dandelion head in the appointed space.

Alf was especially excited to be back on his homeworld. Johnny, Bentley (his fur still matted with orange goo) and, reluctantly, Clara followed the android down the antigrav lifts to the main doors at the foot of the *Spirit of London*. Clara might be able to fold space, but it didn't stop her being terrified of heights – stepping into thin air to be transported through the ship never seemed to get easier for her. Johnny and Bentley both loved it. It reminded Johnny of cartoons where a character like the Pink Panther would walk off a cliff and be able to keep going for a few moments before realizing he was in mid-air and plummeting to the ground. Sometimes he'd even hum the theme tune as he entered the seemingly empty shaft but, unlike with the Pink Panther, he was glad the 'falling' part aboard the *Spirit of London* was rather more controlled. As they reached the bottom, Johnny slapped the statue of the giant silver alien in the lobby for luck.

It didn't seem to have worked. When he looked out through the clear walls it wasn't Bram he saw. Instead, a familiar-looking three-metre high Phasmeer was standing outside the revolving doors. It might simply have been the sunlight, but its robes were glowing pink. This was the new Chancellor, whom Johnny had found himself speaking to only the other night. Considering the previous incumbent of the role, Chancellor Gronack, turned out to have been spying for the Andromedans, he'd developed a dislike for the species that his only conversation with the new Chancellor had simply reinforced.

'Can't take no for an answer, can you?' squeaked the Phasmeer, as Johnny stepped out of one of the four sets of revolving doors, keeping a tight hold of Bentley's lead. As soon as he was outside, he felt crushed by his own weight. One of the drawbacks of Melania he'd forgotten was the strong gravity. The Chancellor, with the benefit of a portable antigrav assist, hovered about half a metre above the ground in front of them. 'I told you he wouldn't see you,' it continued, speaking loudly and slowly in Universal, as though its audience might not understand.

'Why not? Where is he?' Johnny asked.

'I do not discuss the whereabouts of His Divine Imperial

Majesty Emperor Bram Khari with barbarians from the periphery,' squawked the Phasmeer, turning an ever deeper red.

'I do believe there must be some mistake,' said Alf, stepping in front of Johnny. 'I was formerly Chief of His Majesty's Household . . .'

'Ah yes, the robot,' interrupted the Phasmeer. It was a label Alf hated. 'There is no mistake. If I had my way you would be sent back to whatever unspeakable planet it is you came from, but you will have an audience.'

'Thank you,' said Alf. Johnny was always impressed by the android's self-control.

'For some inexplicable reason, you have been granted an audience with the Regent,' said the Phasmeer. 'Follow me.' At which point it turned and floated away up some wide marble steps.

Alf followed without difficulty, but Johnny, Clara and Bentley struggled to keep up, until the Phasmeer slowed, having lost control of its antigrav device, and began to bash repeatedly into the stone staircase. Johnny laughed and turned to Clara. She was smiling too, but concentrating hard at the same time. The silver flecks in her eyes were shining brightly.

'I've got to practise,' she said innocently, as she repeatedly folded and unfolded the space between the Chancellor and the marble steps.

Reaching the top, in the area known as the Senate Platform, the view opened out and the warm, dry air engulfed them. Johnny glanced longingly towards the needle-like blue tower, many kilometres high, far away on the horizon. Closer to hand, immediately in front of them, was a moving walkway, a travelator wider than a motorway, that led towards a large, domed building. Still bouncing up and down, the Chancellor fell onto it and got to its feet with its robes even redder. The others followed. It was a relief not to have to climb any more stairs. Bentley lay down on the walkway, his tongue hanging out as he panted loudly.

Johnny swatted away a couple of insects buzzing around him and turned to look behind. The nosecone of the *Spirit of London* was visible above the top of the steps. He was proud his ship didn't look at all out of place. He turned back to find Clara and Bentley peering through the walkway, which was solid yet see-through. Melania didn't stop on the surface. Beneath their feet the vast city continued, many kilometres down, buzzing with activity like an ant colony. Flying ships and winged aliens wove their way at frightening speeds between the tops of underground towers, reaching up from below like enormous stalagmites. Clara nudged Johnny and he looked up. The walkway was flanked on one side by seven statues, tens of metres high, ancient yet still recognizable as they glittered red, their diamond structures reflecting the sunlight.

'The other emperors,' said Alf. 'From Themissa to Ophion.'

Clara caught Johnny's eye. The very first statue wore a powerful, yet kindly face. It reminded Johnny of their mum.

'Themissa created the Empire after the fall of Lysentia,' the android continued. 'She brought order out of the chaos – the galaxy has been grateful ever since.'

'The galaxy has outgrown such fairytales,' squeaked the Chancellor. 'It is the Senate that maintains order. Speaking of which, we have arrived.' The wide travelator ended in front of a giant, curved wall, made of some sort of smooth black shiny stone. 'The Senate sits in emergency session. You will wait in an anteroom until you are summoned.'

The Chancellor led Johnny and the others through a massive entrance, thirty metres high, that opened into a courtyard, covered by a clear domed roof through which one of Melania's twin suns shone weakly. At the centre of the courtyard stood a round building, made of white stone, crumbling in parts, which looked so ancient it smelt of history. This had to be the Senate itself. But they turned away from it and walked across the giant flagstones (engraved with strange hieroglyphs), passing aliens of many different shapes and sizes. Their hides like elephants, the floating balls that were Hundras hovered above spots where different species gathered, glowing red as they translated the various interstellar languages. Johnny had to stop Bentley barking at them and was glad he'd put the Old English sheepdog on a lead.

Eventually, they went through another oversized opening and into a side chamber with golden walls and a spectacular ceiling glistening with precious stones. As Johnny stared upwards, he saw that they had been positioned to represent specific stars – massive rubies twinkled in place of red giants, while occasional sapphires showed the few young blue stars that were visible in the skies above Melania. What dominated the ceiling, though, was a vast circle of blackness – the supermassive black hole at the very heart of the galaxy.

Although the room was indoors and covered, a stream ran through it, lined by trees with long leaves like ribbons that swayed in a non-existent breeze. Bentley collapsed underneath one of them and began to lap at the water.

The Chancellor gave the sheepdog a look of total disdain, but didn't prevent Bentley drinking. 'Wait here,' said the Phasmeer, and floated away out of the room.

Clara sat down by the stream to get her own breath back and started stroking Bentley. Alf disappeared in search of some sort of news service to catch up on what had been happening, leaving Johnny to gaze around the antechamber. Just this one room was the size of a football ground. Around the walls were inscriptions carved into the golden stone – Johnny had to rely on his lessons from Alf to try to make sense of the writing, as the fleck of the Hundra's soul inside him could only translate spoken languages. It proved beyond him. Instead, he looked around at the few different aliens scattered about. All were alone and it was odd that he had to squint to focus properly on them – as though they were surrounded by some sort of haze. For a few moments Johnny studied a curiously blurred hexapod fairly close by. All six of its legs were moving forward, yet it remained exactly where it was.

Puzzled, he lay down on his back on top of the springy floor and gazed up at the ceiling. In the outer reaches of the Milky Way, stars were spread out. The Toliman system had been the closest to Earth's Sun (which the rest of the galaxy called Sol), but even that was four light years away. Here, at the galaxy's core, stars were much more tightly packed. That was why the night sky remained so bright, despite the lights of Melania trying to blot them out. During the time he'd spent at the Imperial Palace, the view had been nothing short of spectacular. As Johnny studied the ceiling now, he thought he could identify a few stars and, if he was right, could even see the diamond-shaped constellation Portia (Bram had said it meant 'the doorkeeper' in an ancient tongue) that was the Emperor's symbol.

The jewelled sky became fuzzy. Johnny sat up and found his face squidged against something he couldn't see, as if clingfilm had been stretched across it. For a moment he panicked, but the next thing he knew he'd passed through the strange membrane and found himself inside a clear sphere, four or five metres across. As he got to his feet a smug voice, backed by eerie high tempo music, spoke from all around, saying, 'Thank you for choosing the Milky Way News Network – the number one Vermalcast of all the news, all of the time, from all across the galaxy.' Johnny had never heard of a Vermalcast but presumed he was in it. Against background music, the voice continued, 'In the news this hour . . . **Senate Stalemate** – today's crucial vote on war funding hangs in the balance. **Hundra Horror** – at a ceremony welcoming five threatened star systems under Regency protection, the local President touches a hovering translator and is instantly killed. Hear Chancellor Karragon explain the diplomatic oversight. **The Absent Emperor** – a special report by Z'habar Z'habar Estagog. And **Sport** – the latest stage of the Aldebaran to Mizar Rally. Can anyone catch Sebes Kiksapongo? Approach your story now. To the left and right and in front and behind, an image from each of the options had been projected onto the clear walls of the bubble.

Johnny moved to his right towards Bram Khari's familiar face, hoping this was how he chose the story he wanted. It seemed to work. He couldn't reach the side of the sphere – it rotated beneath him as he walked – but the figure of a far younger Bram, very like the one he'd met in the distant past, crystallized before him, fully three-dimensional. The Emperor was wearing a white top displaying the four stars of Portia, with black trousers, as he stepped out of an enormous spaceship and waved to massed crowds surrounding Johnny. It was just like being there. Hovering only a little above Bram was a very curious, six-legged alien with two sets of thin, insect-like wings which were beating so quickly they formed a solid blur. The creature had a long, twisted neck like a double helix, above which sat two completely separate, but apparently identical, heads. One of them began speaking and, after a few seconds, the other joined in.

'We've all seen the footage. Long before almost any of today's Imperial citizens were alive – *ignoring the unfeasibly odorous Erumpeton of Deneb Six, who claims the secret to her hundred millennia lifespan is imbibing those bodily waste products the rest of us prefer to discard* – a young Senator, Bram Khari, returned to Melania with a mysterious being from Atlantis (*a civilization that had threatened to seize control of the galaxy*).'

Johnny ignored the double-headed commentator, who looked out of place with the rest of the scene. Instead, unbelievably, he found himself staring at his mum. She was standing right in front of him, dressed in a one-piece silver outfit that flowed like liquid over her body, and smiling, her pale blonde hair glinting in the soft red glow of both Arros and Deynar. He reached out to touch her but his hand simply passed through the projection, causing her image to blink out of existence until he withdrew. It was torture – he wanted more than anything for her to take him in her arms and hold him. The voiceover continued.

'After millennia of chaos following the death of Ophion, the people demanded a new Emperor. Khari seemed eager (*some would say too eager*) for the top job and had soon set up home in the Imperial Palace.

'It would be churlish not to acknowledge the prosperity that followed. *The peace dividend from the next few thousands of years saw the Empire restored, perhaps surpassing its former glories.* The entire civilized galaxy (*and plenty of parts that weren't*) seemed under the spell of the fresh-faced Emperor, who made little effort to justify his claims to be descended from a Lysentian.'

As the commentary continued, the bubble of illusion within which Johnny stood changed, the only constant being the hovering narrators. Numerous scenes depicted the young Bram's travels around the galaxy, often with Johnny's mum smiling in the background – whenever Johnny glimpsed her, he had eyes for nothing else.

'Here on Melania, a new outer layer of the capital was built – *both the Imperial Palace and Senate were raised to the new level and restored.* Later – *much later* – came the Great Tower of Themissa, which reached from the surface into orbit. All seemed well, *but appearances can be deceptive.*'

The scene shifted again, returning to Melania to show the entire surface covered over by gigantic machines, sometimes operated by cheery aliens, enabling yet more building to take place on the new top layer. The twin narrators' tone became more serious.

'The cares of running an empire weighed heavily on the once-youthful Senator's broad shoulders. *Following an unscheduled visit to the Large Magellanic Cloud, he aged visibly.* Perhaps increasingly obsessed with threats to his leadership, *he created the elite Imperial Guard*.'

Fearsome soldiers being drilled now stood before Johnny, who was glad they weren't real. That didn't stop him putting his hand through the nearest just to be sure.

'His Divine Imperial Majesty withdrew further and further from public life – *day-to-day control of the Empire passed to the First Senator*. While everyone knew who was really in charge, the whispering campaign grew louder – *who would follow when, dare it be said, the Emperor was no longer with us?* With no heir, who would lead the galaxy in future aeons? Then, *as every citizen of the Empire knows*, His Divine Imperial Majesty disappeared altogether. *The first of what have now been five regents was installed*, and rumours of Khari's actual – *or at least imminent* – death swept all the way from the hub to the outer rim. Despite assertions from the Regency Civil Service that they maintained constant links with the Emperor, he remained incommunicado for almost a century. *War broke out, the Andromedans somehow folding the vast emptiness of intergalactic space, to bring terror to the very heart of the galaxy*.'

Now the view before Johnny was of giant, terrifying space battles, with whole planets disintegrating, as though burning from the inside out. Lines of vessels from opposing sides passed each other, firing bright bolts of energy, but it was the white ships of the Imperial Navy that seemed to suffer the most, while dark, prickly spheres appeared nearly undamaged.

'If ever there was a time a people needed their Emperor, this had to be it. *The galaxy waited*, but the Emperor they hoped for did not appear. *Surely, we thought, he must have passed beyond?* Then – *only months ago* – the Imperial Guard finally set forth from their island base, arriving at the Senate Platform.'

Johnny couldn't believe it – he was within the scene that had greeted him the very first time he arrived on Melania. He could see himself in the distance, supported by a strange, four-winged alien and holding a barely conscious Clara. The Regent, and then Captain Valdour, made speeches, but their words were drowned by the continuing commentary.

'Crowds the like of which had not been seen for decades filled the Senate Platform to welcome back the courageous Dauphin – *offspring and heir apparent of the mighty Regent* – who had bravely tried to sue for piece with the merciless Andromedan General Nymac.'

It was hard to fathom how the commentator had got things so wrong – the Dauphin was about the most annoying, pompous alien Johnny'd had the misfortune to encounter on all his travels. For 'courageous', he thought, substitute 'idiotic'.

'Maverick, *and frankly batty*, Imperial Captain Valdour – *a relic from some imagined bygone age of heroic deeds* – did his best to deflect attention away from the worthy Dauphin, but was himself trumped when the Imperial Guard came to arrest these beings, *later discovered to come from the faraway Sol system.*'

The view was now a close-up of the Johnny from six months ago, holding his sister. He was amazed how young he looked, and wanted to strangle the ridiculous, double-headed reporter. He had most definitely not been arrested – he and Clara had been guests of the Emperor. He watched as his past self was finally able to relax his grip on his sister, allowing an invisible, floating platform to ferry them into the distance towards the great tower on the horizon.

'It was presumed the two criminals had been imprisoned

indefinitely within the Imperial Palace, yet this very morning they arrived at Talamine Spaceport in one of the ugliest Imperial Starships ever seen. *Not best pleased at the presence of MWNN cameras* [Johnny could be seen lashing out at whatever was creating the projection – to his amazement he realized it must have been the "insects" he'd tried to swat], we filmed their visit to the Senate, *accompanied by an alien of unknown origin* [Bentley came into close-up] and a robot thought to have once served in the Imperial Household.'

The scene on the travelator froze and disappeared, leaving only the flying alien buzzing in front of Johnny on its two pairs of wings. The long, twisted neck began to unwind as it continued speaking.

'As if this story weren't strange enough, we can now exclusively reveal for the Milky Way News Network – *first for all the most important galactic gossip* – that the planet these beings call home, *a world known as Terra*, is the world of Atlantis – *the very same world from which our glorious and noble monarch returned more than thirty millennia ago*. His victory over the Atlanteans was already shrouded in mystery. Now these products of that defeated civilization walk freely among us, *appearing to hold the Emperor and even our dynamic Regent in their thrall*. Who are they, *and what is their sinister purpose for visiting Melania?*'

By this point the alien's twin heads had fully unwound and were smiling together towards Johnny. They finished off with, 'This is Z'habar *Z'habar* Estagog with another special report for the Milky Way News Network. And always remember – *two heads are better than one.*'

4 ✧

The Bunker ✧

For a moment, Johnny found himself alone inside the clear bubble with the twinkling stars of the chamber's ceiling shining down on him. Then the original music and smug background voice returned, saying:

'Viewers of this Vermalcast have also chosen to experience:

'**Noble Dauphin** – secret journey of a brave young Phasmeer;
'**Melania Uncovered** – the historic capital beneath the upper levels;
'**An Audience with the Regent** – citizens pose the questions while special guests The Quasars perform live;
'**Disappearing Diaquant** – a special report from Z'habar Z'habar Estagog on what really became of the secret power behind the Imperial throne.
'Select next story.'

Again, Johnny's heart leapt at the sight of his mum and he moved towards the final screen hoping to discover more about her. Outside of the sphere, a single, crystal clear chime sounded and the walls changed colour from gold to olive green. Before the programme could play, the bubble lifted into the air, passing through Johnny's body and over his head with a faint plop, leaving him standing alone on the springy floor. For the first time he realized that the few aliens scattered around the chamber must have been inside their own Vermalcasts which, too, had terminated. Now they were moving, using all sorts of different methods, towards the giant doors. Alf returned, a blur of arms and legs approaching at lightning speed, but stopping instantly just before Johnny.

'Master Johnny,' said the android. 'The Senate has finished sitting.' As he spoke, a shadow fell across both of them. A massive six-metre tall Phasmeer with black robes, followed by the Chancellor and surrounded by several little bow-legged Mannigles, had just entered the chamber. It was the Regent.

'Johnny Mackintosh,' said the giant creature. Its voice was far deeper than any other Phasmeer Johnny had heard. 'I would speak with you. Come . . .'

'Your Highness. I must protest,' squeaked the Chancellor, robes glowing bright pink. 'You cannot treat this inferior as . . .'

'Silence!' boomed the Regent, brushing the Chancellor out of the way with a sweep of its long, spindly arm.

Johnny, Alf and Clara (dragging Bentley), started to move towards the huge doors, but the Regent raised an elongated limb commanding them to halt.

'I would speak with Johnny Mackintosh alone. Chancellor Karragon and my Mannigles will ensure your companions are . . . comfortable.'

Johnny didn't know who looked the more upset – Clara or the Chancellor. He shrugged at his sister, who stopped, while Johnny followed the Regent out into the central courtyard. The Phasmeer soared into the air, supported by some sort of antigrav generator, which enveloped Johnny too, lifting him far from the ground, level with the Regent's head. It felt quite like standing in the *Spirit of London*'s lifts.

'We can talk freely,' boomed the Phasmeer. 'Within this field, no one can hear us.' That was all very well, thought Johnny, but he didn't have anything to say. The Regent stopped walking and turned to face Johnny, its bulbous eyes (set either side of its long, thin face) focused on him. 'Tell me. Why will the Emperor not show himself? His people need him. His galaxy needs him.'

Johnny didn't answer at first, but the Regent refused to shift its gaze. When it became clear that he would stay floating in the middle of the Senate courtyard until he said something, Johnny forced himself to open his mouth. 'I think that's for Bram, not me, to say. So if I knew, I probably wouldn't tell you, but I don't anyway.'

'Yet he welcomed you on your last visit,' continued the Regent, who began moving again with Johnny in tow, drifting towards the ancient Senate building in the centre of the courtyard. As they approached, crumbling white stone doors opened before them and they continued inside. Dim lights floated unsupported at different heights throughout a huge chamber, but wherever Johnny and the Regent moved they brightened, illuminating fading murals depicting scenes from across the galaxy – Johnny thought he recognized the Horsehead Nebula. The Regent led him to the very centre, where they settled softly atop a giant disc of black stone, like obsidian. Johnny looked around to see if he could identify any more space scenes, but he had less than a second before the black floor beneath his feet vanished and he began to fall. The Regent remained beside him, but its antigrav shield no longer extended to include Johnny, whose arms and legs windmilled helplessly as he picked up more and more speed.

Beneath the Senate House the underground world of the capital, seen earlier through the travelator, was revealed. Clara would have died of fright and Johnny wondered if he might too. It might be the best way – a lot less painful than splatting into the ground when he hit bottom. It could easily be over before then if something collided with him on the way down. All around, transports and aliens flew by at terrifying speeds, sending him spinning one way then another. The wind whistled painfully around Johnny's ears and tore at his flapping tunic, shredding the sleeves as he fell faster and faster between the enormous, needle-like towers that rose from the original, inner surface, far taller than any skyscraper on Earth and lit by floating, miniature suns. Fighting hard, he somehow managed to hold his arms and legs out to right himself and then angled his fall towards the Regent's antigrav generator, but whenever he came close a force from the device repelled him.

They were plunging downwards at exactly the same rate, but the Regent remained comfortably within its bubble. Johnny would hit that surface at any moment. He could see a growing black dot – a circular patch of ground – rushing upwards to meet him. He closed his eyes, bracing for impact. Nothing happened. When he opened them he was still falling, but inside a tube, the black shiny mirrored walls matching the stone on the Senate House floor. It was a vertical bore hole leading deep into the planet's original surface. He looked down but could see no sign of the bottom.

The Regent turned its face to him. 'How do you imagine the Emperor would feel if his chosen heir were to meet with an untimely end?'

It was just Johnny's luck to meet another mad Phasmeer. 'I don't know what you're talking about.' Johnny had tried to shout, but the wind seemed to push the words back down his throat. He wasn't sure the Regent had heard.

'Khari is old. He has no natural successor. You must have discussed it, plotting to deny my offspring, the Dauphin, its birthright.'

'Never,' shouted Johnny. Finally, far below, he could see a very bright point of light. The seemingly neverending tunnel did have a bottom and, now he'd spotted it, he saw it was rushing towards him at alarming speed. He tried to warn Clara and Alf, but moving the wristcom to his mouth sent him tumbling out of control again.

'At least tell me where he goes when he leaves Melania. You claim he doesn't visit you?'

Though his eyes were streaming, Johnny could now see tiny creatures walking below. They would hit in any second and this time there was no further shaft to fall through. He had to hope his sister and Alf would get away – that they could find the ships to protect Earth. Johnny forced himself to look away from the onrushing ground and into the Regent's eyes. As loud and clear as he could, he shouted, 'I don't know where he goes. It's not to see me. If it was, I wouldn't be here.' As he forced the final words out of his mouth, the wind stopped and the antigrav field enveloped him again.

They touched the ground, softly as a soap bubble, and the Regent said, 'There's no need to shout. I was simply making conversation on our descent. So tell me, Johnny Mackintosh. Why did you come here?'

Johnny crouched on all fours, trying to suck some of the stale air into his lungs. He flattened his hair and felt for the chain around his neck. The locket was still there, as was his wristcom, which flickered briefly green through Johnny's tattered sleeves, before returning to its normal red glow. He couldn't believe the gall of the Regent, who was acting as though the two of them were simply out for an afternoon stroll, totally ignoring the fact that Johnny could easily have been killed. They were so deep inside Melania that he felt less heavy than when they'd landed. He drew himself up to his full height, and looked up at the Regent towering over him. 'I came to ask for help,' he told the Phasmeer. 'Our nearest star system was turned into a supernova. Earth . . . Terra . . . could be under attack. We need ships to defend ourselves.'

The Regent started chirruping, louder and louder. It took a

while for Johnny to realize the giant creature was laughing. 'You have seen, no doubt, I am surrounded by idiots,' said the Phasmeer. 'It had not occurred to me that you might be one of them.' Johnny felt his face begin to burn bright red. 'We all want ships, little Terran. Just what did you think the Fourth Fleet was doing in the Toliman system?' Johnny looked blankly at the Regent, who went on, 'It was there, at the Emperor's insistence, to protect your pathetic, worthless planet. Do you have any idea how many ships were lost when Star Blaze commenced? Well, do you?'

Johnny shook his head. 'I'm sorry. I didn't know,' he said.

'Well, perhaps you know what this place is?' asked the Regent.

For the first time since his feet had touched solid ground, Johnny was able to look around. Cut from rock deep beneath the planet's surface, an immense cavern stretched far away from the foot of the shaft down which he had fallen. As it opened out into the distance, it was lit up and dominated by a model of the galaxy, many kilometres across, within which billions of tiny sparkles of light were slowly rotating, each representing an individual sun.

'It is my bunker,' said the Regent, 'from where I direct the war effort. A war that goes badly. Come.' With that it began walking towards the light.

Johnny followed behind, jogging to keep up. The outer walls were a hive of activity with aliens of all shapes and sizes (with varying numbers of wings, limbs, wheels and other mysterious appendages) moving backwards and forwards or standing or hovering in front of different terminals, but Johnny had difficulty taking his eyes away from the massive model of the Milky Way. Within it, space was divided into distinct regions using crude blocks of at least three transparent colours, superimposed on top of the different, glowing stars. In the very far distance, most of the dense bulging centre was overlaid with gold and, in some places this colour stretched nearly as far as the outermost spiral arms. Johnny supposed this must represent the Empire. Surrounding the gold, sometimes making deep inroads into it, with one narrow spike reaching to the very heart of the galaxy, were regions of navy blue – the invading Andromedans. Most of the outer rim, and some small pockets inside, were green – perhaps neutral territory.

As they drew closer to the green border of a glowing outer spiral arm, the antigrav field engulfed him once more and he was lifted high off the ground, above the beautiful whirlpool of light. He saw, scattered throughout the slowly rotating model, a handful of humanoid shapes wearing flowing, hooded cloaks and flying between the stars. Their blood-red garments matched the colour of the central galactic hub, shining through the superimposed block of gold. Further out, the suns were brighter, with more blue and yellow.

As Johnny and the Regent flew further across the starry disc, one of the robed aliens rose out of the model to greet them. Johnny's heart skipped a beat – the creature's head . . . was missing. Johnny found himself staring into fuzzy blackness within the cloak's hood. As he looked closer it became clear the thing had no visible body at all, yet the robes were enclosing *something* solid.

'Do not be alarmed,' said the Regent from beside him. 'You are in the presence of greatness. This is an Owlessan Monk, one of only twenty in all the Milky Way. After combing the galaxy, each and every one has been brought here.' The Monk bowed before Johnny. 'You cannot see it, because it is out of phase with non-owlein species. Years of worshiping the galaxy have placed it in this state.'

Johnny had heard the word 'owlein' before. It was the quality, the ability to fold space, possessed by the Plicans and a very few others. Bram had said Clara was owlein. That particular detail wasn't something Johnny thought that the Regent should know. 'They worship the Milky Way?' he asked instead. 'Why would they do that?'

'They believe the galaxy to be the source of their power.'

Johnny was about to ask what power, when his arm became numb. He looked down to see two long, bony fingers had hooked themselves around it. They came from beneath the cloak. He looked to the giant Phasmeer, who seemed not to have noticed anything unusual. But when Johnny turned directly to face the cloaked creature, he could now make out multiple eye sockets staring back at him from out of a skeletal face – it looked as if there were eight of them, equally spaced around a bulging layer of bone that encircled the off-white hollow skull. Johnny stared as an arm of bone rose from beneath the cloak, pressing a long finger over a circular mouth (lined with needle teeth) to indicate silence. Even had he wanted to, Johnny couldn't have spoken – it was as if his vocal chords had iced over. The other Monks were leaving their positions and floating up to surround Johnny. He could see all of them, or at least their skeletons. They pressed against him and all the warmth began to leach away from his body.

'You see them crowding together, to focus their strength,' said the Regent. 'Take one Monk on its own and it can do very little. But bring two together and their power is doubled. Add a third and it doubles again, and so on. With twenty here, all in this one small space, imagine what they can do.'

'And no one can see them?' Johnny forced the words out of his mouth. As he spoke, the breath from his lips condensed into an icy cloud. If it weren't for the warmth of the locket around his neck, he felt he would have frozen solid.

'No one,' the Regent replied. 'They have passed beyond. Observe – they are sensing a change in the galaxy. Witness their strength.' As Johnny watched, the view shifted. He was no longer above an enormous *model* inside the cavern deep within Melania. It was as though he was *really* there, hovering above the plane of the Milky Way itself. It was the most magnificent thing he had ever seen. The Regent and its bunker had vanished, but the scarlet-robed figures remained all around, one clamped tightly to him. Johnny was turned so his face pointed towards a dazzling pink nebula, about halfway from the edge to the centre. He began to move . . . silently . . . effortlessly . . . and very, very fast, accompanied by the posse of Monks. Star systems of all different shapes and sizes blurred past as they swooped down from above the galactic plane into the cloud of stars and dust. It was as if they were crossing thousands, maybe millions, of star systems in the blink of an eye, but their target was clear – a giant sun surrounded by two vast, near-circular lobes of luminous gas, one on either side.

Over the last few months, Johnny had seen many stars on his travels, but this one was special. It was huge – by far the biggest of them all. The blue giant looked a hundred times larger than the Sun, its edges blurred by great plumes of glowing gas breaking away from a surface that swirled with great currents of light and dark in constant turmoil. In the foreground, in the glare of this monster, space teemed with countless ships. He could not have imagined that so many spacecraft could be in one place – black ships, set against the blackness of space. The more he looked the more he could see, until two icy fingers of bone from underneath a scarlet sleeve hooked themselves around his neck and pulled him backwards. Johnny flew up and away.

While one Monk maintained its grip on Johnny's neck and arm, the others floated apart from each other. There was a blinding flash of light before the feeling of suddenly, jerkily, falling, like he sometimes had when he was drifting off to sleep. Johnny found himself back in the bunker, above the immense model. The Regent was speaking. 'Did you sense it too? Finally, I have him,' it was saying. 'My Monks have seen further and clearer than ever before. They tell me of Nymac's centre of operations – what he has kept hidden for so long. If we can only surround him . . . move the First Fleet to the Keyhole Nebula . . . and the Third Fleet behind the great star Carinae itself, then I will have no need of our absent Emperor. Victory will be mine.'

As the last Monk finally released Johnny and all the scarlet-robed figures descended once more into the starry mass below, a wave of exhaustion washed over him – without the Regent's antigrav field, he would have collapsed. He forced himself to keep his eyes open and watch as winged aliens swooped into the giant three-dimensional model, carrying miniature replicas of Imperial fleets. Like a switch being pressed, the entire Milky Way turned the solid gold of Empire, producing a smug smile on the Phasmeer's face. Although now separate from the Monks, Johnny sensed the stirring of large numbers of Imperial ships, like a faraway echo, as though the orders had already gone out and great fleets were manoeuvring according to the Regent's instructions. He rather doubted any actual victory would be achieved quite so easily.

'You are present on a momentous day,' said the Phasmeer, a mad gleam in its bulbous eyes. 'Never has the Milky Way appeared so transparent to us. You will not need ships for Terra, Johnny Mackintosh. The Andromedan fleet will be destroyed. And, when I am victorious, whether you like it or not it is I who shall become the true ruler of this galaxy, the Dauphin as my heir.'

5 ✧✧

Sailing Ships ✧✧

Johnny couldn't believe he'd travelled halfway across the galaxy and not seen Bram. He cursed himself for leaving Earth unprotected. Even having one ship patrolling the solar system was a lot better than none – especially when she was the *Spirit of London* – and the Emperor was bound to have returned within range of his Wormhole at some point. The time would have been far better spent going after Nicky and explaining to his brother about the Krun. He could have had his family together, and with his brother's spaceship to help protect Earth. The Regent might have sounded confident about stopping Nymac, but Johnny was far from convinced. All he knew for certain, was that the giant Phasmeer was deranged and out of control, sending Johnny plunging halfway to Melania's core and accusing him of scheming to inherit the Empire. After everything he'd heard about Nymac, Johnny suspected the Andromedan general would easily outwit the deluded Regent.

Had it been Bram claiming victory, Johnny would have been able to relax about the prospect of the Sun being turned into a supernova, but until he'd witnessed the Vermalcast, he'd not fully appreciated how withdrawn from Melanian life the Emperor had become. He didn't know what Bram was doing, but was certain it wasn't anything on the capital and, in the Emperor's absence, the Imperial Palace remained frustratingly inaccessible to all except Chancellor Karragon. He hoped Bram would return soon, but couldn't afford to hang around so far from Earth on the off-chance.

He'd told Clara and Alf everything that had happened as soon as they were safely back aboard the *Spirit of London*. There didn't seem any reason not to and he hated keeping secrets – not saying anything about Nicky was doing his head in, but he didn't want to get Clara's hopes up until he knew more about their prodigal brother. For her part, Clara was fascinated by the Owlessan Monks and Johnny's eerie journey with them across the galaxy. As she didn't have school work, she decided she would study them during the many folds of the journey home.

Johnny was only too aware how far behind he must be getting at Castle Dudbury Comprehensive, so he lay in the gel pod trying, once again, to concentrate on his history homework. It proved hard as ever. What use was it to know all about the Battle of Trafalgar when you had your own spaceship in which you could search for your missing brother, protect your home planet or even traverse the galaxy? Somehow he didn't think nineteenth-century naval warfare was especially relevant. Worn out, he closed his eyes. He'd asked Sol to read to him from his textbook while he was sleeping, in the hope it would somehow seep through into his unconscious mind in much the same way as the thick orange fluid filled his body. The ship began talking but, once the folds began, Sol's voice became as distant as the *Spirit of London*'s walls and Johnny drifted into a deep sleep.

✡ ✡ ✡
✡ ✡

It was dawn on 21st October 1805. The sky still bore a faint red tinge and the sea was calm. Johnny stood with a few others, including Admiral Horatio Nelson, on the wooden quarterdeck of HMS *Victory*. The great admiral was wearing his full dress uniform, with two huge epaulettes on his shoulders and parallel rows of shiny brass buttons, while numerous medals randomly adorned the front of his navy-blue jacket. Johnny couldn't help thinking that all this, underneath the trademark bicorn, made him a rather obvious target. He wondered why their leader wasn't wearing his sword. Nelson's flagship was bigger than he'd expected, though still loads smaller than the *Spirit of London*. Close up, everyone smelled like they'd not washed for weeks, though this was partly masked by the scent of rum and raisin ice cream that was coming from the galley. The night before, the admiral had briefed his captains about their new tactics – Villeneuve, the French admiral, was finally putting to sea, and wouldn't know what hit him. The British fleet would cut across the line of enemy ships, rather than sail parallel to the French and Spanish – the name 'Trafalgar', the Spanish cape off which the battle would be fought, was sure to go down in history. Now, as they tipped sand over the deck in preparation for battle, Nelson ordered Lieutenant Pasco, the Signal Officer, to run a message reading, 'Nelson confides every man will do his duty'.

'If I may suggest, sir,' said Captain Hardy from the side, 'instead of "Nelson confides" why not "England expects"?'

'It uses fewer flags,' added Pasco in agreement.

'England expects . . . England expects every man will do his duty. Yes, an excellent suggestion, gentlemen,' said the admiral. 'Make it so.' Then Nelson turned and looked directly at Johnny, who felt his face turning beetroot red underneath his regulation round hat. 'What are you doing standing there gawping, Midshipman? Get up the main mast and tell me what the devil's going on.'

'Aye aye, sir,' Johnny replied, not sure if he should salute or not. Instead he turned and half ran to the foot of the biggest of the three masts onboard, about as high as the *Victory* was long. Oh for a gravity assist, but Johnny didn't suppose his midshipman's uniform came with one installed. He stood underneath the towering wooden pole and jumped, grabbing hold of the rope at the bottom of the rigging. Hanging there feeling pretty silly, Johnny pulled for all he was worth, but his arms weren't strong enough and he found his grip slowly slackening. By the time he was only clinging on by his fingertips it was clearly hopeless and, the next moment, he fell, ending up flat on his back with laughter ringing out all around him. His hands were burning from holding the rope, but that was nothing to how his face felt.

'Let's give 'im an 'and shall we, lads?' said a burly sailor from nearby. Four men approached, surrounding Johnny, each grabbing hold of an arm or a leg. Their breath reeked of stale alcohol. He wanted to tell them to stop, but nothing would come out of his throat. 'On three, I think, boys,' said the sailor, before beginning the count.

'One . . .' Johnny was lifted up to near the bottom of the rigging.

'Two . . .' His arms were nearly wrenched from their sockets and his hat flew off, revealing his blond hair.

'Three . . .' He was shot upwards, flying through the damp air, arms and legs flailing. As he levelled out and came to a stop, about five metres up, sheer terror gave Johnny the strength to twist his body and grab hold of the ropes to stop him crashing back down. The men beneath cheered and he managed to place his feet onto some ropes lower down. With arms and legs in position, he began to climb.

Looking up rather than down, Johnny was nearly thrown when the *Victory* suddenly changed course. They were tacking, sailing at an angle into the wind to establish the prime position for Nelson's attack. He clung on, steadied himself, focused on a platform partway to the top and set off again. By the time he reached it, his hands were raw and his arms aching, so he was grateful for a rest and the chance to take in his surroundings.

From his perch he counted twenty-six other English ships preparing to sail towards the French and Spanish lines. In front, through the rigging, were red and blue figureheads, leaning out over the ocean, either side of the bowsprit. The wind began to blow stronger and waves broke over the bows.

Johnny couldn't stay on the platform forever – there was another one twice as high again, from where he might be able to see the enemy. Nelson was counting on him and he wasn't about to let the admiral down. He began again, getting into a rhythm to match the roll of the ship which was far more pronounced the higher he climbed. It was exhilarating being so far above everything, but his arms were soon aching again and it was a huge relief to finally place his hands around the rim of the topmost platform and haul himself onto it.

The waves were gone . . . the ocean was gone. He was still on a ship, but sailing through space itself. The masts were thin and elegant, while the vast sails pulling the vessel shimmered silver, but almost liquid, like mercury. Looking down, there were only two people on the enclosed deck – a boy and a girl – and he only had to think it to float down, through the hull so he was standing just behind them. The boy held a large brass steering wheel, while the girl stood over a table covered in star charts, peering down, her long, purple hair brushing the surface.

Johnny moved forward and glanced over her shoulder. Projected onto the charts he saw the image of a tiny ship – instinctively he knew it was the one he was on – sailing through a narrow band of darkness. Surrounding the little craft were numerous circles of light, illuminating almost all of the mapped area, each centred on other, much larger ships nearby.

The girl turned round and looked straight through Johnny. Her eyes were orange, with long black slits for pupils. Johnny remembered his chemistry partner from school, Alisha Leow, wearing contact lenses that had made her eyes look reptilian like that, until Mrs Devonshire insisted she take them out. Alisha, though, didn't have the same glistening scales that were a trademark of these and many other aliens he'd encountered. Even on Earth, furry mammals would never have become dominant had the scaly dinosaurs not been wiped out by the asteroid impact that had been all Johnny's fault.

The very first time the *Spirit of London* had folded, he'd ordered the baby Plican to go much too far, stretching the space–time continuum so incredibly thin that a nearby explosion had punctured it, sending the ship spiralling into the distant past. When they re-emerged, the force of their entry into normal space deflected the massive rock onto its collision course with the prehistoric planet. Due to Johnny's efforts, a group of rescued dinosaurs were now living happily inside Triton, Neptune's largest moon.

The purple-haired girl spoke: 'Someone's here.' It wasn't a language Johnny had ever heard, but the rasping hiss made perfect sense to him. Next, from the girl's slightly protruding mouth, shot a very long, forked, silver tongue that darted back and forth as though trying to sniff something out.

The boy looked over his shoulder away from the wheel. He was shorter, very stocky with just a few wisps of orange hair centred on the top of his scalp between two, stubby horns. While he, too, had mainly light-coloured glistening scales, his face was framed with six dark scabs forming a near perfect hexagon. 'Don't be stupid, Zeta,' he growled. 'There's no one here. Concentrate – I need you to help or they'll find us.'

'I thought you didn't want my help,' the girl replied.

'For once, sister, I was wrong,' said the boy. 'Their search pattern's cleverer than I expected.' He turned round and looked across to the tabletop charts. Johnny realized the circular pools of light were sensor sweeps from the larger craft, which the sailing ship must be trying to avoid.

He floated over the heads of the two aliens so he could take a closer look himself. The girl's tongue shot straight out in his direction, passing right through him, but he felt nothing.

'Zeta – pay attention,' said the boy.

Zeta shrugged and looked down at the ever narrowing strip of darkness they were sailing within, but then she jumped back as the boy's fist hammered down onto the table, scattering the carefully constructed view of surrounding space. 'That doesn't help, you know,' hissed the girl.

'It's too late,' said the boy. 'Whatever we do now they can't miss us.' He kicked hard with his boots on the base of the steering wheel, generating a metallic clang. Johnny felt very sorry for the ship. 'We've got about thirty minutes,' the boy said. 'Then it's all over.'

'But we're so close,' said Zeta. 'I can feel it.' She slumped onto the deck and buried her face in her hands.

The boy ignored her and floated down, with no obvious means of support, into a bubble protruding from the underside of the hull where he sat down behind what was unmistakably a giant gun. Johnny found himself following. The space was cramped so he hovered just to one side of the weapon. From his angle he could see complicated fractals engraved along the bottom of the ship.

'We're going down fighting,' shouted the boy. 'I can take a few out with the cannon.' As he spoke, a black ball of swirling energy was somehow growing between his hands.

The girl looked down to where her brother was sitting. 'No,' she said firmly. 'We mustn't hurt them. It's not their fault.'

'I don't care. They're in our way and they're going to hurt us.' The boy brought the cannon round past Johnny so the barrel was pointing towards a distant black ship, slowly coming closer.

Zeta floated down in front of the gun and placed a hand over its end. 'No,' she said again and she blew on the black sphere, causing it to change colour so it looked as if the boy was holding a miniature sun between his palms. The girl reached out a finger and touched the glowing orb, causing whatever it was made from to flow out of the boy's hands and into the long barrel.

'Light will always overcome darkness,' she said. 'Fire between the ships. It can be a laser, a distress beacon. Someone could rescue us.'

The boy snorted but, with surprising strength, the girl pulled the long cylinder round so it was pointing directly at Johnny's head. Although it was only a dream, he started to feel uncomfortable.

'Now,' said the girl.

Everything turned bright orange.

☆ ☆ ☆
☆ ☆

Johnny sat upright with his eyes wide open. His heart was racing and everything was still orange. He wondered if the laser had blinded him. Sol was speaking. Something about an automatic response, an Andromedan fleet and prematurely ending the fold. It took a while but, as the fluid began to drain away, Johnny realized he was in the gel pod – that it was just a dream, already fading as the here and now demanded his attention. With his slightly inflated hands he wiped the goo out of his eyes and directed the vacuum trunk around his clothes to suck up the rest as quickly as possible. The lights on his left wrist flickered from red to green, but then they changed back. Johnny pressed the switch on the side of the pod and stepped out onto the bridge. Clara wasn't there. He'd never woken from a fold and not seen her before, but then he remembered she'd gone to the library on deck 7. Calming himself, he asked Sol, 'What was that again?'

'We have unfolded prematurely,' the ship replied, 'close to a large concentration of unknown ships – almost certainly Andromedan.' As Sol spoke, bands of light on a large display near the main viewscreen flickered in time to her words.

Still groggy, Johnny seated himself at the centre of the bridge. He'd not heard of anyone being able to track a ship while outside normal space, let alone pull it out of a fold. The air next to him shimmered and Clara unfolded close by, immediately asking, 'What's going on? That was horrid. The poor Plican . . .' She hurried over to the tank behind Johnny's chair and placed her hands on it. Alf exited his gel pod, unusually with little patches of orange still covering his suit.

Now Johnny looked, the Plican did seem very pale and two of its eight tentacles were dangling limply outside of its body. It didn't help that the *Spirit of London* lurched suddenly, banking very sharply, pushing the injured creature up against the walls of its cylindrical home. Johnny looked past it and through the ship's hull beyond, where the stars were rotating. They were turning unusually fast.

'My apologies,' said Sol. 'I observed a long-range sensor sweep emanating from the fleet ahead. Any power signature, including my own, would be detected within the region of space two light seconds away.'

'Do you think they spotted us?' Johnny asked, now totally alert.

'Certainly not,' Sol replied. 'The sensors are of unusual design. Embedded within them is a secondary carrier wave that appears to act as both a targeting beacon and a dispersion field. Once a power source has been identified, it is instantly fired upon. Observe . . .' The viewscreen changed to reveal a small convoy of Ke Kwan transports, the long rectangular vessels that carried freight across the galaxy. The end vessel was clearly marked as a medical supply ship. Sol cleverly highlighted the limit of the sensor sweep with a shimmering band of particles,

79

which the lead ship was passing through.

'We've got to warn them,' shouted Johnny.

'It is already too late,' replied Sol. 'I began recording this on leaving the fold. The ships are on the far side of the search area. The greater the distance from us, the further back in time we are looking. This took place approximately 27 light minutes and 18.281 8284 light seconds away. It has already happened.'

There were four ships in the convoy, each resembling an interstellar brick rather than the streamlined designs of science fiction stories. In the near vacuum of space, sleek aerodynamic designs weren't always necessary. The first had only just crossed the boundary when the front of its dull brown hull began to glow, quickly turning bright orange, as the particles that comprised it were excited beyond their safe limits. Slowly, and horribly, the whole thing began to disintegrate from front to back. Once the leading edge of the hull had been vaporized, the guts of the transport were exposed. It was like watching someone's internal organs spilling out of their body. Any crew inside must have suffered an equally horrific fate. A freezing vacuum normally made short shrift of organic tissue, but a couple of escape pods had been launched. Then, only seconds later, the same orange glow reached them and they were efficiently and completely destroyed.

The second ship must have witnessed it all happening and tried to steer clear but, though it narrowly avoided a collision, it quickly fell victim to the same dispersion field, which began to take effect in one corner. It was like watching a horrific car crash in slow motion. Johnny, Clara and Alf were all shouting, urging the transport to escape, but its outer hull was soon breached and cargo began to leak from the open decks, as fires blazed. Volatile elements simply bubbled away into nothingness, while the rest were once again left to be systematically torn apart, until only their very atoms remained to be scattered across nearby space.

While all this was happening, the third ship ploughed straight into the disintegrating remnants of the first two, explosions ripping through one side of its hull until anything that was left of all three vessels disappeared into one, slowly expanding, gigantic fireball.

The very last Ke Kwan transport, the medical supply ship which would have received the most warning, looked to be OK. Though its turning circle was large and slow, it had begun early and, unlike its sister vessels, only grazed the inside of the kill zone.

'They're going to make it,' said Clara, her hand tightly squeezing Johnny's arm as she stood behind him.

'Come on,' shouted Johnny, urging the lumbering ship to move through the curtain, out of danger and into normal space.

Then the rear of the transport began to change colour, a wave of orange destruction passing rapidly along it, far faster than the snail-like vessel was able to fly. Although a small portion at the very front end remained intact, there could have been no survivors.

A long silence followed on the *Spirit of London*'s bridge. Alf removed his bowler hat and bowed his head a little. Johnny felt the anger rising inside him. The transports' crews had simply been doing their jobs, minding their own business. They didn't deserve those terrifying final few seconds. They were in the wrong place at the wrong time and he knew it could just as easily have happened to his own ship – at least if Sol hadn't been as alert as she was. 'How many on board?' he asked.

'I think Ke Kwan transports are lightly crewed,' said Clara. 'Less than a dozen on each.' Her voice was shaking and her face red.

'Four ships too,' said Sol, bitterly. 'Unable to defend themselves or their crew. One carrying nothing but medical supplies. They should be avenged.'

It was rare for Johnny to hear the ship so angry. He left his chair and walked forward. Although Sol was everywhere in the ship, it made him feel closer to her and he knew she was hurting. He could only guess at the connections between the minds of the different craft that ploughed the emptiness of space together. He rested his palm on Sol's vocal display screen – through the special link he had with his own ship he sensed Sol's loss and tried to comfort her.

'They will be, I promise,' he said quietly. Johnny peered at a nearby display. 'But there must be more than twenty Andromedan ships out there at least. You can't fight them all.' Given half the chance, Johnny was quite sure that at this particular moment there was nothing more that Sol wanted to do. 'I don't think there's much point hanging around,' he went on, quietly. 'It's important we get back to Earth.' The other gel pod at the back of the bridge opened and out came a bedraggled Bentley, shaking the remaining goo from his coat. 'Not so fast, Bents,' said Johnny. 'Sol – get us out of here.'

'I don't think we can,' said Clara. 'The Plican's really sore – it's like someone's burnt the ends of its tentacles. Couldn't we just go round for now?' She looked at Johnny hopefully.

Sol cut in, the anger still present in her voice. 'There is another reason why we shouldn't leave yet. All Imperial ships are designed to respond automatically to distress beacons. That is why I unfolded prematurely. It may be we can still offer assistance.'

After witnessing four innocent ships destroyed, everyone was minded to help if they could. Alf walked quickly over to a navigation terminal near the front of the bridge. He placed a finger directly into the console and became rigid while absorbing the data. When he loosened up, he turned to Johnny and said, 'That is interesting. The signal did not come from the Ke Kwan transports – it originated from deep within the dispersion field.'

'Whoever they were, I suppose that was why they were in distress,' said Clara.

Johnny was thinking, absent-mindedly stroking underneath Bentley's collar as the sheepdog nuzzled his head against Johnny's legs.

'It does not compute,' said Sol. 'Perhaps it is a trap . . . a lure to draw us inside to the rescue. No ship could have sent that message as she would automatically have been destroyed.'

'Unless,' said Johnny, wondering if he was really about to say what had just occurred to him. 'Unless the ship didn't have a power signature.'

'Master Johnny,' Alf replied, throwing his hands in the air. 'In all our spaceship design lessons there is one feature that has remained constant. Every propulsion system requires some sort of energy source – ours is the dark energy core. Do you not remember the laws of thermodynamics? None is one hundred percent efficient – they all leak energy and radiate some sort of power signature.'

'There's one design we haven't covered,' said Johnny. 'What if the crew knew about the dispersion field? What if they used a solar sail?' Alf and Clara looked at Johnny as if he'd gone mad. He tried to explain. 'Earth . . . Terran scientists think you can fly a spaceship with the stellar wind, the particles a star gives off when it shines. If the sail's big and light enough.'

'But that couldn't work,' said Clara. 'Every time you got near a star you'd be blown away from it.'

'You could tack,' said Johnny. 'It was part of my homework. You can't sail straight into the wind, but you can go towards it, at an angle.'

Clara didn't look at all convinced, but Alf said, 'I suppose it would be possible . . . theoretically.'

'Sol – what form did the distress signal take?' Johnny asked.

'It was an ancient, universal distress code,' Sol replied.

'Delivered in the form of a monochromatic pulse.'

Johnny hadn't heard that phrase before, but was pretty sure another word for it would be 'laser'. An image flashed into his mind – a purple-haired girl pointing a gigantic cannon into his face. 'It's not a trap,' he said. 'There's a ship, powered by a solar sail, out there and we're going to rescue it. If we don't, the Andromedans will either kill or capture them – and we're not going to let that happen.'

'Master Johnny – do you really think that is wise?' asked Alf. The android was fiddling with his bowler hat, twiddling it round between his fingers. 'You saw what happened when the other ships approached.'

'That's why we have to do it,' Johnny replied.

'Even though I cannot fold, I can power down all my systems before we enter the dispersion field.' The determination in Sol's voice was there for all to hear. The ship continued, 'The distress beacon lasted for 0.318 31 seconds – from that I can extrapolate the future position of the target vessel. Entering the search field at full speed, cutting engines and power, we can intersect her flight path in 12 minutes 56.637 0614 seconds.'

'Let's do it,' said Johnny.

☆ ☆ ☆
☆ ☆

They were flying blind, but after coasting through space at around eighty percent of the speed of light for nearly ten minutes, they had to be close – so long as the other ship hadn't altered course, in which case they would never find it. Alf was in the shuttle bay with the entire deck already open to space, preparing the grappling hooks to pull the sailing ship inside. Before turning her gravity generators off, Sol had set herself spinning about her long axis, like a giant bullet shooting towards her target. By aligning himself with the centre of the ship, Johnny was able to remain weightless, but the further away from the axis you went, the heavier you became. Bentley was bounding around the outside of the bridge, tongue dangling out as he panted from the exercise, occasionally lapping from his water bowl, perched on a nearby console. Meanwhile, Clara floated close to the Plican, trying to coax the creature into being ready to fold when the need arose. It didn't look to be working.

Bentley growled. Johnny looked over to see the dog's legs moving while remaining stationary, having cleverly matched his speed to Sol's rotation. The Old English sheepdog was staring fixedly out at the same patch of empty space and, the next moment, began barking furiously. Johnny used the top of the chair to push off and floated across. As he went, he quickly became heavier and ended up crashing into the transparent walls. He dusted himself down and began to jog along, matching his speed with Bentley's. It was difficult, but he stooped down and tried to soothe his friend's barks by stroking his coat as they ran. He followed the sheepdog's gaze, but Bentley seemed to be barking at nothing at all.

Then he saw it, blacker than space itself. The exact shape was hard to make out – the only way to see it was to look for the background stars that were missing. As he stared, a structure began to take shape out of the darkness, stretching towards him like a giant space urchin akin to the sea urchins he'd seen pictures of. The Andromedan vessel was covered everywhere in needle-like spikes of different sizes (some many times bigger than the ship itself), all barrels for the fearsome weapons systems it doubtless carried. They were going to pass very, very close – probably less than ten kilometres. Johnny gulped and held Bentley's collar, slowing the sheepdog until the pair of them were rotating with the spinning hull. Every few seconds the sinister black craft came into view. Now he knew what to look for, Johnny was able to survey the whole sky. The thorny black ships slowly revealed themselves as his eyes became more accustomed to them, every one converging on the same spot towards which the *Spirit of London* was also heading.

He'd seen films where submarines in danger of detection ran totally silent, when even a hint of noise could give them away. It couldn't hurt to try that now so he softly held Bentley's jaw closed until the sheepdog ceased barking. Then he pushed off the wall towards the captain's chair in the very centre of the bridge. Weightless again, he shut out the image forming in his mind of Captain Valdour impaled on *Cheybora*'s bridge, and strapped himself in. It was vital to be ready the instant he might need to act.

The monstrous blackness obliterated the stars outside while the only sound on the strangely quiet bridge was Bentley lapping from his bowl. Even the sheepdog must have sensed the danger and he didn't so much as growl. Sol's mind had withdrawn to a deep recess where the alien sensors shouldn't penetrate, but the reassuring aura of power she exuded was noticeably absent. Johnny and Clara both held their breath as the *Spirit of London* drew level with the huge ship and passed within a whisker of the deadly looking quills. Up close, an otherworldly glow hung around the tips of the black ship's spines. Although they were travelling at amazing speed, the thorny sphere was heading in the same direction and must have been at least a hundred times bigger, so overtaking it was agonizingly slow. As they passed alongside, it appeared that at least the Andromedan ship had no windows. It had seemed inconceivable that they wouldn't be spotted – they could only hope that the aliens aboard the other vessel were just using sensors rather than the evidence of their own eyes.

It didn't help when the silver tray holding Bentley's water bowl slid off a console in slow motion, crashing onto the floor with the metal, like a clashing cymbal, taking an age to stop vibrating. Johnny and Clara stared at it, then each other and then the grey and white sheepdog, who lay down with his paws over his face to hide his embarrassment. They cleared the last few black thorns and Johnny finally exhaled. The sight that met them was beautiful. The sailing ship's oval, silver hull, with three silver side-sails like fins, may have been minute, but what impressed was the size of her four mainsails. Johnny remembered them from his dream – together they formed a vast diamond, glinting in the light of a pair of nearby stars and dwarfing the little capsule they pulled.

Clara turned her attention to the Plican while, to his utter astonishment, Johnny heard Sol's voice counting down in his head. Since he'd given form to his wonderful ship he'd always known they shared a unique bond, but he'd never felt it so closely before. Sol told him they were entering the final minute before their high-speed encounter. He wondered how Alf was getting on in the shuttle bay and hoped the android's targeting mechanism was ready. At the speed they were travelling, they'd only get one shot at snagging the little sailing ship as they flew by. All the time the surrounding space was filling with more and more black craft, their sweeping search pattern becoming ever narrower.

Johnny worried for a moment that the *Spirit of London* might actually collide with the sailing ship, but then he marvelled at the accuracy of Sol's calculations as he realized they would pass about a hundred metres apart. Somewhere in his head he knew Sol was happy that he was impressed.

It appeared the crew of the sailing ship – it had to be the boy and girl he'd seen in the dream – had spotted them coming. The liquid silver mainsails were being taken down and reeled in. Johnny hoped it would be done in time. A volley of enormous four-fingered grappling hooks, fired by Alf from the *Spirit of London*'s belly, overtook her nosecone, reaching out towards the tiny silver capsule. The first hook missed. The second overshot

87

too. They simply hadn't had time to come up with a better plan than to snag the little craft, and their efforts were beginning to look foolish. The third and the fourth attempts also failed. It was becoming desperate – they were nearly past the gleaming vessel – yet if anyone could do it, it had to be Alf. Then the fifth hook found its target and held on. The sixth bounced off the hull, but the seventh, again, held firm. The *Spirit of London* flew on, taking up the slack. Johnny hoped the boy and girl had some sort of dampening field as the giant ropes (made, he knew, of carbon nanotubes) took hold and dragged the sailing ship behind. Otherwise, whoever the strange occupants of the little craft were, they could never survive the enormous g-forces they'd been subjected to.

The problem with any dampening field was that it needed power, and power signatures were exactly what the Andromedans had been hoping for. Almost at once, one of the smaller fin-like side-sails began to glow orange, disintegrating from its wingtip inwards just as the Ke Kwan transports had done before. It was jettisoned before the field reached the main hull, the beautiful liquid silver atoms of the sail boiling away into space. The danger wasn't over. The position of the sailing ship – and with it the *Spirit of London* – had finally been revealed.

There was a searing pain inside Johnny's skull, as though his head was being torn apart from the inside. The agony of the dispersion field ended almost before it had begun, yet he almost lost consciousness. Dimly he was aware of the bridge coming to life and Sol's voice saying, 'Full shields in operation.'

Alf was speaking too, saying he needed more time to reel the sailing craft inside. The *Spirit of London*'s engines screamed louder than Johnny had ever heard them, as Sol turned impossibly sharply, ensuring the little ship (continuing on its own trajectory) immediately found itself within the confines of the shuttle bay.

88

'Shields down to 20 percent,' said Sol as the starship flew between the spines of an Andromedan vessel. It bought them a moment's breathing space as the alien ships couldn't fire so close to one of their own.

They would have one chance before the shields failed completely. 'Clara – it's now or never,' said Johnny.

His sister closed her eyes while, with both hands, she massaged the Plican's tank around where the stray tentacles drooped sorrily down. The creature's arms curled up inside its body and at once the whole tank pulsed with blue light. Bentley howled, but the noise was somehow distant. The *Spirit of London*'s hull passed through Johnny and out the other side. Then he saw the spines of an Andromedan ship fly towards him. Even within the fold, there was something horrible about them. The next stage began. They were pulled so fast vertically down that the background stars became streaks of light. Another ninety-degree turn, past a nebula he dimly recognized, before another turn and then another. Then, finally, there was stillness. The *Spirit of London*'s hull was back where it belonged and poor Bentley lay unconscious on the floor nearby.

Johnny felt horribly sick, but was pleased to have remained conscious. He undid the straps holding him in the chair and ran across to the stricken sheepdog, laying his ear on Bentley's chest. The double thump of a heartbeat, albeit very fast, filled him with relief. Johnny looked over to Clara for reassurance.

Her eyes met his. 'We're safe,' she said. 'No one can follow us through a fold. Is Bents OK?'

'I think so,' Johnny replied. 'Let's take him to sickbay. Then we'd better go and meet our guests.'

☆ ☆ ☆
☆ ☆

The first thing Johnny and Clara saw when they stepped out of the antigrav lifts was the sleek silver-hulled vessel, berthed in perfect alignment with the *Jubilee*, its sister shuttle the *Bakerloo* and the bigger *Piccadilly*. Again Johnny marvelled briefly at Sol's precision. He didn't dwell on it, for there were two aliens out on the deck. A squat, powerful boy with wispy orange hair was inspecting the *Piccadilly*, running his stubby hands along the sides of the red double-decker bus. Meanwhile, a girl with long purple hair was sitting on the floor, bent over the prone figure of Alf who lay motionless, his bowler hat forlorn on the floor beside him. Johnny and Clara started walking over, Clara shouting, in Universal, 'Leave him alone. He'll be OK.'

Before they could come close to the android, a long forked tongue shot from the girl's mouth across Alf's face. His body twitched, he coughed and sat up, looking puzzled. As Clara reached her, the girl looked up and smiled, a gleam in her eye. Then Johnny arrived and her expression changed. She turned round and shouted across the shuttle bay to the boy in a strange, rasping language, 'Erin – it's the one I told you about. The one who was aboard the *Falling Star*.' Johnny didn't let on that he understood every word.

The boy walked over, sizing up Johnny and Clara as he came. It was hard to read the expression on his face, but Johnny didn't think he looked impressed.

'Fanciful nonsense,' he said to the girl on the floor. 'Your imagination makes you weak – there was no one there. Now get up. You demean yourself on the floor in front of these commoners.'

The girl got to her feet, scowling. 'I tell you – it is he.'

Before a full-blown argument could develop between the newcomers, Johnny coughed and spoke in Universal, concentrating on making it sound like that to the new arrivals. 'Who are you? Why were the Andromedans after you?'

It was the girl who answered, this time in Universal. 'Thank you for coming to our aid – the galaxy looks after its own. We were searching for . . .'

'It was a pleasure voyage – nothing more,' interrupted the orange-haired boy. 'I am Erin, son of Marin, King and ruler of the Alnitak Hegemony,'

'I do not believe I have heard of it,' said Alf, offering his hand to the alien in the gesture Johnny had taught him and adding, 'My name is Alf.'

'Then you are woefully ill-informed,' King Erin replied, ignoring Alf's outstretched arm.

From all around, Sol's voice explained, 'Alnitak is a binary system that, from Earth, appears as the left-most star of Orion's belt.'

'My name's Johnny,' said Johnny, but he didn't offer to shake hands.

'And I'm Clara,' added Johnny's sister, more to the girl than the boy.

'Your voyage didn't look very pleasurable,' said Johnny. 'The Andromedans were swarming all over you.'

'Insects are drawn to the honey,' said the girl.

'Silence!' roared the boy, reverting to his own language. 'You will speak only when I permit it.' Erin turned his back on the girl and, in Universal, continued, 'This is my sister, Princess . . .'

'Zeta,' Johnny interrupted, before the little king could finish. He knew he shouldn't have said anything, but he wanted to bring the other boy down a peg or two.

'Princess Zeta, daughter of Zola. Clearly you and your ship have heard of us, Johnny,' replied Erin. 'You must be the captain of this vessel.' He looked around the shuttle bay. 'It will prove an acceptable form of transport. You will return us to Novolis, the fifteenth planet of the Alnitak system. During the journey, I shall remain with the Royal Carrier, the *Falling Star*, but I am not unaware of your particular methods of faster-than-light travel. My sister is of a more delicate disposition – you will escort her to your gel pods. That will be all.'

Alf and Clara both looked at Johnny, wondering how he would react. He simply replied, 'Of course, King Erin. We'll let you know as soon as we arrive.'

The boy nodded, but added in his native tongue, 'These commoners are puny. We should seize their ship – it would make a fitting trophy.'

As Erin turned and began walking back towards the silver-hulled craft, the purple-haired girl's tongue shot out, hissing after her brother. 'Come with us,' Johnny said to Zeta, again in Universal, and set off towards the lift with Clara and Alf.

On the bridge, Clara went over to the Plican's tank. She peered inside, checking how the folder was, and then asked Johnny, in English, 'So we're not going to Earth?'

'Of course we are,' Johnny replied. 'We've got to stop Nymac. And I think our new friend needs to learn some manners.'

The purple-haired girl smiled knowingly and Johnny realized he hadn't disguised his speech. Because of the Hundra inside him, she'd understood every word. Johnny shrugged, touched a button on the control panel by his chair and a gel pod rose from out of the floor below them. Princess Zeta, grinning broadly, stepped inside.

✧ ✧ ✧
✧ ✧

Clara had coaxed the Plican through the remaining legs of the journey back to the solar system, where they'd unfolded somewhere close to Saturn. The gel pods were all open and Bentley, now fully recovered, was enjoying having Zeta pick the remaining globules of orange gel out of his coat.

'Your home is spectacular,' said Zeta, looking at the giant ringed world that dominated the view. 'I did not know a planet could be so thickly encircled by rings.'

'It's not ours,' Clara replied, frowning a little. 'But we're close. I'll find out why the Plican didn't fold all the way.'

Johnny had sent Alf to sickbay, partly for a checkup after his rather unusual reboot, but also so he could ask Princess Zeta what she'd done.

'On Novolis I am considered a healer,' she responded. 'I am loath to be away from there for a great sickness has befallen my people, but we are on a quest.'

'Enough!' shouted Erin, stepping out of the lifts and marching across the bridge. Zeta fell silent, but Bentley growled as the boy king approached. Erin ignored the sheepdog and stopped directly in front of Johnny, blocking his view. 'I did not recognize these stars. Your ship refused to tell me where we were, but I forced it out of her.'

'You did what?' said Johnny as he rose slowly from the chair.

'You have betrayed us. You promised to take us home, yet you have brought us here. I do not tolerate treachery.' Zeta touched her brother's arm to stop him, but Erin shrugged her off, looked straight at Johnny and closed his fist. Johnny felt as if he'd swallowed a whole cup full of ice. He clutched at his chest – it was as though a freezing-cold hand had grabbed hold of his heart to stop it beating. As he fell to his knees he looked up and saw a cruel smile spreading across Erin's scaly face. There were sounds in the background, but a buzzing filled Johnny's ears as the blood drained away from his face, and everything started to go white. He closed his eyes and then he saw, in the strange way he was becoming able to do, that his heart had been cut off . . . insulated, preventing any electric charge getting through to the giant muscle – as if a cage had been erected all around it. Johnny couldn't remember such quiet stillness. For the first time in his life, he didn't have a heartbeat.

With no oxygen reaching his brain, he had to force himself to think. He remembered reviving Captain Valdour and drew on

93

all the strength he could find to fire an electric charge towards the idle pump in his chest. Blue sparks flew inside him. They circled Erin's cage, but couldn't penetrate. There seemed no way through the finest of the fine bars of the cardiac prison. He fell forward. His face was wet, which was strange, but Johnny forced his eyes open and they met Bentley's. The Old English sheepdog's rough tongue was frantically slopping over him.

Johnny could no longer move his body, but he stared through the white fringe before him and focused on Bentley's one blue and one brown eye. Then he rolled his own eyes upward towards Erin. Bentley followed Johnny's gaze. The big dog leaned back on his haunches and sprang towards the boy king.

Immediately, there was a slackening in Johnny's chest. Amid the shouts and yelps that shattered the silence, Johnny willed apart the bars of the cage and sent through more sparks. His heart twitched and then, above the background noise, he heard the welcome double thud of it beating. As the blood began to flow again, Johnny got gingerly to his feet. For a moment, the *Spirit of London*'s bridge swam out of focus, but he stayed standing and the sensation passed. His vision clearing, Johnny saw a grey and white Old English sheepdog standing guard over a frightened boy while, nearby, Clara's face beamed with relief. Princess Zeta was smiling too, albeit a little more sheepishly.

'My brother,' hissed Zeta. 'We are guests on this starship. We should start behaving accordingly.'

Johnny walked over to his dog and stroked Bentley's coat, saying, 'Good boy. Good boy, Bents.'

Bentley growled one last time in Erin's face, which was screwed up in a look of deep loathing, making the six dark scabs appear much closer together.

As the sheepdog stepped away, Johnny said, 'Do that again, or do anything to my ship, and you're history,' trying really hard to sound convincing. Now it was beating again, his heart seemed to be making up for lost time and thumping faster than ever. 'I will get you home, I promise. But it might take a few days. Our folder is exhausted and we have things to do on Earth, our homeworld.' Erin lay on the floor glaring up at Johnny, who continued, 'The ships that were searching for you – the Andromedans. We think they may come here. We need to build up our defences.' Finally, Erin nodded. Johnny reached out his hand to help the orange-haired boy to his feet.

Erin was halfway up when the whole bridge shook and everyone fell to the floor. The view of space blurred beyond the hull, Clara cried out and Sol calmly said, 'I am detecting a massive spatial disturbance in our immediate vicinity.'

Johnny was first to rise. 'What's happening?' he shouted as he ran for the captain's chair and sat himself down. He was pretty sure he wouldn't like the ship's answer. On the viewscreen was the largest of the black vessels he thought they'd left behind, some of its long thorns just a whisker away from the *Spirit of London*'s hull.

'I am being hailed,' Sol replied.

'On screen,' said Johnny. 'But make it narrow – just show me.'

Sol displayed a humanoid figure, with long scraggly black hair and matching black uniform. The man's face was half-covered in a mask, from which a single, brilliant white star seemed to shine. It was Nicky. 'This is General Nymac, Commander-in-Chief of the Andromedan Fleets and Captain of the *Astricida*.' As Johnny's brother spoke the last word, he gestured at the ship around him. 'Surrender yourself to me, Johnny Mackintosh, and I give you my word that your ship and crew will remain unharmed. You have one minute.'

6 ☆☆

In the Belly of the Star Killer ☆☆

Johnny needed time to process the crazy information he had just received, but the seconds were rushing by while his brain had simply seized up. Nicky was his older brother, from Earth; Nymac, the most feared general anyone had ever seen, came from the Andromeda Galaxy. They couldn't be the same person yet, as the cogs slowly whirred inside Johnny's head, bits of it, pieces of the puzzle, began to make sense. He needed to know more.

From one side, Erin shouted, 'Treachery – I *knew* it!' but only his sister responded. Zeta's eyes narrowed and she rolled her long tongue out towards him like a party streamer, slapping his face. The boy king fell silent.

Alf came flapping out of the lifts and Johnny put him to work at once, analysing the *Astricida* – every one of its deathly spikes dwarfed the *Spirit of London*. Johnny was desperate to buy more time – to work this out and somehow (he had no idea how) tell Clara that General Nymac was their brother.

He knew his ship must seem like an annoying gnat in comparison with the black supersphere but, even so, Sol's voice boomed across the bridge, defiantly cutting through the dread stillness that had settled. 'I am fully battle ready. It would be an honour to fight.'

Johnny sensed her power and determination – it lifted him. He was proud that Sol packed a powerful sting, but he wouldn't let her be swatted out of existence. Moving towards the Plican's tank, he placed a hand on it and asked, 'Can we fold?' But he knew the answer before Clara shook her head slowly and silently. 'Then there's nothing for it,' he went on, trying to sound braver than he felt, as though he was plucking up the courage to knock on Mrs Devonshire's door having been sent to the headmistress's office to be expelled. 'I have to go.'

'No!' said Clara, fiercely. 'You can't. You mustn't. I won't let you.' She grabbed hold of her brother and clung to him, burying her face in his chest.

Johnny was used to thinking of her as brave and capable of almost anything. He hadn't held her since the day they'd lost their parents six months before and he'd stopped noticing how small and fragile she was. He moved his hands to her shoulders and stepped back, so she was at arm's length. 'You know there's no choice,' he said. 'If I don't go we'll be killed – all of us.'

'Then I'll come too.'

Johnny shook his head. 'I need you here. You're in command now.' He'd been stupid not to tell Clara about his weird meeting with Nicky, but he couldn't come out with it now and then just disappear – that wasn't fair. He simply said, 'There's no time to explain, but I'll be OK. You've got to protect Earth and, if there's anyone in the whole galaxy I want looking for me – who can get me out of there if I need – it's got to be you.'

'The *Astricida* has powered her weapons, which are formidable,' said Sol. 'I am being hailed.'

Johnny pushed Clara out of view, but held her gaze for a second more.

'What is your answer?' demanded Nymac, whose image had reappeared on the screen.

'I'm ready,' he said quietly. 'How do you want me to come aboard?'

'A wise decision.' The figure who spoke sounded every bit

like the cruel Krun-killing person who had taken Nicky over, rather than the long-lost brother Johnny had fleetingly first met. 'There is no need for shuttlecraft or transit tubes – I have the power to fold space. You will enter through the anomaly.'

As Johnny watched, the centre of Sol's viewscreen distorted. If he looked to the side, then everything appeared normal, but when he stared straight at it, a circle of nothingness was spreading outward. It solidified as it grew, becoming a narrow tunnel, beginning in mid-air and sloping away from Johnny. Out of it poured a dense, white mist, seeping across the floor of the *Spirit of London*'s bridge.

'Please don't, Johnny,' said Clara.

He couldn't look at her. He'd never felt so guilty, or so scared, both at the same time. Facing straight ahead, he ran forward and dived, headfirst with arms outstretched, into the opening.

☆ ☆ ☆
☆ ☆

The fold was poorly constructed. Whereas Clara's were instantaneous, allowing you to step straight from one piece of space to another, in this one the different pieces hadn't quite matched up. It was freezing – the vacuum of space just a hair's breadth away, as though he could fall through at any moment. As Johnny slid down the tunnel, the walls narrowed and his progress slowed. He felt as if he were inside a giant intestine, with white mist seeping in where the walls were stretched thinnest. It seemed to be attracted to Johnny and as it swirled around his exposed hands, thrust out in front of him, he flinched. Its touch told him he was tiny and totally insignificant – such a small cog in the cosmic wheel that it wasn't worth carrying on. This was the very fabric of space and time, as close to infinity as it was possible to get and he was as nothing in comparison.

There was no going back. The fold had sealed itself behind

and the tunnel's walls closed around Johnny's feet, forcing him slowly forward like a mouse inside a python, pushing his face into ever thicker whiteness. The tunnel pressed against his torso, squeezing the breath out of his lungs as it propelled him on until, at last, his hands felt warm air and he knew the end was nearby. He summoned all his strength to squirm towards it. His head popped out of the tunnel's mouth and into a world of dazzling bands of blue light, so bright the surrounding detail was lost.

Pausing for a moment, he gulped down the warm air, aware of strange sounds, like a whispering wind, at night, in a dense forest. The burnt electric scent of ozone was everywhere. Johnny wriggled forward once more, then realized he was coming out in mid-air and tried to stop himself. The tunnel walls contracted for one last time, expelling him. Headfirst and hands out in front, he fell, bracing himself for the impact, but the black floor beneath the tunnel's mouth was soft and sticky, like tar. Ending up on all fours, he felt the oily blackness begin to seep up his arms and legs. Something brushed his hair and he rolled over to see a half-empty blood-red cloak billowing just above him. Around the flapping figure were five more dim red dots. Johnny squinted to block out the blue lights and the fuzzy red specks resolved into scarlet robes, swarming not far above his head. From underneath the nearest cloak, he spotted two long skeletal fingers, just like the ones he'd seen in the Regent's bunker. The Phasmeer had been wrong to claim he'd collected every Owlessan Monk in the galaxy – nothing else could have created Nicky's fold. The closest one was reaching out, as though it wanted to touch him, but didn't quite dare. Its cloak flapped in his face and Johnny rolled to the side

He lifted his head to look around. One of the bands of blue light was nearby and the reason for the smell became obvious: the bright line was nothing less than a river of electricity. He traced the flow to a point in the far distance where it joined together with four others. The brilliance of the lights struggled to penetrate the rest of the ship's gloomy interior. When Johnny squinted it looked as if the floor he was standing on curved all the way round to form distant walls, as black as night yet covered with even blacker thick veins that bulged and branched across them. The tar-like material these were made from was moving, snaking slowly over the walls and floor, and pieces nearby had begun creeping across Johnny's top. He stood up, clawing it away, and shivered, fairly sure the strange sounds he was hearing were the workings of a giant organism – and he was inside it.

Something disturbed the floating Monks who briefly parted, allowing Johnny to see directly above. You could have fitted a hundred *Spirit of London*s nose to tail in the cavernous space. Though the insides of the Nicky's ship were mostly hollow, something sparkled at its very centre, like a tiny pearl at the heart of an enormous oyster. Clear tendrils extended away from it in all different directions, tethering it to the black walls.

The next moment, all six Owlessan Monks fled in different directions. Johnny thought he might have heard screams of fear as it happened, but they were so high-pitched he couldn't tell if the sound had come through his ears or simply from inside his head. The reason could only be the two massive, camel-coloured, hairy aliens he saw rushing towards him on a tripod base of three ultrathick legs. Johnny had never seen anything like them – above the waist they were roughly pyramids, a single strong arm centred on each side, and their large, rounded heads came with three pairs of eyes.

They ran very fast, their central leg alternating with the two outside of it, and were on him in a second. A black net shot from one of the creature's hands and wrapped itself around him, leaving just his legs, from the knee down, free. Up close on his left and right, the hairy coats of his tall captors reminded Johnny of Chewbacca in *Star Wars*. But he was a long way from Hollywood and the eyes gazing at him were as black as anything else on the ship, with no detail – just empty pools giving nothing away. He shivered again.

One of the aliens grabbed his boots, the other his shoulders, as they lifted him off the ground. At frightening speed, he was carried parallel to the nearest electric river, the blue lights reflecting off the eyes of his captors. They stopped underneath one of the tubes snaking towards the distant structure that twinkled at the centre of the ship. Johnny was being taken to Nicky's bridge.

Effortlessly, the hairy creature holding Johnny's shoulders stood him upright. Then both of the aliens sprang from their powerful three legs, lifting him high into the air with them. As they rose through the giant tube, they crossed a barrier. Even though he was bound by the net, Johnny felt temporary weightlessness take hold. Then he started to fall – but this time upwards – as a new gravity field took over and Johnny headed towards the clear structure that was now below. Releasing their grip on him, the camel-coloured creatures on either side performed a single graceful somersault, belying their bulk, so they were travelling feet first. Upside down and bound by the net, Johnny knew he had to act fast. Thankful for all his practice in low-gravity environments, he strained forward, shifting his slowly increasing weight, and somersaulted. He landed in a large chamber, knees bent and legs apart, on a hard, diamond surface.

Johnny leapt backwards, as four long limbs from a tall creature with a fly-like snout reached out to grab him. He started to fall, but was caught from behind by a pair of powerful human arms. The man they belonged to laughed from his belly, and Johnny felt his own body shake. 'Even though he is bound, he still eludes you,' roared the man in an alien language Johnny recognized at once. His brother was speaking Krun. That was what the insect-like creature standing before him was, in its true form with no human disguise. It shrank back.

Johnny tried to look around. Here at the heart of Nicky's ship, the *Astricida*, was not one but five large Plicans. Their tentacles were folded inside their fibrous outer skins and squeezed into compartments at the end of clear tubes that joined together in a star shape, floating unaided above his head. The transparent floor on which he stood had five corners with five shallow walls sloping away from its sides. At almost every vertex, stood a motionless camel-coloured soldier, the same as the ones that had brought him there. They weren't simply on his level – there must have been about twenty of the creatures in the chamber, some with their heads facing vertically down while others were at whichever angles the sloping walls dictated. It made it very hard to tell which way was up. The two who'd captured Johnny left his side and marched up the walls to the only remaining gaps.

'Leave my ship,' the man said to the facing Krun. 'The time has come to fetch your pupil and begin his mission. I wish to be alone with the prisoner.'

'But, my Lord – he is too dangerous. You don't know what he is capable of.' Johnny recognized the creature's voice – this was Stevens.

'You dare question me? You forget yourself, slave. Perhaps I should show you what *I* am capable of?' The voice had no warmth, unlike when Johnny had first met his brother. Wrapped tightly in the net, a chill ran down his spine as he felt Nicky's hot breath on the back of his neck. A hand reached past Johnny's side and Stevens's hairy long legs buckled at the sight of the black ring on Nicky's finger. Prostrating himself on the floor, his insect head pressed against the diamond hard surface, the Krun whimpered, 'Never, my Lord.'

'Do I need to ask you again?' said Nicky, and Stevens waddled up the shallow walls and out the same way Johnny had come in. 'Mamluks – you will leave us too.' The huge three-legged creatures at each of the corners snapped to attention, saluting Nicky, before they turned as one and marched in rhythm up and down the different sloping walls, disappearing into several of the clear tubes that led away from the central core.

The hands holding Johnny released him, pushing him forward. For a fraction of a second he thought he might be able to stay on his feet, but the force of the shove was too much. Johnny stumbled and hit the hard floor face first. There was a sickening crunch and it felt as if his nose had been forced into his own skull. Lights flashed in front of Johnny's eyes. He managed to lift his head slightly, his eyes following the slow spread of a rich red film across the floor. Dazed, he was dimly aware it was probably his own blood, but he couldn't watch it for long because a heavy boot rammed under his stomach, flipping him over onto his back.

'You're weaker than I expected,' said the figure, dressed all in black, shifting in and out of focus. Johnny fought against the watering of his eyes from the pain, and concentrated on his brother's face – the brilliant white light shone out of the mask where his brother's right eye should have been. When the beam fell on him, it burnt like a laser. 'You bleed easily.'

'What's wrong with you?' Johnny asked. 'It's me.' The warm blood was pouring down his throat, which was becoming sore, and it was getting harder to breathe.

A puzzled expression spread across Nicky's face. He placed his hands in the air and, from nowhere, a holographic display appeared at his fingertips. From below Johnny could see the dials, but not the screen his brother appeared to be watching. 'You are Johnny Mackintosh, aren't you . . . *the* Johnny

Mackintosh?'

'You know I am,' Johnny replied, spitting some blood so he could get the words out.

Nicky laughed. 'Yes, of course you are,' he said. 'I hadn't realized you were such a coward – who would surrender rather than fight. If it were up to my Krun servants they'd have killed you already.'

'Like they killed Dad?' said Johnny. 'Did Bugface . . . Stevens . . . tell you *that*?'

'You rave like a cornered Saalis at the climax of the hunt,' sneered Nicky. 'Of course you must die, but you should feel honoured. I have been preparing your murderer specially – I think you'll like him.' Nicky laughed manically as if he'd just cracked the funniest joke ever.

'Why are you doing this?' Johnny asked, fighting for breath. 'I don't understand.'

'Of course you don't, little Terran,' said Nicky, crouching on his haunches next to Johnny's head. 'How could you? The plan comes from my master . . . the Nameless One . . . the most ancient of all things. So old that every galaxy in the universe is the outpouring of his breath. If he ever had a name it was forgotten before your insignificant little sun was even born – and, once I've gathered my fleet, it will die like Toliman.' Nicky grabbed hold of Johnny's face and forced him to look into the brilliant white light.

It was like stepping under a waterfall – the pressure pushed Johnny's head backwards as he felt the stream of pure hatred, bashing the back of his skull on the hard floor. At the same time the blood around his face started to bubble and boil, as if heated by the beam.

'Your ship carries the Emperor's mark,' Nicky continued. 'You joined the wrong side. Soon my master will leave his throne in Andromeda and Bram Khari will be dead. But I promise the last thing your precious Emperor does will be to kneel before him, before the Nameless One, the whole galaxy witnessing who is the greatest. Of course, by then you will be long dead.'

Still bound, Johnny had never felt so desperate, but the mention of Bram strengthened him. He remembered the first words the Emperor had spoken when he and Clara knelt before him in the Imperial Palace on Melania, asking them to rise and stand in his presence. Johnny repeated them now. 'The trappings of power are for the weak.' He lifted his head, and forced himself to stare into the white light again. 'This Nameless One can't be very sure of himself if he needs people to kneel.'

Nicky's face twisted in an ugly grimace. He raised his hand to strike Johnny, but a female voice interrupted in a staccato language Johnny had never heard before. 'Fold commencing in 30 seconds. Destination Terra, Sol 3.'

Nicky raised his head and answered in the same strange tongue, 'What are you doing, ship? Cancel this fold at once. The captured vessel is to be boarded – the Krun will return shortly with a new captain.'

'Unable to comply, General,' the ship replied.

'I said cancel.' Nicky's fearsome face turned bright red with anger, as though about to burst.

'You informed me you may try to rescind this command, General,' replied the ship, whose words came sharply, like bullets firing from a gun. 'When placing the order, you said it was a test of my resolve – that on no account was it to be changed.'

The five tanks above Johnny's head began to pulse with blue light, before they opened and the Plicans uncurled their tentacles, extending them towards the centre of the star where they danced around each other in precisely choreographed steps, beginning a fold.

'What madness is this?' Nicky shouted. He wheeled round and looked at Johnny, lying bound and helpless on the floor. 'It's you . . . you did this. I should have listened to the Krun – Stevens was right. I should have destroyed your ship and you with it . . . you have to die . . . now.'

Johnny couldn't believe his brother would do this. With his free feet, he pushed himself away just in time as Nicky lunged towards him. Sliding out of reach, he braced himself for impact against the sloping walls, but it didn't come. Beyond the diamond-shaped compartment, the outsides flew through each other and disappeared. Jupiter and Mars whizzed by. Within it, the walls either side of Johnny had remained firmly in place. He tilted his head back, allowing himself to see where he was going, even if it meant swallowing another mouthful of blood. He was sliding very fast along a diamond-clad tunnel that stretched far into the distance – all the way to Earth.

Nicky leapt on top of him, placed both hands around Johnny's throat and pressed hard on his Adam's apple. Everything began to go dark, but Johnny summoned the last of his strength and hooked his leg under his larger brother. Taken by surprise, Nicky was thrown forward further down the tunnel, towards Earth, which was growing bigger very quickly.

'Stop it, Nicky,' said Johnny, desperately trying to scramble away but knowing it was only delaying the inevitable.

Even as the fold continued, Johnny's brother was able to stand and dust himself down. 'Do you not even know who I am – who it is who is going to kill you? I am Nymac, Captain of the *Astricida,* the Star Killer, and Commander-in-Chief of the Andromedan Fleet.'

'No you're not,' shouted Johnny. 'Nymac . . . it's made up. It's Nicky Mackintosh, just shortened.'

'How dare you speak that name?' replied the figure in black, walking calmly towards Johnny while pulling a curved knife from inside his body suit.

'It's true,' said Johnny, bracing himself for the blade. He stared into the figure's lone eye and said, 'You're my brother.'

The white star shining through Nicky's mask flickered and went out. He thrust the knife forward, but instead of plunging it into Johnny's heart, cut through the net that bound him. Then Nicky collapsed beside his bloodied younger brother and began to shake.

In the background, the walls of the *Astricida* were flying back into their right positions. It was so hard for Johnny to breathe that he had to roll over onto his front and then crouch forward on his knees, allowing the blood to drip from his broken nose onto the floor. He pulled pieces of netting off him, rubbing his arms to get his circulation going, and noticed the lights around the face of his wristcom had all turned green. Johnny lifted his hand, daring himself to touch his nose, but when he placed the index finger on it everything went white and a pain like nothing he'd felt before shot through his skull. He was only dimly aware of his own agonized howl, worse than fingernails being scraped down a blackboard.

'Sorry 'bout that,' said Nicky, speaking English for the first time and rolling onto his side which let Johnny see the look of concern on his face. 'I promise I'll make it up to you.' Johnny wasn't at all sure what had just happened, but Nicky looked different . . . human again. 'I knew you could do it, Johnny,' his brother went on. 'Draw me out of him properly. I've been planning it for days, getting stronger as I lurked in his subconscious, secretly programming the fold to Earth for when Nymac captured you. I think I can keep him buried for a few hours.'

'Orbital docking with Terran platform NY0 completed,' said the ship's voice, all around them. Johnny looked up. There had been an imperceptible thud, but that was the only indication of a joining with another ship. The tunnel was gone, and the bridge was, once again, firmly enclosed. It had been the strangest, least stomach-churning fold he'd ever experienced.

'Thank you, *Astricida*,' said Nicky, slipping effortlessly back into the strange language of before. 'We should leave the ship while we have the chance,' he said, turning to Johnny and speaking in English again. 'Are you able to fly?'

It was such a strange question Johnny didn't know how to respond. Slowly he shook his head, showering the floor with a few more droplets of blood. Nicky turned again to a holographic display in front of him. As his hands brushed a combination of different-coloured dials, the clear pentagonal roof of the diamond bridge changed through a sequence of ever darker tones, until it became black and then vanished. Nicky waved an arm and this time the console disappeared. 'Then hold onto me,' he went on, offering his left hand out to his younger brother. As Johnny placed his palm inside it, the hairs on his arm began to tingle and he felt goosebumps. The sensation travelled around his body and he tried to make sense of it.

An image came into his head of himself lying on a trampoline, seeing the effect his body had on the very fabric of space–time itself. The longer he held Nicky's hand, the less impression he was making on the canvas – it was straightening out and, after a few moments, the sheet became taut and flat and he saw his body leave the surface and begin to float.

At the same moment, he lifted into the air with his brother, soaring towards the junction where the blue rivers of electricity came together. Now he was closer, Johnny could see five huge white monoliths, like giant teeth, standing at the point the currents met, as though enclosing a giant mouth. Above their heads, light streamed into the massive ship as its jaws opened. Greeting them was the most welcoming sight in the galaxy – the view of Earth from space. Somehow able to breathe, he flew, with Nicky, past the teeth and out of the mouth, which slowly closed behind them. The sensation was even better than piloting a shuttle with shields on – there didn't seem any walls around them – just the perfection of the cosmos. Then, beneath Johnny's boots, a piece of the Earth blurred, before his feet touched solid, but invisible ground. It was a clear platform, floating thousands of kilometres above the planet's surface. Nicky let go of his hand and Johnny could sense space–time bowing again, as he returned to his normal mass. He stood with the Earth beneath him and his brother at his side, and could almost forget the deathly spikes of the *Astricida* above.

Nicky turned to Johnny and smiled. 'Alone at last, little bro',' he said, reaching for Johnny and pulling him into another powerful embrace. Finally, after it seemed as though all his ribs were about to crack, Johnny was released. He gulped down some extra air and turned around, trying not to let his discomfort show. Nicky said, 'It's good to see you,' while slapping him hard on the back, sending more shooting pains through Johnny's broken nose.

Johnny steadied himself. He couldn't quite see where the platform ended and empty space began and didn't want to fall over the edge. He felt his brother's arm around his waist, guiding him forward. 'Come, we have much to discuss,' said Nicky. Johnny let himself be led for a few metres, but then the sharp edge of the platform came into view and he tried to dig his feet into the smooth glassy surface to stop himself moving. Nicky laughed. 'Don't worry – we can't fall off. This thing is encased in *that* many fields. It's just the best place to sit and, sadly, I very rarely get the chance. You see I've not been myself very often these last few years. Not since that night.' He let go of Johnny and settled down right at the edge of the platform, his legs dangling over the side pointing down towards North America, which was clearly visible beneath a near cloud-free sky.

Slowly, and very carefully, Johnny followed suit. He couldn't help thinking of Clara. She would never be able to sit here, however beautiful the view. He wondered whether Nicky knew about her. Probably not or he'd have brought their sister aboard the *Astricida* as well. It was only fair not to tell Nicky about their other sibling until he'd told Clara first.

'You see this,' said Nicky, nodding between his feet towards the blue and white globe below. 'All this can be ours when we join together.'

'I don't understand,' said Johnny. 'What do you mean, "ours"?'

'Ours to rule, of course. And not just Earth. You won't know, but there was a time when our homeworld had an empire spanning half the galaxy. We can build that again.'

'Atlantis,' said Johnny, quietly.

His brother stopped and studied him, as though seeing him properly for the first time. 'Yes, Atlantis,' he said. 'The greatest civilization our planet has ever produced, destroyed by that excuse for an emperor.'

'I think he had some help,' said Johnny, remembering how he and Clara had travelled into the past, met a very young Bram and rescued the Diaquant (the mysterious being who powered Atlantean society) from her cruel enslavement, only to discover later that she was their mother.

'Khari has spoken of this?' Nicky asked. 'You must be close to him – another spy on Melania could be useful.'

Johnny bit his lip. He wasn't about to tell Nicky he'd actually been to Atlantis – not yet anyway. 'Bram's my friend,' he said. 'I would never betray him.'

'You're friends with a thief. He stole the Diaquant. If he hadn't, today Earth not Melania would be ruling the galaxy.'

'I think she wanted to go with him,' Johnny replied.

'Well of course that's what he'd say.'

'*He* didn't tell me – *she* did,' said Johnny, cutting across his brother.

'So the Diaquant was a she? I suppose you've met her, have you?' Nicky asked in a tone that indicated he didn't believe a word of it.

'So have you,' said Johnny, exasperated. 'She's our mum.'

For a moment Johnny's brother fell silent. Then he lay down with his back on the platform and his whole body began to shake with laughter.

'What's so funny?' Johnny asked.

'Priceless . . . our mum . . . the Diaquant of Atlantis,' said Nicky, struggling to get the words out between belly laughs. Somehow he composed himself, sat up and placed a hand on Johnny's shoulder. 'I hate to ruin your fairytales, but our mum wasn't the super-powerful galactic force you've been led to believe. She was a cleaner at the Derby Royal Infirmary.' Johnny brushed the hand off him, but his brother carried on. 'OK – if she was, how could she allow a feeble race like the Krun to abduct her eldest son? Answer me that.'

Johnny looked away. The question hit him as if he'd just been thumped in the stomach. It had been nagging at the back of his mind for months. How could his mum have abandoned him, and Dad and Nicky, and unborn Clara? The Diaquant could do anything – it had been nothing for her to stop time, defy gravity and send him and Clara thousands of years forward from the past back to the here and now. Yet the night the Krun came, she didn't lift a finger to stop them. His family had been torn apart – he'd lived alone in a children's home for more than a decade.

'I'm sorry, little bro',' said Nicky, who might have noticed Johnny's eyes watering. 'You're right – we are special. That's because we were chosen, but it wasn't anything to do with Mary Mackintosh from Littleover. It was him – the Nameless One – he reached out from another galaxy, searching for vessels fit to fill with his power. And he found us.'

'It's not true,' were the only words Johnny could get out.

'Look at me,' said Nicky. Johnny refused to turn his head, but his brother continued anyway. 'The thing is, he made mistakes. He made us too powerful. That's why he fashioned this hateful mask.' Johnny looked round and saw his brother's one visible eye was also beginning to water. 'It is his way to control me. He made me Nymac. He sees this galaxy through me. His eye burns through my skull, controlling me. He's made me do terrible things, but has also shown me the path to greatness. And I have learnt to fight. I grow strong – sometimes nearly as powerful as him. If only I'd known earlier that he gave you his power too, we could have thrown off his mantle long ago. Already, just on my own, I can be myself for hours, sometimes days at a time. The battle that rages – the important one – is not the Andromedans fighting the Milky Way. It's in here,' he said tapping his skull. 'It's Nicky Mackintosh versus Nymac. That's what will decide things.' Nicky paused, hugging himself, rubbing his hands up the arms of his black outfit. Less certainly than before, he went on, 'It's just that . . . in any war, you never fully know what your adversary is planning. He is still drawn to this place and has come to realize you're his genetic brother – he sequenced your whole genome to prove it. He's just loath to admit it and not all his schemes are clear to me. I am blocked . . . shut out some of the time, even while I lurk in the shadows, hoping to pounce. But I know one thing – Nymac hates you with the same fury that the Nameless One hates you. He's trying to erase his past. He wants the Sun gone, Earth destroyed, but, most of all, he wants you dead.'

'This Nameless One?' asked Johnny. 'Why? What have I done to him?'

'You escaped – the night he took me. You have the powers he gave you, but he's never been able to control them. You're a loose cannon, when you should have been his most perfect weapon.'

'A weapon like you? Do you know about Alpha Centauri?'

'Ah, the Star Blaze,' Nicky replied. 'I'm not proud, but it had to be done whether I was Nymac or Nicky.' Johnny shrank back, horrified. 'The Tolimi weren't the target – it was Khari's Fourth Fleet. There's a war on. You have to expect casualties – collateral damage.'

'Not like that,' said Johnny. 'Not a whole star system.'

'Did you not notice the *Astricida*?' Nicky asked, raising his head to the foreboding blackness above, blotting out all the distant suns. 'She is the Star Killer. With her weapons and the power of my mind, you would be amazed what is already possible. Imagine if you and I joined forces.'

'It's wrong,' said Johnny. 'You're wrong. He lied to you . . . about everything. I don't know why Mum couldn't save us, but she *was* the Diaquant. That's why we're who we are. Why he wants to control you. Can't you take the mask off?'

'How old are you now?' Nicky asked. 'Ten? Eleven?'

'I'm thirteen and a half,' Johnny replied, feeling his face quickly turning red, probably matching the drying blood across it.

'Exactly. You're too young to understand. When you're older – when we rule together – you will lose your scruples. Sometimes, the ends justify the means.'

Johnny scowled and his brother's face softened, forming a sad smile. 'More than anything I wish I could remove this curse he has given me,' said Nicky touching the blackened side of his face, 'but I would die trying. Or worse still, he would return . . . take me over . . . force me to kill you right here and now. I feel him stirring inside me even as we speak – we don't have long.'

Johnny could see it was pointless to argue. If Nymac was really coming back, he had to get away from his brother before it happened. Behind, a bell chimed and Johnny looked round. A large, wooden box had appeared in the very centre of the platform, with an ornate design on the front that looked a little like a thistle. A door in the box slid open. It was a lift – the top of a new space elevator.

'Come,' said Nicky, standing, his one eye sparkling. 'Let me take you to Earth while I still can.'

7 ✰✰

The Starry Ceiling ✰✰

Johnny followed his brother over the clear floor until they arrived at the lift doors. 'Art deco, mid-1930s design at its best,' said Nicky. He ran his fingers around the outside and carried on, 'Oriental walnut. Just look at this marquetry – the workmanship's stunning.'

Johnny had no idea what any of this meant, but was a little dubious that an old wooden box would safely carry them through the atmosphere all the way down to the Earth's surface. 'Is it safe?' he asked, as Nicky stepped inside.

'It's perfectly safe,' said Nicky smiling. 'You'll love it. I was told the Krun sent you and another prisoner up in one a while ago. Surely you at least enjoyed the ride?'

If Stevens still hadn't said anything to Nymac about Clara, Johnny guessed there'd been no reason to also tell him that they were gassed unconscious during their journey. He hoped the same wasn't about to happen again. 'You have no idea,' he told Nicky, before taking a final look at the beautiful planet below him and then entering the space elevator. The doors closed, there was a slight jolt and the lift began to descend. Once moving, the walls began to glow, a strange blue translucence that matched the colour of Earth's oceans. Soon, walls and ceiling disappeared completely, leaving Johnny and Nicky careering downwards. Above hung the ominous *Astricida*, blacker than the blackness of space, while America lay beneath their feet.

'Impressive isn't it?' said Nicky, as they plunged faster and faster. Johnny simply nodded. 'I don't think I have long,' continued his brother. 'But I will contact you again. Soon, very soon, I shall be myself properly, able to shake off Nymac forever.'

'What's Nymac . . . the Andromedans up to, Nicky?' asked Johnny. 'Is Earth in danger? After Toliman, will the Sun be next?'

'Of course not,' said Nicky, but Johnny's relief was short-lived. 'Yes, he intends to turn the Sun into a supernova, but I will stop him.'

'Let me help you,' said Johnny. 'Let Bram help you.'

Nicky turned from the magnificent view and stared straight and seriously at Johnny. 'The Emperor is simply using you. He is weak – he doesn't have the power that we do. Remember that when the time comes. We're . . . kin. We're all each other's got. You need to trust me.'

Johnny looked away. He felt that his eyes would betray him, that Nicky would be able to peer inside them and see through to Clara. He just nodded and pretended to be distracted by the view. They were descending with ocean on one side and land, together with some massive lakes, on the other, with the space elevator apparently on the boundary. Perhaps Nicky had built a secret base just out to sea? Then they were engulfed in wispy cotton wool clouds, before emerging, definitively above dry land, over a huge city, a gleaming tower of silver directly below, reaching skyward through concentric squares. Johnny braced himself as the space elevator looked to be about to collide with a wide metal spike protruding upwards, but they passed through as though it were simply a hologram. The walls became solid and, soon after the cabin settled, a bell chimed and the doors opened.

They stepped into a wood-panelled corridor, matching the

lift design and his brother pushed Johnny forward through a concealed door that led into a spacious bathroom of white marble. Nicky turned on a chrome tap, picked up a couple of small white towels from a pile of crisply ironed ones and set to work wiping the blood off Johnny's face.

'That's better,' said Nicky, scrubbing hard at the final few splodges. Johnny felt like a little boy who'd got mucky playing football outside. 'Couldn't have you walking the streets looking like that,' his brother went on.

Together they examined Johnny's reflection in a large dark-framed mirror. There were still a few bloodstains on his top, but at least he'd stopped bleeding. He was having to breathe through his mouth and his throat was still sore, so he walked over to a drinking fountain in the corner of the bathroom and took a few glugs of water. 'Where are we?' he asked.

'I'll show you,' his brother replied, leading the way out of the bathroom and opening another door a little way along which led into the most amazing office Johnny had ever seen. He'd always thought Mrs Irvine's was posh, but now it seemed plain and tiny in comparison with the high, painted ceiling and the enormous room that must have been in the very corner of the skyscraper. Giant, upward-pointing triangular windows looked out in two directions. 'Welcome to New York,' said Nicky, as he made a sweeping gesture to the view before them.

Nicky sat down, resting his legs upon a vast, leather-topped desk while Johnny walked across the shiny black stone floor to gaze out of one of the massive windows. Unless he could persuade Nicky to accept help, Nymac would take him over and all this could soon be gone. He was much higher than even Sol's bridge when she was in the middle of London and could see that New York had many more skyscrapers to admire. Below, about a quarter of the way down towards street level, gleaming metal eagles protruded from the building's skin, as if to ward off unwanted guests. Much further down, yellow matchbox cars wove through the traffic on a busy main road.

'Is this the Empire State Building?' Johnny asked. It was the only skyscraper in New York he'd heard of.

Nicky smiled. 'The Empire State's over there,' he said, standing and pointing out of one of the windows to an even taller building, lit up in the evening twilight to show a garish red body with a green top. 'That's the biggest, but this is the most beautiful. We're in the Chrysler Building – Nymac owns the top few floors. The only downside is that, from here, we can't actually see the Chrysler Building.'

Johnny surprised himself and laughed. 'Is it as cool as the Gherkin?' he asked.

'That steel and glass monstrosity you've modelled your ship on?' said Nicky. 'Must be a bummer to hide when you're on Earth. Nymac's pulling his . . . my hair out trying to locate your landing site.' Nicky raised his hand to stop his brother saying anything, not realizing Johnny had no intention of letting the secret out. 'I cannot trust myself to keep it from him. What if he's here now, lurking inside me? Sometimes I wonder if I'm not simply his puppet, dangling on a string.' Nicky gazed out of the window, deep in thought, but then shook himself. He turned to Johnny and forced his frown into a smile. 'Ignore me – where was I? Yes, the Chrysler Building,' Nicky went on. 'It's the tallest brick structure in the world. One day I might turn it into a ship. I imagine it would not look out of place on Melania, when we land, ready to take over.'

'I don't get you,' said Johnny. 'Why do you have to rule anything?'

Nicky's feet slid to the floor with a thud and he clutched his head. 'Nymac is stirring, little bro'. You need to go back to the elevator – get out of here.'

Johnny hesitated. The lights on his wristcom were steadfastly green and there was nothing shining from the mask on his brother's face.

'Don't wait for him,' shouted Nicky, steadying himself by holding onto the desk.

'Let Bram help you,' said Johnny, walking around to be beside his brother. 'He could get that mask off.'

'Weren't you listening? I don't want Khari's help. We can do this together . . . you and me. Just not now . . . not yet. The Nameless One . . . I can feel him. He is coming. Go, Johnny . . . now!'

The white star began to flicker on and off and Johnny saw the lights around his wrist beginning to turn red. He looked at his brother and saw tears rolling down Nicky's exposed cheek. Johnny could feel his own eyes watering.

'Please,' said Nicky. 'I got you back here but I can't stop him. Save yourself.'

After a moment more, Johnny nodded, turned and ran out of the door. He sprinted to the lift and was relieved to see that beside it was a button pointing down that might take him to safety, as well as one that went up, presumably to the platform in the sky. The doors opened immediately. Johnny pressed the very bottom of a few circular knobs, the doors closed and, to his relief, he felt the cabin begin to descend.

Johnny's ears popped. He was sure he was moving quickly, but it still seemed to be taking forever to reach the ground floor. He hoped his brother, possibly already Nymac again, wouldn't stop it before he could get away. Finally the lift came to a halt. Johnny squeezed through the slowly opening doors into a wood-panelled hallway. All around, other lifts chimed as their doors opened, business men and women (with the familiar appearance of those he saw around the Gherkin in London) stepping in and out. Few paid Johnny any attention. The sight of a thirteen year old in the middle of the Chrysler Building was so unusual as to render him near invisible. Their surprised comments were all directed towards the elevator he'd come from, which was apparently always out of order.

He knew he had to get out, and quickly, but the way into the wider lobby was blocked by a burly security guard in an old-fashioned, dark blue uniform with a peaked cap. The guard was standing beside one of two modern glass barriers out of keeping with their surroundings.

There was nothing for it. Johnny ran and hurdled the clear gate.

'Hey you! Come back here,' shouted the man in the cap.

Johnny kept going. More guards moved from behind a counter to block his path, but Johnny dropped onto the shiny brown marble floor and slid beneath their grasping fingers and between two thick pillars. Keeping his momentum, he got to his feet and ran towards the right-hand of a pair of revolving doors that led, he hoped, into the busy street and away from Nicky, or Nymac, or the Nameless One, or whoever it was he should be running from.

Outside, Johnny turned right, began to run and then stopped as he heard someone calling his name above the noise of the traffic.

'Johnny?' A small woman in a navy-blue trouser suit with shoulder-length red hair, was standing on the pavement a little further up. He couldn't believe it – it was Miss Harutunian, his social worker from Halader House. Johnny turned and sped in the opposite direction. He heard shouts of, 'Wait! Come back . . .' tailing off behind him as he ran out into the road, ignoring the horns from hundreds of cars, before turning right down another street, underneath an overhanging building and keeping going for all he was worth, dodging shoppers and a man in a Father Christmas outfit. He passed beneath a bridge where crowds of people were heading through giant doors into a building on the right – Johnny followed, trying to lose himself in the throng.

As soon as he was inside, he stopped running and slowed to the pace of everyone around him, letting himself be carried along down a wide slope and through more doors. The flow quickened, taking him under a huge American flag and out into a spectacular chamber. The crowd hurried on, but Johnny forced his way to the side and paused for a second, mouth wide open, gulping down the air that his lungs were crying out for. All being well, Clara would have been able to bring Sol back to London safely. He had no idea whether or not the wristcom would work at such long range, but he lifted the device to his mouth and spoke anyway.

'Johnny to the *Spirit of London* . . . come in . . . over.'

He strained, listening for a reply, but in the bustle around him it was difficult to hear properly. Johnny tried again, repeating the same message. He turned the volume on his earpiece up to maximum, but there was only static. It was as desperate as calling International Rescue in *Thunderbirds*, but he tried once more with a different message.

'It's me again. If you're receiving this, please come and get me. I'm in New York – long story. Just left the Chrysler Building – that's a really tall skyscraper. Now I'm in a huge hall. It looks like . . . it's a train station. But a lot bigger than Castle Dudbury . . . or even Liverpool Street. There's a gold clock . . . four faces . . . over a round information desk in the middle, massive windows and . . .' Johnny looked up, '. . . and there's this bluey green ceiling – it's full of stars. Hope you're getting this . . . over.'

There was an announcement about the train on Track 21, drowning out any hope of a reply. Johnny waited, staring at the ceiling and spotting the shape of Orion the Hunter. Then he noticed a couple of people paying him a bit too much attention so turned away, joining a queue of people buying tickets from behind old-fashioned golden-grilled windows. Of course it was possible that Miss Harutunian had followed him into the station – but he didn't think she'd seen enough to be certain it was him. Even so, for a moment he wondered about taking a train out of there. The sign above where he was queuing read 'Hudson Line Departures', and two of the trains on the list were going to Poughkeepsie, which sounded a very cool name. If he'd been able he'd have bought a ticket to there, but he had zero pounds let alone dollars in his pockets. At least standing in line was a way of blending in while he thought about what to do next.

'Going somewhere, Johnny?' whispered a woman's voice from behind, very close to his ear, as something cold and hard was pressed into the small of his back. If he'd had any dollars he'd have bet them all that it was a gun. Johnny felt what little blood he had left draining away from his face. 'First rule of the game – don't break radio silence. Especially when you already know we've analysed your radios. Very careless.' The woman tutted.

Johnny had recognized her voice as soon as she'd spoken. This was Colonel Bobbi Hartman, though it wasn't at all clear whose army she was a colonel in. She had, indeed, disabled his wristcom the time he'd encountered her before, back in London. Following a tip-off from Chancellor Gronack, she'd had Johnny and Clara drugged and taken to a room in the American Embassy, but Colonel Hartman had made it perfectly clear she didn't answer to anything so insignificant as a government. She was after alien technology and had been quite prepared to do whatever it took, including dissecting Johnny or his sister, to acquire it.

'Signalling to your ship, were you?' continued the woman. 'If it's nearby, this time I promise we'll find it.'

'I told you before,' said Johnny in a low growl, still staring up at the departure board. 'I don't have a ship.'

'Yet funny how you can suddenly materialize here in Manhattan without coming through immigration. How ever did you manage that?'

'You wouldn't believe me if I told you,' said Johnny, turning slowly around and standing eye-to-eye with the dark-haired colonel. 'Listen to me. The Sun . . . Earth's in terrible danger – you've got to let me go.'

'I don't think you're in any position to make threats, Johnny.'

'It wasn't a threat,' he hissed, before feeling cold metal on the underside of his chin, forcing his head upwards.

'Take a look above you, Johnny,' whispered Bobbi. 'One of those stars yours?'

It had been Colonel Hartman who'd first identified Johnny's half-alien parentage, after ordering Dr Carrington's DNA test. The colonel had gone on to ignore the 'half' element of this, and was obsessed about discovering where in the galaxy Johnny was apparently 'from'. Seeing as he felt a hundred percent human, didn't have the slightest idea about his mum's origins and Colonel Hartman would have been the last person in the world he'd have told had he known, Johnny answered, 'How many times do I have to tell you? I'm *from* Earth – just like you. That's why I'm trying to save it.' A few people around them began to stare. The pistol disappeared from his chin and was quickly wedged in his stomach, but Colonel Hartman was starting to look a little uncomfortable. This gave Johnny an idea – he just had to hope she wanted to take him alive. He spoke again, much louder than before: 'I'm not coming with you – I'm going back to Dad's.'

'What are you talking about?' whispered Colonel Hartman. 'And keep your voice down, or else.'

'Or else, what?' This time Johnny was practically shouting. 'You can't make me. You're not my real mum.'

One of the onlookers made a move forward, but was

intercepted by a big man wearing cleaner's overalls. Johnny hadn't expected Colonel Hartman to be working alone and was pleased to have sprung the man's cover. Quickly, he looked around. There were two more cleaners nearby, taking a very close interest in what was going on. Either this was the world's best kept train station or he had to assume they were hostile too. Johnny tried to back away, but Bobbi kept a tight grip around his waist, moving with him and digging her long fingernails into his side. Surprisingly strong, she was able to force him to stop. Very loudly again, he said, 'I want to go to my dad's and you can't stop me.'

'Stop this right now,' said Colonel Hartman, aware that the pair were drawing quite a crowd.

Most kept a discreet distance, but one large woman moved forward, bravely saying, 'What's going on here? Do you need any help?'

'Mind your own business,' said the colonel.

The woman, clearly shocked, was about to reply when another figure, wearing an immaculately tailored dark suit, stepped through the circle of onlookers. Taking off his sunglasses to reveal ice cold, grey eyes, Stevens said, 'It's OK, ma'am. I'm the boy's father. I'll take it from here.'

Johnny wanted to shout out that it wasn't true, but the look from Stevens strangled any words before they could form. Johnny searched the crowd for more help, but found Krun operatives in matching suits were standing behind the three pretend cleaners. The woman who'd come forward was backing away, taking Johnny's only hope with her.

Colonel Hartman finally released her grip and looked from Johnny to Stevens. 'You!' she said, as her eyes narrowed. 'This is my operation. You don't have jurisdiction here.' She pushed Johnny away and raised her pistol, pointing it at the Krun.

Someone in the crowd screamed and the ring of bystanders

widened as they edged backwards. Oblivious, another station announcement came over the tannoy. Ignoring it, Stevens said, 'I'm changing the terms of our agreement. When I want jurisdiction, I'll take it.' As he spoke, he reached for the blaster he always carried but, even as he pulled it from its holster, three shots rang out in quick succession from Colonel Hartman's gun.

Johnny saw more screams written on the faces of those still watching, but could no longer hear them. The only sound was the ringing in his ears from the gunfire. He watched Stevens wobble from the impact of the bullets, but the Krun didn't fall, instead putting his free hand to his stomach as a mixture of blood and a thick black fluid oozed out. With his right hand he pointed his weapon at the colonel. She sprang at the Krun, forcing the blaster upward just as it fired a bolt of green energy, which struck the starry ceiling, punching a hole through to the darkening sky beyond.

Masonry clattered onto the floor, snapping Johnny out of his trance. The colonel was scratching at Stevens's face and biting his arms, while the cleaners were wrestling with the other Krun on the ground. The other people in the hall were running every which way, trying to reach the various exits. Johnny did the same. He set off towards the big desk at the centre of the concourse but, as he neared it, a bolt of green lightning struck the golden clock, sending it flying through the air, narrowly missing him. He leapt up some stairs, which crumbled just in front as another ray pulverized the stone steps. Turning away, he sped towards and up an escalator, scrambling alongside everyone else fleeing from the shooting. At the top he followed the terrified runners through a narrow corridor that opened into a wide entrance hall and then, through revolving doors, onto the street. The crowd split in two directions and Johnny turned left, running under a bridge and quickly right again round a corner. Steam was rising from a couple of thin red and white drums nearby on the edge of the pavement, so he ran towards and past it, hoping it might help hide him from his pursuers. He had no idea where he was or where he was headed, except away. There was a buzzing in his ear – for a moment he thought it was still the ringing from the gunshots, but then he realized it was someone trying to talk to him.

'Master Johnny – are you there? Master Johnny – please answer if you can hear me.'

'Alf,' Johnny shouted, relief washing over him as he ran with renewed energy, now with his left hand raised to his mouth. 'It's me.'

'Oh thank goodness,' replied the android. 'How on Melania did you escape General Nymac?'

'Later,' Johnny shouted. 'Where are you?'

'I am in the *Jubilee* above, I believe, the Atlantic Ocean. What is your status?'

'Not good,' Johnny replied, thinking that was quite an understatement. 'I've just been attacked by some nasty humans and the Krun. They're probably still after me. And I think I've broken my nose.'

'Oh my goodness,' said the voice inside Johnny's ear.

'And I'm lost,' Johnny went on. 'I'm in New York, but I've no idea where.'

'Stay calm, Master Johnny,' said Alf, which seemed very unfair as it wasn't the android who'd just been shot at. 'I can locate you through the wristcom. Give me a moment and I'll devise a plan – it sounds as though this is a problem for Kovac.'

'Kovac?' said Johnny, but there was only static in his earpiece. He was starting to get a stitch and was now just jogging. At the end of the road he turned left and slowed to walking pace, but even that was too much. Putting his hands on his hips he stopped and stood for a few seconds, gulping down deep breaths, alert to any danger, watching as New Yorkers flowed either side, ignoring him as they went on their way. None looked suspicious. Then, without warning, he found himself standing alone at the centre of a circle of one of the brightest white lights he had ever seen.

Johnny moved to the side but, with just a fractional delay, the light followed. A voice from above, distorted through speakers, said, 'Stay exactly where you are. Do not move. Any attempt to resist arrest will be met by deadly force.' As the words finished, Johnny realized he could just make out the whirring of a helicopter's rotor blades above the sound of the passing traffic.

Very slowly, he raised his hands, looking as if he was surrendering, but really so the left was close to his mouth. 'Alf – if you're there, I need help now.'

'All sorted, Master Johnny. You want to turn right travelling northwest 376.7303 metres, enter . . .'

'Alf!' said Johnny, as calmly as he could. 'There's a helicopter above me – if I move, they'll shoot.'

'Just one moment,' said Alf and, infuriatingly, the static returned in Johnny's ear. Two small black vans, their windows tinted to match, turned the corner only fifty metres down the street and began their slow but unstoppable progress through the rush-hour traffic towards his position. Despite, or perhaps because of, the lack of writing on their sides, they simply oozed security forces.

Johnny looked the other way – to the direction it sounded as if Alf wanted him to go. It seemed clear of danger for now. Then the overhead spotlight blinked off and he heard the rotor blades lifting higher, as the helicopter disappeared out of earshot.

He ran. Looking over his shoulder, two men, still wearing cleaner's overalls, got out of the front van – stuck in traffic down the street – and began chasing after him.

'I have removed the hindrance,' said the voice in Johnny's ear, but it wasn't Alf – it was Kovac. 'Turn right now onto Madison Avenue.'

'Kovac,' shouted Johnny as he ran. 'They're right behind me. What's going on?'

'I reprogrammed the helicopter's computer – though that's perhaps too grand a term for such an antique collection of circuitry – and gave it a new mission. The *Jubilee* will reach Manhattan in 3 minutes 14.159 27 seconds. I have prepared a suitable rendezvous point, extrapolating your fitness levels and maximum running speed for the required duration. Monitoring your position I must say you are not performing optimally – please increase your speed by 1.618 0339 kilometres per hour.'

The stitch had returned in Johnny's side, his nose was agony and he was still struggling to breathe. Even worse, cars started to overtake him – the traffic was moving more freely and the two black vans had turned the corner, passing the men in overalls and were gaining very fast. 'Kovac,' he said, desperate for oxygen as his legs pumped faster. 'I can't outrun a car even when I'm . . . performing optimally. They're right behind me.'

'Why didn't you inform me earlier? I should never have agreed to oversee this mission when there's such an intolerable absence of information.' Ahead, Johnny saw the traffic lights change to red, buying him a few vital seconds from the pursuing vans. The quantum computer continued, '(a) You are a highly unpredictable variable and, if I may say so, behaving absolutely to form, and (b) there are so few CCTV cameras in your surrounding area that I cannot assure myself you are following my instructions to the letter.'

From all around, car horns began to honk, the noise becoming louder and louder. Even as he ran, Johnny realized that no cars seemed to be moving anywhere. *All* the traffic lights seemed to have turned red. He figured Kovac must have something to do with it.

'Finally,' said the computer. 'Turn left now onto East 49th Street. Then cross the main road heading to the right and enter a pedestrian area.'

Johnny could hear his heart thumping furiously in his chest. The stitch was like a knife beneath his ribs and the back of his throat had begun to burn. As he turned the corner he paused, just for a moment, to gather his strength and look behind. The two men in cleaner's outfits were only a few metres back while some others had got out of the vans and were also chasing, not much further behind. Even though his whole body was crying out for him to stop, Johnny knew he had to run faster.

Kovac spoke again, sounding as exasperated as ever. 'Try to keep up. You know I have far more interesting things to do with my time than wait for you to jog to the Rockefeller Center at your leisure.'

'I'm going as fast . . . as I . . . can,' gasped Johnny, while it seemed no air at all was entering his lungs. He reached the next street, Fifth Avenue, which was massive and jammed with cars, their drivers all beeping their horns, many of them shouting out of open windows. The sign at the junction he came to flashed 'WALK' in white letters so he ran straight across, turned right and immediately left through a large entrance. He was off the street and it was downhill, but the path was blocked by hundreds of sightseers. He couldn't afford to ease up, so took the only route available, hurdling a bench into a rectangular fountain and splashing his way through two more identical pools and out onto the far side. He landed in a narrow band of dry tarmac before, like a steeplechaser, he was hurdling again. Three further water jumps took him in front of an open-air ice rink at the base of a tall building, with sides tapering towards its narrow top. As Johnny approached, he saw the skaters shoot to the sides of the rink, like charged particles repelled by each other. Then he understood why. A black helicopter was coming down to land in the very centre of the ice.

'Kovac,' shouted Johnny. 'Another helicopter.'

'Have a little faith in my abilities,' replied the computer. 'I take it you don't want the thing blasted out of the sky unless absolutely necessary – although it might make this whole exercise fractionally more interesting.' Right now, Johnny felt he'd be more than happy to see the chopper blown up. 'Why I bother I don't know,' the computer went on. 'At this rate my circuits might atrophy with boredom – I could be working on my new solution to Fermat's Last Theorem.'

'Kovac!' said Johnny, who felt as if he was running towards certain capture. The men behind had struggled to follow him through the water, but were now gaining again. The whole thing looked desperate, but he couldn't give up. He thought of the horror in Captain Valdour's eyes when recalling the supernova. However much his body ached and wanted to shut down, he wasn't going to let that happen to Earth's Sun.

'The plan remains within acceptable tolerances,' said Kovac. 'Turn right in front of the skating rink, follow the path round onto the street and, by a sign that reads "Radio City", enter the main building through a large door on your left-hand side. Climb one flight of stairs and proceed to the security check, informing the authorities your name is Jonathan Cavok and you are performing an inspection of the tourist elevators.'

Johnny didn't think Kovac's 'plan' sounded worthy of the name, but took another lungful of air and ran even faster.

'I have provided a full description of you, which appears to come from the City of New York's Department of Buildings.'

Johnny turned in front of the ice rink and ran up some steps and past a ticket booth, just as the helicopter touched down. The rink was lined by flags from every country. He knew the

United Nations was based in New York – perhaps Kovac was leading him to some sort of sanctuary within it. The next moment there was an almighty bang – he wondered if someone was shooting at him, but then saw the ice had cracked beneath the helicopter's weight. Its rotors were still spinning furiously as Colonel Bobbi Hartman emerged from the machine onto the ice, only to slip and fall wildly. Johnny was on the main street now. As two men carrying rifles jumped out and lifted the colonel onto her heels, he put his head down and ran for all he was worth. There was an entrance, with a sign reading, 'Radio City' and 'Top of the Rock'. Johnny ducked inside as he heard something whistle past his ear and guessed they really were firing at him now.

Inside, he turned left, following a circular staircase up one floor, his feet squelching as he went. At the top, people stood queuing in front of a rectangular metal arch. Johnny followed his instructions and ran to the front of the line, ignoring the muttering of the waiting tourists. A burly security guard stepped forward and he had to stop.

'Where d'ya think you're going, young man?'

'Inspector . . . elevator inspector,' said Johnny, trying to catch his breath and feeling his already red face turn scarlet as the words spilled out.

Infuriatingly slowly, the guard raised a walkie-talkie to his mouth and said, 'Bif – there's a guy here . . . kind of young looking . . . and wet. Says he's here to check the cattle trucks.'

Johnny picked up a few snippets of the response. 'Five-four . . . blond . . .'

As the man listened he raised his eyebrows in surprise. 'Gee – sure sounds like him,' he said into the device before asking Johnny, 'What's your name, sir?'

'Johnny . . . Jonathan . . . Cavok,' Johnny replied. His brain seemed as exhausted as the rest of him and it was a struggle to remember what Kovac had told him.

'Cavok? That Polish?' asked the man.

'Er . . . something like that.'

'Through you go – I'll bring down the blinds.'

Johnny nodded and ran on through the metal arch which beeped loudly. The guard didn't seem to mind and pressed a switch on the wall, whereupon metal shutters descended from the ceiling, cutting the corridor off from the crowds of people behind.

Colonel Hartman's muffled voice screamed, 'Stop him!' and the metal curtain began to shake violently.

'You took your time,' said the voice in his ear as Johnny forced himself forward, round a bend that led him through one hundred and eighty degrees, right through a door until the words 'Elevators to Observatory' swam before his eyes and he found himself facing a bank of lifts. 'I'll accelerate the elevators,' Kovac continued. 'Once at the top, take the escalator up one level and then stairs onto the roof, rendezvousing with the *Jubilee*.'

There was a ping and one of the lift doors opened. Johnny ran inside, pressed the button for the very top and breathed a sigh of relief as the cabin sealed itself. He knew he should stay on his toes and keep moving – that his job wasn't over yet – but exhaustion took hold. Before he could stop himself he was crouching on the floor, panting like Bentley after they'd been for a run. He felt the acceleration upwards, so fast it was like being weighed down on a really big planet with two or three times the gravity, and collapsed the rest of the way onto the floor, rolling over as he went so he lay on his back. At least it would be over soon. Through the clear roof of the lift he could see rows of blue lights like young stars twinkling in the shaft – the top of the building was approaching very quickly.

As the cabin stopped and the downward pressure subsided,

Johnny pulled himself to his feet with the help of a handrail. The doors opened. With the last of his strength he stumbled out and saw through the wall of windows exactly how high up he was – in front of the Empire State Building, probably above even Nicky's office. Kovac was talking in his ear, but he couldn't concentrate on the words. It was as though his whole body had started to shut down once he'd collapsed in the lift. Some survival instinct, buried deep within his brain, told him to keep going upwards. Falling through a set of revolving doors, he stumbled onto a narrow escalator and grabbed hold of the black rubber handrail either side. The moving staircase carried him out onto a roof space. As he reached the top he staggered forward, but stayed on his feet, though it felt as if the cold air was stabbing at his broken nose.

The edges of the roof were packed with sightseers, their faces pressed up against giant clear perspex screens that looked over the city. He just wanted to lie down again and curl up on the paved ground, but Kovac was still talking, directing him left and left again, into a stairwell. Some primordial force kept Johnny moving and he climbed again. He reached the very top, exposed to the surroundings with no more barriers. Far fewer tourists had found their way to this level and those that had were crouched in front of silver binocular stands, well protected by thick coats against the wintry air. The quantum computer's voice was being drowned out by a whirring noise, becoming louder and louder. Johnny knew he'd heard it before, that it somehow meant danger. Then, like a lightbulb switching on in his head, he realized it was the rotor blades of a helicopter. He looked upwards but, apart from a stack of aerials and antennae spiking into the sky, the view was clear.

Then, Colonel Hartman's black chopper appeared from beneath his feet, rising up close to the very edge of the tower, with the Empire State Building behind. It swung round so it was side-onto him and people on the rooftop began to scream. The few tourists in the line of sight between Johnny and it scattered. He immediately saw why. The helicopter door was open and, kneeling on the ledge, was a lone gunman, aiming a rifle straight at him. He knew he should run for cover, but his legs had turned to lead. He looked down at his top and followed the point of a red laser beam as it settled on the central star of Cassiopeia, before he raised his head to the chopper. The colonel was standing behind the shoulder of the marksman, who fired, sparks erupting into the darkness around. Everything seemed to be happening in slow motion and Johnny even had time to brace himself for the impact, but it still didn't come.

The first ping was followed by several more as the rifleman kept firing, but the bullets were rebounding off an invisible barrier. Then the door of a black London taxi opened out of thin air, between Johnny and the helicopter. The rest of the *Jubilee* materialized, hovering about a metre off the ground and, from somewhere, Johnny found a last ounce of strength to fling himself inside.

The shuttle lifted into the sky, while terrified tourists scrambled to clear the rooftop. The man in the chopper stopped firing. Alf looked at Johnny, a concerned expression on his face. 'It is good to see you, Master Johnny, although you have looked better. I am taking you straight to sickbay when we reach the *Spirit of London*.' The android must have thought *Shields on*, because the shuttle began to disappear around them, followed by Alf and Johnny himself. He wished the pain in his nose would vanish as well but, if anything, it seemed to be getting worse. As the *Jubilee* picked up speed, Johnny wondered if he might have seen a black sphere floating alongside them, but he was too tired to speak. He closed his eyes and fell into a deep, exhausted sleep.

8 ✧✧

Self-Destruct ✧✧

Johnny woke in a blind panic. He couldn't see his arms, or his legs, or any part of him. It took a few seconds to remember he was in the *Jubilee* and still shielded. They were just entering the *Spirit of London*'s shuttle bay. As the black taxi rematerialized around him, he saw there was a welcoming committee, not just of Clara and Bentley, but also Zeta and Erin. Johnny smiled to himself – the boy king was keeping as far away from the Old English sheepdog as possible.

Alf brought the shuttle down with a slight thud and the doors opened. 'Welcome home, Johnny,' came Sol's voice from all around, with just a hint more emotion than normal.

'Thanks,' Johnny replied. Anything more would have been drowned out as Bentley had begun barking the second Johnny stepped onto the reassuringly familiar deck. The grey and white dog bounded over, leaping up onto his hind legs to lick Johnny's face.

With his nose still incredibly tender, Johnny fought the sheepdog off as playfully as he could, pushing him down onto all fours. 'Hello, Bents . . . Hello, Bents,' he said, nestling his chin on top of Bentley's head. Then he caught sight of Clara scowling at him in the background, and stood up.

'Master Johnny – I must insist you come with me to sickbay at once,' said Alf, but no one was listening.

Princess Zeta stepped forward and stretched out one of her

long scaly arms, delicately touching Johnny's nose. At once it began to tingle, like he was about to sneeze, and then he felt a burning sensation spread from the point of contact out across his face. He tried to pull away, but some force kept him glued to her hand. Her lizard-like eyes were firmly shut, a look of fixed concentration across her face. Then her lids opened, she smiled and said, 'It is done – but your aura remains troubled.'

Johnny took a breath and discovered his nose was working again and when he touched it, very gingerly with his forefinger, there wasn't the slightest pain. 'Thanks . . . I think,' he said, looking into her reptilian eyes as she backed away, making room for Clara.

Johnny had never seen that expression on his sister's face before. He stood his ground, not knowing whether to try to give her a hug or run away. It was a mistake. She slapped him really hard across his left cheek as she shouted, 'Don't you ever, ever, abandon me again.' More slaps followed on the two 'evers,' stinging Johnny's face. 'We're all each other's got.' Uncertain what to do, but not wanting to be hit again, Johnny put his arms around his sister, like a boxer hanging on. She tried to push him away, but only half-heartedly.

'If I may interrupt,' said King Erin. 'Now you have resumed command of this vessel it is your primary duty to return my sister and I to our homeworld. I must insist . . .'

Johnny shot the king a look that stopped him in his tracks. 'Not now, lizard boy,' he said and, with an arm still around Clara's shoulder, walked past the smarting orange-haired figure towards the lifts. At the last moment, before she was forced to step into the empty shaft, Clara broke free and folded herself into nothingness. By the time Johnny reached the bridge at the top of the ship, his sister was there waiting for him.

☆ ☆ ☆
☆ ☆

Johnny hated leaving the *Spirit of London* so soon, but he had to get back to Halader House before Miss Harutunian returned from New York. Plus, after everything that had happened, it was more important than ever to speak with Bram. Clara refused point-blank to let her brother take a shuttle and demanded the right to fold Johnny straight into his bedroom, the site of the Cornicula Worm's link with Melania.

Alf's protestations that Clara did altogether too much folding, which couldn't possibly be good for her, were met with such a withering look that the android fell silent.

Holding Bentley and wearing a black T-shirt, jeans and trainers, Johnny said goodbye to his sister and stepped through Clara's portal between his quarters on the *Spirit of London* and the attic room of the children's home. At once it was clear that someone had been in there. That wasn't meant to be allowed under Halader House rules but, whoever they were, they had cleared up. Johnny hated anyone else putting his stuff away. Miss Harutunian had been nagging him about cleaning his room, but she'd never actually tidied up after him before – he knew she'd see that as losing the 'battle of wills'. While Johnny had to hope she was still in New York, he'd rather it had been his social worker going through his things than Mr Wilkins.

Poor Bentley made a half-hearted attempt to sniff around the room, but crossing the fold proved too much for the sheepdog who crawled under the bed to curl up in front of the large, old-fashioned radiator. Johnny sat on his (for once) crumple-free duvet and wondered if, this time, he would be able to speak with the Emperor of the galaxy. Early morning sunlight was streaming through the dormer window, but that only served to disguise the fuzzy, glittering patch of air, just above where Johnny was sitting. He closed his eyes and thrust his neck forward, praying the Wormhole was once again connected at the other end. Cold air washed over his face. Opening just the left eye first, in case an annoying Phasmeer was standing before him, he quickly followed with the right. He found himself gazing towards an eerie blue fire in the centre of an ancient courtyard. It was night on the galaxy's capital, but he could make out the silhouette of a robed figure sitting, with his back to Johnny, in front of the flames. Relief washed over him – finally everything was going to be OK. 'Bram,' he said softly.

His Majesty the Emperor Bram Khari stood up, turned slowly away from the fire, lowered his hood and smiled. As he walked through the darkness towards Johnny, the air around him was lit by the Emperor's sparkling white hair. 'Johnny – it pleases me to stand before you now and see you safely returned to Earth.'

'It wasn't easy,' Johnny replied, 'but it's a long story. Where were you?'

'I am sorry – enormously so – to have missed you, but I was on a quest.' Bram paused, as though deciding how much, if anything, to say. Close up, the Emperor's face was far more lined than Johnny remembered from his first time on the Imperial capital, as though someone had thrown a cobweb across it. 'I deeply regret that you came so far and were not able to wait within the palace for my return. An explanation is in order. I have been searching for the world of my forebears.'

'Weren't you born on Melania?' Johnny asked, hoping he'd guessed the right meaning of 'forebears'.

'Indeed I was, but the Imperial line, bent and part broken though it is, derives from a place named Lysentia.'

'I've heard of it,' said Johnny, remembering Alf's lessons on ancient galactic history, as well as the android's explanation of the statues on the way to the Senate.

'Would that you could tell me its location,' said Bram. 'That world is lost – now no more than a legend from long ago. Yet, were I to locate it, I believe the course of this war would quickly change.

Every day the situation becomes more desperate. If Lysentia cannot be found, there will be no choice but to set forth into the great void between the galaxies and do battle there, as far away as I can from the innocents who would otherwise be harmed. Naturally, I ask you not to recount this conversation to others.'

'Course not.'

'So tell me your "long story".'

Johnny began with meeting Captain Valdour and hearing about the supernova on Alpha Centauri. The smile left the Emperor's face and his eyes dulled, as though he was reliving the horror first hand. Bram knew of the Star Blaze and said this was precisely why he wouldn't wage all-out war within the Milky Way. Johnny described his last attempt to make contact through the mini Wormhole, and being rebuffed by Chancellor Karragon – Bram assured him it would not happen again. Johnny hesitated, deciding against mentioning the mysterious message from Nicky next. He didn't want to give the Emperor, who had much more serious things to worry about, the idea he was being reckless and had gone to such a potentially dangerous rendezvous. Instead he skipped straight to the plan to visit Melania and ask for some ships, describing the audience with the Regent, being taken into the bunker beneath the Senate House and meeting the Owlessan Monks. Bram nodded and made the right noises in the proper places, but didn't interrupt.

Then it was onto the return trip, telling how Sol detected a distress signal and coming out of the fold, how they saw the freighters destroyed but were able to rescue the sailing ship. Bram showed no interest in Erin and Zeta, so Johnny carried on with the story. He'd just reached the point when the *Astricida* had unfolded beside the *Spirit of London* when someone began hammering on the trapdoor that led into the attic room.

'Someone's here,' Johnny whispered, not knowing if he could be overheard outside of the Wormhole. 'I've got to go.'

'I will come to Earth,' was Bram's response, 'as soon as can be arranged. I know you are unlikely to follow my advice, but be careful, Johnny.'

The banging began again and an American woman's voice called, 'Johnny? Are you in there, Johnny?'

'Sorry,' was Johnny's final word to the Emperor, before coming out of the Wormhole, which felt just like pulling a tight jumper over his head. He sat back on his bed, blinking in the bright sunlight. 'Come in,' said Johnny, loud enough that his social worker would hear.

The trapdoor lifted and the top half of Miss Harutunian appeared in the room, wearing a green sweatshirt. 'Who were you talking to?' she asked, still only halfway through the door. 'And what has happened to your hair?'

'Er . . . Bentley,' said Johnny, while using both hands to flatten down his sticking up blond strands. Even he knew he didn't sound convincing.

From her position, only waist high into the room, at least the social worker could see the Old English sheepdog, curled up beside the radiator. 'Humph,' she said, glaring between the dog and Johnny. 'How did you get back here so quickly?' she asked as she climbed awkwardly through the opening and marched over to Johnny's bedside. Her trousers matched the sweatshirt top. '*I've* only just stepped off the plane.'

'What do you mean?' Johnny replied, trying to sound innocent, but feeling his face flush bright red in betrayal, even as the words were leaving his mouth.

'I saw you! You were in New York yesterday.'

'I don't think so,' said Johnny, wondering how he'd get out of this one. He hated lying to Miss Harutunian, but he could hardly tell her the truth. She'd never looked this disappointed with him before and was leaning over him, arms folded, a frown on her face.

'Well, when you've finished thinking, why don't we go and see the Manager?'

Johnny was used to Mr Wilkins dragging him through the Halader House corridors for an appointment with doom, but it was the first ever time Miss Harutunian had wanted to do the same. She was rapidly losing her status as his favourite social worker. 'Now?' Johnny asked. 'What about school?'

'I hadn't noticed this concern for your education before. Yes, now.'

'OK,' he said, getting to his feet.

He followed the American down the spiral staircase beneath his room, dragging his feet along the first-floor corridor that led to Mrs Irvine's office. He was still wondering how on earth he was going to talk his way out of this one when he discovered they were already in front of the dreaded wooden door. Three loud knocks were answered from the other side by the familiar Glaswegian accent. Miss Harutunian turned the brass handle and ushered Johnny inside, before closing the door after them.

'Ah, Katherine,' said Mrs Irvine from behind her large wooden desk, silhouetted by the light streaming in from her floor-to-ceiling window. 'Welcome back. Did you have a good holiday?'

'It was . . . interesting,' Miss Harutunian replied. 'No more so than when I spotted Johnny here on Lexington Avenue.'

'Lexington . . . Lexington,' said the Manager, thinking aloud. 'The one behind the bus station, just past Marks and Spencer?'

'No, Mrs Irvine, it's behind Grand Central Terminal . . . in the middle of Manhattan.'

'Oh,' replied the manager.

'Oh, indeed,' said the social worker. Johnny just stood there feeling about a foot tall, but squeezed his eyes tightly shut and concentrated all his efforts on the thought, 'It wasn't me.' He wondered if he could project it into the brains of the other two in the room.

'Jonathan,' said Mrs Irvine. 'Remember I've been responsible for you since you came here as a two year old. You can trust me and Miss Harutunian. Do you have anything you want to tell us?'

The thought transference clearly wasn't working. 'It wasn't me,' he replied, opening his eyes. Maybe it would work if he said the words out loud?

'C'mon, Johnny – I saw you clear as you're standing here now. Your nose looked all broken and there was blood on your face.'

'But my nose is fine,' said Johnny, seizing on the unexpected lifeline. 'Feel it.' He took hold of his social worker's wrist and placed it onto his face.

'Well it doesn't *feel* damaged, I admit,' she said, sounding unsure for the first time.

'Are you saying you're not certain, Katherine?' asked Mrs Irvine, as she stood up from her chair. 'Perhaps Jonathan has a double? I must say, somewhat unusually, Mr Wilkins hasn't complained once in your absence.' Turning to Johnny she said, 'It appears you've finally won him over.'

Johnny let out a sigh of relief. The cook must have been so glad to be rid of Johnny that he'd clearly not bothered reporting him missing to the Manager.

'What about the school?' asked Miss Harutunian. Johnny felt this was below the belt – his social worker loathed Mrs Devonshire every bit as much as he did.

'Unusually good reports,' replied the Manager.

Johnny made a mental note to thank Kovac for doing such a good job with the computer records.

'Well, of course I'm delighted to hear that,' said Miss Harutunian through gritted teeth. 'Tell you what, Johnny. As it's almost time, why don't I walk you up there myself?'

It was the end of lunch break before Johnny sneaked away from Castle Dudbury Comprehensive School. He'd been having a kickabout in the yard outside the science block, but when the bell went he had no desire to stay for a biology lesson on cloning followed by double chemistry. Instead, he made sure he was out of sight behind an old tractor, fixed into concrete at the far edge of the playground and used his wristcom to ask Clara to create a fold so he could escape.

Alf hadn't looked at all pleased with Clara (or her brother for encouraging her), when Johnny suddenly appeared through an archway into the strategy room on deck 14. When she created another fold to bring Bentley back to the ship from Halader House, the android was apoplectic. It was only when Johnny explained he'd spoken with Bram and that everything was going to be OK, that the android became distracted, given news of an imminent Imperial visit to Earth. Straightaway, Alf embarked on a mission to spruce up the *Spirit of London* and make her 'fit for the Emperor' much to everyone's (especially Sol's) annoyance. The android's whirlwind scrubbing of what looked to Johnny like spotless floors and his polishing of the already gleaming metal (Alf claimed Johnny left his fingerprints everywhere) began in the bridge and continued all the way down to the shuttle deck.

✢ ✢ ✢
✢ ✢

With a visit from Bram due any time, Johnny's immediate fears for the Sun and Earth receded and life could return a little more to normal. Over the next week, he spent much of the time wandering the *Spirit of London* thinking about Nicky. He needed a way of locating his long-lost brother, but that wouldn't help without some way of freeing him from the Nameless One's control. Even more pressing was finding a way of telling Clara about him before things dragged on any longer – he found himself rehearsing numerous conversations in his head, while sitting atop the big rock in the middle of the garden deck, but whenever he saw his sister the words he wanted dried up.

Wherever he went, Johnny seemed to bump into Zeta who was keen to explore the ship, and had worked wonders with all the plants on the hydroponics decks and especially in the garden. Erin, however, spent all his time shut away onboard his silver hulled, solar-sailing ship. So it was quite a surprise when, a few days later, the boy king stormed onto the bridge shouting, once again, that Johnny had betrayed them and demanding to be returned home before the Emperor's arrival which, 'The robot has only just told me all about.'

'Listen,' said Johnny. 'I'm sorry we've not been able to take you straight home after saving your lives and all that, but we'll go as soon as we can.'

'That's not soon enough,' Erin replied, his forked tongue flickering a little way out of his mouth.

Clara stepped forward saying, 'You're so desperate to get back, I don't understand why you ever left in the first place.'

Erin's reptilian eyes narrowed even further on her, before they returned to Johnny. 'Don't make me wait too long or you, the ship and your annoying, commoner sister will be sorry.' Before Johnny could reply the boy king did an about-turn and disappeared into the lift shaft.

Clara perched next to Johnny on the arm of his chair. 'He tried to take over when you weren't here,' she said.

'What happened?'

'I folded him away,' she replied, with a slight shrug. 'I nearly left him there – he was trying to do stuff to Sol.'

'You OK, Sol?' Johnny asked, raising his voice a little to speak to the ship.

'I believe I am undamaged, though a little disturbed,' Sol replied. 'I do not believe it is down to Erin, but I have been running diagnostic subroutines to identify any problems.'

'Let me know if you find anything,' said Johnny. Then, to Clara, he added, 'If he does it again, leave him in there.'

'Don't worry,' she replied. 'I've been practising my Klein fold in case General Nymac comes back for you.'

Johnny smiled weakly and, before he could engage brain, found the words, 'Good idea,' come from his mouth. It had been the perfect opportunity to tell Clara about Nicky and he'd bottled it. Before he could call her back, his sister had folded herself off the bridge.

✼ ✼ ✼
✼ ✼

No one seemed more disappointed over Bram's delayed arrival than Alf, who took his frustration out on Johnny, insisting he settle into as normal a routine as possible, spending time at the children's home and being good about going to school. Despite trying the Wormholes every day, no one was to be found at the other end of the one to Melanian and the Tolimi were so busy on a special project they'd devised that he barely even spoke to them.

Johnny, sitting at the back of the classroom, found the lessons pretty dull, but was fascinated by the complex effects of feedback mechanisms on climate change. It seemed scarily like the feedback loops in the electrical circuits he was so good at, where you could overload a system very quickly. But it was one of very few highlights when set against design and technology, ICT and citizenship.

Secretly, though, he didn't mind school that much but it was nothing to do with his classes. While he sometimes kicked a ball about with Clara and Alf on the *Spirit of London*'s five-a-side deck, it wasn't like the real thing. She was only a girl and Alf was even worse. Despite the two of them playing against him, Johnny always won easily. At least spending time at Castle Dudbury Comprehensive meant he could play some proper football. The next round of the County Cup, the competition they'd won last year, was coming up and PE teacher and coach Mr Davenport was putting on extra training sessions after school.

Tonight they were working on a new corner routine, with Johnny driving the ball to the near post as fast as he could, where Dave Spedding would flick it on. It was beginning to get dark – black clouds raced overhead, carried on cold winds that gusted across the playing fields. Johnny was finding it hard to judge the distance on his kicks, and felt sorry for his teammates who were spending a lot of time getting cold while they waited for him to cross the ball. Mr Davenport, wearing his customary green top, kept shouting at everyone to bounce on their toes to keep their energy levels up, but most of the team looked miserable and desperate to return to the changing rooms.

They'd been using six white footballs, but only a couple remained by the corner flag with Johnny. He picked one up and placed it in the 'D' where the touchline met the goal line. Then he bent down and picked it up again, as though it hadn't been positioned right first off. This was the signal for the near-post corner. Mr Davenport insisted Johnny made it each time, even in practice, so it was drilled into everyone. Johnny took four paces back, stopped, visualized the ball flying straight onto Dave's forehead, and then he ran towards the ball and kicked it. The wind got up, making the cross fall short and allowing Ashvin Gupta to block Dave off and boot the ball back the way it had come. It sailed on the wind over Johnny's head, down a slope and away into the wasteland beneath the football pitch.

'Last one, Johnny,' shouted Mr Davenport. 'Make it a good 'un.'

It started to rain. Johnny steeled himself to shut out the cold and concentrate on the final kick. Again he placed the football in the 'D'. Again he picked it up and repositioned it. Again he took four strides backwards and looked up. Dave was on the penalty spot about to make his run. Joe Pennant stood alongside him, with the job of blocking off the defenders, allowing Dave to reach the near post unopposed. Johnny ran forward and struck the ball well. It ripped through the air into the wind and landed perfectly on top of Dave's head, picking up speed and a little height to carry it to the far post where Micky Elliot, the ginger-haired skipper, forced it home.

Mr Davenport blew three times on his whistle and everyone started to run for the changing rooms. Before Johnny could follow, the coach shouted over asking him to collect the ball that had flown past him down the hill. Johnny nodded, shaking off the icicle of raindrops that had attached itself to his nose. He rolled his socks down and picked out his shinpads, before sliding down the slippery slope towards the bushes at the bottom that marked the edge of the local tip. The smell of rotting rubbish was so strong he held the pads over his nose like a makeshift gasmask. He wasn't sure where the ball had ended up and, with the rain getting heavier, it was quite hard to see. From his left, Johnny saw a flash of white. He turned towards it, felt an arm grab his collar and jerk him through an opening onto the bridge of the *Spirit of London*.

Johnny tripped over Clara and they both fell to the floor. He felt sick – he'd not prepared himself for the fold at all and it was as if his stomach had been tied into several very tight knots. 'What's going on?' he managed to ask.

'We're taking off,' said Clara. 'I couldn't stop Sol.'

'Taking off? You don't mean . . .' Lying on the floor beside each other, Johnny looked at his sister, who nodded back. As if going on an unscheduled journey wasn't bad enough, the *Spirit of London* was actually flying away from the Earth's surface rather than folding. At least, with her dark energy drive, Sol could travel astonishingly fast (harnessing the very force that accelerated the distant galaxies), but even so it was hard to believe they wouldn't have been seen.

'Sol – what are you doing?' Johnny shouted.

'We are proceeding directly to the Alnitak system as instructed, destination Novolis, the fifteenth planet,' replied the ship.

Erin must have done something to Sol to force her to take him and his sister home. Johnny was furious, but before he could act the ship added, 'Folding in three . . . two . . .' Johnny ran towards his chair, but on 'one,' he floated upwards, just in time to see the Plican pass the other way and fall into the main, blue-pulsing tank. Space began to distort and disappear around him. As he was jerked in one direction after another, Johnny tried to hold the contents of his stomach in place, but it was no good. The last thing he saw before slipping into unconsciousness was a wobbling cloud of diced carrots and tinned tomatoes, the leftovers of his school dinner, flying across the *Spirit of London*'s bridge.

✩ ✩ ✩
✩ ✩

'Johnny . . . Johnny.' Someone was calling to him, but they sounded such a long way away. Very slowly he opened his eyes. He was lying down only everything seemed to be spinning. If he didn't hold on it was as if he'd fall off the floor and float away. Clara was standing over him, frowning, but he didn't feel well. He just wanted the spinning to stop, so he closed his eyes and went back to sleep.

✩ ✩ ✩
✩ ✩

Someone was shaking him. Johnny thought about opening his eyes, but the message from his brain was that this would be too hard work. He wished whoever had hold of him would stop. There were two voices in the background now – Sol sounded like she was counting while Clara was screaming at him. Through Johnny's lids everything was blinking an annoying red colour that he could do without. His head hurt so much he just needed a bit of peace and quiet. He drifted away and the voices became fainter until, at last, there was silence.

He could feel a cool breeze on his face. Another voice began to call to him, so insistent that he couldn't shut it out. 'Johnny Mackintosh . . . concentrate.' He thought he recognized the speaker and then Princess Zeta appeared before him. They were standing together aboard her sailing ship where she had been winding a brass handle, but now stopped. 'You need to wake up,' she told Johnny, which made no sense at all considering they were here having a conversation.

'What do you mean?' he asked.

A voice reached them from further down the ship. 'Zeta – why have you stopped? I need more sail.'

The princess looked at Johnny and said, 'You must go now. You must wake up – your ship is in danger.' As she said the last word her tongue shot out and slapped Johnny across the face, spraying him with moisture. Strangely, although the tongue withdrew and Zeta returned to her winch, Johnny's face became wetter and wetter. He felt cold too. He opened his eyes and saw Alf and Clara standing over him with an empty bucket, the contents of which had just been deposited on Johnny's head.

He groaned and asked, 'What did you do that for?' while sitting up and wiping the water away from his face.

'Master Johnny – you have to wake up,' said Alf, skipping on the spot behind Clara, clearly very agitated. All around the bridge, red warning lights were flashing.

'Three hundred seconds to self-destruct,' said Sol, lights on the display flickering in time to her words.

It took less than one of those three hundred seconds for their meaning to sink in. Johnny jumped to his feet, ignoring the blood rushing away from his brain. There didn't appear to be any damage and there was nothing to suggest the *Spirit of London* had been boarded. Sol would only self-destruct if aliens had taken control, but the bridge was still theirs. Alf had moved to the navigation station and was using it without difficulty – Clara must have rebooted the android after the fold. Johnny hoped Bentley was in a gel pod and not unconscious elsewhere. Yet, despite the normality of the scene, Johnny could see the fear written across his sister's face. 'What's going on?' he asked.

'You've got to stop her,' said Clara. 'Sol's going to blow herself up.'

As if on cue, the words, 'Two hundred and fifty seconds to self-destruct,' rang out across the bridge.

'Sol,' Johnny shouted. Although the ship's mind was distributed everywhere, he clattered across the floor with his football boots still on, until he was standing in front of her voice screen. 'What's going on? End self-destruct sequence.'

'I'm sorry, Johnny. I'm afraid I can't do that.'

'Why not? What's the problem?'

'Johnny – I think you know what the problem is just as well as I do.'

'What are you talking about, Sol?'

'When you ordered the self-destruct sequence to begin, you stated that, whatever you were to say later, the command could not be revoked.'

'Stop it, Sol,' said Johnny. 'I didn't order anything.' This sounded weirdly similar to what Nicky's ship had said when he'd been taken aboard the *Astricida*, but Johnny was sure there wasn't a hidden consciousness buried within him, ordering Sol around – it didn't make any sense.

'Two hundred seconds to self-destruct.'

'It must have been Erin,' said Clara. 'We're heading for Alnitak – though we only managed one fold.'

'But, for an initial fold, it was at the very maximum of safe limits,' added Alf, examining the panel in front of him. 'Hence Master Johnny's . . . discomfort. We are entering orbit around a gas giant in the Aldebaran System.'

'Sol – where's Erin? And Zeta?' Johnny asked.

'King Erin and Princess Zeta are no longer on board,' the ship replied. 'They exited in the *Falling Star* 31.415 927 seconds after the self-destruct sequence was initiated.'

'I shouldn't have let them get away,' said Clara, 'but I was too busy trying to wake you.'

'Hey it's not your fault,' said Johnny, before trying again with Sol. 'It wasn't me – it was Erin. He's done something to you.'

'I believe you are mistaken, Johnny. I distinctly remember you giving me the order.'

'Think about it, Sol,' said Johnny, beginning to get desperate. 'I was unconscious – from the fold.'

'One hundred and fifty seconds to self-destruct. The order was pre-programmed,' continued Sol.

'Pre-programmed? What does that mean?' shouted Johnny.

'When issuing the command you insisted it should not take effect until after the next fold. All failsafes were meticulously followed,' the ship replied.

'But we're heading towards Alnitak,' said Johnny. 'I didn't order that – it must have been Erin.'

'I agree that the inference is not without plausibility,' said Sol. 'I will think about it.'

'Please, Sol,' said Clara. 'You've got to stop.'

'I'm sorry, Clara. One hundred seconds to self-destruct.'

'I thought you said you'd think about it,' shouted Johnny.

'I have thought about it,' said Sol as infuriatingly calm as ever. 'After a careful re-examination, I have verified that the order was correct and cannot be changed.'

'Send the Imperial distress signal,' said Johnny. 'All frequencies.'

'As you wish, Johnny, although I do not believe I am in distress.'

'Johnny,' said Clara. 'I don't think you can reason with her – you've got to do something.'

Johnny nodded. He looked to the android standing behind the navigation console and said, 'In case I can't stop this, I need you to get Clara and Bentley to minimum safe distance.'

'Don't you dare. . .' said Clara but, before she could finish, the whirl of arms and legs that was Alf moving at full speed had picked her up and whisked her off the bridge.

'The *Piccadilly*'s fastest,' Johnny shouted after them. Now he stood alone with his ship. 'Sol – I'm not going to let you blow yourself up. You can't die.'

'Johnny – I am not afraid of death. I do not believe it is the end. Fifty seconds to self-destruct.'

'I don't care if it's the end or not. This is stupid – you've got to stop.'

'I shall die content in the knowledge I have carried out your orders. I hope I have done well. I advise you to leave as soon as possible to reach minimum safe distance, before I detonate my dark energy core.'

Johnny didn't know what to do, but he had to try something. 'I'm sorry, Sol,' he said as he closed his eyes and reached out with his mind, trying to connect with the ship. If Erin had done it, it had to be possible.

'What are you doing, Johnny?'

He used the question to look for some sort of disturbance in the electric fields around the bridge and felt he might have sensed something, but it was hard when Sol's presence was everywhere.

'Forty seconds to self-destruct.'

That time he'd definitely seen something – a swirling vortex of thought, of electrons, but moving forwards and backwards in time.

A voice came through Johnny's earpiece. 'If you don't get out of there I'm folding myself back to the bridge and there's nothing you can do to stop me.'

Johnny raised the wristcom to his mouth. 'Clara – if I'm going to stop Sol, I have to concentrate.'

'Promise me you'll abandon ship if you can't stop her.'

'Clara – I haven't got time for this.'

'Promise me!'

'OK . . . I promise.'

'Thirty seconds to self-destruct.' Sol's words jarred Johnny back to reality. He hadn't had any intention of leaving the bridge – every captain went down with their ship – and immediately regretted giving in. Clara's interruption meant he'd lost concentration and vital seconds.

He switched his thoughts back to Sol with the ship's words still ringing in his ears. He followed them as they ebbed into her consciousness, like tracing waves back to their origin when a pebble is thrown into the centre of a pond. Then, when he saw that centre, he couldn't have taken his mind away even if he'd wanted to. Sol was beautiful. Johnny's mind orbited around his ship's, a complex ever-changing, white crystal of pulsating energy, like a giant three-dimensional snowflake. At its many points (the closer he looked, the more he was able to see) lines of electric current, like silken chains, shimmered away from the structure, directing operations right across the *Spirit of London*.

'Twenty seconds to self-destruct.'

As the words were spoken, Johnny saw a stronger stream of electrons leave the glittering snowflake. He cursed Erin for having done this – and for making Johnny do what he was about to do. He knew the only way to stop Sol blowing herself up was to cut her mind off from the rest of the ship. So he began to break the chains. Every link leading away from the beautiful crystal had to be severed – there was no way of knowing (and no time to find out) which was responsible for what commands. Johnny's thoughts became a scalpel, slicing through waves and currents, shutting out the screams of pain he knew he was responsible for.

'Please stop, Johnny. You're hurting me.' Since Sol had been born it had been rare for her to show emotion, but her voice was full of it now. Johnny tried to blot her out and redoubled his efforts, but Sol's mind was so complex he doubted he could finish the job in time. He hated himself – cutting Sol's mind from her body was the only way he could think of to stop her blowing herself up, but it was a dreadful thing. For ten long years Johnny had watched his mum lying in a hospital bed with no spark behind her blue, unfocused eyes, her own brain cut off from her body until his father had returned to release her from her mental prison. Johnny was sentencing Sol to exactly the same fate. He pushed the thought from his mind and continued slicing through the connections.

'Ten seconds . . . to . . . self-destruct.' The voice was deeper and slower than normal.

Almost all of the outer connections had been severed and, in doing so, Johnny could see a single, tightly bound stem of energy remaining, currents winding around each other, leading away from the very heart of the structure. It was the final link to sever. If he didn't keep going now, it would all have been for nothing. Johnny sliced again.

'*If they look out of their windows they will see your world as it is, albeit with a two nanosecond delay.*'

And again . . .

'*I anticipate our destruction in 42.537 32 seconds. The necessary missiles and mines have all been launched. The probability is 100 percent.'*

And again . . .

'Then I shall take the name "Spirit of London". The spirit of your people . . . of this city. But you can call me "Sol" for short. The symmetry is pleasing. Do you like it?'

'I love it, Sol,' said Johnny, quietly. 'I'm so sorry.' These were Sol's memories coming out – key moments she had stored, going back to the time of her creation. It sounded as though she'd stopped the countdown, but Johnny cut the very last connection, opened his eyes and discovered he was floating near the centre of the darkened bridge. The gravity generators, the life support, everything had ceased to function. The only light came reflected from the giant planet they were orbiting.

'Johnny?' The voice was Clara's, direct into his ear.

He raised the wristcom to his mouth, brushing his tear-stained face as he did. 'I'm still here,' was all he could think of to say.

'He did it!' Clara was shouting for joy at Alf, but Johnny simply felt numb.

'We're on our way back,' his sister continued. 'Get Sol to open the shuttle bay doors.'

'No,' said Johnny. 'Listen to me. Sol's not working. She's . . . sleeping for now.'

'Can't you wake her up?'

'I don't know how. And she'd probably blow herself up if I did. We can't stay here – there's no power . . . nothing. Is there anywhere on your scanners we can go?'

'Master Johnny,' said Alf. 'Sensors indicate there are five sizable moons orbiting the gas giant, each capable of sustaining an atmosphere. Closer inspection will be required to determine if any can support life.'

'I'll check some out too,' said Johnny. It makes sense to have a back-up . . . bring another shuttle.'

'An excellent plan,' said the android. 'The Emperor would be proud.'

'Thanks,' Johnny replied. He'd only suggested it because he wanted to be alone.

Already the bridge felt colder than normal. He was close to the Plican and relieved to see the creature looked unconcerned, tentacles squeezed up inside its fibrous body as the design of the tank dictated. Johnny didn't know what the long-term effect of separating Sol from her 'folder' would be, but there was nothing he could do about it now. He pushed off from the tall cylinder towards the antigrav lifts and then peered the one hundred and eighty metres down through the many decks. Kicking off, he floated in total darkness, feeling his way down the long shaft, arms out in front as he zigzagged from side to side. Several times he bashed against the ice-smooth walls, stubbing fingers on the way, before crumpling in a heap beside the three-metre-high statue of the silver alien at the foot of the *Spirit of London*.

Starlight shone through the outer doors, reflecting off the statue and up the shaft. Johnny could see where he needed to go. He pushed off again, carefully angling his approach so he was able to pull himself into the shuttle bay on deck 2, leaving the main shaft behind. He'd only used a spacesuit a few times before, but would need one now. The advanced design moulded itself around his body, as if giving him a second, very strong, outer skin, and wasn't at all like those of NASA astronauts – only the clear bubble helmet indicated he was wearing anything unusual.

With the sound of breathing filling his ears, Johnny took hold of two carbon nanotubes and fixed one end of each to the side of the *Jubilee*, clipping the other onto his suit. Then he made his way over to the massive bay doors and pulled the lever that would expose the deck to the vacuum of space, letting the air out and the starlight in. Johnny was sucked out of the ship, as he knew he would be, but the cables held firm. Bits and pieces not properly anchored to the deck flew past, to be lost forever – a bowl of flowers Zeta must have left there even struck Johnny's suit – but no damage was done and they sailed out into space, to be caught in the gravity well of the giant planet below. In the far distance, something was glinting and Johnny wondered if it was the unfurled sail of the *Falling Star*, carrying its traitorous crew away to safety. If he could have gone after them he would, but he knew that would have to wait.

He gazed towards the blood-red sun. Aldebaran was a giant star near the end of its life – at some point in the next few million years it would naturally become a supernova. If Bram arrived on Earth now and found him and Clara gone, Johnny wondered if the Emperor would stay to stop the Sun's own Star Blaze. Somehow he had to get home. With the inner and outer pressure now equalized, he pulled himself across to the *Jubilee*, opened the door and climbed inside.

He thought *Forward*, and the little black ship responded. As the *Jubilee* flew out through the shuttle bay doors, Johnny turned to look at his ship. 'If you can hear me, Sol, I'm so sorry,' he said. 'I promise, as soon as I can work out how to fix things, I'll be back.'

Using the *Jubilee*'s scanners he reached out into space to sense where the *Piccadilly* was, before pointing his shuttle in the opposite direction, to investigate the large moon that was just rising on the far side of the giant planet below.

9

Freefall

Normally Johnny's command of the *Jubilee* was instinctive, but now he found himself having to concentrate to keep it under control. After the terrible harm he'd caused Sol, he must have been struggling to focus because it took a second or two for his tiny craft to respond. When he was sure he was pointing in at least roughly the right direction, he allowed himself to look back properly, lovingly examining the sleeping ship now adrift, high above the nearby planet.

With no power lighting her up, anyone not knowing what to look for would have struggled to make out the *Spirit of London*'s form properly, but Johnny's eyes went straight to the diamond-patterned hull and the glistening starlight reflecting off the different panels. He wondered if one of those points of light might be Sol's namesake, Earth's Sun, shining faintly and looking like every other average faraway star. Even if it happened tomorrow, from Aldebaran it would take sixty-five years for the light of a supernova to show.

'Clara to Johnny – we've reached the first moon.' His sister's voice reverberated inside his helmet. 'Alf's struggling a bit with the *Piccadilly* – I think we'll have to land.'

'OK,' he replied into the microphone. 'I'll get over once I've checked on mine. Johnny out.'

He switched communications off – it was too hard to talk normally after what he'd just had to do. Johnny took a final, lingering look at his abandoned ship. He knew he had to find a way of returning to Earth as quickly as possible but, right now, all he really cared about was going after Erin – to think he'd once offered his hand to the arrogant boy king.

Grimly, he turned to face forward. The planet orbiting Aldebaran filled the windscreen. It was encircled by stripes of purple, green and brown and spotted by giant storms, one of these a huge blue circle embedded within a larger oval, like an enormous eye staring back at him. The moon he'd been flying towards was in the very corner of the window, as if the *Jubilee* had drifted off course. Johnny fixed its orange and black surface, a little like Jupiter's volcanic satellite Io, in his mind. The shuttle shuddered, but didn't change direction. He tried again, thinking very clearly indeed. Once more, the *Jubilee* jolted, but stubbornly remained on course for the gas giant which by now filled the view down the side windows as well as the windscreen. That definitely wasn't good.

Johnny tried merging his own senses with the shuttle's sensors, but the euphoric buzz this normally produced was missing – everything seemed fuzzy, like being underwater. He wondered if the helmet was somehow blocking him, but it didn't seem wise to take it off. Instead he opted for the readings to be projected onto its curved insides, like a fighter pilot's head-up display. Red warning lights flashed everywhere but he ignored them for a moment to turn the communication system back on.

'Clara, Alf, can anyone hear me? Over.'

The only result of turning the volume to maximum was that the buzzing in his ears grew louder. 'If either of you *can* hear me, something's happened to the *Jubilee*. I'm off course, heading straight for the planet. I'd really appreciate it if you can get over here and rescue me. Please . . .'

His request was met by silence. Something sparkled on the

edge of Johnny's field of vision – for the first time in a while, the face of his wristcom had turned green and showed no sign of changing back. As he stared at the strange gift from his even stranger brother, Johnny couldn't help but think it remarkably rubbish. So what if he knew Nicky had thrown off his alter-ego, Nymac, for the time being? It wasn't much use when he couldn't contact his big brother, especially when he could really do with some help. If Nicky'd had any brains he'd have given Johnny something that was actually useful, like some sort of deep-space walkie-talkie.

Johnny switched his attention to outside and the colourful bands encircling the gas giant. He knew these were boundaries between the ferocious air currents that swept around the globe, but he'd learnt surprisingly little else about this class of planet – largely because very few of the galaxy's spacefaring civilizations came from them and those that did were so odd they tended to keep themselves to themselves.

The *Jubilee* entered the atmosphere and began to shake. Weightless, Johnny bounced around in his seat as the shuttle headed vertically down towards spectacular multicoloured cloud formations. He concentrated hard, desperately trying to take his tiny ship out of its dive, but the London taxi was in freefall. As it plunged through a fine, purple mist, level with the tops of pillars of angry red and blue cloud, the turbulence became so bad that Johnny was flung violently around the cabin. He bashed his bubble helmet on the shuttle roof and was glad of the extra protection of the spacesuit but, just when he thought either he or the *Jubilee* might be shaken apart, the vibrations stopped. He'd crossed into another atmospheric layer and relative calm returned, broken only by occasional, mighty peals of thunder when lightning bolts from massive electrical storms flashed nearby.

Scarily, the little taxi's normally shiny black bonnet was

already glowing red as it heated to beyond safe limits. Johnny pulled himself down underneath the steering wheel, trying to remove the panels that hid the inner workings of the small craft. It was immediately obvious why he'd lost control – the fuel cells were all but exhausted. No wonder the shuttle's communications were down. He couldn't understand how that had happened when they were always fully charged in the shuttle bay. Then Erin's horned face flew into his mind's eye and the full extent of the act of sabotage became clear. The final few drops of energy left had now been diverted to the front shields to try to hold the black cab together. At this rate they would soon fail.

Then something screamed. It was a high-pitched, otherworldly wail that made the hairs of Johnny's neck stand on end. He jumped, smacking his helmet on the bottom of the steering wheel. The language was too primitive for the speck of Hundra inside him to translate, but he picked up enough to know it was some sort of terrible death cry. The voice had sounded close by, only just beyond the *Jubilee*'s cabin, but as his eyes darted this way and that there seemed nothing to see, save for a long twisted green cloud like a colourful unicorn horn, above a solid swirling wall of paler green. Rushing from window to window, he also spotted a cluster of straggly mushroom-shaped clouds, like distant hot-air balloons, but it was only when he peered upwards through the narrow rear window that he found the source of the shrill cries. Swooping down from above was a school of what looked like purple flying sharks, bigger than buses, with tall fins along their backs. They were pumping their powerful bodies from nose to tail to propel themselves on streamlined wings towards him – very fast. Even as Johnny watched, their colouring began to fade and give way to the fainter green of the surroundings, like deadly chameleons, making it harder to see the danger. Johnny, on the other hand, didn't have nearly enough energy left to make the shuttle invisible.

The pack of flying hunters careered towards the *Jubilee* in a V-formation. Totally powerless, Johnny took a deep breath and steadied his hands on the steering wheel. In the rear-view mirror he watched a pair of jaws larger than the shuttle open, ready to swallow his ship whole. The inside of the animal's mouth was like a runway, luminous skin cells pulsing as if landing lights, directing the creature's prey to its doom between row upon row of fearsome curved teeth.

Then Johnny's world turned white. Something exploded all around and he was forced down into the driver's seat, before the pressure lifted and he began somersaulting around the cabin. The light was so bright it took a few moments to realize he'd closed his eyes. As the flash faded, he opened them slowly, wondering if the creature had fired on him. His ship was spinning like the insides of a washing machine, while part of the bonnet had sheared away. Outside, a bolt of lightning arrowed across the sky, lighting the *Jubilee* through the passenger side windows. Only a direct hit, moments before, could have saved him. The bolt would have been drawn towards the *Jubilee*, which had only half-survived it, but the creature behind had come off even worse. Charred and lifeless, both it and the broken shuttle fell together towards and then into the next layer of cloud, a thick blue fog that Johnny could only hope would hide him. Desperate to right itself, the *Jubilee* must have used the very last ounce of remaining power to stabilize the roll. Johnny dropped into the pilot's seat, just as the craft again nosedived into freefall.

Slowly, from out of the gloom, the shadowy outlines of shark-like hunters began to appear. As Johnny's eyes adjusted, he could see more and more lights from their cave-like mouths, circling the shuttle and its lifeless companion. Still plunging downwards, the beasts' shrieks were coming faster and faster and rising higher and higher, as though counting down to the kill. Then the noise stopped. Johnny held his breath as time seemed to stand still.

The creatures poured forward as one, drawn not to the *Jubilee* but to the other of their kind. A terrible feeding frenzy began as the carcass was shredded in only a few seconds, like watching a time-lapsed film speeded up. The *Jubilee* was ignored and left to continue its descent alone, as the flying sharks halted their fall and slowly began to gain altitude, fighting among themselves for the remaining scraps of flesh. Johnny watched as they shrank into the distance, envious of their power, until he was interrupted by a loud bang. This time he was certain the noise had come from within the cabin and then he saw it – a tiny crack in the front windscreen, no longer than a fingernail. Agonizingly slowly, millimetre by millimetre, it began to grow, spidering out in all directions. Next, the roof of his craft buckled and flying glass from the rear window flew all around, bouncing off Johnny's helmet. The front windscreen blew in too, allowing the cabin to fill with purple vapour. The roof peeled away, like the lid of a tin can, leaving Johnny pinned in his seat as the wind whistled around his spacesuit. The passenger door went next as the rest of the black cab disintegrated about him. He watched it tumbling into the distance and held onto his own door handle, more for comfort than anything else. The next thing he knew he was falling forward through the thick atmosphere just in his seat with only the driver's door beside him – the rest of the *Jubilee* had been completely stripped away. He marvelled at the strength of his own spacesuit, but knew it wouldn't be long before he, too, was torn apart.

With a great effort, Johnny was able to haul the door round so it was beneath him, acting as a shield to stop the wind buffeting him as he fell. In doing so, he lost his seat which somersaulted away, disappearing into the ever-thickening mist. Holding either side of the door, he pulled his feet into its middle and crouched, grateful for the shelter it offered, if only for a few minutes until the pressure overcame his suit or he crashed into the gas giant's ocean of metallic liquid hydrogen – Johnny laughed at himself for having remembered that would be the planet's core. Already droplets were forming on the outside of his helmet making it harder to see. Wondering if the air rushing past might blow them away, he rose slowly to his feet until he was standing like a surfer with a fishbowl on his head, riding the biggest wave of anyone in history.

Clara was his only hope. Swooping across the sky of this deadly, unknown world, he tried the wristcom and could have cried when met by the faint sound of a panicked Alf coming through his spacesuit helmet.

'Alf!' Johnny screamed back. 'Am I glad to hear you.'

'The feeling is mutual, Master Johnny. We are having to use geothermal energy from the moon we landed onto power the *Piccadilly* – quite ingenious if I may say so. I based the idea on the Ghordian civilization on Ramos IV, whose cities float on planet wide lava flows and . . .'

'Alf – I don't have time for this. I need you to lock onto my position and have Clara fold me out of here.'

'Master Johnny – I do worry Miss Clara does far too much folding as it . . .'

'Alf! It's urgent – life or death. Get Clara now.'

'Of course, Master Johnny.'

Moments later, Clara's trembling voice came through the spacesuit helmet. 'Johnny! Alf's getting a lock on your position – it's hard cos the atmosphere's so thick. Are you OK?'

'Not especially,' said Johnny, determined not to let his own voice waver. 'The *Jubilee*'s gone. I'm in my spacesuit – just falling. I don't have long.'

'Don't worry. I'll fold you out,' said Clara, her words so distant they were barely audible.

'Clara – it's a huge planet. You might not find me.' As Johnny spoke, the clouds parted and, far below the board on which he stood, he could see the planet's otherworldly, shiny ocean. He'd almost run out of time. 'Listen to me. Someone will hear the distress signal. Bram will come. You've got to protect Earth.' Face to face with death, Johnny was consumed with a new urgency. He'd made a decision. 'I can see the core now. It's almost over. There's something you must know – it's important.'

'I'm not losing you, Johnny.' The signal had almost gone.

'You can't always save me, Clara.' There was no reply and it was now or never. He took advantage of her silence to carry on. 'I've been trying to tell you for ages – you've got another brother.'

He couldn't blame her for saying nothing.

'Nicky's alive. I don't really understand it,' Johnny went on. The ocean was rushing towards him faster than he'd expected. He could see waves now. 'He's Nymac – it's short for Nicky Mackintosh. He doesn't know about you. And something's controlling him. Something bad . . . from Andromeda . . . called "the Nameless One". I'm sorry I couldn't tell you before, Clara. I'm so sorry.'

There was a crystal clear chime in Johnny's ears. Focusing on the inside of his helmet, he saw the thinnest of hairline cracks. Any second now it would implode.

An archway opened in mid-air a couple of hundred metres to the side. By some miracle Clara *had* found him. For a second, he could see his sister, sitting on a rocky outcrop of a dark moon while Alf stood further back, struggling to hold onto Bentley's lead. The bright red *Piccadilly* looked out of place.

He angled his surfboard towards the portal. Clara leant

forward, only just on the other side, arms reaching out to grab hold, but Johnny knew he was losing height too quickly and would never make it through the gap. As he came close Clara reached right down, straining so far she was almost falling through. Johnny stretched his arms upwards, risking losing the board. Then, at the very last moment, he took his hands down. It was instinctive. Their fingertips brushed for a tiny fraction of a second. Any longer and he knew he'd have been pulling his sister down to her death as well.

His helmet cracked, just above the surface of the ocean. Johnny's hand reached for the locket that was his link to his family, but he couldn't hold it – it was tucked inside the spacesuit which had somehow kept him alive till now. His silver reflection, distorted by the waves in the liquid metal ocean, was almost touching him.

Then another silver-haired figure burst through his mirror image, breaking the shimmering surface and rising upwards, its arms outstretched. Johnny thought he must be dead – that he was falling into the arms of his father. Then he understood. The grey-cloaked figure wasn't his dad. Bram Khari, Emperor of the Galaxy, caught hold of Johnny and gathered him in.

10 ✧

Titan's Secret ✧

A great wet tongue slopped across Johnny's face and around his ear, tickling as it rolled onto his neck. He opened one eye to see Bentley's shaggy grey and white face pressed close to his own and wrapped his arms around the Old English sheepdog.

'He's awake,' squealed Clara.

Gently, Johnny pushed Bentley off him and sat up, looking sheepishly across to where her voice had come from. His sister, the fear draining from her face, ran over, flinging her arms around him and burying her head in his chest. It was as if what he'd told her about Nicky didn't matter at all – that everything was forgiven. A great wave of relief washed over him. Awkwardly, he patted her blonde hair and squinted past her to take in his surroundings.

They were in a room looking out across the biggest, brightest, neatest cargo bay Johnny had ever seen. The first thing he spotted, fitting comfortably upright against one wall was the *Spirit of London*. All the lights in Johnny's ship were still out. Above her, hanging from the roof, stacked as far as he could see were row after row of sleek white fighters, ready to be deployed at a moment's notice, while far in the distance was a collection of what looked like giant dandelion seeds. Closer at hand, beneath the floor-to-ceiling gap (which presumably contained a forcefield) and spoiling the neatness just a little, stood a rather grimy red double-decker bus – the *Piccadilly*.

'Welcome to the *Calida Lucia*, the Imperial Starcruiser. I hope she meets with your approval.' His Majesty Emperor Bram Khari stepped smiling into Johnny's field of vision. He was tall, with a mass of grey hair that seemed to slowly weave through the air of its own accord, giving off a little silvery light as it moved. Just as when they'd spoken through the Wormhole, Johnny couldn't help noticing that the Emperor's face looked far older and more lined than he remembered, though there was no dulling of Bram's piercing pale blue eyes. The Emperor of the galaxy wore a simple grey cloak, topping a pair of black trousers and boots.

'We've got to get back to Earth,' said Johnny. 'The supernova . . .'

'I'm sure we can at least say hello first,' said Bram, smiling. 'I was rather glad I caught you in time.'

'Not as glad as me,' Johnny replied.

'When you let go . . .' said Clara, lifting herself off and turning around so Johnny and Bram couldn't see her face.

'Can you fix Sol?' Johnny asked, anxious to change the subject and looking to the Emperor. 'I did something horrid to her.'

'In time I am sure she can be healed,' Bram replied. 'But right now, time is something we do not have. Your distress signal won't only have attracted the *Calida Lucia*. We must leave the Aldebaran system before drawing too much attention to our presence here. I will take you home where we can properly discuss the solar system's defences – Clara has reiterated your desire for ships to prevent another Star Blaze. On the way back though, if I have your permission, we shall take a very slight detour.' The Emperor's eyes twinkled as he spoke. Johnny exchanged glances with his sister. Just for a moment they could relax and forget about the impending supernova, as they both wondered what treat Bram had in store for them.

The gel pods on the Imperial Starcruiser were more luxurious than any Johnny had been in before, but then the *Calida Lucia* was unlike any ship he'd travelled in. Between folds, while discussing the supernova threat, the Emperor had given them what he'd called 'the grand tour'. The time Johnny had saved the dinosaurs from extinction on prehistoric Earth, he'd converted the *Spirit of London*'s five-a-side football pitch into a self-contained habitat which became known as the dinodeck. Now that seemed rather feeble compared with the entire biospheres within the *Calida Lucia*'s massive hold. There was a mini-ocean, populated by all manner of sea creatures; another sphere contained snow-capped mountains; there was some sort of tropical rainforest (though the strange howls from within were rather off-putting); a formal park in one contained a grove of Kanefor trees, bearers of the wonderful fruit tasting of coffee ice cream which was Johnny's favourite (but the trees would only let you pick them if you tickled them in just the right place); and, finally, you could even lie on sandy beaches around a turquoise lagoon, with triple artificial suns to keep you warm. It was here they spent the most time as Bram said he would soon be giving it away.

After several requests and refusing to take no for an answer, Johnny was finally allowed to join in with one of the *Calida Lucia*'s fighter squadrons' practice drills. Although a Starfighter was nearly the same size as a shuttle, and also responded to thought control, that was where the similarities ended. He had no idea any ship could be quite so fast and manoeuvrable. Without the most advanced internal dampeners in the galaxy he'd have been killed instantly by the massive g-forces. By the end of the session he was buzzing and had even managed a weapon's lock on the squadron leader. It had been as he was leaving the cargo bay that the ship announced the final fold to the Sol system and the pilots had rapidly dispersed to their gel pods.

Now the fold was over, Johnny waited while pulses of warm air dried the orange gloop off his clothes, wondering about their destination if it wasn't Earth. The door opened automatically and he stepped out, only to meet Bentley shaking out his coat, spraying Johnny's white tunic top with more of the goo. Cassiopeia's stars were lost against a messy new sky. As the sheepdog rolled over onto his back, Alf joined them in the wide corridor. Johnny was deliberately barefoot so he, like Bentley, could make the most of the lush carpet massaging his feet, just as in his old bedroom in the Imperial Palace on Melania. However, when Alf started to sponge his top, Johnny decided it was definitely time to move so announced they shouldn't be late for the meeting on the bridge. The poor android was clearly torn between not keeping the Emperor waiting while not having Johnny arrive looking messy and, as they began to walk, became a whirr of nervously waving arms.

The ship was so large it would need days to walk across it – they were taking a bullet car to the bridge and Johnny led the way to the nearest transit tube hatch, passing a couple of Viasynths as they went. A capsule was waiting for them. The smooth streamlined cars travelled in tubes that criss-crossed the length and breadth of the ship. Within these tunnels were few reference points by which to gauge your speed, but Johnny suspected it was *very* fast. After an initial surge of acceleration they sped forward for half a minute before the pointed cabin slowed and came to a smooth halt right outside the bridge.

Two soldiers from the Imperial Guard, wearing cream uniforms with four diamond-patterned stars across their chests, stood still as statues, either side of the entrance. Despite their round faces, their eyes were very close together. Johnny had to pull Bentley away to stop him sniffing the squat, powerfully built aliens, before they passed through a forcefield, noticeable only for a slight tingling, and entered. He would have recognized the view anywhere. Bram and Clara were standing side by side, gazing at magnificent Saturn and its rings, with the Sun shining brightly and safely in the background. Everything was still OK.

The ship's powerful external fields prevented all the air on the bridge rushing out through a massive gap, fifty metres high, to create the spectacular viewing platform. Bentley bounded across, barking and Bram turned only just in time to ward off the Old English sheepdog who jumped up on his hind legs, placing his gloop-covered paws on the grey cloak, and attempted to lick the Emperor's face. Alf looked mortified, but Johnny knew Bram would be delighted.

Something about the planet and their position relative to it seemed familiar. 'Isn't this where we found *Cheybora* after the supernova?' he asked as he and Alf followed the line of Bentley's paw prints across the bridge towards his sister and the Emperor.

'Space is creased here,' said Clara. 'I can feel it – like it was folded too deeply once.'

Bram frowned, his face absolutely full of wrinkles. 'It is as well others do not share your talents, Clara. This place is special – I would not wish it to be discovered.'

Johnny pictured a galactic tourist trade springing up around the thickly ringed world – it would be hard to keep all those aliens secret from Earth. 'I always dreamed of seeing it from so close,' he said.

'Aha. And I wasn't even talking about these marvellous rings, as old as your solar system itself. Sadly, in time – admittedly a rather long time – they may break up and disappear. There is something else I wish to keep secret – something on Titan. Something that will last forever.' Still gazing at the view, Bram raised his voice slightly and went on, '*Calida Lucia* – take us into orbit around the largest moon.'

Instantly the view shifted as the great ship banked, rolling over as it changed direction. Clara screamed and grabbed hold of Johnny's arm, even though the ship's gravity field was holding her as tightly as ever to the floor of the observation platform.

'Clara Mackintosh – my sensors are reading biosigns symptomatic with acute stress. I assure you that you are in no danger.' It was the ship speaking, her voice deep and rich.

'Just warn me before you do that next time,' said Clara. Her eyes were closed, but her grip on Johnny's arm began to relax.

The view righted itself as the vast ship entered orbit above a cloudy, orange globe. 'You can open your eyes now,' Johnny whispered in Clara's ear, while Bram and Alf looked away pretending not to notice her discomfort.

'Alf, my old friend,' said Bram. If the android could have blushed, Johnny was sure he would have turned bright pink. 'Would you do me the favour of looking after Bentley while I travel with Johnny and Clara to the surface?'

'It would be an honour, your Majesty,' replied the android, bowing his head a little, which was a mistake because it brought it within reach of Bentley's tongue. As Alf tried to extricate himself from the Old English sheepdog, the Emperor led Johnny and Clara off the bridge towards a waiting bullet car.

☆ ☆ ☆
☆ ☆

The Emperor had declined Clara's offer to fold them all directly to the surface and they were now in the giant bay at the heart of the *Calida Lucia*. Johnny's sister wasted no time in pointing out that he had been granted his wish to fly the overhead Starfighters, but she was never trusted to do anything. Bram's response that, 'Folding may be the fastest way to travel, but that does not mean it is always the best,' only led Clara to screw her face up so tightly Johnny thought she might explode. He did wonder if she was secretly mad at him, instead, for not telling her about Nicky sooner. They hadn't spoken about their elder brother since arriving on the Imperial Starcruiser. Miss Harutunian and Johnny's other social workers were always telling him not to bottle his feelings up and he guessed his sister's mood could be the result of exactly that.

Even though Bram didn't seem able to walk quickly, Clara was lagging behind the other two, dragging her feet on the deck. The Emperor looked so frail, close up, that he might not have wanted to fold in case the stress had finished him off – he'd even struggled to get out of the bullet car. Johnny had always known Bram was old – after all, they'd first met forty thousand years before in Atlantis – but, when it came to the Emperor, he hadn't ever thought that 'old' might also mean 'infirm'.

High above, row after row of Imperial Starfighters reassured Johnny that the Sun would be safe for the time being, but he knew the Emperor's personal starship couldn't stay in the solar system indefinitely. Depressingly, the *Spirit of London* looked as lifeless as ever. Bram had told Johnny that the *Calida Lucia* was a sister ship, born on the same strange moon where Johnny had helped give Sol her form. Since plucking her younger sister from the Aldebaran system, the Imperial Starcruiser had been trying to tease memories from Sol's separated mind, without reconnecting it and restarting the self-destruct sequence. The Emperor likened it to seeing into another person's dreams and trying to make sense of them without waking the sleeper, adding that very few races had such interesting dreams as humans.

As they walked past Johnny's ship, one of the giant dandelion seeds at the far end of the bay, which he now knew were shuttlecraft, lifted away from the pile, floated through the air and settled in front of them. This would be their transport to Titan. The Emperor blew softly on the nearest of the long tips, which parted and a walkway extended towards them. It wasn't clear if it was solid or simply a forcefield, but it took their weight and Bram led the way, slowly hobbling up and into a central hub, from where the ship's quills were transparent. There were no visible controls, but the craft lifted into the air and floated towards the walls of the gigantic chamber. Just when it looked as if they would collide, the wall warped and opened, allowing them through. The process repeated several times until, passing through the final opening, they were clear and flying above the vast ship towards the biggest moon in the solar system.

'You know there's a human probe down there?' Johnny asked, wondering if they might be about to fly over Huygens and confuse Earth-bound scientists.

'No longer broadcasting and not in the place to where we are heading,' Bram replied, 'but I am pleased humanity has taken another step further out.'

As they plunged through the thick, orange clouds, a landscape of mountains, oceans and rivers came into view. From altitude, it looked very like Earth. Johnny tried to tune into the ship's sensors which told him the liquid that had sculpted the moon's surface was methane, not water. He followed their progress until they settled on a rocky outcrop, overlooking a featureless plain that extended for many tens of kilometres towards some low mountains in the distance. Having observed various sections of Titan on their descent, this was without doubt the most boring spot anywhere on its surface.

'Welcome to one of the most special places in the galaxy,' said Bram, his eyes twinkling again. 'Shall we go outside?'

'I didn't bring a spacesuit,' said Clara.

Johnny checked – the atmosphere was almost all nitrogen,

with just a couple of percent methane and the rest trace elements. There was no oxygen to breathe.

Bram, however, laughed. 'It is important to remember that not everything is as it appears. There is no need of spacesuits in this place – your mother made certain of that. Follow me – you will not be disappointed.'

A small circular hole appeared in the side of the craft, which quickly widened. Instinctively, Johnny held his breath, but then watched as Bram shuffled out down the ramp. Halfway along the Emperor vanished, as though he had stepped through an invisible curtain. Johnny stared at the spot and then at Clara, open-mouthed.

Now they were alone, if only for a moment, he wondered again about trying to explain better about Nicky, but Clara smiled, said, 'Here goes,' and set out after Bram. After just a few strides she, too, simply disappeared.

Johnny had no choice but to follow. One moment, as he stepped barefoot onto the walkway, he was looking at a muddy brown landscape beneath a thick layer of orange cloud. The next, under a clear sky dominated by the majestic Saturn, he saw a perfectly circular lake, filled with thick liquid like molten gold. As he gulped the air down it smelled of honey and heather. Bram and Clara stood together near the edge, watching ripples from the centre spreading out and breaking over the sides. Even as they did so, the liquid clumped together, like yellow droplets of mercury, and sucked itself back into the body of the lake, almost as though it was alive.

'Do not touch it,' said Bram. 'You are not yet ready. Come.' Being in this strange place appeared to invigorate the Emperor, who set a quick pace as he strode around the lake's edge to the far side, soon reaching a spectacular grotto of blue crystal pillars, jutting from the ground at all angles. At the centre of the huge, geometric needles, on a striking white crystal plinth, was a clear dome that looked vaguely familiar to Johnny.

'You have seen a thought chamber before?' asked Bram. 'They are a rare, ancient technology.'

'It was on Nereid,' Johnny replied, nodding to himself as much as anyone else as he remembered. 'Neptune's moon where I found Dad. The Krun had one.'

'Clearly the Krun are not to be underestimated,' said Bram. 'They are like locusts, swarming from the rim, devouring technology, new and old. Tell me – what did you see?'

Johnny thought back to the time, many months ago when they'd rescued his father and Louise. 'At first it was the dinosaurs,' he said, recalling the battle on the insides of Triton, Neptune's largest and strangest moon. 'They'd held a council and agreed to fight the Krun – I saw them attacking.'

'The image changed?' prompted the Emperor.

'Yeah . . . to a triple star system,' said Johnny. 'Seen from a ship.'

'Curious,' said Bram. 'Toliman, perhaps. Did you recognize it?'

'Not at all,' Johnny replied.

'The chamber can be controlled by one skilled in its use,' said Bram, 'but, essentially, it connects the observer to people or places that matter to him or her – or are, in some way, linked. What else did you see?'

'At first I thought it was you,' said Johnny, a little awkwardly. He didn't relish recalling the scene. 'Someone was seated in front of a fire. Then they turned round and it wasn't you at all. They wore a mask – all black – except for this white explosion, like a really bright star. I could feel the hatred.'

'I have seen him too,' said Bram. 'He is the Nameless One, from Andromeda . . . the force behind the invasion. Due to his actions, I was delayed in my journey to Earth. Half our fleet was destroyed in an ambush at the hypergiant Carinae. Another Star

Blaze . . .' For a moment the Emperor appeared distant, as if his mind were elsewhere. Then he continued, 'Although we will not win this battle through strength of arms or numbers, it was a bitter blow. But there are better ways to fight and, when the time comes, you two will play your parts.'

As if galvanized by Johnny's report, the Emperor said, 'Stand back – I shall return presently. Whatever happens, do not follow.' This was an instruction and not a request – there was no way Johnny was going to argue.

Bram stepped onto the lip of the lake and then took a stride into it. Instead of his boot disappearing into the thick liquid, it met solid, invisible ground just above the surface and the Emperor began to shuffle towards the centre, as though walking on golden water. As he went, the waves moving past him distorted, flowing around him as if marking lines of force, and welling up and splashing about his feet. Finally, Bram reached the midpoint of the lake. He threw off his cloak, revealing a white tunic top like Johnny and Clara's, stretched his arms out wide and lifted his face to the heavens. The gold liquid all around shot high into the air, hundreds of metres into the sky beneath Saturn, encircling the Emperor with a rippling, shimmering curtain, like an aurora. As some fell back into the lake, more rose to take its place, drenching the figure under a constant golden deluge.

It must have been like standing beneath Niagara Falls. Johnny was worried Bram would be washed away – that he wouldn't be strong enough to survive the deluge. He made a move towards the lake but Clara grabbed hold of his hand and, this time, refused to let go. She shook her head and pointed. The glow from the centre of the lake was no longer only from the glittering liquid. The drenched figure at its heart was shining brightest of all. Bram no longer looked bent over and old. It was almost the same as when they saw him arriving in Atlantis. He strode out from under the golden fountain, which ceased as quickly as it had begun, the liquid falling out of the sky but no longer being replaced, like the slow fade-out of a firework. Striding purposefully, Bram marched along his invisible walkway towards Johnny and Clara. The four diamond-patterned stars of Portia blazed brightly across the chest of his white tunic. His hair was lively, and shining more brightly than Johnny could remember. The Emperor opened his arms and said, 'Behold, the Fountain of Time – that which sustains me.'

'It's amazing,' said Clara.

'The effect is not what it was,' replied Bram, frowning, revealing a face still faintly lined. 'Every time I come here, the impact is less and I find I must return sooner. I would have liked to have waited, but I need my strength for the struggle that lies ahead. Both of you must be strong too – you're special – and, whatever happens, you must stick together. The galaxy needs you.'

Johnny exchanged an awkward glance with his sister, before looking back at the Emperor. He'd failed Sol and knew the Sun was still in terrible danger. Special was the last thing he felt.

'But there are other special ones too,' Bram went on.

'Who?' Clara asked. Johnny waited for her to add, 'Do you mean Nicky?' but the words didn't come.

The Emperor turned to the lake, hands cupped, and scooped up some of the golden liquid. He blew over its surface and, instead of forming a flat layer above Bram's fingers, the fluid began to spin like a whirlpool. Without warning, the Emperor threw it into the air. Johnny's eyes followed as it took on the shape of a galaxy, slowly rotating just over their heads. Clara clapped.

Bram smiled and sat down on the ground, indicating that they should do the same. 'The lake is filled with chronons,' he said. 'Particles of time. They retain an impression of what has gone before. What you see is our galaxy, the Milky Way, as it was in the beginning.'

When you looked through a telescope Johnny knew you were also looking backwards in time. From Earth, even Andromeda appears as it was more than two million years ago – not as it is now – but it was fascinating to see his own galaxy looking so young.

'No one knows *how* the very first life began,' the Emperor went on, 'but it is clear that our galaxy loved and embraced it.'

'I don't understand,' said Clara. 'The galaxy's not got feelings . . . has it?'

'In a way it has. Life was the ultimate in its evolution – the Milky Way made conscious. At first, it is said there was only one. Over time, aeons, others were created or came to be. They were still few, but the life they contained was rich and thick and not like today. They had wondrous gifts – great power. They were the lawmakers and lived, effectively, forever.'

'The Lysentians,' said Johnny.

Bram smiled and nodded. 'Yes . . . the Lysentians were the first ones. But the galaxy that had given birth to such wonders somehow knew it had made a mistake. To concentrate so much life in so few led to terrible problems – trouble in paradise.'

'What happened?' asked Johnny. He and Clara were sitting cross-legged in front of the Emperor, hanging on his every word.

'The story is a long one – no one knows it fully. But there was war . . . the most terrible devastation. The Milky Way realized its error and decided to diversify – life began to spread out. New races were born, vast in number, but short-lived. As consciousness spread into every nook and cranny the galaxy had to offer, it became diluted, individually less spectacular, but more diverse and vibrant and without the destructive power of some first ones.'

'And what happened to the Lysentians?' Clara asked.

'A few stayed behind – guardians of the cosmic order – to

nurture and care for the new races. They created the Hundra, to help the different lifeforms communicate. They built a peaceful civilization. Some of them ruled as the first, benevolent Emperors, moulding the galaxy for different races to flourish. But this busy new Milky Way – buzzing with its fireflies of life – was not for most of them. They went on, clearing the way for the new lifeforms to spread unimpeded.'

'Where to?' Johnny asked. The picture Bram was painting of ancient, ultrapowerful first ones reminded him of someone – his mother. More than anything he wanted to know what had happened to her and where she'd taken their human father. He wanted specifics.

'Alas I cannot say,' Bram replied softly. As if reading Johnny's thoughts, he continued, 'When many of the others left, your mother, the Diaquant, was one of those who stayed behind. Gradually the others departed – I believe she was the very last of the originals to leave.'

'So there are no guardians at all?' Clara asked.

'There are some,' said Bram. 'But we are not first ones – the life in us is not so strong so our power is less. But I sense a new awakening within the galaxy . . . perhaps a longing for what it once held within itself. Give me your hand, Johnny.'

Bram took hold of Johnny's left hand and rolled up the sleeve. In this strange bubble of timelessness the lights on Johnny's wristcom were neither red nor green. Instead, on Johnny's inner arm, something else was glowing.

'This is your Starmark,' said the Emperor, tracing out the five stars of Cassiopeia, the big 'W' on the inside of Johnny's forearm. 'It is a sign – an imprint from the Milky Way. The five stars tell us that, when you were born, you were one of five in all the galaxy imbued with some of the first ones' life and powers. This pattern of stars was the brightest in the sky on that day – it tells us where in the galaxy you came from.'

'I'm . . . like a first one?' Johnny couldn't believe it. He knew he had strange abilities – he could do stuff with electricity – but he couldn't control it very well and most of the time he felt very ordinary.

'Not yet,' Bram replied, his eyes smiling, 'and we don't know how you will develop. Let's just say you have potential – with a mother like yours, it would be hard not to. But with great power comes great responsibility – never forget that.'

'Who are the others?' asked Clara.

'A very good question,' Bram replied. 'When I was born, I was one of four.' He turned and lifted up his top, revealing a smooth back except for four splashes of glowing green, perfectly matching the stars of Portia. 'I cannot be sure, but I believe you met one of my contemporaries.'

'Neith!' shouted Clara.

'Very good,' said Bram. 'Queen Neith of Atlantis . . . she had undoubted power.'

'But now there are seven,' said Clara, rolling up her trouser leg to reveal her own pattern of freckles, now glowing, in the shape of the Plough. They were the only marks on her otherwise clear skin.

'Yes – now there are seven,' said Bram, nodding. 'The galaxy has been busy. One was born between you and Johnny, doubtless somewhere undiscovered but with a Starmark in a pattern of six.'

'Erin,' said Johnny, as much confirming it to himself as announcing it to anyone else.

'Erin? The boy you rescued?' asked the Emperor, his blue eyes narrowing.

'Erin son of Marin, King and ruler of the Alnitak Hegemony – apparently. He's the one who hurt Sol,' said Johnny bitterly. 'He had a hexagon on his face . . . great big splodge.'

'And I just thought he was ugly,' Clara added. 'Like his sister.'

Johnny had thought Zeta was quite pretty, but that was before they'd tried to kill Sol. Now he was in full agreement with Clara.

'Fascinating,' said Bram. 'I had heard rumours – whispers from Orion's clouds. I've been searching for this pair and all the time they were on the *Spirit of London*. The galaxy works in mysterious ways.'

'General Nymac was looking for them too,' said Clara. 'The Andromedan fleet was hunting them.' Johnny guessed the Emperor knew she was talking about their brother. It hurt to use his real name when he was trying to destroy their Sun.

'As I feared,' said Bram. 'They, too, are young, but were they to fall into Nymac's hands or, worse still, the Nameless One who commands him, the damage may be irreparable. They could take over the galaxy and enslave everyone. Tell me all you can about this Erin and his sister – did she have a Starmark too?'

So Johnny and Clara told Bram nearly everything they could think of about the strange pair and their solar sailing ship, the *Falling Star* – how Erin had stopped Johnny's heart beating on the bridge, but how his sister had resuscitated Alf after a fold without rebooting him, and then healed Johnny's nose after it had been broken. And how Erin must have used his power to force Sol's self-destruct sequence to begin. The Emperor was troubled as to how such a thing could have happened to a ship he thought secure, but Johnny couldn't see any other explanation.

When they'd finished, Bram sat in silence for a couple of minutes, eyes closed. Johnny stood, shaking out the pins and needles from his legs and walking to the very edge of the lake. Clara joined him. Together they watched their reflections in the rippled surface. Behind, Bram stirred, jumped to his feet as easily as a young man and came to stand beside them. He bent down and scooped another handful of chronons which, in his palms, grew six golden spikes. The Emperor cast them into the air above the golden lake where they hovered for a while, a hexagon of golden stars, before slowly drifting down and rejoining the lake.

'I will send you Captain Valdour and a fleet of ships,' said Bram. 'It will more than suffice – he is a fine, resourceful officer and your detection system will ensure the Andromedans do not gain a foothold. And I will go to Alnitak to see if these stars truly adorn the skies from that system. Bur first we must heal Sol and take you home.'

'It's different . . . peaceful here,' said Clara. 'Can I try what you did to make the Milky Way?'

She bent to scoop up a little of the golden liquid herself.

'No!' said Bram, sternly, and where Clara was reaching the liquid receded, as though repelled, making a semicircle of gold with her at its centre and leaving absolutely nothing in its place. It was a vast void of nothingness, stretching down for as far as Johnny could see. Clara peered into the depths and overbalanced. Johnny grabbed her and pulled her away from the edge, allowing the fluid to return to the side as though nothing had happened.

Bram tried to smile. 'Of course you like it here – your mother built it,' he said, 'but you are still so very young that one touch of the Fountain of Time and you might even cease to be at all.'

'Mum? How?' Johnny asked.

'I don't know how,' Bram replied, 'but I think I know why.' Johnny knew so little about their mum that he was hungry for even the tiniest smidgeon of information about her. 'This surface was once perfectly smooth,' the Emperor went on, 'until after she sent you forward through time from Atlantis. We came here together that same day, forty thousand years ago, when she first showed me Titan's secret. She told me the disturbance in the cosmos after what she'd just done was very great, so she'd used the fountain, and the lake, to soften it. It was very important for her that you got home.'

'I wish she was here now,' said Clara.

'So do I,' replied Bram. 'So do I.'

✩ ✩ ✩
✩ ✩

Finally, once the dandelion-head shuttle was safely back in the *Calida Lucia*'s cargo bay, Clara had her wish to practise folding. She, Johnny and Bram stepped through an arch-shaped opening onto the deserted and dead bridge of the *Spirit of London*. It was dark and cold. Johnny's breath condensed into a white cloud as it left his mouth. He put his hands into his pockets but somehow it didn't make him any warmer. Secretly, he knew he'd been hoping for a miracle – that Sol would have magically healed herself and the words 'Hello, Johnny' would have welcomed him onto his ship. Sadly, the only sound was squeaking, as Clara used her sleeve to wipe the condensation from the Plican's tank. The strange creature opened an eye, as though proving to his sister that it was still alive.

Bram surveyed the scene. 'Johnny – I have something to show you,' he said. 'You may find it disturbing, but you must see it.'

Johnny nodded.

The Emperor walked over, placing a reassuring hand on Johnny's shoulder. 'It is one of Sol's memories – the *Calida Lucia* believes it to be important.' From nowhere, a second Johnny appeared, sitting at the centre of the bridge. 'Do not be alarmed,' said Bram. 'It is a simulation . . . a recreation of what Sol believes took place.'

'Can he see us?' Clara asked, peering uncertainly round the Plican's tank. The Emperor shook his head.

'Ship,' said the other Johnny, stretching out in the comfort of the captain's chair. 'I demand you do something for me.'

'Yes, Johnny,' replied Sol.

For a moment, it was as if everything was back to normal, but then Johnny realized Sol's soothing voice was also part of the recreation.

The other Johnny continued, 'The thing is I want you to blow yourself up . . . kill yourself . . . not right now, of course.'

'I don't understand,' said Sol, the lights flashing on her vocal display as she spoke.

Both Bram and Clara turned to the real Johnny, who was gesticulating for them to look back at the figure in the chair. 'It's not me – it's Erin,' he hissed. 'Look at him. It's like he's never sat in that chair before.'

'You don't need to understand,' said the seated Johnny. 'Think of it as a test. To prove how far you will go to follow my orders.'

'You know I will do anything you ask me to,' Sol replied. 'Even this, however much it grieves me.'

The real Johnny had taken his hands out of his pockets and his fingernails were digging into his palms. If he could have throttled the impostor sitting in his chair, he would happily have done so.

'Whatever,' said the hateful figure, 'but that's not all. You will only begin the self-destruct after you have emerged from the next fold; you will not discuss this instruction with anyone else; and, in the event that I should attempt to countermand the order, know that I am testing you. You must not stop the countdown for any reason. Is that understood?'

'It is, Johnny,' said Sol. 'May I at least discuss . . .'

'This is not a debating society, ship,' said the other Johnny. 'One more thing. The moment you take off on your final journey, you will drain the fuel cells of your shuttlecraft – there will be no survivors.'

'Johnny – you know I will die if you ask it, but I cannot believe you want Clara and . . .'

'Silence!' roared the figure in the chair. 'You dare defy me?'

'Of course not, Johnny.'

'Then you have your orders – that will be all.' The impostor rose and turned as if leaving the bridge before the scene froze.

Bram walked forward and peered at the statuesque Johnny. 'He does look like you,' said the Emperor. 'And a DNA analysis shows that only you, Clara, your mother and Bentley have ever sat in that chair.'

'You've got to believe me,' said Johnny. 'I promise *this* is not me – it's Erin.' As he said 'this' Johnny waved his arm through the projection which disappeared for a moment.

'Of course I believe you,' said Bram. 'That is axiomatic. It's just that the evidence is compelling. Convincing Sol may be more difficult than I had hoped.'

'Surely she should be able to tell,' said Clara. 'This other Johnny's too . . . neat . . . and clean.'

'Thanks very much,' said Johnny, though he realized it was true. The projection in front of him had his Cassiopeia-emblazoned tunic top tucked inside his black trousers, which he hoped he never did. And he could almost see his reflection in his double's shiny black boots.

'You're welcome,' Clara replied, smiling innocently.

'*Calida Lucia* – if you can, probe Sol's memories and show me this Erin.' At once a frozen image of the boy king appeared on the bridge close to the lifts. 'Fascinating,' said Bram, examining the hexagonal markings surrounding Erin's face. 'I can sense his power growing, but it is unclear to me how he would have fooled your ship's DNA sensors.'

'But what about Sol?' Johnny asked, stepping between the Emperor and Erin's hologram. 'Can you heal her?'

'You're right – that is the matter in hand,' said Bram. 'I'm afraid my answer has to be "nearly".'

'Nearly? What does that mean?'

'It means she will have to revert to an earlier state . . . of consciousness. If we reconnected her with her current mindset, I do not believe I could stop her self-destructing. You mustn't feel bad about the action you took, Johnny. I see now it was the only way to save your ship's life.'

'So what *can* we do?' asked Johnny.

'If Sol's the good ship I think she is,' Bram replied, 'she will have built a mind cache.' In response to Johnny and Clara's questioning looks, he went on, 'snapshots of her being at previous points in time. This memory of Johnny . . . of Erin in the chair,' the Emperor corrected himself, 'has a date stamp. If we restore Sol to a point before then, she can recover, but it will be a great trauma and she will need looking after.'

'How do you mean?' asked Clara.

'Every second Sol senses vast quantities of information, processing and evaluating it and performing more calculations than there are atoms in the universe. She thinks deeply. When she recovers, there will be a discontinuity in the data – like a vast, ominous black hole she cannot ever enter.'

'It's got to be done,' said Johnny. 'I'll make it up to her and explain everything that's happened.'

'I know you will,' said Bram. 'Your ship is in good hands.'

'Where's the cache?' Johnny asked. 'Let's do it now.'

The Emperor turned to Clara. 'Sometimes folding *is* the only way.' Johnny's sister smiled again, but looked uncertain. Bram continued, 'Your Plican friend is the gatekeeper, but I trust it will let you pass.'

The smile on Clara's face broadened. 'That's brilliant,' she said, as the realization struck, before rushing over to the tank at the centre of the bridge. She placed her hands on the curved cylinder and closed her eyes. Next, the tank disappeared. In its place was nothing . . . and everything . . . at the same time. 'Welcome to hyperspace,' said Clara.

It might have been Johnny's imagination, but when his sister opened her eyes they looked as if they had many more silver flecks than normal. He hoped she could still see properly.

'Follow me,' she said, smiling and stepping into the nothing. She disappeared.

'Come,' said Bram, placing an arm around Johnny's shoulder and steering him into the void.

It was like looking at a world reflected in a shattered mirror, broken into a million fragments, set against a swirling backdrop of pink, purple and black. The Plican existed here and was huge. How stupid, Johnny thought to himself, to presume a creature that could fold space was confined to its little tank on the *Spirit of London*. Instead it protruded into all these other dimensions, myriad tentacles capable of manipulating every one – three of the arms were writhing towards Johnny, Clara and Bram.

'Don't be afraid,' said Clara, as one of the huge sucker-covered limbs wrapped itself around each of them and plucked them, not forward or backward, or left or right, or up or down, but in a different direction entirely. They were carried through just one of the dimensional fragments, a cone-shaped space that seemed to go on forever, yet folded back in on itself. There, spiralling through its heart was a beautiful, sparkling double-helix, built from the different mind states Sol had asked the Plican to store here. Johnny shivered, remembering what he had done the last time he had seen one of these glorious crystal snowflakes. The folder retracted its tentacles, releasing them.

'Come on,' said Clara. Seemingly without effort, she began to move towards the glittering structure, yet she remained in her original position. It was as if she was everywhere at once along the path she was taking.

Bram followed and exactly the same thing happened to him. Johnny had no choice but to push off from the nothing he was standing on and join the others in inspecting the stored minds. As Sol had aged, her different mind states had become bigger. The first caches were only the size of a pea, if size had any meaning here. The later ones, near the end of the spirals, were a metre or so across, more like the mind Johnny had forced himself to sever from the rest of the ship. In this place, Johnny could understand their structure, how they were folded in on themselves, dimension upon dimension, saving space yet still storing the vast sum of all Sol's experiences to date. Here, Johnny could follow and understand those dimensions perfectly. He could see the timeline of his ship's experiences – her memories – all the way to her near destruction. He picked out the spot before the reconstruction he'd just witnessed, back on the bridge in the regular universe. A tentacle from the Plican appeared from nowhere, wrapped itself around the particular crystal and detached it from the double-helix. It spoilt the symmetry, like having a tooth missing in a previously perfect mouth. The folder offered the glittering structure to Clara, but she shook her head before pointing in Johnny's direction, and it pressed the mind into his arms.

'Let's go home,' said Clara and Johnny found himself on the floor of the *Spirit of London*'s bridge, between Bram and Clara who'd stayed standing. The Plican's tank was back to normal, Clara's eyes were fading to blue and the mind Johnny had briefly carried had disappeared. He tried to move, but instantly waves of nausea washed over him and he began to be violently sick.

'Are you OK, Johnny?' Even in the midst of feeling absolutely dreadful, Johnny couldn't have been happier. It was Sol who had asked the question.

'Never better,' he replied, before throwing up again.

11 ☆

End of Term ☆☆

The solar system's defences were in place or on their way, meaning Bram could now leave for Alnitak. The *Calida Lucia* had spent the last fortnight putting her sister ship to the test in the form of gruelling space trials. The *Spirit of London* had responded magnificently and seemed completely back to normal, so the two Imperial vessels moved onto battle drills, flying side by side into the outer solar system, taking the opportunity to probe and test Alf's defence net for any signs of weakness. Johnny's ship's already powerful weapons had been upgraded so they would even be a match for the giant Andromedan Stardestroyers. He'd had to give up his five-a-side football pitch to make room for new machinery, but it seemed a small sacrifice considering. Reinforcements, in the shape of Captain Valdour's fleet, were gathering around Melania and due to leave within the next week.

Meanwhile, on Pluto Base, the little Tolimi had been busy. A huge cylinder now snaked across the surface of the dwarf planet. When he first saw it, Johnny assumed it was some sort of pipeline, but he quickly discovered it was the massive barrel of a nearly finished super gun, capable of accelerating projectiles to relativistic speeds and firing them at enemy ships. Johnny couldn't help but be impressed by how these aliens, used to living with three suns, were adapting to life with just one very distant one. Although the Sun was tiny in the sky it was still surprisingly bright, but couldn't provide the tropical conditions the Tolimi were used to, which meant the Emperor's gift of the *Calida Lucia*'s beach habitat, especially modelled on their home planet, went down especially well. To provide additional entertainment, Sol transmitted instructions on how to build televisions meaning Johnny was able to watch a football match with the aliens and explain what was happening. When a Tolimus asked Clara what was meant by offside, she beat a hasty retreat back to the beach.

Now, though, the fun was over and a new seriousness had gripped the *Spirit of London*. The Emperor stood tall, his eyes bright and earnest. 'I must search for Erin and Zeta – before the trail goes cold or they do any more damage,' said Bram, looking around the bridge, 'or fall into the wrong hands. And you . . . you must return to Earth.'

Johnny pulled a face – he hadn't forgotten the promise he'd made to himself to also go after Erin to avenge Sol.

'Your place is here,' said Bram. 'The net is closing – the Andromedans will come sooner rather than later. I have vowed to protect humanity in the coming conflict and need someone I can trust on the ground. But remember this – should anything happen before the fleet arrives, contact me by Cornicula Worm. Be patient if I am not in attendance – it will take a few days for any Andromedan fleet to assemble and it is inadvisable for you to return to Melania for the time being . . . given your last visit.'

'Of course, Your Majesty,' said Alf, taking his hat off and making a low bow.

Bram walked over and, in turn, hugged Clara and Alf – the android turned red as a traffic light. Next, he saluted Johnny, accompanied with the word 'captain' as though to emphasize there really was a war on, before turning and disappearing through a fold Clara was holding open.

From the bridge they watched the *Calida Lucia* break orbit

and pass in front of Pluto's giant moon, Charon, before space appeared to collapse in on itself and the Imperial Starcruiser vanished from sight. With such a massive spatial disturbance, the *Spirit of London* wouldn't be able to fold straight home. Instead, Johnny brought the dark energy drive online and set course for Earth.

✦ ✦ ✦
✦ ✦

It was December and the streets of London without a coat were far colder than the surface of Pluto from inside a spacesuit. Christmas shoppers, wrapped in woolly hats and scarves, scrambled to buy presents, oblivious to the fact that the wintry Sun shining above them might explode at any time. Johnny stood on the pavement as the world went by around him. He knew he had to return to the children's home to stay close to the Wormholes, even if it meant leaving Sol for a few days. The ship declared she would be fine, so long as Johnny didn't spend all his time sending messages through 'that annoying bundle of silicon, Kovac'. Johnny tried to put on a brave face in return. After weeks in space, it seemed even more unfair that Clara could remain aboard the *Spirit of London* and didn't even have to go to school.

Alf had insisted he take the *Bakerloo* to Castle Dudbury. The android had claimed it was important for Johnny to have a shuttle at his disposal, but Johnny suspected it was at least as much to do with not wanting Clara to fold space any more than necessary. Johnny had been thrilled to see Bram had placed an Imperial Starfighter in the shuttle bay, filling the hole left by the missing *Jubilee*. If only it had the same camouflage modes as the other shuttles he could have travelled to Halader House in that. As it was, he and Bentley flew invisibly, but rather more slowly, over the outskirts of the capital. As they left the city behind, patches of snow dotted the countryside and, by the time they reached Castle Dudbury, the ground below was a continuous band of white. Stepping from the shuttle, the snow crunched satisfyingly beneath Johnny's boots, as more flakes fell all around. Bentley was off straightaway, leaving a trail of muddy pawprints in his wake. Johnny chased after him, cornering his friend in front of a group of tightly packed cars. He dived on top of the Old English sheepdog, rolling Bentley over in a mock fight.

Then, just as Johnny began to get up, he was forced to duck down as a snowball flew a whisker over his head.

'Get 'im!' someone shouted from behind the cars, and a volley of missiles rained down. If it was Spencer Mitchell and his gang, Johnny wouldn't put it past them for their snowballs to have rocky cores – he was lucky they were such bad shots.

Johnny rolled out of the way of the incoming fire and propped his back against one of the vehicles as he made his own ammunition to fight back – even if the odds were against him, nothing beat a good snowball fight. Sadly, before he had chance to retaliate, Bentley had chased the rabble away.

Johnny gave the dog a half-hearted pat of thanks. On his feet again, holding a firmly compacted ball in each palm, he lobbed the left-hand snowball high into the air and then took aim with his right, scoring a direct hit high above his head. Then, with his numbing fingers, he picked up Bentley's lead, smiled grimly at the Old English sheepdog, took a deep breath and said, 'Here goes, Bents.'

The pair set off towards the corner of the carpark. Almost inevitably, as they reached the rear gate into the Halader House backyard, the last person in the world Johnny wanted to see happened to be standing beside the back door.

'Thought you'd got rid of that mutt, sonny,' said Mr Wilkins.

'Course not,' Johnny replied. He had no choice but to tie Bentley's lead to the snow-covered kennel near the gate, despite the sheepdog's unhappy whimpering. Johnny lifted his friend's shaggy fringe and looked into the different-coloured eyes. 'Sorry, Bents,' he whispered. 'Promise I'll get you soon as I can.'

Bentley pulled away and lay down in the snow, not even making use of the little shelter on offer.

'So long as it stays there I s'pose there's no harm,' said Mr Wilkins. 'Come on, sonny. You'll catch your death out here.' The cook took hold of Johnny's elbow and steered him through the doorway into the warmth of the children's home. This weird behaviour was compounded when the huge man added, 'You hungry then? I've got your favourite for supper.'

'You've cooked fish 'n chips?' Johnny asked, incredulous.

'Nah – roast beef and Yorkshire puddings,' replied the cook.

'OK . . .' said Johnny, thoroughly confused. 'Better go and get changed first.' He ducked out of Mr Wilkins's grasp and ran down the corridor before the cook could stop him.

✿ ✿ ✿
✿ ✿

Entering his bedroom felt less like coming home than ever and Johnny soon found himself longing for his quarters on the *Spirit of London*. Someone had taken all his space posters down and most of his favourite clothes had been thrown away. He knew he should probably go and find Miss Harutunian and make up a cover story for his latest absence, but right now he couldn't face lying to her again. Besides, judging from Mr Wilkins's strange behaviour, it was just possible he'd somehow managed not to be missed. Whatever, he didn't fancy the thought of going down to the dining room and eating with everyone else and was quite sure Mr Wilkins had to be lying about the Yorkshire puddings.

He'd have liked to have spoken some more with Bram, but there was no way he could right now as the Emperor had been going straight to Alnitak. Instead, he used the other Wormhole to speak briefly with Frago, one of the leaders of the Tolimi. Johnny promised to stay close by in case any ships were detected.

He sat back on the bed feeling hungry. Once he was sure dinner was in full swing, he crept downstairs and sneaked into the computer room to say a belated hello to Kovac. Eventually, he managed to get away and made the short walk to the nearby chippy. On the way back he collected a very cold and unhappy Bentley from the little kennel and, as soon as they were safely upstairs in the attic bedroom, tried to pacify him with a large portion of chips all to himself. The sheepdog soon stopped sulking and, after polishing off some of Johnny's fish as well, retired underneath Johnny's bed beside the radiator in front of the window.

Bentley's contented snores lifted Johnny's spirits. He ventured down to the common room, but no one seemed very interested in chatting to him and his arrival had the effect of emptying the entire place. A few weeks away and it felt as if he hadn't lived there for eleven and a half years. With nothing worth watching on the TV, he climbed the stairs all the way up to the top, pulled down the trapdoor with its 'no entry' sign screwed on and climbed into his room to prepare for school the next day. He really didn't want to go, but at least it was the very last day of term before the Christmas holidays. It would be good to catch up with his friends in the football team, before returning to check the two Wormholes.

✧ ✧ ✧
✧ ✧

Double chemistry was never one of Johnny's favourite subjects, but today was worse than ever. Alisha Leow was his chemistry partner solely because 'L' came next to 'M' in the alphabet and, on this particular morning, she kept moving her stool closer to his while Miss Hewitt at the front talked about potassium permanganate and swimming pools. Johnny edged his own stool away, but Alisha seemed to find this very funny and kept following. Then, when Miss Hewitt had her back turned and was writing a chemical formula on the whiteboard, a hand placed itself unexpectedly on Johnny's thigh. He yelped, jumped up and knocked over the Bunsen burner, which clattered to the floor.

'Whatever is going on, Jonathan?' asked Miss Hewitt sternly. 'Will you kindly stop messing around and start paying attention?'

'It wasn't my fault,' Johnny replied lamely. Alisha giggled.

'Well, if you and Alisha can't keep your hands off each other, I shall have to separate you. Come and sit next to David,' said the teacher, tapping the bench at the front, 'and you, Ashvin, can swap places.'

Red-faced but relieved, Johnny grabbed his schoolbag and set off to sit next to Dave Spedding at the front. When he reached there, it proved the opposite of Alisha. Dave moved his stool so far away that Johnny couldn't even whisper to him safely so, instead of catching up on what had been happening, he had to follow the lesson. When the bell went, Dave threw everything into his bag and rushed out of the door without even a backward glance. Johnny sat at his bench, slowly gathering up his own things. He'd hoped his best friend at school would have been pleased to see him, but the prolonged absences must be taking their toll.

'Chop chop, Jonathan. Haven't you got lessons to go to?'

'Yes, Miss . . . sorry,' Johnny replied. He stood up, hoisted his bag over his shoulder and was quite horrified to see Alisha standing in the doorway waiting for him. As he swiped his schoolcard, she scowled and folded her arms. Johnny tried to slip by to one side, but found his way blocked by a sixth former with messy hair.

'You Jonathan Mackintosh?' the boy asked.

'Who wants to know?' Johnny replied.

'Don't get clever with me – Headmistress's office . . . now.'

'What for?' Johnny asked.

'I don't know, do I?' replied the boy. 'Let's just hope it's something bad. Come on.' He steered Johnny through the crowded corridor away from Alisha, who looked furious to be left behind. Johnny managed an apologetic shrug in her direction.

It had probably been too much to hope that Kovac's manipulation of his attendance records would go unnoticed, but Johnny was disappointed to be summoned to see Mrs Devonshire on his first day back. He knew he should have had some sort of explanation prepared, but of course he hadn't and now he tried to think of one his mind simply blanked over. In no time at all, the sixth former was knocking on the door of the Headmistress's office.

'Come in,' said the dreaded voice from the other side.

Johnny's escort opened the door and said, 'Mackintosh for you, Headmistress.'

'Thank you, William,' replied Mrs Devonshire. 'That will be all.'

The door closed leaving Johnny standing in front of a large desk which was entirely free from clutter, save for a small leather briefcase on one end. Behind the desk sat Mrs Devonshire, wearing a very hairy purple jumper. Standing beside her, by a row of shiny new filing cabinets, was a tall balding man with round, steel-framed glasses, wearing a long white coat – Dr Carrington.

'Jonathan,' said Mrs Devonshire. 'Thank you for coming. Dr Carrington's here with the results of your medical. And to discuss your Personal Healthcare Plan.' Johnny must have looked confused, because the Headmistress added, 'It's a government initiative.'

'Right,' Johnny replied, composing himself. Although he'd missed his medical weeks ago, the doctor must be using some fake results as cover to arrange a meeting.

Dr Carrington was a mystery. As well as officially looking after Johnny's mum for years, he'd been the physician at the Proteus Institute for the Gifted, the Krun 'school' where Johnny had found Clara. But Johnny hadn't forgotten that, six months ago, when he and Clara were being held prisoner by Colonel Hartman and about to be placed on the dissection table, it was Dr Carrington who had engineered their escape. Still – that didn't mean Johnny had to start liking him.

'As I have just been reminded,' said Mrs Devonshire, 'health matters are confidential between you and the doctor, Jonathan. You can use my office – I'll be in the staffroom.' With that the Headmistress gathered some papers together, got up and left.

'Ah . . . we meet again, Jonathan . . . again,' said the doctor, taking a step towards Johnny, who took a matching one backwards, closer to the door. Dr Carrington stopped and raised both hands in the air. 'I'm not here to hurt you . . . no . . . not at all,' he continued. 'But to warn . . . yes . . . warn.'

'Warn me about what?' Johnny asked, now standing his ground.

'That stunt you pulled in New York. That was foolish . . . and risky . . . risky, yes. Don't do anything like that again.'

'It wasn't my fault,' Johnny found himself saying again. 'Anyway – how do you know about it?'

'It's my business to know,' snapped the doctor. 'Though the whole world knew something had happened . . . everyone. You made the evening news.'

'I couldn't help it,' said Johnny. 'It was your friends who started shooting.'

It was Johnny's turn to move towards the doctor, who

retreated, saying, 'They're no friends of mine – neither the Krun . . . nor the Corporation . . . the Corporation . . . no. I had hoped to have convinced you of that.'

'What's the Corporation?' Johnny asked, backing Dr Carrington into a corner.

'I . . . I . . . I didn't come here to talk about them.'

'You work for them . . . and the Krun.'

'I do what I have to . . . what's needed . . . yes,' said Dr Carrington, recovering his composure. 'But I'm on your side . . . yes, your side. Remember that.'

Johnny took pity on the nervous figure cringing in the corner and relented. 'OK,' he said. 'Truce . . . for now. And thanks for not landing me in it with Mrs Devonshire.'

'I . . . I don't follow,' replied the doctor.

'That stuff about the medical,' said Johnny. 'Thanks for not telling her I missed it.'

'But you didn't,' said the doctor, looking puzzled. 'What are you talking about?'

'I wasn't here,' said Johnny. 'I was . . . well let's just say I had to go away.' He might have called a truce, but wasn't about to tell Dr Carrington that he hadn't turned up because he was flying his spaceship to the capital of the galaxy.

'Interesting . . . very interesting,' said the doctor, taking a stethoscope from out of the small leather case on the desk and inserting the two pieces into his ears. He approached Johnny holding out the other end, but Johnny pushed it away.

'What are you doing?' Johnny asked. 'You're not examining me – I won't let you.'

'Relax . . . yes . . . relax,' said Dr Carrington. 'I just wondered if you'd had any more of these . . . these blackouts . . . losses of memory.'

'I haven't had any blackouts.'

'Are you sure?'

'Of course I'm sure,' said Johnny, very firmly, despite the sudden, awful doubt that had surfaced in his mind. He thought back to the reconstruction he'd witnessed on the *Spirit of London*'s bridge . . . when the figure who looked so absolutely like him had ordered the self-destruct. It couldn't have been him after all . . . could it?

'Well, you must have had at least one,' Dr Carrington replied. 'I came here several weeks ago . . . several weeks . . . when I warned you about keeping a low profile. And I performed a DNA test.'

'You did what?' shouted Johnny.

'And I need to do another – it's important . . . yes.'

'If I recall correctly, you did one before,' said Johnny, 'when me and Clara were your prisoners – at the Embassy. Or have *you* been having blackouts?'

'It's changed,' said the doctor, stepping forward and taking hold of Johnny with both hands. 'Minute differences . . . subtle mutations. So small no one else would have noticed.'

'DNA can't change . . . can it?' Johnny asked.

'Not normally . . . no . . . not at all,' said the doctor, letting go. 'But it might explain your blackouts. I *need* to do another test – a full examination.'

There was a knock on the door and it opened without any invitation. Into the room, wearing his shabby green sweatshirt, came Johnny's PE teacher and football coach, Mr Davenport. 'Found you. If you ever want to play for the team again, get changed now. Kickoff's in twenty minutes. Cup match.'

'What? OK . . .' said Johnny, moving towards the door.

'What about my examination?' shouted Dr Carrington.

'I told you,' Johnny replied. 'No more tests – I'm not your guinea pig.' Before the doctor could respond, Johnny had followed Mr Davenport out of the door. 'Sorry, coach – I didn't know there was a game today.'

'Look, Johnny . . . don't take this the wrong way, but you weren't exactly my first choice. It's just that with all our bad luck over injuries, I need some cover. Go and get changed and I'll see you out on the playing fields.'

Mr Davenport set off at a fast pace leaving Johnny alone in the corridor, bemused that his place in the team was threatened. He was definitely one of the best players, and last year had scored the winning goal in the County Cup Final. Still, there was no time to dwell on it. He ran in the other direction, hurrying to reach his locker, hoping his boots were in there – he was sure he'd not seen them at Halader House the night before. Thankfully the corridors were empty and Johnny soon arrived outside his empty form room. His luck continued when he opened the metal door – his best-case scenario had been that the boots would be there, but wrapped in a carrier bag at the bottom of his locker, probably covered in mud or mould or even both. Instead, by some miracle they sat neatly on the shelves, cleaned and even polished – he could smell the wax on them.

On the way to the playing fields, Johnny spoke to Clara on the wristcom, suggesting she come to watch the match with Bentley – the Old English sheepdog had always proved lucky in his unofficial role as Castle Dudbury Comprehensive School mascot. Clara might not be a football fan but, as it meant performing a couple of folds, she agreed straightaway.

Johnny reached the changing rooms just as the rest of the team were heading onto the pitch, psyched up and ready to go. Hanging forlornly on one peg was a single white shirt with the number 13 on the back. Johnny hated the thought of wearing it, not because it was unlucky – he didn't believe in that – but because it meant he must be a substitute.

He changed as quickly as he could, putting his school jumper on over his football shirt as he didn't have a tracksuit, and ran outside. The match was taking place on the very farthest pitch, close to the local rubbish tip. By the time Johnny had run all the way over, the game had already kicked off and he joined Mr Davenport and two other subs – boys from the year below – on the touchline. A smattering of other kids and parents who'd come to watch stood on the far side, with a trickle of other people making their way from out of the school buildings. Luckily, Clara was able to use the tip as cover for her fold. She and Bentley clambered up the slope beside the pitch and joined Johnny.

'How come you're not playing?' she asked.

Johnny shrugged his shoulders. 'Guess I've missed too much training,' he whispered.

'Amazed you're in the squad at all, blondie,' said one of the other subs who'd been near enough to overhear. 'You're useless.'

Johnny couldn't believe his ears. Watching the match take shape, he was desperate to get on the pitch sooner rather than later to prove the new boy wrong. From the look of things, he was certainly needed and it wasn't long before Castle Dudbury were a goal down. Micky Elliot, the regular captain and centre half, was off school ill. It meant their opponents, Stortford School, were able to slice through the home defence with ease and, when the goal came, keeper Simon Bakewell had no chance with the one-on-one.

From the touchline, Johnny could see the Castle Dudbury midfield weren't pressuring their opponents nearly enough, making it all too easy for the Stortford midfielders to play dangerous through balls to their strikers. Johnny didn't want anything bad to happen to his own team, but when Naresh Choudhary (playing in Johnny's preferred position in central midfield) twisted his ankle, he thought it might have been for the best. Mr Davenport ran straight over, carrying a yellow bucket with icy cold water sloshing over the sides and from which he produced his 'magic' sponge. Even that didn't seem to be helping and the coach shouted, 'Get warmed up,' to the touchline.

Johnny started with a few stretches, before skipping along the side of the pitch, with Bentley running alongside him. He pulled his jumper over his head as Mr Davenport helped Naresh hobble off the pitch, but the coach looked to the cheeky new boy and said, 'On you go, Owen. More pressure on the ball.'

The boy nodded to the coach, but whispered, 'Loser!' to Johnny as he ran past him onto the field of play.

Johnny put his jumper back on and walked down the line to where Clara and Bentley were standing. With no tracksuit bottoms his thighs were numb with cold and he looked enviously at his sister's woolly hat and mittens. 'I should be out there,' said Johnny, shivering.

'Come on,' said Clara. 'You're not exactly a regular at school at the moment.'

'I go more than you,' said Johnny. He knew it was unfair to pick on his sister, but it was even more unfair that he was standing on the touchline freezing to death and not playing.

'Johnny!' shouted Mr Davenport. 'Get back here and concentrate on the game.'

'Such a shame I don't have teachers yelling at me all the time,' Clara said after him as Johnny trudged away up the touchline to rejoin his coach, Naresh and the other sub. As he went, Stortford scored again. This time it was Simon's fault in goal, but that didn't stop him berating his defence. There was no leadership or team spirit. At least it wasn't too much longer before the referee blew for half-time and the white-shirted Castle Dudbury players trudged, silently with heads bowed, across to Mr Davenport.

The coach was rummaging through his sports bag looking

for something, clearly without much success. As the players began to arrive he turned to Johnny and said, 'I've forgotten the oranges. Run back to the changing rooms and get them will you? Should be in the kit bag.'

'Why me?' asked Johnny, who rather thought the other sub from the year below was a much more obvious candidate. He struggled to physically speak the words – it was so cold his lips were beginning to freeze up.

'Because I said so,' replied the coach. 'Get going.'

Owen winked at Johnny, who gritted his teeth and began the long jog back towards the changing rooms. 'Faster, Johnny!' Mr Davenport shouted after him and Johnny heard the rest of the team laughing as he picked up the pace.

It took an age for Johnny to find Mr Davenport's other bag and, when he did, there were no orange segments. At least there was a tub of petroleum jelly – Johnny smeared a handful over his face to keep it warm enough for him to be able to shout in the second half. Someone would have to take charge on the field. The oranges turned out to be in the small kitchen area nearby. Johnny flung them into a plastic tub and ran back out into the cold. By the time he reached the huddle on the touchline, half-time was almost over. Johnny held the container out into the semicircle and greedy hands reached in to grab the segments, leaving none for the subs.

'Ash – I'm taking you off,' said Mr Davenport. 'You should be happy – all half you looked like this football pitch was the last place you wanted to be.'

'Whatever,' Ashvin Gupta replied.

Johnny was disappointed – he normally linked up really well when the two of them played together in midfield. He was even more disappointed, though, when the coach turned to the other sub and said, 'Carlton – this is your chance. Don't disappoint me.' Next, Mr Davenport picked up the matchball and held it out in front of the team. 'You seem to have forgotten this is your friend,' he said sternly. 'Look after it, want to be with it and, whatever you do, *don't* keep giving it away.'

'Yes, coach,' mumbled the team, not sounding very convinced.

The referee blew his whistle and shouted, 'Let's get going.'

The semicircle broke and the Castle Dudbury players jogged listlessly onto the pitch to take up their positions. Johnny looked round to commiserate with Ashvin, only to see him already halfway towards the changing rooms, kicking an empty tin can with plenty of venom as he went.

The second half didn't begin much better than the first had ended, but Simon partly redeemed himself with a string of fine saves. Johnny hated to admit it, but the only other player doing anything like a decent job was Owen from the year below, who looked as if he could be quite useful. Dave Spedding was the stand-in skipper, but was being just as quiet as in the chemistry lesson earlier in the day. Johnny started to warm up again, hoping Mr Davenport would take the hint, but the coach showed no sign of wanting to make his last remaining substitution.

Twenty minutes into the second half, his chance finally came. Owen and Ian Marden jumped for the same ball, but neither of them called. There was a sickening crack as their heads came together, leaving both of them lying on the ground. Owen rolled around for a while before getting up, while Ian just lay near the centre circle, totally dazed. Johnny ran straight over with Mr Davenport as soon as it happened, but it was fully five minutes before it became clear it was safe to carry Ian off the pitch.

Johnny whisked his jumper off, threw it over the touchline, and ran back onto the field of play, immediately incurring the displeasure of the referee, who ordered him to remove his locket and the wristcom. Reluctantly, he took them over to Clara and then had to wait a while before he was finally allowed to return. Once the ref eventually waved him on, he struggled to pick up the pace of the game – he'd been so worried about Ian, he hadn't had time to warm up properly and his muscles tightened as soon as he tried to sprint. What made it worse was that no one on his own team seemed to want to pass the ball to him. He was stuck out on the left wing, which was where Ian played, but everything was going down the right-hand side instead. When he finally got to touch the ball it was only because the Stortford right back smashed it straight into his face.

☆ ☆ ☆
☆ ☆

Johnny was lying on a patch of rock-hard ground while someone wiped his face with icy cold water. It took a few moments for him to remember where he was – then he recognized Mr Davenport's silhouette leaning over him. The thing in his teacher's hand – a yellow sponge – was slowly turning red.

'Just a slight nosebleed,' said the coach. 'But if you want to come off . . .'

'Course not,' Johnny cut in. 'I'll be fine.' He stood up and, for a second, his surroundings seemed to blur, but he knew he had to hang on. He touched his nose. It hurt, but not as badly as after the encounter with Nicky. Zeta had done a good job on it.

'Sure you're OK, son?' asked the ref, as he pressed a button on his stopwatch.

Johnny nodded and the game restarted. If no one was going to pass him the ball, he decided he'd just have to go and get it himself – he didn't have to wait long for the chance. Joe Pennant played a one-two with Dave, but ran into trouble, a couple of defenders converging on him. Johnny was the obvious outlet, but when the ball didn't come he joined the opposition in what became a four-way fight for the ball and, after several ricochets, emerged victorious. Finally, with the football at his feet, he could forget about the cold or his nose or having been sub, or even the fact that the Sun could soon explode, and he started running. With a clever stepover he beat his fullback on the outside and put in a left-footed hanging cross, which was headed behind for a corner.

Johnny ran down the small slope to collect the ball. When he climbed back, Owen was waiting by the corner flag to take the kick. Johnny held onto the ball and said, 'Late run to the far post – Dave's going to flick it on for you.'

Owen stood his ground.

'Listen,' said Johnny. 'Micky's not playing – you've got to take his place.'

'It's your own time you're wasting,' said the referee before jogging into position and, reluctantly, Owen turned and ran into the penalty area. Johnny placed the ball carefully in the 'D' by the flag. Then he picked it up again, turned it through his fingers and put it back down.

'Get on with it,' shouted the referee.

Johnny took four paces back and looked up. Dave and Joe were in their right positions, close to each other near the penalty spot. Owen was looking disinterested on the edge of the area – Johnny hoped it was a ruse. He stepped forward and struck the ball hard, so it flew flat at head height. Joe blocked off Dave's marker, allowing the stand-in skipper to reach the near post unopposed and flick the ball on. It sailed over the keeper, as though in slow motion, before Owen arrived with a spectacular diving header at the back stick, powering the ball into the net.

The other Castle Dudbury players up for the corner chased after Owen who ran to the halfway line with both arms in the air, as if he'd just scored the winner in the Champions League Final. It seemed just a little excessive, thought Johnny, as with less than five minutes to go they were still a goal down. He collected the ball from the net and carried it quickly with him to the halfway line.

No one congratulated Johnny on a great corner, but the next time Joe Pennant won the ball he played it straight out to the left wing. Johnny ran at his defender, who backed away. Johnny did a stepover to the right, as before, but followed with another to the left and then cut inside the fullback on the corner of the penalty area. Desperate to tackle Johnny, the Stortford boy stretched out his leg, but he wasn't quick enough and the ball had long gone. Johnny was sent tumbling a metre inside the box. As he was falling, he could already hear the whistle blowing. It was a penalty.

As Johnny lay on the ground he saw Owen run for the ball, picking it up and placing it on the spot. Johnny had always been the designated penalty taker and went across, but Owen said, 'This one's mine, blondie – everyone knows you can't hit a barn door.'

Before Johnny could respond, Dave Spedding picked the ball up and handed it to Johnny. 'You won it – it's your penalty,' he said. It was the first time he'd spoken to Johnny all day.

'Get on with it or no one'll take it,' said the referee. 'Time's up already – this is the last kick.'

'I'm ready,' said Johnny, walking to the penalty spot and putting the ball down.

'No pressure,' said Owen, as he walked out of the area.

Johnny ignored him. He took four paces straight backwards so he was in line with the ball and the goalkeeper. With that run-up, if the goalie was any good Johnny hoped he'd think he was going to strike to the keeper's right. Focusing on the back of the ball, he pictured exactly what he was going to do – whatever happened he knew he mustn't change his mind.

He could hear voices in the background, several people shouting 'come on, Johnny,' including Clara and then, strangely, one that sounded like Alisha Leow. That was mad as he knew she wouldn't be seen dead watching a football match. Johnny shut out the noise, took a deep breath and ran forwards. He struck the ball as hard as he could, but with the outside of his foot. As hoped, the goalie dived the wrong way, but even if he hadn't he'd never have saved it. The ball struck the net high up, just inside the post. Johnny sank to his knees as three blasts came on the whistle and the next thing he knew it felt as if the whole team had dived on top of him.

It was a while before the scrum pressing down on him lifted and Johnny was finally able to breathe. Everyone was smiling and taking turns to say they'd never seen a better penalty, and when Mr Davenport saw Clara coming over with Bentley he said, 'First time we've had our mascot for a while, Johnny. Just make sure he's there for the replay.'

Some of the other kids in Johnny's year were on the pitch celebrating with the team. Clara handed over Johnny's locket, which he slipped over his head – as soon as he did he felt a little warmer – and his wristcom, which he strapped into place, the red lights clearly visible.

'Good goal,' she said, smiling broadly. 'Probably not offside.'

Before Johnny could respond an icy voice behind him said, 'Who's she?' Johnny turned round to come face to face with Alisha.

'What? Er . . . hi Alisha,' he mumbled.

'Don't you "Hi Alisha" me,' she shouted, sounding absolutely furious.

Johnny could sense his team mates backing away.

'I'm sorry,' he said. 'I don't . . .'

'Oh you're sorry, are you?' Alisha interrupted. 'You don't know the meaning of the word – yet.' With that she marched past Johnny, stopped to look Clara up and down, giving her an evil stare, before continuing on towards the school buildings without a backwards glance.

'What was that about?' Clara asked.

'I have absolutely no idea,' Johnny replied.

With Bentley wagging his tail by their side, they started walking slowly towards the changing rooms, not wanting to overtake Alisha who'd been joined by a few of her girlfriends. Johnny was partway through telling Clara about his strange meeting with Dr Carrington when she whirled round, pointing at two figures, one much taller than the other, silhouetted against the setting sun at the very end of the playing fields.

'Is that Bugface?' she asked, suddenly serious.

Johnny squinted into the bright light. They were too far away to make out clearly and, at that moment, turned and walked down the slope and out of sight. 'Stevens? Can't be . . . can it?' he said hopefully. 'I've never seen a short Krun – it must have been a dad with his son, come to watch the match.'

'Maybe you're right,' said Clara, but she stayed staring across towards the tip.

'Come on,' said Johnny. 'I'm freezing.' He resumed the walk to the changing rooms and, after a couple of seconds, Clara followed.

12 ✢

The Christmas Surprise ✢

It was only nine o'clock at night, but an exhausted, fully clothed Johnny lay on his bed in the attic room of Halader House, with Bentley curled across his feet. The curtains intended to cover the large, dormer window were open, allowing the stars to shine down from out of a clear, moonless sky. Bram had only been gone a couple of days, but Johnny wished Captain Valdour would hurry up with the promised reinforcements. Of course he knew his friend would never let him down and coordinating a lot of ships so they unfolded in the same place was a difficult task, but he'd feel much happier with an Imperial fleet patrolling the solar system. Johnny gazed at the stars while absentmindedly reaching to rub his Old English sheepdog under the collar. At least it was the holidays – it was nearly Christmas – and Johnny looked to have gotten away with all his various absences from school and the children's home over the last few months. If he could have thought of anything suitable, he'd give it to Kovac as an extra special Christmas and thank you present rolled into one, but the quantum computer wasn't the sort of thing it was easy to buy for.

With the solar system defence net reassuringly silent, Valdour's absence and Dr Carrington's odd claims were the only clouds on the horizon, but after the game and spending so much time outside in the cold, fresh air, Johnny was far too tired to think about them now. It could wait till tomorrow, when

Johnny had decided he was off to the *Spirit of London*. Without school, uniforms and homework, it would be much easier to pretend he was simply away from Halader House during the day having fun. By showing his face briefly in the common room and messing up his bed to make it look slept in, no one would know he was actually living elsewhere. Of course he'd return for regular chats with the Tolimi and try Bram at the same time (and have Sol scan every frequency for a message from *Cheybora*). He was also planning a few upgrades to his bedroom that meant the Wormholes would not be left unattended.

Orion the Hunter took pride of place in tonight's sky. Its two brightest stars, Rigel and Betelgeuse, marked the foot and the head, but Johnny was drawn more to the constellation's centre. The left-most star of the three forming the belt was Alnitak, whose fifteenth planet, Novolis, was home to Erin and Zeta. As soon as the Sun and Earth were out of danger, Johnny promised himself he'd go after the brother and sister pair. Briefly, he wondered where in the galaxy the *Falling Star* might have reached and if Bram had caught up with them.

His wristcom filled the bedroom with a faint red glow – Johnny couldn't remember the last time the lights were green. It seemed as though his brother was losing the fight against the nameless being from Andromeda that enslaved him. Johnny opened the locket, swinging from around his neck. There, standing in a line that had never actually existed, were Nicky, himself and Clara. When he'd first acquired the locket, it looked as though his brother's face was simply in shadow. Now he realized Nicky was hiding the mask that covered nearly half of his face – as though he were ashamed of it.

Johnny had always been more interested in the pictures of his family than the locket itself. Now he'd found out a little more about his mum, he wondered where the beautiful object she'd given him came from. Was it forged in Lysentia? Might she even have made it herself? If she'd created the Fountain of Time, it seemed she could do almost anything. Knowing that to be true led him once more to the question he couldn't avoid – why had she not saved herself and her family that fateful night the Krun came and ripped Johnny's life apart, almost before it had begun?

Footsteps were clanging up the spiral staircase – Johnny slipped the locket under his shirt as someone rapped on the trapdoor. It was pulled down and in climbed Miss Harutunian, armed with a steaming mug of hot chocolate and some toasted marshmallows. There was no time to hide Bentley under the bed, but Johnny hoped she wouldn't tell him off.

'Bentley!' shouted the social worker, putting the food and drink down on the bedside table and fussing over the Old English sheepdog. 'I haven't seen you for, like, ever,' she continued.

Relieved, Johnny said, 'Hi,' as he slid his legs over the side of the bed and sat up, helping himself to a marshmallow – straightaway it started to melt on his tongue.

'Thought I'd come and ask how the last day of term went,' said Miss Harutunian. 'Haven't seen you in the common room lately – I hope you're not avoiding me.'

'No, absolutely not,' said Johnny, his mouth still full. 'Thanks, by the way,' he added as he sipped from the mug by his bedside. 'I was there yesterday. I'm just tired from football – we had a match this afternoon.'

'You're back on the team? That's great news.'

'I scored with the last kick,' said Johnny. 'It was a penalty, but I won that too.'

'I'm really pleased,' said the social worker. 'And no more trouble at school?'

'No, all fine,' Johnny replied, crossing his fingers underneath the marshmallow plate in the hope Mrs Devonshire wouldn't return to Halader House any time soon to question his disappearances. 'Can Bentley have one of these?' he asked, eager to change the subject.

'If it's just one,' Miss Harutunian replied. 'It's good you're getting on so much better with Gilbey, too,' she went on, adding, 'Mr Wilkins,' when she saw the lack of comprehension on Johnny's face.

He had to try very hard to suppress a snort. It was incredible the cook had lasted so long at Halader House without his ridiculous first name being exposed. 'Yeah, much better,' Johnny replied, a whisker away from bursting out laughing. He supposed that managing to walk a little way down the corridor alongside the huge bearded man without being beaten, shouted at or taken to see the Manager had to count as some sort of improvement.

'Excellent,' said the social worker. 'Well, I also came to tell you that, now it's the holidays I've got to go home – just for a few days. New York . . .'

'New York,' Johnny repeated, not meeting Miss Harutunian's eyes.

'You promise to behave yourself when I'm gone?'

'Cross my heart,' said Johnny. This time he could meet her gaze as he absolutely meant it.

She seemed to believe him. 'OK then. I'll see you in a couple of weeks,' she said, walking over to the trapdoor.

'So long,' said Johnny, remembering what Miss Harutunian had told him about American goodbyes.

'So long, Johnny,' replied the social worker, before making her way a little unsteadily down the stairs.

Johnny finished off the marshmallows, splitting them half and half with Bentley, before getting ready for bed. The last thing he remembered seeing before drifting off into a deep sleep was the left-most star of Orion's belt – Alnitak.

A door opened and light flooded into a darkened corridor, revealing endless other doors of different shapes and sizes as far as Johnny could see. Zeta stood in the entrance. 'What are you doing out here?' she asked. 'Come.' She took Johnny's hand and pulled him through the opening. The next moment, Johnny and the purple-haired alien were sitting on a soft, spongy plant right by a seashore. In front of them, the vast disc of a blue giant star, far larger than Earth's Sun, was sinking into the ocean. A band of turquoise stretched all the way from the horizon to where the waves lapped over their feet. Zeta only had four toes on each.

The air behind buzzed and, when Johnny turned, he saw little flashes of red light, suspended above strange plants with large triangular greeny-blue leaves. A long forked tongue shot from beside him, aimed at one of the flashes, before retracting into Zeta's mouth. Smiling, she picked a bulbous, beetle-like creature from between her teeth and offered it to Johnny.

'Try it,' she said. 'Here on Novolis, Phosphoric Sulaflies are a delicacy.'

'Er . . . no thanks,' Johnny replied.

Alnitak was setting very quickly, making Johnny think they must be near the equator, or that the planet rotated especially fast. In the evening twilight, stars were beginning to twinkle in a pink, near cloudless sky. As he looked a little longer he could make out an almost perfect hexagon above them.

'Erin's stars,' said Johnny.

Zeta nodded. 'He didn't mean any harm – it's important you know that.'

'Not much,' Johnny replied angrily, moving a little away from the alien girl. 'He sabotaged my ship.'

'He was desperate to get away.'

'His mistake,' said Johnny. 'No one messes with Sol.'

'The Emperor was coming. You said so yourself. We couldn't let him find us – we had to continue our quest. Everything depends on it.'

'Was it worth destroying my ship at the same time? And me and my friends with it?'

'You see that cross?' asked Zeta, pointing to a triangle of bright stars near the horizon, with an especially bright fourth one lower down, only just above the ocean.

Johnny nodded.

'Those are my sign,' she went on, 'my Starmark.' She rolled up her trousers to confirm a matching pattern of dark scales along her otherwise pale leg. 'I swear on my stars that neither I nor Erin were responsible for the self-destruct sequence.'

'Yeah, right,' said Johnny.

'I know it was wrong to force the takeoff – to head for Novolis. I've told Erin that, but he has sworn he didn't try to destroy your ship.'

Everything was fading, becoming darker.

'You have to believe me, Johnny. It's important,' said Zeta.

Johnny made to stand up, but Zeta placed an arm across his legs to keep him sitting beside her.

They were back in the corridor.

'Johnny!'

He awoke with Zeta's disembodied cry still ringing in his ears. For a moment, Johnny couldn't work out what was happening, but then he realized the pressure on his legs was only Bentley, and that he'd been dreaming, asleep in his bed at Halader House. Through the window Alnitak, which a moment ago had seemed so close, was no longer visible. Orion was out of sight. Johnny tried to remember his dream, but it began slipping away, like water running through his fingers. He turned over and, moments later, was sound asleep. When he woke up the next morning, he'd forgotten all about it.

After fixing up some new equipment in his bedroom, Johnny was late for breakfast. All the bacon sandwiches had gone, so he had to allow Mr Wilkins to pour a large helping of runny grey porridge into his bowl. Johnny thought he'd get his own back by saying, 'Thanks, Gilbey,' rather loudly – he couldn't resist it – but the joke fell a bit flat when the bearded cook simply replied, 'No problem, Jonathan.' Worse, Spencer Mitchell and the rest moved their trays to ensure there was no room for Johnny at the older kids' table so he had to sit with the others. Clearly it didn't pay to be on first name terms with the massive chef.

With Mr Wilkins's beady black eyes fixed on him, Johnny did his best to force his way through the watery grey sludge in his bowl. Never having eaten salted cardboard after it had been soaked in lukewarm dishwater for several days he couldn't be sure, but Johnny suspected this would be how it tasted – and what it looked like. Finally, the cook turned his back to do something in the kitchen and in a flash Johnny swapped his almost full bowl with an empty one sitting on an unattended tray nearby. As Mr Wilkins looked round, Johnny pretended to savour a final spoonful before licking his lips and pushing the bowl away from him. Then he stood up and slipped out of the door before he could be ordered back to do the washing up.

He willed the lock to open on the next door along the corridor and heard the satisfying click well before he reached for the handle. Inside the Halader House computer room, Johnny walked over to the master terminal and switched it on.

'About time,' said Kovac. 'I was wondering when you might deign to come and actually talk to me.'

'Listen – I've been busy,' Johnny replied.

'You think I don't know what you've been up to? It was you who tasked me with monitoring your records. I can only imagine you've come in here to marvel at how a machine with a brain as immense as mine could survive a task that was quite so boring.'

'Well, I've got just the thing to interest you,' said Johnny hopefully.

'I doubt it – you'd have to go a long way to interest me,' the computer replied.

'I'm talking seriously further than even you can imagine,' said Johnny. 'I want you to monitor transmissions from Pluto Base and, if that's not far enough, Melania – that's near the centre of the galaxy. We could have to respond at a moment's notice.'

'May I remind you that the centre of the galaxy is 27,182.28 light years away . . . approximately. Even someone with a brain the size of yours must realize that any communication will have originated more than 27,000 years ago – it's hardly likely to be urgent. You also appear to have forgotten that messages to and from Pluto take several hours.'

'Ah . . . that's where you're wrong,' said Johnny, smiling. 'But if you're not interested in what happens on the galactic capital . . .'

'I didn't say I wasn't interested,' the quantum computer replied. 'I was merely pointing out potential problems with your request that you may not be aware of.'

'What you're clearly not aware of,' said Johnny, 'is that my bedroom upstairs contains the end points of two trans-dimensional Wormholes that link directly – and instantaneously – to both places.'

'Instantaneously?' Kovac asked.

'I've placed wireless transmitters at the openings of both,' said Johnny. 'Perhaps you could use these to study them?'

'Intriguing . . . but why?' asked the quantum computer. 'Where will you be when I'm "monitoring transmissions"?'

'On the *Spirit of London*,' Johnny replied. 'It's Christmas.'

'Ah yes. By my understanding, which is clearly limited in some areas, Christmas is traditionally a time spent with family and friends.'

'I guess so,' said Johnny, wondering where this was leading.

'Yet you're abandoning me and spending it with that jumped-up spaceship.'

'That jumped-up spaceship designed your quantum processor,' said Johnny. 'You wouldn't exist without her.'

'You call this existence?' said Kovac.

The room fell silent – Johnny didn't know what to say. Breakfast must have finished as there were voices in the corridor outside. Someone tried the door handle, but found it locked.

'Take me with you,' said Kovac, changing tack.

'What?'

'Take me with you. I'm . . . I'm lonely. Stuck here in this children's home with no one to talk to.'

Johnny was amazed to be hearing this, but knew a little of how the computer felt. 'I'm sorry,' he said. 'I didn't realize.'

'So you will? My very own Christmas holiday . . .'

'I can't,' said Johnny, hating himself. 'You're not exactly portable, are you?'

'One plastic box is much the same as another,' said Kovac. 'We could soon remedy that.'

'Who'd monitor the signals?' said Johnny. 'That's so important.'

'After everything I've done for you,' said Kovac. 'Bringing you out of New York – your precious spaceship couldn't have done that.'

'And I'm glad you did . . . but it doesn't change anything,' said Johnny. There was no reply – he wasn't used to silence from Kovac. 'Look – study the Wormholes. If there's a way you can find to check on them remotely then . . .'

'You promise?' Kovac asked.

'Maybe,' Johnny replied.

☆ ☆ ☆
☆ ☆

The conversation with Kovac stayed with Johnny until he and Bentley entered the revolving doors at the foot of the *Spirit of London*. There in front of them was the three metre high statue of the silver alien, bedecked in tinsel and wearing a santa hat. Clara told Johnny she was in the ship's garden, so they took the lifts straight to deck 18. As soon as they stepped out, the smell of fresh baking hit Johnny and, despite his shouts, Bentley shot ahead, following his nose to a large pine tree with Clara at its base and Alf some way up. The android was floating in an antigrav harness, and both of them were hanging different-shaped, golden brown ornaments on the tree's branches.

Clara offered Bentley one of them still in her hand, which he promptly began to eat. Then, clearly delighted, the Old English sheepdog rolled onto his back holding his paws in the air, hoping for a tummy rub. It was almost impossible not to succumb and, by the time Johnny reached the base of the tree, Bentley was giving Johnny's sister a little thank you kiss.

'Miss Clara,' shouted Alf from several metres up. 'We will never finish if you keep allowing yourself to be interrupted.'

'Don't be silly,' she said, looking up at the android hovering in mid-air. 'You know very well you don't need me – you and the drones could do it more quickly and I'm definitely not helping up there. There's no point doing something if you can't enjoy it.'

'You mean like me having to go to school,' said Johnny.

Clara jumped and looked across. 'Well, you're on holiday now,' she said a little sheepishly, 'so let's have some fun.'

'OK – I'll start by having one of these,' said Johnny, taking a snowman-shaped biscuit from Clara's hand and, before she could protest, biting its head off. 'It's all right for you,' he mumbled through a mouthful of beautiful buttery crumbs. 'I had Mr Wilkins's porridge for breakfast.'

✵ ✵ ✵
✵ ✵

After a day spent decorating the *Spirit of London*, the ship looked more Christmassy than Santa's grotto. As well as streamers everywhere and snow paintings on the windows, the corridors and larger decks had been hung with copies of the illuminated Oxford and Regent Street decorations that Clara had apparently taken Alf to see the night before. It was the garden, though, that was the centrepiece. Sol had somehow made it snow without it becoming too cold for the plants, so everything was covered in several centimetres of crisp white carpet that miraculously wasn't melting. Finally, floating unaided directly above the decorated pine tree, shone a single, bright, beautiful, miniature star.

As the day wore on, Alf went to the galley to prepare supper. Bentley had worn himself out rolling around in the warm snow and was now snoring peacefully underneath a nearby oak tree. Conscious that he had to pretend to be spending his evenings out in Essex, Johnny asked Clara to fold him quickly to Castle Dudbury – there was still no sign of Captain Valdour's fleet, so he wanted to see if Kovac had heard anything. She was delighted to agree and seconds later an archway appeared that led directly into the attic of the children's home.

The immaculate bedroom was nearly unrecognizable. The unmade bed he'd left that morning had been stripped and replaced with freshly laundered, perfectly ironed sheets. His mud-spattered football boots from the match had been cleaned – and polished – and placed neatly in the corner of the room. There wasn't a hint of dust anywhere and the cardboard box containing the few mementos Johnny had of their parents, normally tucked under his bed, was poking out of the wastepaper bin in the far corner. That was too much. Johnny rescued it and placed it on a shelf inside the wardrobe.

'You're sure this is your bedroom?' asked Clara. Over the months she'd grown used to his messy quarters aboard the *Spirit of London*.

'It's weird,' Johnny agreed. 'I promise it's not normally like this.'

Clara lifted the trapdoor, keen to have a look around the whole children's home, but Johnny stopped her. It was too risky – if she were spotted, they'd have some difficult questions to answer. Instead, he asked her to make the room appear 'lived in' while he showed his face downstairs and caught up with Kovac.

He needn't have worried – Clara could have come. The children's home was almost deserted with just a couple of younger boys in the common room, making the most of everyone being away by sitting on the best sofa right in front of the TV. Johnny said hi to make sure they'd noticed him in case anyone asked, and then went down the corridor into the computer room.

Even Kovac couldn't pretend to be bored by his examination of the Cornicula Wormholes. He'd received a message from Pluto Base, but nothing from the centre of the galaxy. Captain Valdour's continued non-appearance was becoming a little disturbing.

The quantum computer had also printed off the blueprints for a device he claimed would let him monitor them from any Earth-based location, if it were possible to build it. Weighed down by the large pile of paper, Johnny climbed his spiral staircase, opened the trapdoor and entered his impressively messy bedroom to find it deserted.

'Clara?' he whispered, looking round as he pulled the trapdoor closed. Sheets were now hanging off the bed so he had to get down on his knees to look underneath – no one was there.

He tried the wristcom. 'Clara – where are you?' and from behind he heard the creak of the wardrobe door opening.

'I wasn't sure it was you,' whispered his sister, parting some hanging shirts to show her face.

'Who else would be it be?' Johnny whispered back, not clear why he was keeping his voice down. The next moment though, footsteps clanged on the foot of the wrought-iron staircase. Johnny looked at his sister, whose fearful eyes met his. Her hands reached out and yanked him into the wardrobe, before pulling the door to just as the trapdoor opened.

'It's only you who mustn't be seen,' whispered Johnny.

Clara elbowed him in the ribs to shut him up while, outside in the room, somebody let out a long sigh. Of course Johnny could simply open the door, but having whoever was in his room tell the rest of the children's home that they found him hiding inside his own wardrobe didn't bear thinking about. The intruder must have gone straight to the hifi on top of Johnny's chest of drawers, because the room was instantly filled with very loud, extremely dull, classical music. Next, the person in the room began a one-way conversation, presumably on a mobile phone, but the music was so loud Johnny couldn't hear what was being said. Something about the voice sounded familiar, but he couldn't put his finger on it. The call ended and, from the noises filtering into the wardrobe, it sounded as though whoever they were was now tidying up. Johnny was pleased to still be holding the pile of papers, or they might have ended up in the bin. Moving them to underneath one arm, he very carefully opened the door just a sliver to try and see who was there – and cringed as the hinges creaked. The mystery intruder was out of sight, but then some fingers curled around the inside of the door and began to pull it open. Johnny felt as if his heart had stopped beating, but then his arm was grabbed and the next thing he knew he was lying in the snow on deck 18 of the *Spirit of London*, with Clara beside him and Bentley lolloping over to say hello.

'Thanks,' said Johnny. 'Though I wish I'd seen who was in my room.'

'It was probably just a cleaner,' said Clara, laughing nervously.

Johnny rather thought she was showing her ignorance of children's homes, but he laughed too, relieved at not being discovered.

'And you know what?' his sister added.

'What?'

'Tomorrow's Christmas Eve. For once let's forget everything and have some fun – I can't wait for everyone to see what I've bought them.'

Johnny felt himself turn even paler than normal. In one fell swoop all thoughts of the mysterious bedroom invader and even Captain Valdour's absence were instantly dismissed. Much more important was that he had only a day to buy Christmas presents for everyone on board.

☆ ☆ ☆
☆ ☆

First thing the next morning, Johnny presented Sol with Kovac's blueprints for making the quantum computer portable. He could tell the ship didn't think much of the idea, but to her credit Sol set about manufacturing the device. Meanwhile, Johnny ransacked his quarters trying – and failing – to find where he'd put his money. Somewhere he knew he had about thirty pounds. He lifted the same piles of clothes and magazines over and over again, moving them from one spot to another, but there was simply no sign.

To make matters worse, in the snow-covered garden Clara and Alf had placed a selection of intriguing and beautifully wrapped presents under the branches of the fir tree, while some of Sol's repair drones had built a magnificent snowman and were now in the process of carving a circular dining table and matching curved benches from an enormous and curiously non-melting block of ice, on which tomorrow's dinner would be served.

Sol told Johnny that Kovac's carrying case had been finished, with a little help from Clara, so he took the lift to the engineering deck where it was waiting, all the time wondering how he was going to buy anyone anything for Christmas.

'A present for Kovac,' said Clara, as she held out a clear container into which Kovac's casing could be slipped, before the open end was folded over and sealed shut. 'It looks like a smaller rectangle inside a bigger one,' she said, which was exactly what Johnny thought, until she added, 'but this is simply the three-dimensional shadow of the four-dimensional container,' which hadn't occurred to him at all. 'It means Kovac can be here, on board, but also there, in Halader House, at the same time – it's brilliant.'

'I'll take your word for it,' he said, picking up the box and inserting a regular PC which Sol had handily supplied as a replacement.

The only hope was that he'd left his money at Halader House so he went directly to the foot of the ship and out through the revolving doors, across the deserted little square, up a few steps and into the waiting *Bakerloo*. In no time at all, the shuttle was coming to a halt in the snow-covered carpark of Castle Dudbury Railway Station, lit by a watery low sun.

Johnny went straight to his room. Again, everything had been tidied and cleaned. Again, the cardboard box with his parents' things lay in the corner waste bin, topped by a punctured football Johnny had kept for ages as a souvenir of a hat-trick he scored for his junior school team. He didn't mind so much about the ball, but rescued the box, putting it on his bed with

Kovac's container while he looked for a pen. There were several, neatly lined up in one of his drawers – Johnny took one and wrote 'DO NOT THROW AWAY' on the side of the box in very big letters.

The problem with having such an orderly room was that there were very few places the money could actually be. After Johnny had searched all of them at least three times, he had to admit defeat and sat on the edge of the bed with his head in his hands, wondering what he was going to do.

Half an hour passed. The shops would probably start shutting fairly soon. Though even if he found the money, Johnny didn't know what he'd buy for anyone. He searched the room twice more, opening every cupboard and drawer and checking the pockets of all his trousers just in case, but there was still nothing. Back on the bed, Johnny picked up the box of his parents' stuff. He was absolutely positive the money wasn't there, but it was the only place he hadn't looked.

Opening the box, he quickly saw there was a total absence of notes or pound coins, but as he held his dad's battered geologist's journal in his hands, he had an idea. Rummaging through for more, he also found a faded burgundy portable chess set (with only one white pawn missing, which he replaced with a small metal peg) and, getting really desperate, an old gyroscope. There was even a ball of string – he could use some of that to start the gyroscope spinning. These would be his presents – the journal for Clara, the chess set for Sol and the gyroscope for Alf. Kovac was getting his four-dimensional casing anyway. Johnny stood up and bagged his goodies, before walking past the trapdoor to the corner of the room and retrieving the football from the bin for Bentley's present.

Relieved to have solved the Christmas dilemma, Johnny was far too careless on his way to see Kovac. Just as he was about to open the door, who should step out into the corridor but Mr Wilkins.

The huge cook cast his beady eyes over the bag Johnny was carrying and said, 'Throwing more stuff out, Johnny? That's the spirit.'

Nonplussed, Johnny stood there, his hand placed incriminatingly on the door handle, without replying.

'Can you pop by the kitchens when you've done that?' asked the cook. 'Could do with some help with the sprouts for tomorrow.'

'OK,' said Johnny uncertainly, with no intention of doing any such thing.

'Thanks, sonny,' said Mr Wilkins, before setting off again down the corridor, whistling a Christmas song as he went.

Johnny wished it could be Christmas every day if it meant the cook wouldn't shout at him. Quickly, he slipped into the computer room. Kovac was beside himself with excitement as Johnny prepared to place him into Clara's four-dimensional hyperbox.

'Happy Christmas!' he said, before sliding the quantum computer into the casing and sealing it shut.

It was an age before Kovac replied – so much so that Johnny thought something must have gone wrong – but finally the computer said, 'I think I'm going to enjoy this.' The casing lit up as Kovac spoke.

As a bonus, Johnny found some plain brown parcel paper in the corner of the room, which he added to his bag – it would be better than nothing. Then, with the replacement PC wired up and working, he slipped out of the children's home weighed down with Kovac and all his gifts. For the first time he could remember, he was actually looking forward to a Christmas Day.

☆ ☆ ☆
☆ ☆

Johnny's Christmas treat to himself was a long lie-in. When he finally awoke, it was to the sound of Christmas carols being piped into his quarters. A familiar voice from the ledge in front of the mirror said, 'How can I be expected to think with that racket in the background? Is this a spaceship or a holiday camp? At least at Ben Halader House I had some peace and quiet.'

Johnny made a mental note to find somewhere other than his quarters to keep Kovac. 'Happy Christmas, Sol,' he said sleepily, sitting up in bed and rubbing his eyes.

'Happy Christmas, Johnny,' the ship replied. 'You'll be pleased to know that Alf is already in the galley, preparing a special lunch, and has insisted no one needs to help him at all – you're to have a complete day off.'

'Thanks,' he replied. 'Is Clara up?'

'Clara is on deck 18 in the garden.'

Gently, Johnny took hold of Bentley's head, nuzzled his nose against the Old English sheepdog's and said, 'Wake up, Bents. It's Christmas.' Throwing on some clothes he walked to the door which swished open.

Bentley skipped through and Johnny was about to follow when a voice from the ledge on the other side of his quarters said, 'What about me?'

Johnny stopped. 'As it's Christmas,' he said. 'If you *promise* not to annoy anyone, I suppose you can come too.'

Bentley ran out of the lift shaft first, followed by Johnny carrying Kovac. A snowball flew past, missing the end of his nose by a fraction. Clara frowned, deeply disappointed, but before she could fire again Johnny said, 'Truce! I've got Kovac.'

He carried the computer over to beside the decorated pine tree, all the time scanning the ground for ammunition for a quick counterattack, but there weren't any snowball-shaped clumps nearby. Under the tree, Clara and Alf's parcels had been joined by the presents Johnny had wrapped the night before, tying them up using some of the white string.

'Nice paper, by the way,' said Clara.

Johnny felt his face start to go red, but then realized his sister actually meant it.

Though they were both eager to start opening presents straightaway, they decided to just have each other's until Alf joined them with dinner. Clara handed hers to Johnny first. It was heavy and rectangular and felt like a book, which was a little disappointing as Johnny didn't have a lot of time for reading nowadays. That was until he opened it. Although it was, indeed, a book, it was unlike any Johnny had ever seen before. The title was *Set Pieces: Winning through Freekicks and Corners* by Stuart Mackay, the former manager of one of those smaller teams who'd done far better in the Premier League than they had any right to expect. Johnny had expected to see diagrams accompanied by explanations of what each player did, which would have been great, but what he found was even better. Where there were pictures, they somehow came out of the page in true, miniature 3D, while the images weren't static – they actually showed the set piece taking place step-by-step.

'Is it OK?' asked Clara. 'I'm getting loads better at dimensional manipulation and this was a great way to practise.'

'It's brilliant,' said Johnny. 'Absolutely brilliant. The only problem is I can't show it to Mr Davenport or anyone in the team.'

Clara laughed.

In comparison, Johnny's present to his sister suddenly felt even more rubbish, but there was nothing for it. He picked it out of the pile and handed over the brown package.

Clara undid the white string binding it and the parcel paper fell away. She held the battered, hardback notebook in her hand and, very carefully, opened a few pages. 'Is this what I think it is?' she asked, looking at Johnny. Her eyes were watering.

'It's Dad's,' Johnny replied. 'Some trip he made to Russia. I hope it's OK – I didn't have any money and . . .'

Before Johnny could continue a mane of blonde hair covered his face and Clara flung her arms around him. 'It's more than OK,' she said. 'It's the best present ever.'

✧ ✧ ✧
✧ ✧

The circular ice table had the five stars of Cassiopeia carved into where Johnny should sit and Clara's Starmark of the Plough for her position. Between them sat Alf, whose place was marked by the Emperor's diamond-shaped Melanian constellation, Portia. Johnny wondered if the lure of the food (carried in by one of Sol's repair drones which had been decorated to look like a sled) would overcome the uncomfortable look of the seats for Bentley, but he needn't have worried. The sheepdog was first into position, his tongue hanging out and salivating over the delicious feast well before Johnny sat down and discovered the ice benches were heated, soft when you sat on them and hugely comfy as they moulded themselves around your bottom.

Sol had gone above and beyond the call of duty by creating a groove at the fifth and final position, into which Kovac's new casing fitted perfectly. Once everyone was seated, Sol announced, 'Happy Christmas!' and it started to snow again, the giant flakes cleverly missing all the food. Crackers were soon being pulled, Bentley gripping them in his mouth, and even Kovac ended up with a paper crown perched on the top of his case, while telling bad Christmas jokes adapted from supposedly funny web pages.

Alf lifted the lid on the upside-down silver bowl at the centre of the table, to reveal an enormous bronzed turkey, surrounded by balls of stuffing and chipolata sausages, and said, 'Dinner is served.'

Soon everyone was tucking into the bird, together with roast and mashed potatoes, steaming blue Magule tips (a delicacy from the planet Naverene that Clara and Alf were keen on), roast parsnips coated in cheese, minted carrots, purple broccoli and, of course, the Brussels sprouts. If Johnny had found his thirty pounds, he'd have happily bet every penny that Alf's were a million times tastier than the ones Mr Wilkins would be cooking at Halader House. There was bread sauce and gravy and Johnny had never eaten such crispy roast spuds. Alf looked especially pleased to hear this and explained that he had fanned them to increase the surface area exposed to the fat. Johnny and Clara both laughed.

Everyone was so full after the first course that they decided to take a break and open a few more presents before pudding. Bentley tore straight into his, little pieces of wrapping paper flying into the air and joining the snow. Clara had bought the sheepdog a pair of reindeer antlers that she took great delight in placing on his head, while Alf's present was even funnier – a soft doll in the form of treacherous Chancellor Gronack. Bentley growled and immediately started chewing his present, before Johnny distracted him by helping unwrap the old football. The dog absolutely loved it, though no one else had enough energy to join in and chase the ball around the snow-covered garden.

Sol was delighted with the modified miniature London Gherkin in a snow globe that Clara had bought her, which repeatedly folded in and out of the scene, and loved the chess set from Johnny. When Kovac discovered he wasn't getting any more presents, the computer instantly challenged the ship to a game. Sol accepted and soon they were engrossed in a battle of intellects, the board projected in mid-air above the table so everyone else could follow the play. Clara's present to Alf was a book of cryptic crossword puzzles and how to solve them, which the android loved nearly as much as his gyroscope. He started the device spinning on the very edge of the ice table, so it was soon hanging right over, yet somehow didn't fall to the ground. Alf gave Johnny some new space posters for his room at Halader House, but they weren't the kind anyone could buy in a shop. Instead, the images had all been taken from the android's own memory chip and depicted some of the favourite places Johnny had visited.

It was the best Christmas Johnny could remember, but he had to admit something was bothering him. At first, when they'd returned from the Fountain of Time, he'd been relieved that Clara showed no signs of wanting to talk about Nicky. Then, as the weeks passed, a dreadful idea had begun to form in Johnny's head – one he hadn't been able to dismiss. Over and over he re-ran his last conversation with Clara as he'd been falling towards the heart of the gas giant orbiting Aldebaran. It was more than possible – in fact now it seemed likely – that his confession about Nicky, spoken as he plunged to his doom, had never reached his sister. How else could he explain her continued silence when any link to their family, like his dad's journal, was so important to her? He braced himself. If he couldn't talk about Nicky now – on Christmas Day itself – he knew he'd never be able to.

'Clara,' he said, getting to his feet. 'Can I have a word?' He nodded in the direction of a rocky outcrop where they could sit down, close to the Christmas star.

Clara looked puzzled, but stood up, holding her stomach. She looked as full as he felt.

'Where do you think you two are going?' asked Alf, also standing.

'Just for a chat,' Johnny replied, feeling his face warming under the android's scrutiny.

'Master Johnny – there will be all the time you want for chats once dinner is finished. Will you please sit down. You too, Miss Clara.'

Clara shrugged and resumed her place around the table.

Reluctantly, Johnny followed suit – at least he'd started the ball rolling. A few minutes more wouldn't make much difference.

Alf picked up the Christmas pudding and, even without asking, all the lights on the deck went out, leaving the only illumination coming from the ongoing chess match. The android placed a finger on top of the dessert next to a couple of holly leaves, and the whole, rich black hemisphere burst into ghostly blue flames, reminding Johnny for a moment of the blue sparks on the *Astricida*. He joined in with Clara's applause while Bentley barked his approval.

Once the flames went out, Alf divided up the pudding in the darkness, and placed bowls in front of Clara, Johnny and Bentley. To see exactly what he was eating, Johnny said, 'Sol, can we have the lights back?'

Nothing happened.

'Ah, I forget my infrared vision is somewhat more developed,' said Alf. 'Lights please, Sol.'

Still nothing happened, although the garden was brightening up a little, but only because Kovac's casing had started to glow.

Johnny put his hand on the table and found it was wet – and cold. 'Sol – what's going on?' he asked, suddenly wary.

'I am a little busy,' the ship replied, very slowly. She wasn't wrong. Moves on the chess board were happening at lightning quick speed. Johnny stood up and reached over to Kovac – the computer's casing was too hot to touch. He studied the board – the position looked incredibly complex. It sounded crazy, but it was as if Sol and Kovac had diverted all their thinking power into the match, at the expense of pretty much everything else.

Then Kovac blundered. Johnny wasn't even that good at chess, but he could see the quantum computer had made a losing move.

'Checkmate,' said Sol, as she captured Kovac's queen and checkmated him all in one move. The ship's lights flickered on all around.

'That's not fair,' said Kovac. 'I was distracted. Let's play again.'

Clara laughed. 'Distracted how?'

'I want to play again,' said Kovac, becoming more insistent. 'Something was bothering me.'

'What?' Johnny asked, wondering if the computer was going to blame the way Alf had cut the Christmas pudding, or something similar.

'It's those annoying Wormholes,' said Kovac. 'Someone keeps shouting down one to say the defence net has been activated and Andromedan ships are entering the solar system.'

13 ✬

Fight or Flight

'*What?* Play the message,' said Johnny.

'If I do, do you promise we can have a rematch afterwards?' asked Kovac.

'Now!' Johnny shouted.

'All right – keep your follicles in place,' the computer replied. 'Displaying message.'

The final image of the chessboard was replaced by a frantic Tolimus shouting, 'Can anybody hear me? I'm reading three, no make that four . . . five Andromedan ships gathering in the Oort Cloud. It's just how it began with our suns. Can anybody hear me?'

'It's Johnny here . . . Johnny Mackintosh,' he shouted to the figure. 'Frago? Is that you?' Johnny hadn't worked out a good way to tell which Tolimi was which.

'Please respond . . . it's now eight ships,' said the Tolimus. 'The Krun are here too.'

'I'm here,' shouted Johnny. 'What's your status? Has Pluto Base been detected?'

'Please . . . is Johnny Mackintosh there?'

'Why can't he hear me?' Johnny asked around the ice table.

'Didn't you read my blueprints?' said Kovac. 'This is purely a projection of the Wormhole. I never said you could communicate through it.'

The snow that had covered the deck was melting away and

Johnny heard Sol say, 'Switching to battle stations.' He knew the ship wouldn't flinch from the fight, however long the odds of survival. He turned to Clara who understood at once what was needed. The very next second, the attic room of Halader House came into view and Johnny stepped through, followed by his sister and Alf. There was a thud, as though the trapdoor had just been pushed shut, but then Johnny realized that Alf was on the floor, having been unable to cope with the fold. Clara bent down to reboot the android, while Johnny pushed his head into one of the hazy patches of light, glinting above the bed.

The scene that confronted him was chaotic. Several little Tolimi were running around the control centre, silencing one alarm after another, only for more to keep going off. There was no room for Johnny's hands in the Wormhole or he'd have been covering his ears. It took a few seconds to make himself heard.

'Oh thank the Maker,' said Frago, turning round and almost running into Johnny's face. 'We're reading ten Andromedan Stardestroyers already, with a score of smaller Krun ships.'

'When Toliman . . . your sun, exploded,' said Johnny, 'how many ships did they have?'

'Several hundred,' the little alien replied. 'We think they needed enough vessels to surround the star with their tachyon beams.' There was a look of horror in the alien's large, black eyes as it recalled the dreadful day its own sun was blown up, but it mingled with a burning fire – the determination to have its revenge.

'Is the base secure?' Johnny asked.

'So far – we don't think they know we're here. Well, they're in for one very big surprise.'

'Don't do anything stupid,' said Johnny. 'The fleet have got to be here any time now – Captain Valdour would never let us down. You can't fight them on your own.'

'Humph,' was the only response.

'Listen,' said Johnny. 'Alf's talking to Melania right now, to find out what's happening.'

'We'll see,' said Frago. As more and more alarms continued to wail in the background, it added, 'The super gun will be ready in three days – though I imagine it will take at least that long for the Andromedans to gather enough ships, I think he should tell this Valdour to hurry up.'

'Don't worry,' said Johnny. He pulled his face out of the hole to find Alf standing beside Clara shaking his head.

'No sign of His Majesty,' said the android.

'Well, the Tolimi are OK . . . for now,' said Johnny, 'but I'm worried. They don't sound like they want to lie low. I'll try Bram – just in case.' He paused for just a moment to flatten his hair and then stuck his face into the adjacent Wormhole. The Imperial Palace was bathed in a red glow, the two strong shadows of the buildings indicating that Arros and Deynar were both high in the sky.

'Hello,' shouted Johnny. 'Can anybody hear me? Bram? Anyone?'

A figure appeared in front of Johnny. He was relieved to see it wasn't Chancellor Karragon, or any Phasmeer for that matter. This alien had a blotchy blue and white face, spotted with fur, and was wearing very baggy orange trousers with a gap at the back for a long, curling tail. It looked a little like a cat, standing on two legs.

'Is that the Terran?' asked the creature.

'Yes . . . Yes it is,' said Johnny, amazed to be recognized.

'Massenko Felix Dinaster at your service,' said the alien, bowing slightly. 'What can I do for the mysterious Johnny Mackintosh?'

'We're under attack,' Johnny replied. 'Or we will be any time now. The Andromedans have entered our system – Bram . . . the Emperor promised us ships.'

'Hmmmm . . . I'm afraid, Johnny Mackintosh, that His Divine Imperial Majesty Emperor Bram Khari is not in residence. I will, of course, pass your request on as soon as he returns.'

'But that'll be too late,' said Johnny. 'Captain Valdour needs to get here now.'

'Valdour, you say?' The cat-like alien cupped its head in its hands as though deep in thought. 'I believe the Captain has been seconded on official Senate business, reporting to the Regent.'

'No!' shouted Johnny.

'Do not fear,' said the alien. 'It so happens I have Its Highness's representative, the Chancellor, standing beside me – I shall ask.'

'Don't bother,' said Johnny. 'There's more chance of a Sulafat tortoise winning the Imperial Speed Medal than Chancellor Karragon wanting to help Terra.'

'But you are behind the times,' said the alien. 'Karragon was not considered up to the difficult task ahead . . . and has been replaced.' Johnny's spirits rose. 'The new Chancellor is familiar with your planet,' continued the alien. 'I'm sure a request to release Captain Valdour from his duties would be looked on favourably.'

'Brilliant,' said Johnny. It was about time he had some good news. 'Can you ask him . . . her . . . it, sorry, what I need to do?'

There was a pause as though the creature was clarifying instructions. Johnny crossed his fingers behind his back, hoping for all he was worth.

'The Chancellor apologizes,' said the blue-headed alien. 'While we are sympathetic, and would support your request, there are procedures to be followed. Now the Senate is involved, the only way for Captain Valdour and his fleet to be released is to present yourself before the Imperial Senate and petition for it in person. It is purely a formality, you understand.'

Johnny gulped a huge lungful of Melanian air. 'But . . . I'm not meant to go to Melania,' he said. 'And there isn't time.'

'I am truly sorry,' said the creature. 'Sadly, we do not make the rules.'

'No . . . I'll come. I'm on my way,' said Johnny. As the alien bowed its head, Johnny pulled his own out of the Wormhole and into his bedroom.

'That didn't sound good,' said Clara.

Johnny shook his head. 'The Regent's got Valdour working for the Senate – we've got to ask for his release in person.'

'There can be no question of going,' said Alf. 'The Emperor was very clear – on no account were you to return to Melania in his absence.'

'Alf – we have to,' said Johnny.

'Our whole planet's in danger,' added Clara.

'Does either of you believe for one nanosecond that the Regent or his . . . highly objectionable Chancellor will give you ships to defend Earth?'

Johnny could tell Alf felt incredibly strongly – he'd never heard the android openly criticize a chancellor before. 'There's a new chancellor,' he said, 'who's on our side. It might make the difference.'

'We have to try,' Clara added.

'If Captain Valdour doesn't get here soon, the Tolimi will start fighting,' said Johnny. 'You know they don't stand a chance.'

'You two are impossible,' said the android. 'One of these days I will blow my neural detonator and it will be all your fault.'

'Not today, I hope,' said Johnny 'I've a feeling we're going to need you.'

Clara reopened the fold, this time leading straight to the *Spirit of London*'s bridge.

'We'll never get there in time,' said Johnny, to no one in particular as he rebooted the prone android before walking across to the captain's chair.

'Yes we will,' said Clara from beside the Plican's tank. 'Remember, we have two folders on board. I'll take turns with the Plican.' Johnny's sister looked fiercely determined.

☆ ☆ ☆
☆ ☆

It was the first time he'd ever felt a jolt from within a gel pod. Johnny knew it had been madness for Clara to attempt to fold the entire ship across thousands of light years – only Plicans could do something like that. He hoped the *Spirit of London* hadn't been spliced in half, left a piece of herself behind or been accidentally crushed. He thought about leaving the capsule to check on things, but draining the gel pod would only delay them even more. If there was a problem, he'd find out soon enough. For the hundredth time, he revisited his decision to leave for Melania and plead for Captain Valdour's release – perhaps, with the upgraded weapons, it would have been better to stand and fight. Even if, by some miracle, the fleet was waiting and ready to go the instant they reached the capital, the round trip would take at least a week. It was cutting everything so fine.

From what Frago had said, it sounded as if the entire Andromedan fleet would be coming to the solar system. He knew that, because of the way folds distorted the surrounding space, it would take time for Nymac to gather that many ships together, but Johnny would never forgive himself – or his brother – if the Sun was turned into a supernova before he could return home to at least try to prevent it.

Johnny looked at his inflated arm. Even through the orange haze, there was no mistaking the colour of the lights on the wristcom. He was fed up with the permanent circle of red and decided, when he had a moment, to swap the device for another version without Nicky's enhancements.

If Bram were still elsewhere and out of contact, it hardly bore thinking about. Johnny would have to make a personal appeal in the ancient Senate building – the very idea made him feel queasy. If anything, he'd rather face a hundred Andromedan Stardestroyers. The only tiny consolation with the journey taking so long was that he had a couple of days to plan what to say. As he drifted into an uneasy sleep, he hoped the new Chancellor would be willing to go through things with him beforehand.

✧ ✧ ✧
✧ ✧

When Johnny awoke, he discovered the last globules of gel were being hoovered off him by the trunk at the top of the capsule. His body had returned to normal size and, as ever, he had to grab hold of the locket around his neck to stop it being sucked up the tube and lost. Something must have gone wrong, mid-journey – with speed of the essence, he'd instructed Sol not to drain the pod until they reached Melania.

'Sol – where are we? What's happening?' asked Johnny as he sat up and opened the gel pod door.

'We have arrived at Talamine Spaceport,' the ship replied. 'All systems are in order, although I believe Clara may require assistance.

'What?' shouted Johnny. He ran onto the bridge and saw his sister, sprawled on the floor beside the Plican's tank. 'Clara,' said Johnny, kneeling down and cradling her head in his hands. 'Talk to me.'

Slowly, Clara opened her eyes and Johnny almost dropped her head in shock. Instead of looking their usual blue with silver flecks, her entire eyeballs were shining silver. She smiled weakly and said, 'Did I do it? Are we there?'

'You're amazing,' said Johnny, nodding. He felt his sister go limp in his arms. Alf arrived beside him 'Get Clara to sickbay,' he went on. 'I'm off to the Senate.'

'Master Johnny – I think you should wait until I am ready to accompany you.'

'There isn't time,' he replied. 'Clara's much more important.' Alf disappeared down the lift shafts as Bentley emerged from his own gel pod, shaking the gloop from his fur. 'Sorry, Bents,' said Johnny. 'I think it's best you stay here. Guard the bridge – don't let any strange aliens you don't know on here. OK?' Johnny headed for the lifts and looked over his shoulder, to see Bentley jumping up into the captain's chair.

First stop, briefly, was his quarters. He gave himself two minutes to dress as smartly as possible. Now he stood in front of the long mirror wearing the white tunic top with the golden stars of Cassiopeia, and the black trousers with matching gold stripe. Instead of trainers, he'd changed into his black boots. Lastly, he tucked his locket underneath the tunic and stepped out into the corridor. Reaching the lift, he asked Sol if Bram was contactable. She promised she would be trying constantly, but for the time being there was no response. With no other options, Johnny stepped into the lift shaft and said, 'Deck zero.'

At the foot of the ship, he touched the silver statue for luck, before exiting through the revolving doors. No one was there to meet him and, unusually, it was raining, both red suns hidden behind a thick mass of cloud. Despite the strong gravity pushing him down, he hurried up the steps away from the *Spirit of London*. His chest tight, he reached the top, breathing heavily, and turned to take a last look at the ship. Berthed very nearby was another spacecraft Johnny recognized – *Cheybora*. Straightaway he asked Sol to patch him through to the warship, who turned out to be raring to go into battle. She assured

Johnny her captain felt just the same, but sadly he had been asked (yet again) to address the Senate. At least knowing Valdour would be there gave Johnny a huge boost and he set out on the wide, transparent travelator at a sprint – every second could be vital. Soon he'd passed the statues of the old emperors and reached the giant curved wall and doorway barring his entrance. For just a moment, Johnny was unsure what to do – there was absolutely no sign of a bell – but then, agonizingly slowly, the two huge slabs of black stone swung outwards, granting him access.

'You have a fast ship, Terran.' Standing alone in the Senate courtyard was Massenko Felix Dinaster, the same blue-faced cat-like alien he had spoken with through the Wormhole.

Johnny couldn't reply – his lungs were crying out for oxygen. With his hands on his legs, he was bent double, his face flushed.

'Fortune smiles on you,' the alien continued. 'Captain Valdour and the other commanders are presently addressing the Senate, with the Regent itself in attendance. After you have petitioned the Senators, can you communicate the result to your ship?'

Johnny nodded, holding up the wristcom with its red dial that he'd forgotten to change.

'Follow me.' The creature turned and began walking, its tail curling upwards, across the giant flagstones engraved with hieroglyphs towards the ancient, circular white stone building at the centre of the courtyard.

'Wait!' said Johnny, still gasping for breath, but the alien was already too far away to hear. It was now or never. Johnny had no idea what he was going to say to the Senate, but took a last deep breath and followed.

As he hurried to catch up with the cat-like creature prancing ahead, Johnny heard snatches of the debate being conducted inside the Senate chamber – it didn't sound good. The atmospheric controls on Melania had been switched to a very basic level to conserve energy that could be diverted into growing more spaceships. According to the different commanders giving their reports, the Imperial Navy had suffered a number of heavy defeats.

The blue-headed alien was waiting for him at the crumbling white stone entrance to the ancient chamber, but as soon as Johnny caught up the doors opened and his guide disappeared inside. He had no option but to follow, keen to keep up.

The chamber was only dimly lit and Johnny couldn't see what had become of the alien. It was packed with all manner of strange lifeforms, Senators representing civilizations from across the galaxy, some seated, others floating at different heights. Still more were swimming encased in transparent spheres, while several wore face masks – Johnny supposed they couldn't all be oxygen breathers. At the front, in a chair built for a giant, sat the Regent. It, and all the Senators surrounding it, were facing towards the black circular disk that had once disappeared underneath Johnny's feet. Standing spotlit, dressed in the full ceremonial uniform of the Imperial Navy, was Captain Valdour himself, speaking in midflow.

'I concur with Admiral Chad. The only explanation is espionage – we are being betrayed.'

Gazing towards his friend, Johnny felt as if a huge weight had been lifted. He was sure Valdour would be keen to join him, and the captain, covered in battle scars, looked so menacing that not even the Senators would dare refuse.

In the shadows behind Valdour, Johnny spotted the blue-headed alien whispering into the earhole of a tall Phasmeer, before Massenko Felix Dinaster stepped forward to stand beside the captain in the light, interrupting the speaker.

'Apologies to Captain Valdour and the Senate,' said the alien. 'The Terran, Johnny Mackintosh, has entered the Chamber and demands the right to address this House.'

There was uproar. Johnny fumed at the cat-like creature – he'd not demanded anything of the sort and the Senators were clearly not amused. He had no choice other than to make his way towards the black stone stage, feeling his face becoming redder and redder as he went. As he climbed up, the Phasmeer stepped out of the shadows into the spotlight, quieting the hubbub. Johnny couldn't believe it – in front of him was none other than the traitor Gronack.

Before he could shout out, the Phasmeer began to speak. 'Apologies to our unannounced guest,' it said. Close up, Johnny could see its thin mouth had curled into a smile. 'Before the Terran, Johnny Mackintosh, addresses the House, it is my unpleasant duty as Chancellor to report that surveillance systems have detected unauthorized hyperspatial transmissions from within this very Chamber. Noble Senators – we have heard the Imperial officers speak of espionage. It appears that, today, there is a spy in our very midst.'

'You're the spy,' shouted Johnny. Seeing Gronack again made him so angry he couldn't contain himself. Standing on the black platform, it was as if he was speaking into a microphone – as his words echoed around the Chamber, he went on, 'You've been working for the Andromedans . . . and the Krun all . . .'

'Silence!' boomed a powerful voice from nearby – it was the Regent. The huge Phasmeer rose from its chair. 'How dare you enter the Senate Chamber, making such accusations?'

'Your Highness.' It was Captain Valdour who spoke. 'I would remind the House that this is the Terran trusted by the Emperor himself.'

Johnny was conscious of how loud his breathing and heartbeat both were. He could not believe the gall of the alien who'd plotted to hand him over to Colonel Hartman's Corporation and, when that backfired, brought in the Krun to sell Johnny and his sister to the Andromedans.

It was Chancellor Gronack who responded. 'Alas it is one of the burdens of high office, that some will always seek to undermine we servants of the people. It matters not. What is important is that, in the long history of the Senate,' it said, its robes turning red in mock anger, 'we can count on one Deraxli finger the times when this noble House has been bugged. All know the new penalty for such bass treachery – death by firing squad.'

There was uproar all around the Chamber.

The Regent raised its arms for quiet. 'As our new Chancellor has stated, the law is clear. If anyone in this House is in communication with outside agencies . . . with the enemy, they are in for a surprise. A simple test is now possible.' There was no need to ask for silence – the Senators were hanging on its every word. 'Beneath the Senate House is a small community of Owlessan Monks.' Johnny could hear the sounds of surprise from the onlookers – even Captain Valdour looked shocked. 'They have been summoned,' the Regent continued. 'If messages are being sent through tunnels in space – the only means out of here – there will be residual echoes. They will know.'

Half a dozen scarlet robes, billowing in a nonexistent breeze, unfolded throughout the building. They separated and sped around the chamber, darting between the astonished Senators, in and out of the tanks. Some tried to beat them away, while others stood still as statues. It didn't make any difference – all were being tested. Johnny could just about make out the skeletal faces and limbs of the strange Monks, but had the distinct impression he was alone in this. He couldn't help watching, fascinated, as the creatures came closer, until they circled the black stone disk.

'Get off,' squeaked the Chancellor, as it attempted to keep one of the faceless Monks at bay with its spindly arms, while its robes turned pink. Another of the creatures flew to Captain

Valdour, who stood, impervious, as the blood-red cloak flapped in his face and moved on.

All six Monks now swooped across to where Johnny was standing. The long bony fingers reached out from beneath their cloaks and prodded and poked him. He felt a chill, which could have engulfed him had it not been for the warmth of the locket around his neck. One of the Monks attempted to take hold of the chain from which it hung, but Johnny pushed the skeletal hand away and it withdrew. Another of the Monks was examining the wristcom. As its finger touched the red dial of the device, it disappeared within it, followed by half the creature's forearm. Another reached out and did the same, and another. A fourth Owlessan Monk began to undo the Velcro strap of the device.

'Hey – I need that,' said Johnny. 'It's my communicator – for my ship,' but the creature ignored him and removed the wristcom, before all six flew with it to the Regent.

The huge Phasmeer stood, surrounded by the Monks, and said, 'But it is more than a simple link to your ship, is it not?'

'What do you mean?' asked Johnny, defiantly.

'I am informed it is a hyperspatial transmitter.'

Johnny went cold. He wondered exactly what Nicky had affixed to the wristcom's face.

The Regent continued, 'We will analyse your signals, but already the evidence is damning. Members of the Senate – it appears we have found our spy.'

The next moment, two squat, muscular aliens clad in blue body armour grabbed Johnny, easily wrestling him to the floor. Winded, he was forced face-down onto his front. One sat on him, grabbing hold of his arms and forcing them behind his back.

As he struggled, Johnny heard Captain Valdour's voice cut across the hubbub, shouting, 'There must be some mistake. I owe Johnny Mackintosh my life and will gladly vouch for him.'

'As his Second you are aware you would face the same sentence as the accused?' boomed the Regent.

'I am,' replied Captain Valdour, nodding towards Johnny. The alien's battle-scarred smile looked none too reassuring.

'While I would be loath to execute a capable officer and holder of the Regency Medal of Honour, the law must be followed. Arrest them both.'

More armour-clad guards were flooding into the Chamber and a pneumatic syringe was pressed against Johnny's neck.

14 ✢

Trial and Retribution ✢

'*Johnny? Where are you? Can you hear me?*' It was Clara's voice coming through his earpiece, but it wasn't possible to respond. Even if he'd still been wearing his wristcom, Johnny wouldn't have been able to lift his arm to his mouth to talk. The chair in which he'd awoken came complete with metal bands, tightly binding his arms and legs. His head hurt and everything was hazy, as if he'd been drugged, but there was no way of telling how much time had passed since his arrest in the Senate Chamber. He wondered what was happening back in the solar system. He had to get out of here, wherever 'here' was.

The stabbing pains in his temple were made worse by the annoying little insects buzzing around Johnny's face, that he was powerless to swat away. It looked as if his trial was already about to begin, but the large room in which he found himself wasn't like any courtroom Johnny had seen. Parts were old and worn, but modern fittings had been grafted onto the old stone ceiling so that, if anything, it looked more like a TV studio. The impression wasn't helped by the excited aliens, of all different shapes and sizes, who'd taken their places on the rows of stone steps, like an amphitheatre, facing Johnny and Captain Valdour – who had been seated, about ten metres apart, on a narrow, crumbling stone stage. They were separated from the audience by a dry moat, filled with soldiers clad in blue body armour. Next to the captain was a set of steps leading to an empty, hexagonal platform, a couple of metres higher than its surroundings, overhanging the moat.

The watching aliens were chattering in a mixture of languages, clicks and whistles (he only caught snatches of it) while pointing at Johnny and the captain and, for some reason, the wall behind them. Then the lights above the audience dimmed and a single beam lit up a spectacular side entrance. Buzzing into view, to enormous applause, came a double-headed alien with two identical pointy faces, supported on four wings which were beating so fast they moved as a solid blur.

'Thank you . . . *thank you*,' came a voice from each of the creature's twin mouths. At first it looked to be flying towards Captain Valdour, but then it diverted to hover above the front two rows of the audience, extending six long, thin legs, jointed very high up, which were grasped fleetingly by different aliens seated below. There were squeals of delight from the audience.

'Welcome to this Milky Way News Network Special,' said the flying speaker. 'We may Vermalcast around the galaxy, around the clock, *but once in a Big Bang we give you a show even more spectacular than normal.* This is one of those rare occasions. Citizens of the galaxy – We, Z'habar *Z'habar* Estagog, present The Trial of the Terran.'

The audience cheered wildly.

'Yes, all you intelligent life forms out there, this is no ordinary trial – the Terran, Johnny Mackintosh, and his Second, Captain Valdour, are charged with nothing less than High Treason.'

The audience hushed.

'*A crime so heinous, that it has been made . . . punishable by death!*'

At this the audience roared.

'Everyone who's anyone is here, in this very studio. We have Gilgadon!'

250

A spotlight fell on the front row of the audience, picking out an alien with a triangular-shaped body, covered in sparkling gold fur, across which fell a pink sash. It stood up, opened a very wide mouth, and emitted a steady, high-pitched squeal so powerful that Johnny was pressed into the back of his chair and momentarily deafened. The ringing in his ears only stopped after two further, quieter aliens had been picked out and introduced. If Clara had been speaking again, he wouldn't have heard.

'But that's not all,' the flying, buzzing alien carried on as Johnny's hearing returned. 'I've Vermalcasted with celebrities before, but today, my fellow citizens, is special. We're not simply joined by the stars of the galaxy – *we have its political elite*. With more gravitas than a Carabine Bear declaiming the twelve cycles of the new ascension – *while standing on one leg* – I give you Gronack, Chancellor of Melania!'

With robes of the deepest purple, the Phasmeer swept into the studio through the same entrance Z'habar Z'habar Estagog had used, its antennae wrapping around each other in delight at the audience's rapturous response.

'And finally, whisper it among yourselves – step into your Vermaldomes to be in the presence of greatness. And give the loudest acclamation you have yet for the wisest, most benevolent and – *according to the latest and most comprehensive survey of galactic opinion by Mizar Magazine* – most admired ruler of all the galaxy since Themissa herself.'

For a fleeting moment, Johnny thought Bram had returned to Melania just in time, but it was the gigantic Regent who came through the entrance as the presenter shouted its name. The tall Phasmeer was flanked by an escort of squat soldiers in blue armour carrying very powerful looking blasters. The loudest applause yet followed, but Johnny realized it wasn't coming from the aliens sitting in front of him, but was being piped into the studio.

'Two of the greats of the galaxy, here to enjoy the show,' continued the alien presenter. 'Incidentally, it's down to Chancellor Gronack that we're casting from the highest-security courtroom in all the empire. Designed by Ophion himself, this studio is guaranteed one hundred percent Plican-proof, so there's no chance of rescue – our two accused have to hope they'll be found innocent. *Like that's really going to happen when you're caught red-handed in the Senate chamber.*'

The audience laughed. Johnny couldn't believe this was happening – it was like a bad dream. He thought courts were meant to be serious places, but this one looked like some sort of light entertainment show. He didn't know much about laws, but enough to see it was outrageous that the host had pronounced his guilt before anything had even begun.

As if reading his mind, Z'habar Z'habar Estagog continued, 'But it's not up to me to mete out the verdict. *Though we have two heads' worth of memory engrams full of messages wishing it were* . . . oh yes. But, citizens of the galaxy. For justice to be done, and to be seen to be done – *maybe with just a tinsy winsy bit of fun along the way* – we demand a judge!'

What Johnny had thought was a wall beside his chair vanished. Now the stage extended further back and, between him and Captain Valdour, was a gigantic brain, with thick trailing tentacles, floating in a clear vat. Flanked on either side were massive three-dimensional close-ups of Johnny's head, above two discs, one white and one black, supported on pillars of the same colours. Johnny stared wide-eyed and his gigantic doubles stared back – the little insects buzzing around his head must be more cameras.

'Court is in session,' boomed a deep voice and, as it did, the fluid in which the brain was suspended flashed with light. The audience cheered even louder, this time without any need at all for assistance. Johnny tried to look across to Captain Valdour, but was only able to see his friend's eye patch.

'*Johnny – what's going on? Alf says you're on trial.*' It was Clara again, coming in through his earpiece. '*He's watching some broadcast thing and says you're there with Captain Valdour. Look, I know you probably can't speak to me, but maybe you can still hear. We'll get you both out of there . . . I promise.*'

Johnny wished he shared his sister's confidence. He had to get out of here and back to Earth, but even Clara probably wouldn't be able to fold into a Plican-proof courtroom designed by a former Emperor and, if she did, Alf wouldn't be able to come with her without collapsing. Then, supposing they could rescue him before the Regent's highly armed soldiers intervened, there was no way they'd be able to free Captain Valdour who was out of reach on the far side of the studio.

'Johnny Mackintosh of the planet Terra,' said the Judge. 'You are charged with High Treason against the State. Under the Emergency War Act, the penalty for this crime is death by firing squad. How do you plead?'

Johnny felt as if all the air had been squeezed from his lungs and his voicebox crushed. He managed a feeble, 'Not guilty.'

'Very well. I call the first witness,' said the Judge, the fluid in its tank again lighting up in time to the words. I call Chancellor Gronack of Melania.'

Z'habar Z'habar Estagog, hovering overhead, whispered its running commentary, 'As the youngest chancellor the Emperor ever appointed and then the Regent reappointed takes to the stand, no one can doubt its eloquence and grace alone will prove more than enough to convict the Terran. I hear the firing squad is already being prepared – *watch the execution live on the Milky Way News Network.*'

The Phasmeer rose against a background of excited whispers from the audience. It walked slowly across the stage, its antennae proudly vertical and its robes a rich, shining turquoise, as it milked the attention for all it was worth. Finally it reached the stone steps, but tripped on the way up, falling flat on its elongated face. Nobody dared laugh. Once on its feet its robes glowed bright pink as it stood atop the hexagonal platform, its head now higher than even the Regent's as it surveyed the audience as though a fiery preacher about to begin a sermon.

'Members of the jury,' began the Phasmeer, addressing the aliens sitting on the stone steps at the front of the courtroom. 'While it is doubtless unusual for such an important official to take to the stand, I am uniquely placed to report on the activities of the accused.'

'Remarkable though it sounds,' whispered Z'habar Z'habar Estagog, 'during its first term, our beloved Gronack travelled aboard the accused's spaceship – *immediately before the Chancellor's mysterious disappearance*. Until now, nothing has been known of that time. But in a live Milky Way News Network exclusive, *sources tell us that all will now be revealed*.'

The Phasmeer considered its congregation. 'You have been led to believe that the accused, the Terran Johnny Mackintosh, is especially favoured by our much-loved but reclusive, ageing Emperor. Nothing could be further from the truth. You may be surprised to hear that, when this Terran first came to Melania, His Divine Imperial Majesty only sent forth the Imperial Guard – for the first time in a century – precisely because the threat from the defendant was so great.'

Johnny rolled his eyes, wondering when he'd have the chance to speak himself. He wriggled in his chair, but it was impossible to free his arms or legs.

'That is the reason,' the Chancellor went on, 'our sadly feeble Emperor sent me to Terra – to keep watch over Johnny Mackintosh and report on his loathsome activities.'

Johnny was seething. How dare Gronack lie so blatantly to the court.

'What I found was so shocking, that I struggled to believe it. The accused wasn't only openly working with the evil Krun, the very dregs of sentient life in our galaxy.'

Screams of 'No!' and 'Shame!' came from the audience.

The Chancellor paused before saying, 'Oh yes, but it was far, far worse. He was also in contact with the Andromedans.'

'That was you,' shouted Johnny. He tried to carry on talking, but a band from the neck of the chair instantly slid across his lips, gagging him. He could taste the cold metal in his mouth. A matching, golden metal band had slid across his faces projected either side of the brain's tank.

'Silence!' boomed the Judge. 'Any more interruptions and you will be in contempt of court and executed on the spot. Your counsel can cross-examine the witness in due course.'

'Your Honour,' said Captain Valdour from across the stage, his voice level and controlled. 'It has doubtless, quite understandably, escaped your attention, but we do not appear to have counsel.'

'The oversight is not my own, Captain Valdour. You have had two days to assemble the defence team of your choosing before this trial began. Failure to do so cannot . . .'

'This isn't justice,' shouted Valdour, before he too was gagged in the same manner as Johnny.

'Proceed,' said the Judge to the elevated witness.

Johnny wasn't listening. Two Melanian days were the equivalent of three on Earth. While he'd been drugged unconscious, waiting for the trial to be organized, the Andromedans would have been preparing their attack. They would be ready to strike any time now.

'Indeed I sought sanctuary with one of their ruling powers, but the accused now sitting before you ordered that I be . . . dissected.' The Phasmeer raised a weedy arm to silence the horrified jury. 'The planet is primitive – we must remember that. It is why it took me so many months to return to my post. Its inhabitants did not comprehend what Johnny Mackintosh demanded of them. While others might not, I forgive them. And as you will discover,' Gronack continued, 'there are some brave souls on his homeworld who have opposed him.'

Z'habar Z'habar Estagog maintained its hushed commentary. 'What an exclusive. Observe the hate-filled eyes of the watching Terran, wishing it had completed its dastardly plan and the gracious Chancellor was no more. *Too late now, Johnny Mackintosh.*'

'Questions from the defence?' asked the Judge. Both Johnny and Captain Valdour writhed in their chairs, but neither could make a sound. 'Very well,' the huge brain went on as the lights from its tank flashed. 'I call the next witness – another Terran, I see.'

For a moment, Johnny wondered if Clara had somehow been captured. Then he heard Z'habar Z'habar Estagog at it again, quietly commentating for a faraway audience. 'In an early, unexpected twist, a leader from the Terran's home planet steps into the courtroom. Has she arrived to help the traitor wriggle out of his certain guilt?'

Johnny opened his eyes wide with surprise as the suited figure of Colonel Hartman, hunched and frightened, was led into the studio. A Hundra about a metre across floated above her head. The colonel stopped and looked around, as if unable to understand where she found herself. Her normally immaculate hair was sticking out in all directions, globules of orange goo left over from the gel pod she'd been transported in. Her huge, round, disbelieving eyes fell first on Chancellor Gronack and the Regent beside it, then on the brain and, finally, on Johnny himself. As though the sight of him bound and gagged gave her confidence, she appeared to grow a few inches and set off again, clunking more steadily across the studio on her high heels. She reached the steps and climbed into the raised witness box.

'You are Colonel Roberta Hartman of the planet Terra?' asked the Judge, speaking in Universal. The floating Hundra glowed as it translated the question.

'Yes . . . yes, your Honour,' replied the colonel. 'Though we call it Earth.'

'It is a primitive world without formal first contact and not under Imperial jurisdiction?' asked the Judge.

'Some of us, your Honour, have been aware of, and had dealings with extraterrestrials, though I never imagined all this.' Colonel Hartman's gaze swept across the audience.

'That is to be expected,' the Judge replied. 'By definition, primitive imaginations are limited.' Colonel Hartman's lips narrowed as the translated words sank in, but she did not respond. The brain continued, 'Tell me – is the accused, Johnny Mackintosh, known on your planet?'

'He is, your Honour, known to those of us who try to maintain law and order. It is to my deep regret that I did not cooperate more fully with Chancellor Gronack over his arrest, some months ago.'

Johnny thought that this was a bit of an understatement. It was actually Colonel Hartman who'd ordered the Chancellor to be dissected.

She went on, 'My organization has observed the accused's dealings with alien races.'

'Do you know the names of these races?' the Judge asked.

'I believe they are called the Krun . . .' Colonel Hartman paused as there were murmurings among the audience, 'and the Andromedans.'

Uproar broke out in the courtroom. Johnny couldn't believe even Colonel Hartman would sink so low.

'Order . . . order,' boomed the Judge. Gradually, the chattering aliens hushed each other. Once the studio was silent, the brain continued, 'Do you have evidence to corroborate your claims?'

257

'I do, your Honour,' Colonel Hartman replied, confidently. 'This memory chip,' she said holding up a little card in her hand, 'contains video of a recent encounter.'

The Judge said, 'Approach and deposit this . . . video.'

The colonel did as she was asked, the echo of her heels on the stone steps reverberating around the expectant courtroom as the Hundra followed, drifting out of reach above her. As she stopped before the Judge, two long grey tentacles slid up the wall of the tank and out. They moved over the top of Colonel Hartman's head, hesitated for a moment and then, surprisingly delicately, plucked something from out of her palm. Holding it between the two sucker-covered limbs as though between thumb and forefinger, the tentacles retracted into the vat. The fluid inside fizzed for a moment.

Johnny came to a decision. However much he hated this woman, if he could he had to warn her about what was happening back home. She might be able to evacuate some people – some of humanity could still survive.

'Interesting,' said the Judge, lighting up the courtroom as it spoke. 'Observe . . .'

Everything went dark and then a large projection appeared for all the court to see. The huge brain cleverly processed the images on the fly so that they appeared three-dimensional. Even so, the pictures were slightly grainy, from a CCTV camera. Johnny recognized the location – the grassy moat surrounding the Tower of London, with Tower Bridge in the background. It was evening. The air shimmered and a black, spherical craft materialized on the lawns in front of the castle walls. It was a Krun shuttle. As a ramp extended onto the grass, Stevens, in human form, accompanied by another suit-wearing Krun, descended, followed by a smaller blond figure in a white tunic top on which were emblazoned the five gold stars of Cassiopeia. There was no doubt it was meant to be Johnny, and was an excellent likeness. Behind him, with a single bright light shining out of a mask that covered nearly half his face, was Nymac.

The CCTV camera followed their progress as they climbed a set of wide stone steps, before the viewpoint shifted as the foursome made their way through the darkened streets of the City of London and its mixture of old and new buildings. The more he thought about it, Johnny realized he shouldn't be surprised. Colonel Hartman would probably go to any lengths to ingratiate herself with these new, more powerful aliens she had recently encountered. He knew she'd had some dealings with the Krun too – that much was obvious from New York. Presumably Chancellor Gronack or the Regent itself had promised her and her Corporation even greater rewards – perhaps the ship she coveted. Even now, it might be the means by which some of humanity could escape the supernova.

The four were now around the corner from the London Gherkin – or the *Spirit of London* depending if Sol had been on Earth during the filming. Nymac was talking to the Johnny lookalike, who nodded as though he understood. A reassuring hand from Stevens was placed on the blond boy's shoulder and the camera followed the lone figure in his white top as he turned the corner and strode across the small square, and into the beautiful curved glass and metal building at its centre.

'For the benefit of the court,' said the Judge, 'I have analysed this primitive footage.' The projection reverted to the original scene of the four figures descending the ramp from the small Krun ship. 'While the craft is undoubtedly of Krun design, the final figure following the accused is believed to be none other than General Nymac himself.'

Horrified gasps and more shouts of 'No!' came from the amazed audience.

'Does the defence wish to cross-examine the witness?' asked the Judge.

Johnny struggled against his bonds, but a familiar voice from behind him shouted, 'It most certainly does.' Into view, by way of a blur of fast-moving arms and legs that stopped instantly, right in front of the huge brain, came Alf. Colonel Hartman had jumped out of the way and now lay spreadeagled on the studio floor.

Z'habar Z'habar Estagog was already buzzing just above Alf's head. 'We promised you drama, but here's a twist no one anticipated. A robot has burst, unopposed into the courtroom, claiming to represent the defendants – *like any sentient being would want the job.* Another exclusive story brought to you by Z'habar *Z'habar* Estagog on the Milky Way News Network.'

'Who might you be?' asked the Judge, as the armour-clad soldiers exchanged glances, wondering if they should intervene.

'My name, your Honour, is Alf. I am an artificial lifeform who has previously served as a member of the household of His Majesty Bram Khari himself.'

'Objection!' squeaked a figure to the side of the audience. Chancellor Gronack stood, adding, 'Surely it demeans the court to have a robot involved in these proceedings. Only independent lifeforms are considered acceptable witnesses and, presumably, court officials.'

'Objection . . . overruled,' said the Judge. Johnny smiled underneath his metal gag. It was the first thing all day that had gone right. 'By Imperial decree I understand the android Alf has been declared fully sentient and a Citizen of Melania.'

'Thank you, your Honour,' said Alf as he straightened his bowler hat. 'May I first request a recess so I can communicate with the defendants?'

'Objection!' squeaked Chancellor Gronack again. 'Once the proceedings have begun, they cannot be interrupted for these stalling tactics at the whim of the defence – the guilt of the accused is clear.'

'The case rests on a knife edge as the Judge ponders a dramatic request from defence counsel.' Z'habar Z'habar Estagog was hovering close to Johnny's chair. *Which way will our wise court arbiter decide? Find out after more special messages from our sponsors.*

'Objection . . .' began the Judge. There was an agonizing pause as Johnny's eyes flickered between the brain in the vat, Captain Valdour and Alf. Finally, after pondering for at least a minute, the Judge added, 'Overruled. Court will recess for ten minutes only. Escort the defendants and their counsel to an antechamber.'

☆ ☆ ☆
☆ ☆

Johnny and Captain Valdour's chairs floated a few centimetres above the floor, as the pair, accompanied by armed guards either side, followed Alf through the side doorway, along a short corridor and into a tiny room beside the main studio. It might as well have been a large wardrobe. The walls and ceiling were hung with several sets of blue body armour matching those of the security guards while, through a small window, a public square was visible, dotted with strange black domes.

Johnny's metal gag finally retracted, though all the other bands remained in place. The soldiers brushed the hanging clothes away to point their blasters at him and Valdour, as though either prisoner might spit deadly poison in a bid to make their escape. Johnny wished it were possible.

'Oh, Master Johnny,' said Alf. 'If only you had waited for me, none of this would have happened.'

'Alf – we were in a hurry. I was set up.'

'But why would anyone want to do a thing like that?' asked the puzzled android.

It was Captain Valdour who replied. 'I believe the Regent is moving against the Emperor,' he snarled. 'Killing Johnny will be a way of establishing its authority.'

Even with the extra gravity of Melania, hearing the words spoken out loud made Johnny's stomach weigh at least a hundred times more than normal. He thought he might be sick.

'No one is going to be killed,' said Alf quickly. 'I am well versed in Melanian and Imperial law and there are plenty of avenues we can try.'

'Get Gronack back on the stand,' said Johnny. 'That was all lies.'

'I regret, Master Johnny, that Chancellor Gronack's evidence is set in the court record. It was not challenged at the time, so cannot be contested now.' Alf looked up from his feet to meet Johnny's furious eyes and added, 'But there are many more things we can do. I am transmitting the latest footage to Kovac so we can demonstrate it was faked.'

'The most important thing,' said Captain Valdour, 'is to get word to the Emperor. Can your ship take off without you?'

Johnny nodded. He hated the thought of Clara and Sol leaving now, but knew it might be the only way.

'Come closer, Alf,' said the captain. 'Send these coordinates to the *Spirit of London*.'

As the android leaned forward so his ear was beside Valdour's scarred face, the guards trained their blasters on the pair, but Alf quickly stepped away and said, 'It is done. Though I do hope Miss Clara will return soon.'

Johnny butted in. 'Tell her, if she can't find Bram in the next twelve hours, she must get home. Evacuate as many people as she can.'

'Both Sol and Miss Clara say they are not leaving without you,' the android replied.

'Tell them it's an order,' said Johnny.

A clear chime sounded and one of the guards said, 'Time's up.'

'I have not finished,' said Alf, but he was powerless to do anything as the chairs holding Johnny and Captain Valdour immobile lifted off the ground and propelled their captives out of the antechamber and along the short corridor towards the courtroom. The android had no choice but to follow.

No sooner had the trio re-entered the studio when the Judge boomed, 'Court is in session.'

As the audience cheered, Z'habar Z'habar Estagog rose into the air off six spindly legs and began again. 'The defence returns from their scheming. *What fiendish plan have they concocted to prevent justice being done, when the Terran's guilt is clear?*'

The huge brain was continuing with the proceedings, and asked 'Does the defence wish to question the witness?' Colonel Hartman stood in front of the vat beside Alf, glaring at the bowler-hat wearing android.

'No questions, your Honour,' replied Alf.

'What?' hissed Johnny from his chair. 'What about the fake footage?'

'Kovac assures me it is genuine.' Alf had tried to whisper, but his reply was so loud the whole courtroom must have heard.

'Well it's not – ask him to check again.'

'I . . . I cannot, Master Johnny. The *Spirit of London* has now taken off.'

'Oh,' said Johnny. He wilted in his chair. Even with the android nearby, he couldn't remember ever feeling quite so alone. There was nothing for it, but to warn Colonel Hartman. 'Bobbi!' Johnny shouted. 'Earth's in danger – you've . . .'

'Silence in court,' boomed the Judge, and the metal gag once again slid across Johnny's mouth. The startled colonel stared at Johnny as she was led away, while the brain continued, 'I call the next witness.'

'The moment has come,' whispered Z'habar Z'habar

Estagog. 'The time to hammer the final nail into the traitor's coffin – *to bury him alive* (metaphorically speaking).'

Into the courtroom slithered one of the largest, most grotesque creatures Johnny had ever seen. It was like a giant, brown slug, as big as a tractor, with dark liver spots along its body. The thing slid across the studio to the foot of the stone stairs, leaving a trail of silvery slime behind it. At the ends of two long stalks, giant eyeballs swivelled first to Captain Valdour, then to Johnny and then straight upwards towards the roof of the chamber. A crane began moving along the ceiling. Once in position, a harness was lowered and the huge slug was hoisted into the air. The jib groaned, but didn't buckle as it swung the creature across the courtroom, showering Johnny with slime, and then lowered it onto the hexagonal platform. The whole studio was buzzing with excitement. Once settled, its eyes turned and lowered to face the giant brain.

'You are Limax Maximus VII, Chief of Defence Staff, are you not?' asked the Judge.

'I am, your Honour.' As the alien replied, saliva spat from its mouth, spraying the stage.

'Proceed,' said the giant brain.

'Thank you,' replied the creature. 'And might I add what an honour it is to be here addressing the court on this historic day.'

'Limax Maximus VII captures the feelings of all of us,' whispered Z'habar Z'habar Estagog. '*We are indeed witnessing history in the making.*'

'While the Terran, Johnny Mackintosh, is quite rightly on trial for treason, I would like to draw attention to the role played by his Second, and accomplice, Captain Valdour of the Imperial Navy.' The giant slug paused for effect while a wave of murmuring swept across the audience and Z'habar Z'habar Estagog flew in for a closeup. 'If it pleases the court, I would draw your attention to the events of Galactic Standard Date

8.854 187 817. Every lifeform in this courtroom knows the significance of 187/817 – we all watched the Vermalcasts with horror, however magnificently produced they were.'

The slug's eyes swivelled upwards to the hovering presenter, who whispered, 'Winner of five Galactrons for best current affairs Vermalcast – *including best presenter*.'

Limax Maximus VII went on, 'It was the day a star in the galaxy's Orion Spiral Arm went unexpectedly Star Blaze, thought at the time to be solely the work of General Nymac and his invading Andromedan hordes. It was the day our own Fourth Fleet was totally destroyed.' Apart from the voice of the Chief of Defence Staff, the studio was now deathly quiet. 'Captain Valdour – can you tell the court where you were that fateful day?'

'You know very well where I was,' said Valdour. 'Fighting with the Fourth.'

'Aha! So you see,' the slug replied, turning to face the audience. 'Not all the Fourth Fleet was destroyed. Perhaps the reports were misleading?' Z'habar Z'habar Estagog buzzed away in the background as the eyes of the slug pointed forward, straining towards Captain Valdour. 'Tell me, Captain. How many other ships from your fleet survived that attack?'

'None,' replied Valdour in a whisper. He looked haunted, being forced to remember the deaths of his fellow soldiers.

'I didn't quite catch that,' Limax Maximus VII replied. 'For the benefit of the court, could you repeat it a little louder?'

'None,' bellowed Captain Valdour. 'It was the most terrible thing I have ever witnessed.'

'Yes, I suppose you would have to say that, wouldn't you,' spat the alien. Slime began dripping from the witness platform onto the guards in the moat. 'So how do you explain your own survival?'

'I almost died. Had it not been for Johnny Mackintosh here, I would have. He revived me – my ship avoided the full force of the Star Blaze as we were already en route to rendezvous with him. I was all but dead, but *Cheybora* folded close to the agreed coordinates and we were saved.'

'Condemned by his own words,' said the creature, its stalks swivelling to the audience. 'Captain Valdour clearly didn't suffer the fate of his brave comrades because he was running away – running away from the ambush he had planted with Johnny Mackintosh. How else can we explain such a fortuitously timed rendezvous?' Limax Maximus VII stretched its brown body forwards, out of the harness towards the bound captain. 'I put it to you that you are both in league with General Nymac!'

With his one eye, Captain Valdour stared at the giant slug as though it were the vilest creature in the galaxy. 'How dare you, sir?' he snarled.

Johnny watched, amazed, as the metal bonds holding the captain began to lose their shape. There was a sharp crack as the one around his massive chest broke, followed by another and another. Captain Valdour forced his way out of the chair and staggered to his feet. He howled with rage and lurched towards the raised platform as the creature shrank back. Several aliens in the audience screamed and then four lightning-like bolts converged at the centre of Valdour's chest, fired from the security guards' blasters.

For a moment, it looked as if the captain might keep going forward, but then the combined force of the blasters lifted him off his feet and sent him flying backwards, landing with a loud thud on the stone floor of the stage. Johnny bit down on his metal gag in horror, as he stared, eyes wide, at the motionless body. He could feel the blood trickling from the roof of his mouth.

'Oh my goodness,' said Alf as he ran towards the prone figure.

'Counsel,' boomed the Judge.' You will control your defendants or, the next time, the blasts will prove fatal.'

'Your Honour,' said Alf, who was now leaning over Captain Valdour's body. 'It appears they already have,' he added bitterly.

Johnny couldn't let this happen. He felt the anger welling up inside him and, before he knew what was happening, two bolts of electricity zapped out of his bound hands all the way across the stage, linking him to the hearts underneath each of Valdour's arms. The captain's body twitched and he coughed. There was uproar in the courtroom, with the Judge calling for order but being ignored. Aliens were running in all directions, but Johnny was losing focus. All the energy seemed to have drained out of his body. From somewhere, a heavy red blanket had been thrown over him and it felt as if he was suffocating, impossible to breathe let alone keep his eyes open.

15 ✿

Into the Fire ✿✿

'We have completed our examination of the hyperspatial device.' Several voices were speaking the words at once, not quite in sync with each other.

'Have transmissions been sent?' The voice sounded familiar – Johnny thought it was probably the Regent, but he didn't want anyone to know he was awake and his eyelids felt almost too heavy to open anyway.

'They have, frequently,' the many voices replied.

'Can you determine the recipient?'

'Without doubt it was General Nymac.'

There were gasps. Johnny decided he must still be in the courtroom cum studio. He didn't feel he'd been unconscious for long, but it was impossible to know. Had Clara followed orders and taken the *Spirit of London* back to Earth? Was there still time? Vaguely he could hear Z'habar Z'habar Estagog adding some extra commentary.

'Have you been able to reconstruct any of the transmissions?' It was definitely the Regent speaking.

'Some,' replied the voices.

'Then show the court,' said the Regent.

Slowly, Johnny opened one eye. Captain Valdour was bound to a floating stretcher nearby, with Alf standing over him anxiously. The collective voices came from four Owlessan Monks, floating beside one of Johnny's giant heads near the

Judge's tank. New images were being projected in the air above the big brain – they had an odd, dreamlike quality to them, but Johnny instantly identified the location as Pluto Base. The little Tolimi were saying farewells to Johnny and Clara, while the dwarf planet's massive moon, Charon, hung against a sky full of brilliant stars.

'I would not have thought it possible,' said the Regent. 'This image would have provided enough information for Nymac to wipe out the few remaining Tolimi who escaped him. A grand prize indeed.'

There were murmurs of disgust from the audience.

Turning towards the Monks, it added, 'Show the court what else there is.' The images changed to the insides of the *Calida Lucia*, followed by a view of Saturn and then Titan. 'Yes,' said the Regent. 'I am certain General Nymac would find the layout and capabilities of the Imperial Starcruiser most useful, as well as the locations His Divine Imperial Majesty visits. Treachery against our noble Emperor himself.'

Johnny wanted to shout out that it wasn't true – it wasn't his fault. He'd never spy against Bram – he wouldn't even spy against the Regent.

'Is there more?' the Phasmeer asked the four Monks. Again the images changed – this time they showed the Regent's bunker deep beneath the Senate. The giant alien was ordering ship movements, eager to encircle the Andromedan fleet by moving 'the First Fleet to the Keyhole Nebula and the Third behind the great star Carinae itself.'

'Right at the heart of government,' said the Regent. 'I welcomed him to our most secret place, and my battle plans were laid bare. How he must have laughed.' The Phasmeer looked up and saw Johnny stirring. Walking across, it asked, 'Was it sending Toliman Star Blaze that gave you the idea for this, even more deadly, ambush?'

Johnny could taste the metal of his gag – he tried to speak but no words could pass the barrier.

'Do you know how much energy is released when a hypergiant explodes?'

Johnny simply shook his head, numbed not only by the thought of one of the biggest explosions the galaxy had ever seen, but also by the way his own brother had used him to kill so many people. He'd been the unwitting pawn in Nymac's game of chess with the Empire, sending a constant stream of information through the wristcom all this time. Although he'd known nothing about it, the destruction of those Imperial fleets had been his fault. It was him who'd given their position away to his brother. He tried to summon the strength to free himself from the bonds of the chair, but he had none.

'Attempting to escape, Johnny Mackintosh?' asked the Regent, who stooped and peered into Johnny's eyes.

'After the Terran's last outburst,' said Z'habar Z'habar Estagog overhead, 'he was wrapped in a most unusual fabric. Woven into the fibres is a particularly useful mineral – *we call it orichalcum*. In certain configurations it might enhance the strange abilities we witnessed earlier. *But here, asymmetric and heaped chaotically over him, they are deadened.*'

'You cannot free yourself,' the large Phasmeer went on. 'You will sit and listen to the verdict. Then you shall be executed for being the dirty little traitor you are.'

'Objection,' said Alf, but the android's voice carried little conviction. 'The Regent is leading the jury.'

'Objection overruled,' said the Judge, without hesitation. 'The defendant's guilt is clear for all to see. It is time for the verdict.'

Johnny couldn't believe it. He'd not had the chance to speak and Alf hadn't questioned anyone yet. Lights fell on the audience of aliens, all looking forward, eager and alert, and on

Z'habar Z'habar Estagog, who once more was taking centre stage.

'It's almost over,' said the double-headed commentator, speaking directly to the rows of aliens on the stone steps. 'You've heard the evidence – *and seen the drama*. Secret dealings with the Andromedans – *the mysterious sole survivor of the 187/817 attack*. Sparks have flown – *literally as well as metaphorically*. And you saw, with your own eyes, transmissions sent by the Terran, Johnny Mackintosh, that led to the destruction of over half our ships – and the deaths of their crews. Now you must decide. Are the defendants guilty – *or are they guilty?*' The first head swivelled to look at the second as though it had made a mistake, but then a smile spread across both faces. 'The evidence is compelling as you weigh the fate of the accused and his Second. It is time for you, *members of this exclusive Milky Way News Network Vermalcast jury*, to vote.'

Lights flashed everywhere as dramatic music was broadcast into the courtroom. The central focus switched to Johnny's two massive heads, projected either side of the Judge's tank. The one on the black disc was swelling and looked lower down than the one on the white which, in turn, was shrinking as it rose higher into the air. The black disc hit the floor of the courtroom with a loud clang while, at the same time, the head projected above the white disc shrank to nothing and disappeared with a faint plop.

Johnny didn't know exactly what was happening, but could see it wasn't good. He hardly had the energy to react and wished Alf could take the orichalcum covering off him, but the android stood alone on the far side of the courtroom, fingers stuck in his ears as if he didn't want to hear the worst. All other eyes were on the giant tank which lit up as the Judge began to speak.

'Terran, Johnny Mackintosh, and your Second, Captain Valdour of the Imperial Navy – you have been weighed upon the scales of justice and found guilty of High Treason, one of the most heinous crimes in the galaxy. The evidence of your guilt was clear and compelling – as a result of your treason, many trillions of lives have been lost. That blood is on your hands and you will atone. You will be taken from this place to the steps of the Senate Platform, where you will be led before a firing squad and shot.'

The commentary from above only served to reinforce the terrible unfairness of it all. 'As is the custom, the accused will be executed first while the Second watches – *contemplating their misguided support*. The accused's body will be cut down and his Second's put in its place. Once dead, both will be left as carrion – *a reminder to the people of the punishment for these crimes*.'

The Judge concluded, 'I hereby delegate authority to the Regent to oversee the execution. Approach and take the prisoners away – court is dismissed.'

The audience rose as one, clapping and cheering. The giant Phasmeer also stood, before walking forward on its long, spindly legs. Guards flanked it on either side and Johnny's chair, together with Captain Valdour's stretcher, left the ground and followed. The party turned in the direction of the side exit and was almost out of the courtroom whcn, far faster than an Olympic sprinter, Alf appeared beside the Regent and attached something to the creature's long neck.

Everybody stopped and the armour-clad guards encircled the android, pointing their blasters at him.

'You would be wise not to fire,' said Alf. Johnny had never seen the android look so steely and determined. 'I am sorry . . . truly, but I have attached my neural detonator to the base of the Regent's brain stem.'

The Regent and its escort exchanged glances – none seemed to know what this actually meant, but the area of the Phasmeer's robes close to the device had turned white.

'The curse of being a, rather well-constructed, artificial lifeform,' Alf went on, 'is that I might have the misfortune to live forever. So, when the Emperor made me, he built in a fail-safe . . . the chance, before the darkness comes, to destroy my own brain – my own consciousness.'

The guards closed in, their weapons now practically touching the android's pinstriped suit.

'A brain comprising seventeen quadrillion positronic neurons,' Alf continued, raising his voice. 'And all it needs is for me to think one simple thought and you, sir, will die.'

'No one saw this coming – *even with two pairs of eyes*,' said Z'habar Z'habar Estagog who was now hovering above.

'This is an outrage,' said the Regent.

'I could not agree more,' the android replied. 'This trial makes a mockery of the word – faked evidence and biased witnesses. It is not justice.'

'It was necessary,' said the Phasmeer. 'If your brain were as large as you claim, you would understand that.'

'As this is necessary,' said Alf. 'You will release Johnny Mackintosh and Captain Valdour or you will die.'

Even Z'habar Z'habar Estagog had fallen silent. Johnny watched as his android friend and the Regent fixed eyes on each other, neither one blinking. Surrounding them he saw the soldiers' fingers twitching around the triggers of their blasters. He hoped none would panic and open fire. Finally, as if out-stared, the Regent turned slowly to its guards and growled, 'Do as the robot says.'

The bands holding Johnny prisoner in his chair slid away and he was able to push the suffocating orichalcum blanket to the floor – he felt better at once. Captain Valdour groaned. Johnny stood, shakily, and went over to the stretcher. Half the guns followed him while half remained trained on Alf.

'Are you OK?' Johnny asked.

'I've been better, but I'll live,' Valdour replied.

'That remains a matter of doubt,' said the Regent.

Johnny ignored it. 'Can you walk?'

'If I have to.'

With a little help, the captain swung his legs over the side of the stretcher and, leaning heavily on Johnny, got to his feet.

'Alf,' said Johnny quietly. 'I think we should go.'

'Master Johnny,' the android replied, not taking his eyes off the blasters trained on him. 'The *Spirit of London* is on her way back to Melania and will land within the hour. Take Captain Valdour and find somewhere to lie low. Miss Clara will come for you.'

'I'm not going without you – I'm not leaving you here.'

'I . . . I will be fine,' said the android, 'but I need to maintain my proximity to the Regent.'

'I assure you, you will most definitely not be fine,' said the Phasmeer. 'I will have your head for this, robot.'

'When His Majesty Emperor Bram Khari returns, I will place myself under his protection.'

A chirruping came from the Regent's middle as it shook with laughter. 'The Emperor has shown himself here once in a hundred years. He will not help you. It's over – he's finished. You have chosen the wrong side.'

'You are misguided,' Alf replied. It was strange for the android to be so calm when the tiniest thing would normally excite him. 'Go, Johnny – now.'

'I'll come back for you,' said Johnny. 'With Bram – we won't be long.'

'You are not to return to this place, Master Johnny. If His Majesty were here, he would say that is an order.'

'We'll see,' Johnny replied as, reluctantly, he turned away and, from somewhere, found the strength to half-drag, half-carry Captain Valdour out of the door.

Some of the soldiers made to follow but, after a warning look from Alf, the Regent said, 'Let them go. They won't get far.'

With a last backward glance to his android friend, Johnny hauled Captain Valdour out of the courtroom and down a short corridor, past the little room they'd been in before. With the strong Melanian gravity and the captain weighing him down, he knew he wouldn't be able to keep going for long – already his muscles were burning with the effort they were being asked to make. Another door slid open in front of him and the pair stepped outside into stale air. Johnny marched his friend forward, while scanning their surroundings for signs of danger.

High in the sky above them was the second, translucent surface that had been added to the planet early in Bram's reign. Looking back, the courthouse was the dull red of orichalcum, but its shape was hard to make out. It took a moment before Johnny realized it was like a giant three-dimensional Mandelbrot set, infinitely detailed and complex. In front was the square he'd seen earlier, thankfully deserted apart from the large black domes scattered randomly like half-buried Krun shuttles. He struggled past several of these, until he thought he could hear Z'habar Z'habar Estagog's voice coming from inside one. He froze and tried to listen, but the captain began to speak.

'You must flee, Johnny – go without me. I'm only holding you back.' Just speaking the words seemed to have taken the last of Valdour's strength. His legs stopped moving altogether and he would have fallen without Johnny holding him up.

'Shut up – I'm not leaving you too,' said Johnny, even though he knew that, carrying his injured friend, they wouldn't even make it to the edge of the square. 'Rest here, get your breath back,' he added as he tried to prop the captain against the nearby dome.

Instead of leaning against it, Valdour fell backwards and disappeared inside, with just his boots sticking out at the

275

bottom. Johnny touched the black surface and found his fingers, after a moment's resistance, passed straight through. Behind he heard the trampling of feet and looked to see a group of soldiers marching out of the courthouse. Desperately hoping he'd not been spotted, he jumped into the black dome – it felt like leaping through a spider's web – and found himself inside with Captain Valdour and Z'habar Z'habar Estagog itself. He lashed out at the presenter, who simply vanished – they were in another Vermaldome. He pulled at Valdour's feet so they were completely inside the bubble, and then turned to face the spot where the two-headed presenter had reappeared and began to speak.

'More breaking news from the trial of the century – *the Regent is safe and the robot defence counsel has been disarmed.*'

Johnny watched, aghast at the three-dimensional image of Alf lying motionless, surrounded by guards on the floor of the courtroom.

'I said I would have his head,' said the Regent, peering down from above the circle of soldiers. 'As a government official, it is important to keep my promises. Chop it off – now. And bring me Johnny Mackintosh.'

'Sir,' said one of the guards. 'Request permission to . . . to bring cutting apparatus.'

'How long will that take?' asked the Regent, raising itself up to its full height.

'Ten minutes, sir. No more.'

'You have five,' boomed the Phasmeer. 'What are you waiting for? Go! And the rest of you – find the Terran.' As one, the guards ran from the courtroom.

'We might have missed one execution, but it seems that here, live on the Milky Way News Network, we can bring you another – and I do love an impromptu beheading. *So long as it's not one of ours.*' The two faces looked at each other, smiling, before one added, 'We'll return after these special messages.'

'I've got to go back,' said Johnny.

'It's suicide,' whispered Valdour, who tried to hold onto Johnny's arm, but it was easy to brush him away.

'He's my friend – we've been through a lot,' said Johnny. 'He's not going to die in my place.'

'Then let me give you something,' said the captain. He lay back, opened his mouth wide and began unscrewing one of his front teeth, but even that effort now seemed too much for him. 'Help me,' he whispered. 'Pull it out – you'll see.'

Johnny looked inside Valdour's mouth at the prominent, half unscrewed yellowed incisor. He hesitated for a moment, but took a deep breath and then did as he was asked. The tooth came away easily in his hand and began to vibrate.

'Put it down,' said the captain.

On the floor of the dome, the grimy incisor began to change shape. Soon it had been replaced with something very similar to the particle beam disruptors carried by the armour-clad guards.

'I am a soldier,' whispered Captain Valdour, 'and never without my weapons.' He smiled weakly at Johnny, his gap-toothed, scarred face looking horribly disfigured.

'Thanks,' said Johnny, picking up the disruptor. He had no idea what, but he had to do something.

From inside the Vermaldome it was just possible to see out into the square. He watched and waited as several soldiers in their blue armour ran past. As soon as the coast was clear, he stepped out of the bubble. Johnny sprinted between the black domes, using them as cover, to reach the outer wall of the courthouse. Up close it was made of thousands of miniature copies of the larger structure. He sidled along the bumpy wall until he was standing in front of the main doors, which opened automatically, onto an empty corridor. He ran inside, pointing the disruptor ahead of him, and then darted into the little side room where he'd been taken with Alf. The blue armour hanging there looked far too big but, when he threw a set over his tunic, it moulded itself to fit his body shape making him look quite muscly.

Placing the disruptor into an empty holster, Johnny returned to the corridor. A couple of short aliens who were probably court officials were coming the other way. He held his breath, but they scuttled past without even glancing up at him.

He entered the near empty courtroom. The audience had left. The Regent and Chancellor Gronack were standing in front of the wall which obscured the brain's tank, peering over Alf's body which was strapped to the same stretcher that, not long before, had held Captain Valdour. The android's bowler hat lay discarded on the floor nearby. A single soldier stood by Alf's head, holding the ends of what looked like a rope made of pure blue light in its two hands. As it stretched its hands wide, the beam went taut above Alf's exposed neck. Above the scene hovered the figure of Z'habar Z'habar Estagog.

The aliens around Alf's stretcher didn't notice Johnny until he came quite close – it was Z'habar Z'habar Estagog's shriek that alerted the others.

'Nobody move,' Johnny shouted, taking the disruptor from its holster and waving it at the assorted aliens gathered around Alf. He ran to the far side of the stretcher, took the cord from the soldier and tossed it away. Then he stood with his back to the wall so he could also cover the side exit.

'Oh please,' squealed Chancellor Gronack. 'This is too good to be true. You came back for this sub-sentient mechanoid? Not even I thought you were that stupid.'

'Shut up,' said Johnny as he waved the others away from the stretcher with the end of the gun. 'You too,' he added, looking up at Z'habar Z'habar Estagog who had begun whispering renewed commentary. Hoping it would work, he fumbled for

Alf's left ear, pulled it out and rotated it three hundred and sixty degrees, all the time keeping the blaster moving between the different aliens.

'Master Johnny,' came the voice from the stretcher. 'I told you not to return.'

'I wasn't leaving you behind,' said Johnny. 'We're . . . family.' He pointed the disruptor at Chancellor Gronack's face and said, 'Release him.'

'Or what?' asked Gronack. 'You'll shoot me? You haven't got the nerve.' Behind the Phasmeer, a dozen soldiers ran into the courtroom, fanned out and took up aim.

'I mean it,' said Johnny, trying to sound convincing but, before he could decide what to do, the weapon was snatched from his hand and he found himself dangling upside down, suspended by the ankle from one of the Judge's giant tentacles. The wall behind him had once again vanished.

'You cannot escape justice, Johnny Mackintosh,' said the giant brain, 'and it must be seen to be done.'

'I don't think so.'

Everyone's heads, including both of Z'habar Z'habar Estagog's, swivelled to face the side entrance. Captain Valdour, a blaster in each hand and a bright orange antigrav harness strapped around his waist, lifted into the air, just as a volley of disruptor fire flashed into the space where he'd been standing. The captain returned fire and three of the Regent's guards were struck down, falling into the moat running in front of the stage.

Valdour landed on top of the raised witness box and crouched for cover. The remaining soldiers encircled his position, spraying the hexagonal platform with more energy bolts so that the air was soon thick with pieces of shrapnel. The captain fired upwards and not at them, sending the crane crashing down on his attackers, felling two more.

Still hanging by his ankles, Johnny was powerless to help. He looked on, horrified, as the witness platform finally exploded into smithereens, filling the studio with a cloud of purple smoke. Nervously, the remaining soldiers advanced through the dust, which slowly cleared to leave them staring nose-to-nose at each other in a tight circle.

'Looking for someone?'

As one, the soldiers' heads swivelled vertically upwards to where Captain Valdour hovered right underneath the battered ceiling.

'Kill him!' shrieked Chancellor Gronack.

Before the soldiers could fire, the captain undid his harness to leave it floating above him as he fell. He landed on top of the remaining guards. It was clear none of them would be getting up for a long time.

Z'habar Z'habar Estagog buzzed over towards the debris, hovering a few metres above it, and began to describe the carnage below. Before the commentator had got very far, a single warning shot fired straight up from the floor, narrowly missing its beating wings. The two heads turned to each other, screamed and the creature fled from the courtroom.

There was movement in the pile of bodies and, slowly and awkwardly, Captain Valdour struggled to his feet, blasters now trained on Chancellor Gronack and the Regent. He limped forward towards the group around the stretcher, smiling a toothless smile. It was all too apparent where his extra disruptors and probably the harness had come from.

'Order your Judge to release Johnny Mackintosh,' he said to the Regent.

'It is not mine to command,' the large Phasmeer replied, but Johnny still found himself being lowered, head first and rather too quickly to be comfortable, onto the floor. He stood up as the brain's tentacles retracted into the vat.

'What are we waiting for, Johnny?' said Captain Valdour.

'Haven't you got a planet to save?'

The smile was still forming on Johnny's face when it happened. A single blast came from behind him. The place on Valdour's chest from where Alf had once extracted the metal rod, was now smoking, a new hole burnt through it. Johnny stared at the blackened spot and then up to the captain's face. Lifeless eyes, still wide open with shock, didn't meet his own. In slow motion, Captain Valdour's dead body fell backwards. In slow motion, Johnny turned to confront his friend's killer. As he did a wall of sticky fluid gushing out from the brain's shattered tank broke over him. The last thing he saw was his disruptor still pointing outward, held tightly by one of the brain's tentacles.

✧ ✧
✧ ✧

Johnny was tied, with orichalcum-entwined ropes, to a red post fixed not far beyond the top of the steps in front of the Senate House. He could see one long shadow stretching out across Talamine Spaceport. Z'habar Z'habar Estagog hovered above him, with more of the annoying little insect-like cameras in his face to capture his final moments. Alf was tied up and under guard some way away and would be next. After threatening its life, the Regent had ordered the android to be executed as Johnny's Second, since Captain Valdour was already dead.

In the heavily armoured transport to the execution site, the android had bitterly explained his earlier collapse – that his positronic circuits must have overloaded. He had realized, too late, that he was unable to take another sentient life except in self-defence. Johnny listened, but felt numb. He managed to tell the android it wasn't his fault. He knew there was no one to blame but himself – Alf had tried to stop him coming here. He'd not listened, Captain Valdour was dead and he, Alf, and probably everyone on Earth, were about to be next.

A dozen blue-uniformed soldiers marched into view forming

a line in front, each carrying a long laser rifle. The Regent, also armed, followed and stood at the end. Only Gronack was missing from the scene. Johnny was surprised the Chancellor hadn't come to gloat, but the evil Phasmeer had been keen to return to the Senate.

Following the Regent's lead, the soldiers lifted the rifles to their shoulders. Johnny ignored the excited commentary above him. He gazed beyond the soldiers, scanning the spaceport, but another ship he didn't recognize was now berthed at the foot of the steps. There was no sign of the *Spirit of London*.

He thought about the first time he'd met Captain Valdour, when *Cheybora* had rescued him and Clara and brought them here to Melania to begin their adventures. It had all started when Kovac had found an alien signal. Then there was the visit to his mum's hospital bedside where, somehow she had given him the locket that now hung forlornly around his neck. He wished he could open it to take one last look at the pictures of his family inside.

The soldiers took aim.

He remembered finding out about Clara, and being taken into orbit with her in the space elevator and, from there, out into the galaxy. He hoped she'd be OK – that she'd be able to look after Bentley and Sol.

'I hold this rifle and stand beside my soldiers as is my right and duty,' said the Regent. Johnny was hardly listening as the Phasmeer's faraway voice added, 'I would ask no one to do what I would not do myself.'

He remembered the day, much later, in the Krun base masquerading as St Catharine's Hospital, when his mum revealed herself to be the Diaquant, one of the galaxy's first ones – when she had taken his human dad and they had left. She'd said they had to take different paths. When he died, Johnny wondered if that would be it – or would he somehow then take the road his parents were now on. He was clutching at straws – and it would be terrible for Clara to be left behind. He'd still not told her about Nicky and now he never would.

'Johnny – we've landed. I found Bram – we're coming. We'll be there in a moment.'

'Fire,' said the Regent. Clara was too late.

Ruby-red beams from all thirteen laser rifles converged on him and Johnny couldn't help but close his eyes. It didn't shut out the light, which was the brightest he'd ever seen, searing through his eyelids. A burning in the middle of his chest spread through his body and a whining started in his ears, quickly becoming louder. He was surprised it was taking so long to die.

'Johnny!' It was Clara again. She was screaming in stereo – through the earpiece and because she must be somewhere close by.

He didn't want her to see this. He opened his eyes and was nearly blinded by the white light surrounding him, shining like the brightest star in the sky from the centre of his chest – from his locket. The beams from the laser rifles were still targeted on him, but couldn't penetrate a sphere of whiteness that was surrounding him and growing. The high-pitched whine was also coming from his chest. It was as if the locket were absorbing all the energy being directed at him, but Johnny knew that couldn't last much longer.

The noise stopped. For a moment there was utter silence.

Johnny wondered if his eardrums had burst but then, with a whoosh, thirteen golden beams shot from the crystals in his locket, returning the fire it had soaked up and burning huge round holes straight through the bodies of the soldiers and the Regent. For a second, Johnny could see the spaceport through their chests; then the dead bodies crumpled to the floor.

Clara ran into view and sped towards him with Bram striding imperiously behind, followed by members of the Imperial

Guard. She reached Johnny and flung her arms around him, even as he was still bound to the post.

'Johnny – are you OK? Johnny?'

He couldn't speak. Nothing made sense.

Clara struggled to untie him, still asking if he was all right.

Johnny looked skyward. Z'habar Z'habar Estagog hovered five metres above, unscathed from the shootings. 'Murder . . . *murder*,' screamed the two heads. 'The Regent is dead – *killed by the Terran.*'

Bram reached Johnny and Clara and, instantly, Johnny's bonds fell away. He sank to the ground. The sound of marching footsteps warned of more soldiers approaching.

'Listen to me,' said the Emperor, placing an arm on Johnny and Clara's shoulders. 'I regret deeply that I could not return to stop the trial, but I knew, long ago, that your locket was a personal shield – from the time you returned the fragment of my own soul to me in Atlantis. Nothing else could have contained such a thing. You were not in danger as the evidence is now clear for all to see.' Briefly, Bram looked round at the fallen bodies. Behind them, Alf was being freed by the Emperor's soldiers. 'Wear them always – both of you. They are a precious gift from your mother. But, even so, Melania is not safe for you. The Empire is fractured and needs healing – my hold on it has grown weak. My own quests and obsessions made me blind to the oppression of my people and the actions of the Regent and its Chancellors.'

'Captain Valdour . . .' said Johnny.

'Died as bravely as he lived,' said the Emperor. 'As your Second, I thought him safe. The fault is all my own. I will honour him and *Cheybora* will do his memory proud.'

Alf rushed over to join them. The android was unscathed.

'Earth?' Johnny asked.

'Survives . . . just,' the Emperor replied, looking between

Johnny and his sister. 'A fleet will follow you, but remember what I said on Titan. You are the lawmakers now. I have no doubt that, together, you will save your Sun – it is for you to believe it too.'

Hordes of soldiers in blue Regency armour reached the top of the steps, spilling out into the space above. They stopped and stared at the bodies on the ground and the ring of troops surrounding the Emperor. Z'habar Z'habar Estagog began talking above.

'Go now,' said Bram. 'There isn't much time.'

Clara nodded and an archway opened leading to the *Spirit of London*. As she pulled Johnny through, he saw more blue uniforms on the bridge.

16 ✧

The Twin Paradox ✧

Bentley lay bleeding near the captain's chair, but lifted his head and barked weakly as Johnny, Clara and Alf appeared. The android collapsed, his bowler hat rolling across the floor.

'Hello, Johnny . . . Clara,' said Sol, ignoring the four soldiers busy encasing the Plican's tank in a strange red foam (smelling of air freshener) and the several others performing different tasks around the bridge.

All of them turned, clearly puzzled by the sudden appearance of the unlikely trio before them. At least five had bite marks showing on different parts of their anatomy. The one in charge stepped forward, saying, 'I don't know who you are or where you came from, but this vessel has been impounded by order of the Regent. You will come with me.'

'What have you done to our Plican?' demanded Clara. Her face radiated anger and power.

It wasn't the response the officer expected and he backed away as the girl half his size marched towards the tank. 'Come any further and I'll shoot,' he said.

'No!' screamed Johnny. He was finding it hard to think after the events of the last few minutes, but the one thing he was sure of was that he didn't want any more killing. He grabbed hold of Clara and shouted, 'Sol – forcefields.'

Blaster fire reached halfway across the bridge before fizzling out against an invisible wall.

'Do that again and you'll all be dead,' said Johnny, as Clara fought to break free from him. If she did, Johnny was sure the forcefields wouldn't hold.

'Sir,' said another of the soldiers. 'The Regent – it's . . . it's dead. All troops are ordered to report to barracks.'

'What?' said the officer, his face quickly losing colour. He took a couple of steps towards Johnny, Clara and the prone android, but was stopped by an invisible wall. Clearly flustered, he said, 'Don't think you've heard the last of this. It's impossible for you to take off but, should you try, your vessel will be destroyed.' With that he clicked his heels and led his men to the lifts.

Johnny breathed a sigh of relief. The soldiers clearly didn't know whose ship they were on or he was sure they wouldn't have dreamed of leaving. He relaxed his grip on his sister and bent down to check on Bentley, while she rebooted Alf. The Old English sheepdog must have put up a good fight, but was suffering for it now. 'Sol – can we take off?' he asked.

'Not officially,' the ship replied, 'but I am capable. However, I estimate the Plican will be unable to fold for 1.618 034 days.'

'I'll get us home,' said Clara.

Johnny nodded. 'Do it, Sol,' he said, 'as soon as those soldiers have left.'

'More soldiers?' asked Alf, standing up and going to collect his hat.

'Gel pod, Alf,' said Johnny. 'We're getting out of here.'

'Not a moment too soon, Master Johnny,' said the android, entering one of the two capsules that had risen up through the floor of the bridge.

As gently as he could, Johnny scooped Bentley in his arms and carried him to the remaining empty chamber. The pool of warm blood on the floor didn't bear thinking about, but there was no time to get to sickbay and folding without protection would probably finish the sheepdog off. He lowered his oldest friend, as carefully as he could, onto the floor of the pod; the dog whined, but licked Johnny's fingers.

Johnny stood, stepped backwards and sealed the door behind him. As he turned, the view outside was already changing from pink to black as the *Spirit of London* careered out of Melania's upper atmosphere.

Just beyond the hull, an explosion lit up the bridge before Sol darkened the windows. The ship shuddered, but carried on. 'Planetary defences include batteries of hyperspatial gravimetric charges,' she said. 'Apparently, that one was a warning shot. I am informed it will be our last.'

'Clara – now's a good time,' said Johnny.

He floated away from the floor as Sol switched the gravity generators off. Nearby, globules of Bentley's bright red blood did the same, but somehow Clara remained exactly where she was, her legs apart and her hands stretched upwards. It began. Johnny felt himself flying through the *Spirit of London*'s hull above the familiar sight of the Imperial Palace and its giant tower. Next moment he was jerked sideways at unfathomable speed, passing close to a fiery red giant star. Then he flew upwards through the blackness of space, the background stars becoming lines alongside him. He was pulled backwards through an orange and green nebula. The sides of the ship flew through and past him into their right positions and he was back on the bridge. Slowly, Sol turned the gravity on and Johnny floated to the floor. For all the world he wanted to be sick, but he fought back the feeling in order to rush Bentley out of the gel pod and to sickbay.

✵   ✵   ✵
✵   ✵

The journey had taken nearly a day so far and Johnny had lain awake the whole time. He replayed the events in the courtroom over again, unable to believe Valdour could really be dead. If only he hadn't let the Judge disarm him. He hoped the giant brain had suffered in destroying its own tank to kill the captain.

Afterwards, facing the firing squad had been the most terrifying moment of his life, but it had brought him closer to his mum. He knew now more than ever that she'd given much to protect him and Clara – their shields were proof of that. It wasn't fair that he'd never had the chance to talk to her properly. He hated how everything important seemed to happen so quickly – even with Bram returning, but telling him and Clara to leave the capital at once. If they ever came through this and made it home, he was determined to pin the Emperor down and find out more about his mum, the Diaquant. That was if home still existed. It was all very well Bram saying Johnny and Clara could protect Earth themselves. There'd been no chance to question it at the time and it all sounded fine when the Emperor was oozing power and reassurance beside him. Lying there on his own he didn't feel at all confident about standing in the way of a few hundred Andromedan and Krun destroyers. He hoped the fleet wasn't far behind.

His thoughts drifted to Nicky and how he might breach his brother's outer shell that was Nymac. Again he cursed himself for not telling Clara about her other brother straight after the meeting in Derby – the longer he'd waited, the worse it had become. As soon as they finished folding, he promised himself he would do it. He rehearsed the words in his head. He'd step straight out of the gel pod and say, 'Clara – I've got something important to tell you that I'm really sorry I've not told you before.' It wasn't going to be a good conversation, but it would be better once it was over.

He felt such a useless passenger lying in the gel pod while his sister remained on the bridge, manipulating great swathes of the fabric of space in huge folds to speed them home. *She* had real power – if only he was as strong, they might yet stop the Andromedans.

✦ ✦ ✦
✦ ✦

Johnny sensed the change even before Sol announced the last fold to be over – it was something he was getting better at. It was time to face the music. He didn't want to wait any longer. Still covered in gloop as the vacuum suckers had only just begun their work, he opened the door all ready to make his announcement. A moment's relief – the yellow Sun was shining through the clear walls of the ship – but something had gone wrong. Outside, it was Saturn, not Earth, which hung majestically against the backdrop of blazing stars. The ringed planet filled the viewscreen and most of the windows while Johnny's sister was lying on the floor before him, her body filling the bridge with a silvery glow.

He ran over to Clara and bent down beside her, desperate to check she was still alive. As he touched her wrist, his fingers tingled. Her pulse was strong, but her eyes were closed and he couldn't wake her. He'd half-carried Captain Valdour in the far stronger gravity of Melania, so getting his little sister to sickbay shouldn't be a problem. He made to pick her up, but nearly dropped her in surprise – she weighed next to nothing. It was just like the time he'd had to carry their mum all the way back from the Atlantean tower to the *Spirit of London*. If she'd not made herself incredibly light, they would never have reached the ship.

Once in sickbay, Johnny placed Clara on one of the beds, from where her silvery aura filled the room. Moments later, Alf appeared, very flustered, and promptly took over. Johnny watched as the android ran various checks and finally announced that, given time and plenty of rest, Clara would be all right. In the nearby open gel pod, Bentley was well on the way to recovering. At least the sheepdog could keep Clara company when she woke up.

Returning to the bridge, Johnny asked Sol to scan the solar system for hostile vessels. The news was bad. Five hundred and twelve Stardestroyers had gathered in the Oort Cloud and were spreading out, encircling the Sun. Johnny considered whether to head straight out to face the Andromedans single-handed or make a last stand with the Tolimi on Pluto. Neither would save the Sun. It was all very well Bram saying he and Clara could stop the Andromedans together, but his sister was unconscious and Johnny doubted that him firing a few electric sparks in Nymac's direction would be enough to send his brother into retreat.

Clara had folded them here at incredible speed and he wondered how long it would take the Imperial ships to join them. Then he remembered the thought chamber beside the Fountain of Time, 'connecting the observer to people or places that matter to him'. What mattered more than anything to Johnny was to connect to Bram – the Emperor could still tell him what to do and when the fleet would arrive. He shouted for Sol to enter orbit around Titan.

Telling Alf that he was in charge and should maintain their position, and ignoring the android's protests, Johnny descended the lifts to the shuttle bay. For a moment he wondered about flying the Starfighter to the surface, but something told him it was wrong – that it would violate the peaceful place his mum had created to take weapons into its vicinity. Instead he settled into the one remaining black London taxi, checking it was fully powered, and then flew the *Bakerloo* out of the open bay doors. There was no time to admire Saturn's rings. The *Spirit of London* was soon out of sight on the far side of the orange, cloud-covered moon. Johnny merged his thoughts with the shuttle's sensors so he could locate the landing site, but as he probed outwards his mind suddenly recoiled in horror. It had touched death and darkness. They came in the shape of long, deadly spines, protruding from a ship. Johnny didn't know how, but he knew they belonged to the *Astricida*. Desperately hoping he'd not been detected, he willed the *Bakerloo* quickly into the moon's upper atmosphere while thinking, *Shields on*. He didn't dare contact the *Spirit of London* – he hoped Sol could look after herself and he wasn't about to give her position away. With Nymac's flagship so far inside the solar system things were more desperate than ever.

The descent was bumpier than it should have been, as Johnny pressed the *Bakerloo* through the thick clouds at the absolute limit of the shuttle's tolerances. He landed on a rocky outcrop which looked out across a vast, nondescript plane. Feeling beyond the craft, everything told him the atmosphere was a poisonous cocktail of nitrogen and methane, but Johnny still thought, *Doors open*, and the *Bakerloo* responded, rematerializing around him. He stepped onto the rock and immediately through an invisible curtain.

The sweet smell of honey welcomed him, but Johnny didn't stop to enjoy it. He kicked himself for not thinking properly – he'd shown Nymac Saturn and Titan through the wristcom. His brother, or rather the Nameless One controlling him, was bound to be curious – pausing to survey the moon might even be what, until now, had spared the Sun from its supernova fate. Johnny sprinted around the edge of the golden lake, careful not to step in any of the liquid, continually spilling over the sides before being sucked back in.

Partway round he reached the crystal grotto where, at its heart, sat the domed communicator. Johnny placed his hands on the crystal plinth and peered inside, willing the Emperor to be there looking back. At first he could see only murky shapes, swirling in a thick mist like at the very centre of a nebula.

Johnny thought only of Bram and, through the fog, a face appeared – but it was completely encased by a mask as black as space itself with a single white star painted on. The person's eyes were even blacker than the mask that surrounded them and, as they stared at Johnny, he knew the only time he'd felt such hatred before was on Nereid many months ago when he'd first seen this same figure. Now he understood that the explosion of white against the dark mask represented a Starmark. It was a first one looking back at him. With a single star, it could even be *the* first one – it was certainly the Nameless One. The dome above the projection began to vibrate. Rippling waves of pure hatred were being directed towards him, deforming the surface which, any second now, looked likely to break, allowing the thing inside to come through. Johnny couldn't take his eyes away but managed to slap the controls.

The ripples remained, but they were softer and formed part of a new picture. The scene had changed. The place was one Johnny recognized, even though he'd never been there in real life. Now he saw it again, it was so vivid he couldn't understand how he'd ever forgotten it. It was where he'd sat beside Zeta in his dream, on her faraway planet. She was there now, on the spongy plants that lined the seashore, with her back to him, facing the ocean. He didn't have time to speak with her – it was Bram he had to talk to. His hands stroked the crystal controls, desperate to see the Emperor. Instead he found himself staring into the *Spirit of London*'s sickbay. From the look of his twitching eyes and limbs, Bentley was asleep but dreaming of chasing after cats. Clara remained motionless, her body still glowing but less silvery bright than before.

Exasperated by the hopeless device, Johnny kicked the plinth. He had to do a double take. The viewer wasn't useless after all – it could see through time. He was now watching himself running around the border of the lake, just as he'd done a few minutes earlier. He'd never seen himself sprinting before and it was, frankly, embarrassing. He couldn't believe no one in the football team or Mr Davenport had said anything – he ran like a girl. He made a mental note to work on his style if he ever got back to Earth.

An idea came to him, almost too incredible to contemplate. For just a moment, all his fears about the Sun and Earth left him as he dared wonder if he could look more than just a few minutes back through time. What if he might be able to see his parents? What if that was the real reason his mum had built this here? Johnny concentrated on his mum and dad. In the thought chamber, his past self had reached the crystal grotto and was running towards its centre – what was odd was that now he could also see another version of himself standing by the plinth. His past self stopped right behind the projection of him now – this couldn't be right. Johnny turned round. There, right in front of him, was . . . *him*. It wasn't the same as standing before his own reflection – his face looked the wrong way round – but then he normally saw himself in a mirror rather than in real life. His other self reached out a hand as if to shake.

'Are we allowed to touch?' asked Johnny. Alf had warned him of the dangers of seeing yourself when time travelling and Johnny had read loads of science fiction stories that warned of instant mutual annihilation if you had any physical contact with your double. The particular version of himself standing with his arm outstretched nodded – Johnny took the hand that was offered. The next thing he knew, the other Johnny had pulled him forward while kneeing him in the groin. He bent over in a mixture of pain and shock, but was then knocked off balance by a punch on the ear. As he fell, he was still looking behind unable to grasp why his double was acting like this. Too late he saw a particularly thick spike of blue crystal which met his skull with a dull thud. He lay on the ground, dazed and trying to come to terms with how much his head hurt and exactly what was happening. When he rolled over, the last thing he saw was the other Johnny wielding the broken off shard of crystal in both hands, like a baseball bat. He brought it crashing down, with a sickening crunch, on the bridge of Johnny's nose.

☆ ☆ ☆
☆ ☆

Somebody nearby was humming classical music, but stopped when Johnny groaned. His broken nose throbbed like never before, his throat was sore from swallowing warm blood and his head was being squeezed by something stuck on top of it that felt as if it was burrowing into his brain. For the first time in his life, he could feel movement inside his skull. His hands had been tied to something sharp and solid behind him, while his ankles were also bound together. Opening his eyes, he found himself propped up against one of the crystal growths facing the other version of himself, who was sporting an ugly smile.

'We meet at last, Johnny Mackintosh,' said the figure facing him.

'I don't understand,' said Johnny. 'Who are you?'

'Of course you don't understand,' the other boy replied. 'Because you're so dumb. In case you hadn't noticed, I'm you.'

'But . . . how? Why?' Johnny asked.

His double kicked him quite hard. 'That's for making Alisha break up with me,' he said.

'Alisha? Alisha Leow?' None of this was making any sense whatsoever. 'Do I go out with her in the future? But she's horrid.'

'You still don't get it, do you?' said the other Johnny, kicking him again. 'I'm not you from the future or the past. I'm you now. While you've been flying around the galaxy, who else do you think has been living at Halader House, going to your school and playing that stupid football you think you're so good at? And now I'm going to kill you and fully take your place. That thing on your head – it's recording your memories.' The double pointed to some images, flickering inside the nearby dome. 'Soon we'll know everything you know and then your pathetic excuse for a life can be over.'

From where he was tied up, Johnny could see only a little of the thought chamber, but the projections inside were so familiar he still recognized them. Playing out backwards, was the scene the *Calida Lucia* had reconstructed from Sol's dreams, with Johnny, Bram and Clara as spectators on the *Spirit of London*'s lifeless bridge. A figure in the captain's chair had just ordered Sol to self-destruct. '*You* tried to kill Sol,' said Johnny. The anger he felt was clearing his senses. 'It wasn't Erin – it wasn't me. *You* programmed the self-destruct.'

The figure facing Johnny began a slow clap. 'Ladies and gentleman – I do believe we have a winner. Penny's beginning to drop, is it? I don't know who Erin is – but I'll soon find out,' he said tapping his head to indicate the device on top of Johnny's. 'I was only doing you a favour – that must be the ugliest spaceship anyone's ever built. But I guess I'll just have to get used to it.'

Johnny growled – he'd never been so angry. He fought to get to his feet, but the cords holding him were too tight.

His double laughed. 'Is ickle Johnny upset about his ickle spaceship?' He kicked Johnny again, before examining the contraption around Johnny's head. 'Don't worry – you won't have to cry about your precious Gherkin much longer. I think we're nearly done – knew there wouldn't be much in that tiny brain of yours.'

'How is this possible?' asked Johnny. He was completely helpless. The only thing he could think of was to play for time and keep the impostor talking.

It was a different, older voice, standing behind him, that

answered. 'Because, little brother, I cloned you.' Nymac stepped forward, dressed all in black, the bright light shining from the mask which covered nearly half his face. 'It wasn't my idea – it was my master's. And, as I see now, quite brilliant. After we accelerated the growth, I left my new Johnny Mackintosh in the hands of the Krun to complete his education. I think we can agree he's fitted in very well.'

'Mr Wilkins helped too,' said the other Johnny. 'I'd have hated that place without him – and your bedroom's a pigsty.'

The world Johnny thought he'd been living in for the last few months was crashing around his ears. If he didn't do anything, he knew he'd be dead soon. Maybe, even at this stage, he could reach his real brother. 'Nicky,' he said urgently. 'I know you're in there somewhere. You've got to fight him. We can still help each other – we're family.'

'Yes, I admit that we are, but I made a new brother, you see,' said Nymac. 'And I'm sorry to disappoint you, but Nicky's gone forever. He had his uses – getting closer to you being the main one – but he's history. I was always in control.'

'I don't believe you,' said Johnny.

'No – you just don't *want* to believe me. I adapted his silly device to turn you into my spy. He didn't know it, but he even helped me clone you – that day we first met. His finest hour.'

'The mosquito,' said Johnny, remembering the annoying insect that had settled on his arm and drawn blood. Now he was used to them, but back when he first went to meet Nicky he'd not come across miniature flying machines like little bugs.

'He's definitely catching on,' said Nymac to the other Johnny, who smiled back.

Johnny tried rubbing the ropes holding him against the crystal support, but he knew it would take far too long to free himself.

'You had your chance,' Nymac said to him. 'If you, too, had

been willing to serve, I have no doubt my master would have let us rule this galaxy together.' Johnny rolled his eyes while the figure in black continued, 'Who would not be interested in such an opportunity? Yet that headpiece you're wearing is the closest you'll ever come to a crown. Now I have the genes,' he went on, turning to Johnny's double, 'but without the wishy-washy attitude.'

'Bram will stop you,' said Johnny, but it was hard to form the words, as though his brain was slowing down. Projected into the thought chamber behind Nymac, he saw the carpet of a familiar but long-forgotten child's bedroom. He was hiding under the bed with Bentley beside him.

'I don't see your precious Emperor now,' said Nymac, turning three hundred and sixty degrees while pretending to look around. 'Oh – there he is!' he said, pointing to behind the post to which Johnny was tied.

For just a second Johnny wondered if there was hope, but then both his double and Nymac began to laugh.

'Ah – we seem to be finished,' said Nymac, gazing into the nearby, now empty, dome. 'Or rather, you do,' he added, turning to Johnny with a cruel smile. He touched something on the side of Johnny's head, there was a whirring noise and Johnny felt dozens of needles withdrawing from inside his skull. As they retracted, air rushed into the holes, like hundreds of miniature daggers stabbing his brain.

'You don't get to be king after all,' said Nicky, holding up the crown of strange metal, inlaid all along the inside with hundreds of spikes of varying lengths, some up to several centimetres, all of them dripping with blood. Johnny felt sick – it looked like something from a medieval torture chamber.

'Let me have it,' said Johnny's double, greedily reaching for the headpiece.

Nymac held it away from the impostor's grasp. 'This is not

for you, little brother,' he said. 'I have not gone to the trouble of making you, only to give you the memories of the Emperor's puppet here. Gain those and you might become him.'

The clone didn't look happy, but withdrew his hand. 'He said something about an Erin – he might be important – you should find out. And there's his girlfriend too.'

'Yes – I have wondered about her,' said Nymac. 'Often, I see her face through my little spy camera. You two have become close.'

'What are you talking about?' said Johnny. 'I don't have a girlfriend.' He was still rubbing his ropes against the pillar behind. The crystal was cutting into the skin around his wrists, but he could feel a few of the strands breaking – if only he had more time.

'I'd be embarrassed, too, if I was going out with that,' said the double. 'What's her name? Clara?'

'Clara?' said Johnny as another strand broke. 'She's my sister, durr-brain.' At once he regretted saying it, but he couldn't suck the words back into his mouth.

'I have a sister,' said the clone, a stupid grin spreading across his face.

Johnny wanted to tell him that of course he didn't – that he was making it up – but Nymac had bent down so close that Johnny could feel the hot breath on his face. His brother was looking furiously into Johnny's eyes.

'Sister?' said Nymac. 'What do you mean, sister? Why did I know nothing of this?'

'Probably because the Krun took her education in hand too,' said Johnny. 'Like durr-brain behind you.'

'Liar!' shouted Nymac. 'It's not possible.'

'She went to their Proteus Institute,' Johnny replied, as calmly as he could. He might be able to stay alive a little longer if he could turn Nymac's anger on the Krun. 'Perhaps Bugface

'. . . the one called Stevens . . . forgot to tell you?'

'How dare he hide this from me? He goes too far – it is the last time,' said Nicky. A vein in his forehead was throbbing and looked as if it might burst. He stood up, turned to the clone and said, 'Finish him and take his shuttle back to his ship. I shall return to the *Astricida* at once and see if this is true.'

'General,' said the clone, who'd backed away from Nymac as he'd turned angry. 'I understand if you won't give me the memories, but might I borrow your blaster?'

'Didn't you see the Vermalcasts?' shouted Nymac. 'Or are you an inferior copy with mush for brains?' The clone looked frightened as Johnny's brother went on, 'He has a personal shield – that's why I told you not to shoot him in the first place.'

'Not any more, he doesn't,' said the other Johnny, reaching underneath his tunic and pulling out a golden chain with the gold and crystal locket sparkling at the end of it. 'Now it's mine.'

'That doesn't belong to you,' said Johnny, working even harder. How dare the impostor steal this link to his parents? More strands snapped behind his back. He was nearly there.

'You have redeemed yourself, brother,' said Nymac to the double. 'Your time has come – the first great purpose for which you were born. Indeed you may take my gun – you are right not to leave anything to chance.' The figure in black removed a weapon from a pouch built into his body armour and handed it to the clone. 'The act of taking a life is a doorway through which only the strongest can pass. But once they do, the rewards are without equal.' Nymac's smile was twisted and terrible. 'Bring his ship and rendezvous with the fleet when you are done. When you are truly Johnny Mackintosh.'

'Yes, General,' said Johnny's double as Nymac strode out of the crystal garden and away. As the impostor watched Nymac walking around the outside of the lake, Johnny took the chance to rub the ropes some more against the crystal. He was very close.

The clone turned to Johnny. 'I'd love to stay and chat,' he said, pointing the blaster at Johnny's chest, 'but I've got a sister to get to know.' He squeezed the trigger.

Johnny watched as the bolt of energy left the end of the gun. It was strange that it hadn't reached him yet. No longer caring if the clone could see him, he rubbed his wrists frantically against the post behind him. His double didn't move a muscle but the lake, which had been almost still, was now covered with ripples, some of them quite large. From nowhere, roaring waves broke across its surface – they reminded Johnny of the ocean crashing over Atlantis. That day it had looked as though he, Clara, Bram and the Diaquant would all be swept away, yet somehow Johnny's mum had stopped time so they could escape.

The energy bolt was halfway towards him. Johnny's wrists felt as if they'd been sliced to shreds by rubbing against the crystal, while his head ached like never before from the memory transfer, but he summoned the energy for one last effort. The final cord snapped and he rolled out of the firing line.

The spell was broken. The beam of energy smashed into the pillar to which Johnny had been tied a moment earlier. It shattered in a dazzling explosion, covering the ground in hundreds of slivers of crystal. He grabbed one and was able to slice straight through the ropes binding his ankles. Getting up, he turned to charge the impostor, but another bolt of energy blew a hole in the ground right in front of Johnny's feet.

'How did you do that?' asked the clone. 'Tell me and you might live a little longer.'

Johnny hadn't the slightest idea if he'd just caused time to slow and, if so, how he'd done it. If it had been him, he was certain he couldn't do it again – his head hurt so much it felt as if it might shatter like the crystal pillar.

'Tell me now,' said the impostor.

'I'll show you,' said Johnny. 'Put the blaster down and I'll teach you how it's done.'

'You must think I'm stupid,' said the clone, who fired again.

The ground in front of Johnny's feet disintegrated and he jumped backwards to avoid falling into the hole that opened up, landing close to the edge of the lake.

The clone laughed. 'I want to see you dance,' he said, firing several more shots around Johnny's feet.

Johnny jumped high as shrapnel from the explosions flew around his legs. He was teetering right on the boundary of the golden liquid. The blaster fire hit the ground between his feet and he fell forward, but the clone stopped shooting.

'You're good at skipping – like a girl,' said the clone. 'Is that why you're in the football team?'

'You run like a girl,' Johnny replied, getting to his feet but not taking his eyes off his double. 'Is that why you're not?' It looked as if he'd struck a nerve.

The clone lifted the blaster from Johnny's feet, instead pointing it at his chest. 'I'm bored of you now,' he said. 'Time to die.' He fired.

Johnny leapt backwards out of the way. As he twisted in mid-air, the beam of charged particles, like a lightning bolt, just missed him, but he saw he was heading into the lake with no way to stop himself. Then, just above the surface, he landed on something solid which he couldn't see. By the confused look on the clone's face, he couldn't see it either. Johnny guessed it was the walkway Bram had stepped onto when they'd been here the last time. He stood up, seemingly supported by nothing at all and laughed. He knew it would annoy the clone and must look as if he was defying gravity.

'Stop it,' said the other Johnny. 'It's not funny – you know I'll kill you in the end.'

'You'll have to catch me first,' Johnny replied, risking a few steps further along the invisible walkway towards the centre of the lake. 'Or are you too scared to come after me?'

The clone fired a couple more blasts but, further away now, his aim was poor. Very tentatively, he put his feet over the boundary of the lake, searching for something solid to step onto. Much to Johnny's disappointment, he found it, but the impostor looked very unsure as he edged along the invisible bridge.

Johnny took a few confident steps further away. Behind him, columns of chronons, liquid time, shot into the air. He couldn't go any further without stepping under them.

'What's that?' said the clone. He was looking nervously beyond Johnny while inching along the walkway towards him.

'Wouldn't you like to know?' said Johnny. Despite the blood dripping from his wrists, nose and scalp, he was feeling a little more confident now.

Then the clone's eyes turned from green to silver. The space between Johnny and his double collapsed as Johnny found himself being folded forwards towards the impostor. Like Clara, the double could fold space, but for the very first time Johnny was able to understand how it was done. Everything began to straighten out just a metre in front of the clone, who was preparing to fire.

Instinctively, Johnny grabbed hold of a piece of space itself, just behind the impostor, and pulled as hard as he could. The blaster released its energy bolt into thin air as Johnny found himself in normal space, back to back with his double. He turned first, rugby-tackled the impostor and knocked the blaster out of the other boy's hands. It slid along the walkway closer to the fountain. Johnny dived for it with the clone jumping on top of him – the weapon remained out of reach. Johnny twisted his body so he lay on his back, grabbed the clone's wrists which were still grasping for the gun, and placed a foot in the impostor's stomach. He threw the double over his head, closer to the roaring fountain. Quickly Johnny turned to pick up the weapon and point it at the clone now standing before him.

'Can you really kill yourself?' asked the clone, raising an eyebrow as he spoke. Not far behind him, the golden aurora hung high in the sky, while a solid sheet of liquid chronons began raining down into the lake.

'You might have my genes, but you're not me,' Johnny replied. 'I don't want to kill you, but I will if I have to. I'm taking you back to the *Spirit of London* while I work out what to do.'

Despite Johnny's words, a look of pure terror spread across the impostor's face. 'Clara – help me,' he shouted. 'He's gonna shoot.'

Johnny wasn't about to be fooled by the clone's acting and kept the blaster trained on his double – until he heard footsteps hurrying from behind. In the instant he turned and saw Clara running out across the lake, the clone's head caught him full in the stomach, winding him and knocking him to the ground. The impostor snatched the blaster and sat on Johnny's chest, pinning him to the walkway with the cold point of the weapon thrust underneath his chin. He had no breath to speak.

'He's a clone,' said the clone, matter of factly. 'Nymac did it – cloned me. This . . . this thing's been going to school in my place. It wasn't Erin – *he* tried to destroy the *Spirit of London*. I have to kill him – you understand, don't you?' the clone asked, looking at Johnny's sister.

'I understand,' said Clara, nodding and placing her hand on the double's shoulder.

Johnny gasped for air, but found none. This couldn't be happening. He felt the full pressure of the blaster on his windpipe as the impostor's fingers squeezed the trigger. Johnny closed his eyes.

The blast sounded distant. Johnny heard his own scream, even though he'd no breath to make it. The weight on his chest was gone and he dared to open his eyes. There was only his sister beside him, staring horrified at something further along the walkway. Johnny followed her eyes to where she'd folded his clone, now standing right beneath the Fountain of Time.

The clothes the impostor was wearing looked far too big. His hair was retracting into his skull, becoming finer, as his face became less recognizably Johnny's. As chronons from the fountain washed over him, he shrunk to become a toddler – and still he grew younger. Clara stirred as though she was going to rescue it, but Johnny reached up and held her back.

A wrinkled baby crawled out from beneath Johnny's white tunic and black trousers, with only the gold and crystal locket swinging from its neck. It looked questioningly at Johnny and Clara, before reaching the edge of the invisible walkway, its tiny, stubby pink arms grasping at empty space. Then it made a last gurgling noise and toppled, head first, into the lake of liquid time, disappearing under the surface.

Johnny was on his feet, making sure his sister stayed where she was. He only let go once her body sagged and he knew she wasn't about to run under the fountain and try to save the clone.

'It's over,' he said softly.

Tears were falling from eyes that, only a moment before, had burned silvery bright. As Johnny watched, they quickly faded to the pale blue of their mother's.

'Look at us,' she said, snuffling. 'We make a right pair.'

Through the walkway, Johnny caught sight of his reflection in the surface of the golden liquid. A ring of blood encircled his head, his nose looked nearly as bad as the last time while more blood trickled from his wrists. He began to feel faint.

'Come on, you,' said Clara, shepherding him towards the end of the walkway. 'It's your turn for sickbay.'

Once he reached solid ground, scarred and pitted from the clone's blaster, Johnny sank to his knees. Everything was swimming before his eyes. 'The *Astricida*,' he said, fighting to stay conscious so he could warn Clara of the danger.

'It left,' she said.

'There's something else,' he said, holding onto her sleeve for support.

'Shhhhh – it can wait.'

'Not this,' said Johnny. 'It's waited too long already.' He looked up at her tear-stained face as she came into focus. 'Nymac . . .' he went on.

'I told you – he's left,' said Clara.

Johnny shook his head. Blood from his broken nose spattered the ground, but he didn't care. 'It's not that. He's . . . he's Nicky. He's our brother.'

17 ✩

Star Blaze ✩

For a moment Clara looked at him, uncomprehending. Then she grabbed hold of his top and dragged him through the open fold and onto the nearest bed. Immediately, a big ball of grey and white fur bounded across the sickbay floor, barking happily. Bentley reached Johnny, stood on his hind legs and rolled a long wet tongue across Johnny's face. It stung like crazy.

'Bentley thinks I picked the right one,' said Clara. Her voice sounded strained and she wasn't looking at Johnny.

'How'd you know it was me?' he asked.

'I saw you from the edge of the lake,' she said. 'You had a chance to kill him, but didn't want to. He had the chance to kill you and tried to take it. Lucky I know you're such a softie.' Clara looked upwards. Her eyes were watering, but she was refusing to let herself cry again. Her breathing was irregular and heavy. 'I didn't mean him to die, either – I just folded him away to protect you. What happened after . . . it was horrid.'

'I know you didn't mean that,' said Johnny. 'It wasn't your fault.'

'What you said . . . about Nymac,' said Clara. 'I don't understand – I thought Nicky was dead.'

Before Johnny could even think how to respond, Alf burst into sickbay, flapping. 'Oh my goodness, Master Johnny. Whatever happened to your face?'

'It doesn't matter,' Johnny replied, still looking at his sister, pleading for forgiveness. Slowly he turned from her and added, 'The Sun – we've got to stop Nymac.'

'Enough is enough,' shrieked the android, throwing his hands in the air and looking every bit as determined as when threatening the Regent. 'Twice you have not listened to me and both times you have nearly ended up being killed. I cannot allow that again. This is a medical emergency – you need rest and it is up to me to see you get it. You are hereby relieved of command.'

Johnny couldn't believe his ears. He had to stop this happening and raised his blood-soaked hands in front of his face, but the android was too quick. The next moment came a hiss of air as the pneumatic syringe was pressed against his neck. It was like sinking beneath the surface of a great ocean. While sunlight danced above, he couldn't reach it and descended slowly into oblivion.

✧ ✧ ✧
✧ ✧

Dangling his legs over the edge of the clear platform in orbit above the Earth, Johnny was watching events unfold. During the past few hours he had witnessed the Sun swell, becoming bloated and red. There would be panic beneath his feet. No one had foreseen this – the biggest threat to life had seemed a runaway greenhouse effect, meaning the more ice that melted, the faster global warming took hold. Now that particular feedback loop was forgotten as scientists scrambled to explain how the impossible was happening to Earth's supposedly stable star.

What they couldn't know was that the Sun was being bombarded by tachyons, dragging mass from its far future to here in the present. In the course of a single day, it had become a very old, giant star, much of its fuel spent. There was only one thing left – the collapse. Heavy elements that now made up its outer shell headed inwards under the force of gravity, heating the core to unimaginable temperatures and pressures. Something had to give and that something would be the Sun itself.

Johnny knew that, in a way, he was privileged – he had the best seat in the house to watch the greatest explosion in the history of the solar system. The only shame was that he'd not been able to prevent it. A wall of deadly fire, billions of kilometres across, rushed towards him, devouring everything in its path. It felt like standing on a deserted beach watching a wave taller than Mount Everest approaching. Flames licked around the planet beneath his feet. The atmosphere caught fire; the oceans boiled dry. In seconds, the mantle had evaporated and Earth's molten core was exposed, then enveloped, in a mightier furnace. In very little time the world he'd always called home was torn apart, leaving nothing behind.

Gazing at the spot where Earth had disappeared, it struck Johnny how he might have been able to stop it. He wasn't certain, but it could have worked. The words 'Too late now, Johnny Mackintosh' came from an irritating commentator somewhere above. He wished he'd thought of it earlier. Another thing was nagging at the back of Johnny's mind – how was he still alive? Not even Nicky's myriad forcefields could survive a supernova. It didn't make any sense . . . unless what he'd witnessed hadn't happened. Unless it wasn't real. Unless he'd *dreamt* it. He *could* still stop this, but to do that he had to wake up – and quickly.

Normally, the realization that he was dreaming would have been enough, but Alf's sedative must have been powerful. Johnny pinched himself, but nothing happened. He tried screwing his eyes up and blinking hard, then opening them as wide as possible. He was disappointed not to find himself staring at the sickbay ceiling. Instead, he stood in a darkened corridor stretching endlessly on, with many doors of all different shapes and sizes leading off it. He screamed in frustration, but then realized he recognized this place. He'd been here before, in another dream. He stumbled forwards and opened the only door he knew, falling through into the spongy vegetation by the shoreline on Novolis, fifteenth planet in the Alnitak system. He was alone, the landscape now lit by two blue suns, one dwarfing the other. He had no idea what to do except to shout, 'Zeta!'

No time at all later, a purple-haired alien was sitting beside him. 'Johnny . . . your face . . . and your hands.'

'They're not important,' he replied, as she took hold of his wrists and he saw the scars and rope burns begin to fade.

'Shhhh,' said Zeta. 'Let me heal you.'

'I need to wake up,' said Johnny, pulling his hands away. 'I have to stop Nymac.'

Zeta turned her attention to his scalp, rubbing ointment into the wounds that encircled it. 'Do you mean the Andromedan General or your long-lost brother?' she asked.

'How? How could you know that?' asked Johnny in total amazement.

'The memories were still leaking from you,' replied the princess, matter of factly. 'Do not fret – I have stopped them.'

'That's not what I'm worried about,' said Johnny.

Now Zeta was touching his nose. He could feel the tingling, burning sensation spreading across his face.

'It seems we are both burdened by our brothers,' she said. 'We are not responsible for the actions of others – we choose our own paths.'

'I'm sorry I blamed you,' said Johnny. 'And thanks for this.' He could see the scars on his wrists had vanished completely and he could breathe the vinegary air freely through his nostrils.

'You're welcome,' said Zeta, smiling at him. 'I'm glad that your ship, too, has been healed. I hope you will visit me again.'

'I hope so too,' Johnny replied, 'but I've really got to go now.'

'If it's so important, why don't you wake up?' asked the princess.

'I can't – Alf's sedated me. It was the injuries.'

Zeta tutted. 'Check your face,' she said. 'Has all the scarring gone?' She pointed to his reflection in the still waters at their feet.

'I'm sure it's fine,' said Johnny, peering into the great ocean.

'Goodbye, Johnny Mackintosh,' said Zeta, pushing him hard in the back.

Arms flailing and unable to stop his fall, Johnny plunged headfirst into the warm waters. He hadn't taken a breath so, lungs bursting, he kicked hard for the surface above him, patterns of light dancing across it. As his head broke through he opened his eyes properly and found himself staring at the ceiling in sickbay. He'd done it. Zeta had done it. 'Sol – what's happening? Where are we?'

'Hello, Johnny. I hope you're feeling better. We have broken orbit from Titan. I have been asked to fold to Earth to begin an evacuation. You know I would rather counter the Andromedans more directly.'

'Don't worry – change of plan,' said Johnny as the sickbay doors swished open and he ran along the corridor towards the lifts. 'I want you to head straight for the Andromedan fleet – the *Astricida* if you can find her.'

'It will be my pleasure, Johnny,' replied the ship.

☆ ☆ ☆
☆ ☆

'Master Johnny – why aren't you in sickbay? Your scars?'

'No time to explain,' said Johnny, knowing he wouldn't have been able to anyway, considering his wounds had been healed in a dream. He sat down in the captain's chair and said, 'We're going to the Oort Cloud.'

'The tachyon bombardment has already begun,' said Alf. 'The Tolimi are firing, trying to break the circle of ships. They know they don't stand a chance, but they wanted to buy us time while we evacuate who we can.'

'Sol – have you found the *Astricida*? Is she anywhere near Pluto?' Johnny was desperate to kill two birds with one stone.

'The *Astricida* is on the opposite side of the Sun to Pluto Base,' Sol replied.

Johnny's heart sank. He was torn between two locations ten billion kilometres apart. If he turned the ship around to join the fight with the Tolimi, it would be simply be one ship against five hundred – the Sun would still be destroyed and everything with it – but he couldn't just leave them to sacrifice themselves.

Clara was standing beside the Plican's tank, her face even whiter than normal. 'We're too late,' she said. 'There's only a few minutes to save people – we were about to fold to Earth.'

'That is no longer possible,' said the ship. 'Sensors indicate a massive spatial disturbance across the entire solar system. The continuum has become distorted beyond even unsafe limits. I am receiving a transmission.' Was it the supernova? Everyone on the bridge held their breath. 'It is *Cheybora*,' Sol continued, 'with an Imperial fleet. They are engaging the Andromedans around Pluto Base.'

'Yes!' said Johnny, punching the air. They had a chance – it was so slim the odds didn't bear thinking about, but there was still hope. 'Sol – keep going straight for the *Astricida*,' he said. 'Full speed and then some.'

Alf looked far from happy. 'Master Johnny – at those speeds the *Spirit of London* cannot remain shielded. We will be, I believe the term is, sitting ducks. Are you quite certain your place is here and not in sickbay?'

'It's OK,' said Johnny. 'I'm OK. They're expecting us so we don't need to be shielded – we do need to reprogramme your nanobots.' The android looked totally bemused, but it was Clara who Johnny turned to next. 'Remember the box you made for Kovac?' he asked. 'I've got an idea.'

✿ ✿ ✿
✿ ✿

The *Astricida* had taken up position in the Oort Cloud, at the minimum safe distance from which to escape the coming Star Blaze. On the way to meet her, the *Spirit of London* was flying close to the Sun, using its gravity to slingshot them ever faster towards the outer solar system. Through the windows, Earth's nearest star glowed blood-orange, its surface in swirling turmoil as the Andromedan tachyon beams took an ever deeper hold. The ship flew within a giant looping flare that broke free as they sped on their way. Johnny hoped there was nothing in its path.

Travelling so close to the speed of light, the time dilation of relativity theory meant their entire journey would take them only a few minutes, even though hours would pass for both Earth and Sun. Clara had carried Kovac off to the garden so the quantum computer didn't distract Alf and Johnny, who were working together on the bridge, isolating and rewriting key fragments of the nanobots' programming code, hidden within millions of other lines. Johnny glanced out of the windows to see Mars whizz by, far redder than normal. He looked down at the console and went back to work, but it was barely any time later, as the *Spirit of London* careered beyond the orbit of Neptune, that Sol announced, 'I am being hailed – it is the *Astricida*.'

Johnny shooed Alf out of sight and took a deep breath to compose himself – now was not the time to go red. 'On screen,' he said and Nymac was projected into the bridge, but side on without the horrible mask showing. Light still shone from the face, only it was a soft, silvery glow, like Clara's.

'How was your first kill, my brother? Did the weakling cry?'

Johnny was relieved to see Nymac appeared distracted, his hands gliding across the holographic display on his bridge. 'Like a baby, General,' he replied, adding, 'I want more.'

'Yes . . . you're in quite a hurry – in more ways than one,' said the figure on the viewscreen, not looking up.

'I wanted to be by your side, General,' said Johnny. His plan would be a non-starter if he wasn't on board the *Astricida* in the next few minutes.

'So you shall be. I have left room for your ship at my right hand. Tell me – where is our new-found sister? I would have her come aboard to witness my triumph.'

'Er . . . she wasn't compliant,' said Johnny, improvising and hoping Clara wouldn't unfold onto the bridge while he was talking. 'But she will learn.'

'Indeed she will.' Nymac still hadn't looked at him properly. Johnny's brother continued, 'When this is over, I will ensure she is more obedient. We three shall be united in the service of the Nameless One – this galaxy will soon be our plaything.'

It was horrid listening as his brother sneered, but it didn't make Johnny feel any better about what he was planning to do. 'Request permission to come aboard . . . General,' he asked, wondering if the nervousness in his voice would help or hinder.

'Can you not see I am busy?' shouted Nymac, still focused on what he was doing. 'And who would fly your ship after it took so much to win her?'

'There's a robot here for that,' said Johnny. Alf looked up from his console, totally appalled. 'It does what I tell it to,' Johnny added, hoping the android would keep working on their task. 'I want to witness your triumph too.'

'Very well,' snapped Nymac. 'I suppose it is fitting for you to be here, even though our master has not ordered it. I will arrange the fold. Be ready in one minute.'

'Yes, General.'

Nymac had cut the transmission.

'Exactly what is going on, Master Johnny?' demanded Alf. 'Dealing with the Andromedans *and* insulting me all at once? I hope you know what you are doing.'

'I'm sorry,' said Johnny. 'If we get through this, I promise I'll make it up to you. Now can you send the code?'

'But we are not ready.'

'Then we've got about half a minute to finish.'

To Johnny's relief, Alf's fingers began moving across the workstation at lightning speed. 'Johnny to Clara – time's up. It's now or never.'

A moment later Clara appeared on the bridge, holding a new wristcom for Johnny. She looked at him and said, 'It should work, but there wasn't time to test it.' Johnny took the device and fastened the Velcro strap around his wrist.

'Finished, Master Johnny,' said the android, who had a slight sheen across his metallic face.

'Send the code,' said Johnny. He looked out of the windows running along the side of the bridge. The Sun was unrecognizable, blood-red with its disc many times wider than he was used to out here. The Andromedan beams were working well. Worse, Johnny was seeing it as it had looked several hours ago – the supernova might have already happened.

He shook himself – he couldn't afford to think like that. If there was any chance of saving Earth's closest star, he had to act fast. On cue, a patch of nothingness began to appear, obscuring the viewscreen at the front of the bridge. As it widened, a heavy whiteness spilled out of the opening and began to spread across the floor.

'Where is he? I want to see him,' said Clara. 'I'm coming with you.'

'No!' shouted Johnny. 'It's too dangerous.'

'I don't care – he's my brother. It's my right.'

'Please, Clara,' said Johnny. 'There's no time.' As he dived into the open fold, he hoped the furious look emblazoned across his sister's face, wasn't the last he'd see of her.

Johnny felt the fold seal itself behind as he was squeezed forward through the narrow tube. The freezing white mist swirled around his face, seeping inside through his ears and nostrils. Only now did he truly remember how insignificant he'd felt within the Monk's fold before – it was madness to believe for a second that he could save Earth. He should give up now – let the universe get on with being the universe and not interfere. Yet, somehow, he stretched his fingers out in front to pull himself along, working in tandem with the great intestine. Thankfully it wasn't long before his hands reached the end and he hauled himself out into the warmth of the *Astricida* – into the belly of the Star Killer. Everywhere was dazzlingly bright, the currents flowing inside Nymac's ship were working overtime to channel the destructive beams flowing through the entire Andromedan fleet.

He'd wondered if, this time, the fold would lead straight to the bridge, but Johnny found himself on the outer floor of the vast ship, a posse of Owlessan Monks floating around him. He moved quickly so the tarry floor couldn't bind him. With his right hand he pushed the nebulous Monks away while he raised his left wrist to his mouth and whispered, 'I'm in.' There was no response. He tried again . . . nothing. He was on his own.

In asking Clara to adapt the wristcom, Johnny had taken a leaf out of Nicky's book. Hoping it had worked, she'd turned the communicator into a four-dimensional tunnel. The *Spirit of London* should be collecting the reprogrammed nanobots which would travel through the device and into the *Astricida*. Johnny pressed a button to begin the process. The Sun was a poor absorber of tachyons – it would take all Nymac's concentration to keep the reaction going. In contrast, Alf's miniature machines had been reprogrammed to be far more efficient, and build as many extra copies of themselves as possible along the way. Sadly, with communications down, he had no idea if his sister's gateway had opened as planned.

It also meant no hope of rescue, but he pushed that thought from his mind and ran towards the foot of the nearest shaft that would carry him towards the strange bridge, glinting in the distance at the heart of the ship. Reaching the base, Johnny looked up and jumped. As he began to slow, he panicked for a moment, thinking he might simply fall back down, but then the new gravity field took over. Now falling upwards and travelling headfirst, he performed a forward roll in mid-air as he reached the end of the tube, and landed expertly on the diamond floor. None of the three-legged Mamluks at the corners moved a muscle.

'Better than your normal splat,' said Nymac, not taking his eyes off the holographic controls in front of him. In places, the black body suit he always wore was glowing silver.

Johnny found himself standing on a different surface of the diamond shape to his brother, meaning he could overlook the controls. All the power readings were in the red – the *Astricida* was giving Nymac everything she had. Johnny tried to probe the circuits with his mind, but he was too far away to sense them properly. 'Where's Stevens?' he asked, trying to break his brother's concentration.

Nymac didn't look round. 'As you know, we had a disagreement. Happily, I never told your teacher of the plan to create a Star Blaze here. He and the rest of his kind have fled, like the cowards they are, to their base within the solar system. Out of the frying pan and into the fire. Do not mourn them – they are the scavengers of this galaxy – they add nothing. Together we will have no need of their services.'

'But do you . . . we . . . still have enough ships for the beams,

General?' asked Johnny, really hoping the answer would be no.

'I have summoned the whole fleet,' said Nymac. 'The circle is complete. Our ships are linked together through the *Astricida* and they will suffice. We have taken casualties around Pluto, but not enough to thwart the plan. If I use all my power, I can do this. The burden is heavy, but two more minutes – without interruptions – and it will be finished.'

Even presuming they were coming through the wristcom, that was too little time for the nanobots to do their work. If he'd had a blaster, Johnny wondered whether he'd be able to shoot his own brother in the back to save Earth.

The air on the bridge was becoming strangely hazy, so he couldn't see the control panel properly. If he didn't act now, it was all over. His heart pumping at what felt like a million beats per second, Johnny walked as calmly as he could down the wall and onto the same floor level as his silvery brother. The closest Mamluk twitched but did not attempt to intercept.

'What's going on?' shouted Nymac, but only to himself. For an instant, Johnny's brother took his hands away from the controls, raising them high in frustration. 'Ship – that's too much power. I can't control it.'

A staccato female voice from all around said, 'I am having difficulty moderating the tachyon flow – a feedback loop is in operation.'

'That's never happened before,' said Nymac. 'How is it even possible?'

'I am detecting the presence of nanoscale foreign bodies throughout my internal systems,' said the ship. 'They are attempting to overload the tachyon field.'

'Then stop them!' shouted Nymac. He didn't seem to have noticed that Johnny was now right behind him.

'I am compensating,' replied the ship. 'The stellar collapse will still commence in thirty seconds and then Star Blaze can begin.'

318

Johnny had to do something. He closed his eyes and tried again to feel the *Astricida*'s systems – the circuitry was so alien he had no idea where to begin.

'There is a disproportionately large concentration of the nanoscale devices here on my bridge.' As the ship spoke the words, Johnny glimpsed her mind. It was beautiful, but in a very different way to Sol's. The Star Killer was so focused on holding everything together she had left herself defenceless. Even so, Johnny hesitated to do again what he'd been forced to do to his own ship.

'Locate the source and destroy it,' said Nymac.

Johnny's communicator melted while a pain so intense, he couldn't believe he'd felt anything like it before, tore into his wrist, along his arm and through his entire body. At that moment he'd have done anything to make it stop and he lashed out, but not physically. He slashed at the links connecting the ship's mind to her systems. The pain lessened just a fraction, but then roared back as the *Astricida* redoubled the torture. Johnny slashed again and again – it was like using a broadsword rather than a scalpel.

Somewhere, in the distance, he heard Nymac shout that nothing was working, demanding to know what was going on.

In a voice that was slow and unrecognizable, the ship replied, 'Tachyon overload imminent – abandon ship.'

Johnny severed the final bond. When he opened his eyes he found himself and the Mamluks floating, the gravity generators having failed. Only his brother was standing where he'd been before as, beyond him, an explosion ripped through the hull where two of the massive rivers of electricity had come together. His silver glow fading to black, Nymac turned, disbelief etched across his face, which looked properly at Johnny for the first time. The beam of white light, shining out of the mask, fell on Johnny's cheek and burnt like a welder's torch.

'You!' shouted Nymac. 'You're not wearing the locket. You're not the clone. The Nameless One knows you are not the clone.' He raised his head towards Johnny, revealing the black ring and the death it promised. Floating in zero-G, there was nothing for Johnny to push off from to escape the beam. Nothing happened. Nymac roared in frustration and lunged forward, hitting Johnny full in the ribs, winding him and sending them both flying into the wall behind. Johnny couldn't breathe. Nymac was on top of him, hands around Johnny's throat and shouting, 'What have you done to my ship?' while choking him. The bridge was disintegrating all around, debris and pieces of three-legged soldiers flying through the air. Above, the five Plicans had begun their elaborately choreographed moves, perhaps trying to escape before the whole ship was destroyed.

'Nicky?' The new voice, never before heard on the *Astricida*'s bridge, was Clara's. 'Stop it . . . now. The ship's going to explode.'

The grip around Johnny's neck slackened. The beam that had been burning his face blinked, and went out. As he coughed, he heard his brother – not the terrible Nymac but his real brother, Nicky – say, 'Clara?'

Johnny and his brother turned together. Their sister was standing on the shattered floor of the bridge with an open fold to the *Spirit of London* behind. Her hands were reaching out to pull both of them through and they each grabbed hold.

The strange tunnel fold Johnny had witnessed before was forming along the length of the *Astricida*'s bridge and he didn't want them to be swept away. Clara pulled her two brothers backwards towards the sanctuary of the *Spirit of London* as another massive explosion tore through the sides of the *Astricida*. Something – a Mamluk tossed through the air by the blast – glanced off Johnny, but then cannonballed into his brother's and sister's faces. The impact was too strong and their hands fell apart.

Johnny landed hard on the deck of the *Spirit of London*'s bridge, with Clara beside him. She was out cold from the collision, blood trickling down her forehead. He fought to get up, but the fold had already closed behind with no sign of Nicky. Outside, the *Astricida* disappeared within a gigantic fireball.

'Sol – full shields,' said Johnny, still gasping for breath.

'Happily, I anticipated your command,' the ship replied.

From somewhere Alf produced a cushion which he slipped underneath Clara's head.

As the explosion began to die down, another flared in the distance, and then another, and another, like beacons being set alight along the summits of a mountain range. Soon the entire sky was ablaze, forming a chain of lights encircling the distant swollen Sun.

'It appears your plan is working perfectly,' said the ship. 'The tachyon overload begun in the *Astricida* is feeding back through the entire Andromedan fleet.'

'But the Sun? Did we stop it? Please tell me we stopped it?'

'Computing . . . I estimate the Sun came within 6.674 2867 seconds of becoming a supernova. The tachyon potential has peaked and is correcting itself – according to Boloban's Second Law, your Sun will have returned to normal in approximately 2 days, 10 hours, 38 minutes and 32.458 seconds.'

Johnny leaned over Clara who opened her eyes, but looked away. Alf was beside him fidgeting. Johnny said, 'Thanks,' but his sister didn't respond. He took hold of her hand and helped her to her feet – she didn't resist. He led her to the side of the bridge showing where the *Astricida* had disintegrated moments before. There was nothing at all left of Nicky's ship.

'We had to do it,' said Johnny. 'It was the only way to save Earth.'

'What's so special about Earth?' said Clara.

'Miss Clara – you really need to come to sickbay. Let me do something about that cut.'

'Not now, Alf,' said Clara and, before the android could respond, she'd folded herself elsewhere on the ship.

✧ ✧ ✧
✧ ✧

The celebrations were taking place aboard *Cheybora*. Johnny stood on his own sipping a tasteless blue fizzy drink handed to him by a Viasynth. He'd felt he had to be there, but now he wished he was anywhere but. Around him, together with the crew, were several Tolimi he recognized and a few officers from the Imperial Navy he didn't. The only seat on the bridge had been left empty as a mark of respect towards the ship's missing captain. Johnny didn't feel much like partying.

On *Cheybora*'s viewscreen, a distant but reassuringly yellow Sun was lighting up Pluto's surface. Even from this height, the wreckage of the super gun was plain to see, the line of the enormous barrel now twisted and scattered over a wide area. It had taken out four ships before being destroyed. The rest of Pluto Base was largely intact. The small Imperial fleet, led by the captainless ship, had arrived just in time to protect it and engage those Andromedans nearby.

'The galaxy owes you a great debt, Johnny Mackintosh,' said Frago, appearing at his side. The Tolimus's head only came up to Johnny's waist.

'Earth owes the Tolimi, Frago. You were amazing.'

Someone slapped Johnny on the back, spilling his drink.

'Don't care what the Milky Way News Network says. You're all right in my book, Johnny Mackintosh.' Johnny turned and smiled weakly at a red-skinned alien with no hair or ears and a circular toothless mouth. 'Captain Djarjack of the *Angelis Rose*,' he said, saluting.

The alien's stale breath washed over Johnny, but he returned a half–hearted salute.

'Fleet's leaving tomorrow,' said the captain. 'Nothing left for us to do here – you've seen to that.'

Johnny nodded and made his excuses. He slipped away from the bridge, heading towards the shuttle bay.

'Leaving so soon, Johnny Mackintosh?' It was *Cheybora* herself who'd asked the question.

'I've got . . . things to do,' Johnny replied.

'Like you, I do not feel like celebrating,' said the ship.

Johnny had entered the shuttle bay. It was as messy as ever, all manner of oddly shaped space junk pushed to the side to accommodate the various visiting ships. 'I'm so sorry for what happened,' he said to the ship.

'My captain died in battle, doing what he loved best,' *Cheybora* replied. 'I am only sorry I was not with him at the time.'

'Well, I'm glad you're still here,' said Johnny. 'So long – look after yourself.' He climbed into the waiting *Bakerloo*.

'Goodbye, Johnny Mackintosh.'

With the ship's words ringing in his ears, Johnny flew his shuttle out of the open doors and was soon aboard the *Spirit of London*, settling down in the space between the *Piccadilly* and the Imperial Starfighter.

'Sol – where's Clara?' he asked.

'Clara is on deck 18 with Bentley.'

He made his way to the lifts and out into the garden. Bentley stood on his hind legs to greet him, so Johnny rubbed noses with the smelly sheepdog. Then he lowered his friend to the ground and walked towards Clara, who was watching the two of them from her seat on a rocky outcrop. She made room for Johnny to sit down, but looked straight ahead. Johnny stared down at his boots. Bentley settled beneath them, wagging his tail and panting.

It was here on Christmas Day that he'd wanted to tell Clara

about Nicky. He hated himself for finding it so hard to talk to her about their brother. Even now, he had no idea how to begin. Finally, Johnny said, 'He could have survived.'

'How?' asked Clara. 'The whole ship went up – there were no escape pods.' She jumped down from the rock and walked around in circles, waving her hands as she tried to compose herself.

'They fold differently,' said Johnny. 'That strange tunnel. I don't know . . . but it started as you were pulling us out.'

'You're just saying that.'

'I'm not – I promise.' Johnny looked at his sister. He hated how sad she'd been since they saved Earth. The truth was he hadn't seen Nicky die. However unlikely it seemed, he had to hope, if only to give Clara hope.

She climbed back up the rock and sat down, lifting the locket from around her neck and opening it in front of them both. The picture in one half was of their mum, the Diaquant, looking totally human and standing arm in arm with their dad, with a much younger Bentley wagging his tail in front of them. In the other half were Clara, Johnny and, several years older with half his face covered in shadow, Nicky.

'Tell me about him,' said Clara. 'Tell me everything.'

'It's complicated,' said Johnny, taking a deep breath. 'It all started when you were out here – the day you went to Pluto . . .'

The End